Dreams Cor

Victoria Walters is a full-time author living in Surrey. Victoria writes the bestselling women's fiction series GLENDALE HALL, and the cosy crime series THE DEDLEY END MYSTERIES. She has been chosen for WHSmith Fresh Talent and shortlisted for two RNA awards. Victoria was also picked as an Amazon Rising Star.

Follow Victoria on social media here:

Instagram: vickyjwalters
Facebook: Victoria Walters author
YouTube: Victoria Walters
Twitter: Vicky_Walters

Also by Victoria Walters

The Glendale Hall series (in reading order)

The Dedley End Mysteries

Standalone novels

VICTORIA WALTERS

Dreams Come True at Glendale Hall

hera

First published in the United Kingdom in 2022 by

Hera Books
Unit 9 (Canelo), 5th Floor
Cargo Works, 1-2 Hatfields
London, SE1 9PG
United Kingdom

A CIP catalogue record for this book is available from the British Library.

Print ISBN 978 1 80436 000 2
Ebook ISBN 978 1 80436 071 2

Cover design by Aimee Coveney

Look for more great books at www.herabooks.com

Printed and bound in Great Britain by Clays Ltd, Elcograf S.p.A.

I

To all the dreamers

Main cast of characters

Dove House

Lorna Ferguson
Adam Ferguson – brother
Amelia Ferguson, née Kelly – mother
Billy Ferguson – father
Kathleen Ferguson-Donald – sister – married to Hamish
Hamish Ferguson-Donald
Finlay Scott
Thomas Scott – father (deceased)
Grace – Lorna's friend

Glendale Hall

Beth Fraser – married to Drew Fraser
Drew Fraser
Izzy Fraser – their daughter
Caroline Williams – Beth's mother – married to John
Sally – retired housekeeper
Anna Stewart – current housekeeper – Cameron's girlfriend

Fraser and Hilltop Farms

Heather Fraser – married to Rory Fraser – owners of the
    two farms
Rory Fraser – Drew Fraser's older brother
Harry Fraser – their son

Cameron – manager of Hilltop Farm and Anna Stewart's boyfriend

Angus and Luke – farm workers

Don – Heather's father

Glendale Village

Brodie Stewart – minister of Glendale and Anna Stewart's older brother

Emily Stewart – his wife

Iona and Elsie – their daughters

Prologue

Twenty-three years ago...

I held on tightly to my mother's hand as we walked through crunchy fallen leaves.

My cosy beanie hat slipped down my forehead so she stopped us to push it back. 'Now you can see again,' she said, smiling down at me. She looked around where we were. 'Look at that, Lorna,' she said, pointing to the house behind us. Set back from the road, it was half covered by the orange and red leaves of the trees in front of it. It was painted white and was taller than the other houses on the road. I thought it was the biggest house I had ever seen. It looked like something out of a fairy tale. Perhaps Belle from *Beauty and the Beast* lived there. She was my favourite. 'It's the prettiest house in all of Glendale. I thought once that I might live there. I thought we could make it a lovely place for people to stay.'

Then she sighed. 'Life doesn't always work out the way you plan, but it's good to dream, Lorna. You need to imagine the life you want and then work towards it. I want all your dreams to come true.' She turned from the house and smiled at me. 'Come on, we're going to be late.' We set off again and she swung our entwined hands as we walked, making me laugh.

Before we turned the corner, I glanced back and it felt like the white house was watching us walk away.

Part One

Chapter One

'Lorna, there you are!'

My heart sank as my boss, Chris, found me in the lobby of Glenmarshes Inn. I glanced at the clock on the wall behind the reception desk – I only had fifteen minutes left of my shift and I'd finished all that needed to be done, and was already looking forward to heading home.

'There's a big mess in the lounge – can you sort that before you go, please?' Chris barked at me before spinning round and marching off. As manager, he was always rushing around the Inn telling us all what to do. I turned to see the receptionist Clare on the phone but giving me a sympathetic eye-roll. I grimaced in return before I headed towards the lounge.

As Housekeeping Manager, I had come to dread the words 'big mess', and the sight that greeted me reminded me why. Someone had knocked a whole jug of orange juice off a table and it had spilled across the marble floor and covered one of the cream chairs as well. I knew all the housekeeping staff were sorting out the rooms ready for the guest switchover, and with so little of my shift left, I knew it would be faster just to clean it up myself.

Silently cursing whoever had invented sticky orange juice, I tucked in a stray strand of hair that had come out of my bun and set to work with a mop and bucket and industrial-strength fabric cleaner. My shift ended when I was only halfway done.

'You're still here?' One of the housekeeping team, Ellie, spotted me as she passed by with her trolley. 'Oh,' she said, seeing what I was doing. 'Let me finish that, and then you can head home.'

I leaned against the mop and gave her a grateful smile. 'You're a lifesaver. I'm meeting friends for drinks, and I need a large one after today.'

'It's after every day for me,' she replied, taking the mop from me and waving me off. I didn't need telling twice, and I hurried into the staffroom and over to my locker, where I grabbed my bag and pulled my teddy-bear coat on over my Inn uniform of black trousers and white blouse. Then I rushed out of the lobby before anyone else could find something for me to do.

It was a chilly September evening and, once outside, I could see my breath on the air as I walked towards my car. Behind me, the Inn was lit up for the evening. The mock-Tudor building sat in a valley surrounded by rolling green hills, and I had always enjoyed working there until a couple of years ago, when it was taken over by a big chain and refurbished inside taking away all its character, in my opinion. Now we were less about making guests feel like they were in a home from home and more about hosting conferences and hitting sales targets. I no longer loved my job, but I had no idea what to do about it.

Climbing into my car, I turned my phone on and it lit up with several notifications. I checked in case it was my friend rearranging our plans for tonight, but I realised they were all from Facebook and when I saw the name 'Mark Edwards', I couldn't help but take a peek before I drove home. I instantly regretted it when I saw the status update from my ex-boyfriend that had created a frenzy of replies, likes and shares.

Mark Edwards is engaged to Pearl Simmons

'Okay, now I need two large drinks,' I said aloud to myself before switching on the engine, turning up the radio and driving away from the Inn needing the sanctuary of my High-lands village, Glendale, because this really had been a disastrous day.

It was about a twenty-minute drive from Glenmarshes to Glendale and I always felt better once the sights of the village I had lived in all my life came into view, but tonight it wasn't providing quite the same comfort it usually did. I had been feeling stuck at work for a long time, and seeing Mark's news was a reminder that my personal life was just as uninspiring. We had split up when the chain took over as he had been offered a transfer to one of their city hotels and he'd jumped at the opportunity, despite the fact that it meant leaving me behind.

I drove into the Glendale Arms car park, and was relieved to see that my best friend Anna's car was already there. I needed a friendly face right now. I had grown up going to the pub for family meals and then for fun teenage nights out, and now I often met my friends there for a glass of wine after work on a Friday night. I hurried out of my car and walked inside, where the sight of a crackling log fire was immediately welcoming. Summer had not long left but the nights were growing colder in the Highlands already.

Anna waved from the bar where she was buying us a drink, so I found a table in the corner close to the fire and sank into a chair.

'You look like you need this,' Anna said, sitting down next to me and sliding one of the glasses of wine she had carried over across to me. Anna had candyfloss-coloured hair and wore a leather jacket over her dress as usual. 'I thought we could both walk home. It's Friday, after all.'

I smiled. 'Good idea. And you're right, after the day I've had, I definitely need this.' I took a long gulp from my glass.

'Want to tell me about it?' she asked, as she sipped hers.

'It was a long day at the Inn – Chris, my boss, is all het up about a company holding their annual general meeting with us on Monday, so he was even more of a tyrant than usual. Then he made me stay late to clear up what can only be described as a gallon of orange juice all over the lounge. But the worst part...' I showed her the Facebook update on my phone. 'Why is it everyone around me is falling in love or getting engaged or married or having babies, and I can't even get a decent date?'

Anna screwed her face up in sympathy. 'Ugh. I'm sorry. Sounds like a rubbish day at work. But you really don't need to be upset about this,' she said, gesturing to my phone. 'You told me that you weren't really in love with Mark. I know it stings when someone walks away, but if it wasn't meant to be then that was a good thing. This has nothing to do with you. You're lovely. And you will meet someone special soon.'

I knew she was right about Mark. We had dated for about eighteen months, but I had had my doubts about us. When he announced he was leaving, it had still hurt that he hadn't even considered asking me to come with him though. Since then, I'd joined dating apps but nothing ever went anywhere. I was tired of it. 'Let's talk about something else,' I pleaded. 'How was college today?'

Anna told me all about her last cooking class. She was training to be a chef and had almost finished her year-long course at a college in Inverness and was starting to think about what she would do once she had her diploma.

'I love how passionate you are about it,' I said when she had finished, her face lit up with excitement. 'I wish I enjoyed my job half as much as you enjoy cooking.' Anna had a dream of opening her own restaurant, and I had no doubt she would do it.

Anna tilted her head to one side. 'But I thought you'd always wanted to work in hotels.'

'Not exactly. I used to dream of opening my own hotel. Well, a bed and breakfast, but I knew I needed experience, so I started working at Glenmarshes Inn after college and at first I loved it, but lately it's become just a chore. The Inn isn't what it used to be. It's not the cosy retreat it once was, it's more like a corporate chain hotel now. Something I never wanted to work in.' I sighed. 'Listening to you talking about having your own restaurant makes me remember what I had originally planned, I suppose.'

'Well, there's no reason why you can't still make that dream happen. You're only twenty-eight! Look at me, I'm back at college, and I never expected that. You have to follow your heart.' I raised an eyebrow and she chuckled. 'I know, I never thought I'd be giving anyone that advice, but Glendale changed me.' She gestured around the pub with a wry smile.

I smiled. 'Well, I'm glad we did and that you decided to stay,' I replied. Anna had originally come to help out as housekeeper at Glendale Hall, the large estate in our village, just for the summer, but a year later she was still here and we'd become good friends. 'I know you're right, but…' I trailed off. Anna was a go-getter, but I had always been more content doing what was comfortable and familiar, not taking a risk.

'Oh, here are the boys,' Anna said happily then, as the door to the pub opened. In walked her boyfriend, Cameron, and my brother Adam. People always said me and my older brother looked alike with our dark brown eyes and the dimple in one cheek. Adam was taller and stockier than me, though, and his light brown hair was short, whereas mine hung over my shoulders when I let it down. I usually wore it in a messy bun on top of my head though. Cameron went over to the bar but Adam started walking to our table.

'Don't tell them about Mark,' I hissed at Anna. 'I just want to forget about him.' She nodded and I was relieved. If I was honest, it was embarrassing, always being the one unlucky in love. Especially as Anna and Cameron were so loved-up. She had been with Cameron ever since she'd decided to stay in Glendale, and everyone could see how happy they were.

Adam reached our table. 'I have some big news for you,' he said to me in lieu of a hello.

Chapter Two

After his dramatic entrance, Adam sat down and pulled off his coat and told me to wait until he'd had a sip of his beer to explain. I looked at Anna, who was amused. I had no idea what news Adam might have for me. Not much happened in our small Highlands village, which I usually enjoyed but lately had been frustrated by, I had to admit.

'Here we go,' Cameron said, coming over with two beers. Cameron had dark hair and olive skin and he was good-looking. There was a time when I'd wondered if we could be more than just friends, but he'd gone to university and was now with Anna, so he was more like another brother to me. He kissed Anna hello as Adam took a long sip of his drink. 'We've just got new guests over at Hilltop, so I can't stay long,' Cameron said as he sat down. He managed Hilltop Farm out in the countryside, on behalf of the owners, husband and wife Rory and Heather Fraser, and they hired it out for retreats so people could get away from it all. 'Do you want to come back with me, though?' he asked Anna, who nodded eagerly. The way they looked at one another made me take another long sip of wine. I really didn't want to envy something else that Anna had, along with her passion for cooking, but after seeing my ex's news, it was hard not to. The problem with living in the same small village all your life was that I had grown up with practically everyone here, and the idea of getting together with someone I'd been at school with wasn't appealing. There was no one at work that I connected with, and we weren't allowed to 'fraternise' with the guests. And my last date from an app had talked to me about his love of hedges. As in, garden hedges. My mind was still blown about that one. The happy ever after I had always dreamed of wasn't exactly forthcoming.

'How was your boss today?' I asked my older brother. He felt the same about his manager as I did about mine. There were only eighteen months between us, so we had always had the same friendship group. We'd known Cameron and most of our friends since school; I had often hung around with them there and, once we left, when they all played rugby together.

'He's still passing my sales off as his, and he told me I can't even try for a promotion for another year as,' Adam said, holding up his hands to do air quotes, 'I need to "learn the right way to sell a house".'

'There's a wrong way?'

'I'm his top seller, but I'm not doing it right according to him. I'm too focused on finding the right house for people, whereas I should just be focused on my targets.' Adam shrugged. 'He's not from Glendale. He doesn't understand that I want people to be happy with where they move to. He couldn't care less as long as they buy something.'

'Seems very short-sighted to me,' I replied.

'If you have any common sense, but he doesn't.'

'Anyway, what's going on?' Anna asked impatiently.

'What?'

'You said you had news!' I reminded Adam with a roll of my eyes.

'Oh, yes. First of all – how was the Inn today?'

'The same as usual,' I replied. Adam knew how unhappy I was working there. 'Anyway, what's the Inn got to do with your news?'

Cameron's phone beeped and he checked a message. 'Right, I need to drink this quickly and get back to the farm, Heather needs me.'

Adam looked at Cameron. 'You're so lucky working for Heather and Rory Fraser. They wouldn't treat you like my boss, would they?'

'They know I want Hilltop to succeed as much as they do,' Cameron replied. 'Besides, there's so much to do, there's no time to micromanage me.' He turned to Anna. 'I wonder what you'll be like when you're running your own restaurant? Will you be a good boss?'

'I hope so, but my standards will be high – they have to be when you're trying to build a business.' She looked at Adam. 'Maybe your manager is just doing what head office tells him to do. It's not the same, is it, as if he owned the business himself.'

'I think you're right.' Adam sipped his beer. 'But to be honest, I just don't think I'm suited to being managed. I'd much rather be my own boss.' Adam met my eyes and I nodded. We had always felt the same way about that, but we hadn't managed to walk away from our jobs despite how many times we had talked about it over the past few years.

Adam cleared his throat. 'Which brings me back to my news… did you ever tell Anna about our dream?'

I frowned. Why was he bringing that up again? We had both pretty much given up on it. I shrugged, not wanting to talk about it when it seemed impossible.

'Your dream?'

Cameron answered Anna, as I was unwilling to. 'Lorna and Adam have always wanted to open their own hotel one day. Well, a bed and breakfast, right? In this house in the village, but someone else bought it.'

'And we've never found anywhere else we love as much,' I added, dully. It still hurt that we lost out five years ago on our dream place.

Adam leaned back in his chair. He looked kind of smug, and I was just about to throw my beer mat at him when he cleared his throat. 'Well, perhaps that was meant to be, little sister of mine.' He sat forward then, dropping his voice. We all leaned in to listen. 'I've just found out. It's been listed with the estate agent's in Glenmarshes… Dove House is up for sale again.'

My breath caught in my throat.

Chapter Three

'Lorna?' Adam said when I didn't reply.

I was too stunned for a moment to know what to say, but then I shook my head. 'It doesn't matter. We didn't get our offer accepted five years ago – why would we even consider it again?'

'Because there's nowhere like Dove House, is there? We even stopped bothering to look for premises! But we're both stuck in jobs we don't love. We both still wish we could run our own B & B. You know we'd be good at it. Now the opportunity has come up again. Maybe this is a sign. Maybe this time it will go to us,' Adam said, pushing his hair back from his face, looking excited.

My brother was an eternal optimist, and although I had once dreamed as big as he did, I had had my confidence knocked over the past five years and now I wasn't as sure about the future as I once had been. 'Why would we have a chance now when we didn't before?' I asked him. When we had both been at college, we had talked about what we might do for a living. I was studying hotel management and Adam was doing economics, and Mum had suggested we could open up a bed and breakfast together. We knew that it had always been her dream, but she had never managed to fulfil it. She had always thought Dove House would be the perfect place and suddenly, five years ago, it came on the market and the three of us were so excited by the idea of turning it into our own B & B. But despite pooling all our savings, our offer hadn't been accepted, and we had been a bit lost ever since.

'The house needs so much more work doing on it than it did five years ago,' Adam said, interrupting my thoughts. 'You know it's been neglected since Betty lost her husband and fell ill. She's been staying with her daughter for ages. They can't expect top whack for it, plus we've kept on saving these past few years, so we've got more money than we had back then, haven't we?'

'But house prices have gone up in Glendale,' I reminded him. Our village had been thriving since new businesses had popped up in the High Street. I bit my lip. 'I'm just not sure I could bear going through that process again.' Ever since my mum had shown me Dove House, I had been drawn to it, and I had grown up knowing that it had been Mum's dream to own it one day and run it as a bed and breakfast. When it had come up for sale, Mum had said that me and Adam should buy it instead, and it had made so much sense. It had felt right. Like it was meant to be.

But it wasn't the case. I was heartbroken when the owner sold it to a woman called Betty and her husband instead of us. Adam had tried since then to suggest other properties we could buy, but I couldn't get on board. My heart had been fixed on Dove House and still ached for it.

'What's the house like?' Anna asked.

'It's a white house that was built in 1929 in art deco style. It's just off the High Street,' Adam explained in his estate agent voice. 'We've always wanted to restore all the art deco features.'

'We've loved it since we were kids and our mum took us to see it,' I added. 'It's a really special place.'

Adam looked at me. 'It's always felt like it should belong to us.'

'But that's never happened,' I reminded him.

'Can I see it? Let's walk over before we go to Hilltop,' Anna suggested, looking excited. 'It can't hurt to look, can it?'

'I think that's a good idea,' Adam agreed, happily.

'We all know what it looks like,' I said.

'I'm happy to see it again,' Cameron said.

'And I never have,' Anna added. 'Please,' she begged me.

'I'm up for it,' Cameron agreed. They all looked at me.

I sighed, sensing I'd been defeated. 'Fine, we'll go and look. Even though we know it like the backs of our hands,' I said. I often walked past the house and thought about what might have been. When Betty, her husband and her daughter had moved in five years ago, I had thought that was it – they would own it forever. Because who would want to ever let it go? But life had changed their plans – her daughter went off to university and then got married and moved into her own house away from Glendale. Then Betty's husband had sadly passed away, and after falling ill, Betty herself had moved out to be looked after by her daughter, and the house had been empty for months. And they'd obviously decided that they'd never live there again and it was time to let it go. It was hard to deny the stirrings of hope in my heart.

We left the pub together. Outside, the evening chill promised autumn was on the way. I was glad of my coat as we walked down the High Street towards Dove House. At least we were heading into my favourite time of year. I looked up, hoping to see the trees changing colour. They weren't quite there yet, September had only just begun, but I was excited for the start of the season, and then Christmas. Glendale village would be picture-perfect, as it always was.

Our village was small but pretty with hanging baskets full of flowers in between each shop. A few years ago, Glendale had lost some of its spark but Beth Fraser, owner of the largest home in the village, Glendale Hall, had revived it by taking over the shops and helping new businesses to open up and thrive. She had lived in London for ten years after running away when she got pregnant as a teenager, but when she had come back, she had fallen back in love with her childhood sweetheart Drew and she had decided to stay, making it her mission to return the village to how she remembered it.

Now, it was lively and the community was stronger than ever. I also loved that so many of the businesses were run by women. It was inspiring when I longed to start a business myself.

We passed the church, which we attended every Sunday, and the vicarage where our minister, Brodie, Anna's older brother, and his family lived. Then the farm shop owned by Heather and Rory Fraser. Heather had been Beth's best friend before she left and she had ended up marrying Drew's brother Rory and becoming a farmer's wife.

We then passed by the Glendale Hall shop where you could pick things up that were grown on the estate and even Glendale Hall teddies and mugs.

Then we reached my favourite place: Emily's Bakery, which sold the best coffee and cakes for miles around and was always welcoming. Emily was another woman who had found happiness in love and work in Glendale as she owned the bakery and was Brodie's wife and mother to two daughters.

The three friends and Anna had all made their dreams come true in Glendale and I still hoped that I would too.

We walked to the end of the High Street passing the other shops that I visited every week. I loved the village, and I couldn't see myself ever moving anywhere else. Then, we turned off the main road into a small road that I must have walked down a million times.

My heart was bouncing in my chest as we walked towards the house. I remembered taking this walk with my mother when I was a child; she always took the longer way home from school to pass by Dove House, as we were about to do. I remembered her pointing it out to me when I was five years old and me thinking that it was like something out of a fairy tale. If I was honest with myself, I still felt that way about it. The moon above us was full, casting a silvery light down on it. The lamp posts were lit, but with all the trees that lined this road it was still pretty dark. If I hadn't known this route as well as I did, I might have felt lost. But my feet moved towards the house without me having to tell them to.

'Here we are,' Adam said quietly as we stopped in front of it.

'Wow,' Anna said as she leaned into Cameron, who wrapped an arm around her.

I looked at the 'For Sale' sign that now stood outside the closed ornate gates, then lifted my eyes past it and up to the tall white house. I could barely see it in the evening light but I knew it was in a state of disrepair. But still the art deco features made me smile: the distinctive windows, curved white frontage and three floors topped off with a decorative spire.

'It's so unusual. I can see why you both love it so much,' Anna said to me and Adam.

'It'll need a lot of work, but we had it all planned five years ago,' Adam said. 'And like I said, we have more money for the project now.'

'We don't know what they want for it, though, and it will need loads more money spent on it as Betty hasn't been able to look after it or restore it like we know she planned to. If they're asking for offers above a guide price again, we might not be able to make the highest offer,' I pointed out. In Scotland, if the seller wanted offers above a guide price, they usually chose the one who made the highest offer. And you had no way of knowing what other interested parties were offering. You just had to give your best price and hope it would be enough. Five years ago, it wasn't, and Betty and her family secured the house instead of me and Adam. What if that happened all over again?

'I can call the estate agent's in the morning and find out,' Adam said. 'I know them. I bet Jenny is dealing with it – she'll be open with me if other people are interested. We can at least find out what our chances might be. What do you think, sis? Can you really handle wondering "what if" otherwise? Because I don't think I can. And you said it yourself, it's not like we have another plan, is it?'

'If you've wanted this for five years and now you have a shot, you have to try, Lorna, don't you?' Anna asked me. The three of them looked at me and I felt torn.

I lifted my gaze up to the house. For the past five years, I had felt stuck. First losing out on Dove House, and not finding anywhere else that I wanted to turn into a business with Adam; then breaking up with Mark. And I still lived in our family home. I just hadn't had the motivation to move out. I had kept saving for this one-day dream of ours and with each year that passed, it felt less and less likely that it would end up happening. I knew Adam had been frustrated that I didn't like any other properties, but we both wanted to run a bed and breakfast in Glendale. We had lived here all our lives and there was no place to stay in the village. It didn't feel right to do it anywhere else, but the right property never seemed to come up.

But now Dove House was an option again.

'Let me think about it,' I replied, finally. I knew that Anna had a point about me always wondering 'what if', but I was scared. If this really was our last shot and it didn't work out again, then what would we do?

Adam sighed. 'Okay. Come on then. You need to get back, Cameron, and I'll walk you home, Lorna.'

'We'll see you at church on Sunday,' Anna said.

I could tell they were disappointed with my response.

I waited until the last moment, keeping my eyes on the house, before turning around and following them.

Chapter Four

I let Adam and me into our family home, where I had lived since I was born. 'I'm home, Adam's with me,' I called out as Adam closed the door behind us. He had a small flat he rented but was often back at our house. We were a close family and I was fine still living at home, but like working at the Inn, my life was familiar and stable and I longed to shake things up. The problem was, I was also really scared to.

'Kitchen!' my mum called back.

Our childhood home, a three-bedroom semi-detached house, stood on the edge of Glendale. It was perfectly comfortable and full of photographs of our family, of noise and light and familiar scents – my mother's vanilla perfume, cookies being baked in the kitchen, my father's cigars that he was allowed to smoke on a Sunday after church, and my sea salt candles.

I shrugged off my jacket and hung it on the hook by the door, adding my boots to the pile of shoes, and walked through to the kitchen with Adam behind me. 'You won't believe the news,' Adam declared.

My mum was stirring a big pot on the hob, her apron tied around her waist, while my dad sat at the long pine table with my younger twin brothers, still in their school uniform, listening to them talking about what they had done that day. My older sister was there too with her large baby bump.

'What news?' My sister's husband Hamish appeared from the lounge with his phone, his work suit still on. It was a typical busy scene in my house, although only me and the twins actually lived here with my parents. He squeezed past me to sit down next to my sister. 'Pass me a beer, would you?'

Adam looked around. No one was listening to him, I could tell. That was the problem in my family – you often had to shout to be heard. He whistled then, a sharp, loud one that caused everyone to fall silent. He nodded. 'Thanks. So, as I said, you won't believe our news.'

I glanced at our older sister Kathleen – I knew she was going to have something to say about this. And we probably weren't going to like it.

'What is it, loves?' my mother asked us.

'Dove House is up for sale,' Adam said.

'Not this again,' my sister groaned, as I had expected. 'I thought you had given up on all that.'

'It's up for sale?' my mum repeated excitedly, ignoring her.

'There's a sign up and everything,' I confirmed. 'We've just been to see it.'

'It's not actually called Dove House, is it?' my sister's husband Hamish asked.

'We just call it that,' my mum explained. 'It doesn't have a name really, but everyone in Glendale has always used that name. Do you know how much they're asking for it?'

'We don't know the guide price yet. I'd need to phone the agent for all the details,' Adam said. He looked at me. 'If Lorna wants me to.'

'Why wouldn't you?' Mum asked in surprise. 'This is great news!'

'That's what I said,' Adam agreed.

I opened my mouth to speak but my sister beat me to it.

'There's no way you can afford it, you never could,' Kathleen said, pushing back her blonde bob off her face. Honestly, sometimes my sister's pessimistic attitude made me want to cry, but tonight she was saying exactly what I was worrying about.

'Now then, we don't know that,' my dad said, smiling kindly at us, then at my mother. He knew how much that house meant to us. 'Let's wait and see how much the guide price is first.'

'It's in such a bad state. Surely the price must have been dropped from last time,' Adam said.

I walked over to where Mum was and looked down at the hob. She was making one of her delicious hearty stews for dinner. My stomach rumbled on cue. 'But that means we'd need to spend more on restoring it,' I said.

'We'll do it on a budget,' Adam countered as he sat down at the table. His eyes were twinkling. I could see how excited he was. I just couldn't let myself feel the same way.

Mum looked at me. She could always read me far too well. 'I know how upset you were last time…'

'Exactly,' Kathleen called out. 'You pinned all your hopes on that house, and it didn't work out. Why are you going to do the same thing again? Why can't you find somewhere else?'

'There isn't anywhere else,' I flung back crossly. 'We've never found anywhere that would work as well.'

Kathleen shook her head. 'You've never really tried, Lorna. The last place Adam saw, you refused to even go and look round it. You gave up trying to have a bed and breakfast when you lost out on Dove House five years ago, and you can't pretend otherwise.'

I sighed inwardly. She was right. I had begun to think I couldn't do it, and had let myself just stay where I was instead of trying.

'All the more reason not to let it go this time,' Adam broke into our exchange, as always trying to be the peacemaker.

'Well, you and Mum shouldn't have let Lorna believe that only Dove House would work. There has to be something else out there that you could turn into a bed and breakfast, if you'd only be bothered to try and find it,' Kathleen continued.

'Maybe you should let us decide what we want,' I said, trying not to get upset; that only made my sister lecture me more.

'I'm trying to be the voice of reason here,' Kathleen replied. 'Which someone should have been years ago.'

'Is the wine open?' Mum said in despair. I reached behind us and poured us both a glass. The problem was, Kathleen was sort of right. My mum had loved that house since she was a teenager, when she had become friendly with the family who had lived there, and she had fantasised that one day it would belong to her. And then when she had her family, I think she changed the dream to it belonging to us instead.

'I think the house has become a noose around your necks,' Kathleen continued to lecture. Sometimes, she acted more like my mother than my mum did. 'You've become so fixated on it that nothing else will do, but what's happened is, it's caused you to become stuck in your lives. You keep moaning about your jobs, but you won't do anything about it because anything other than that house isn't good enough.'

'That's not fair,' Adam said. I wasn't sure how he could still sound so reasonable. 'When you want something as much as we do, it's really hard to settle for second best. But maybe we won't have to. This is an opportunity again. You must admit, we'd be crazy not to try, if we're as stuck as you say we are.'

Kathleen sighed. He had got her there. 'But what if you don't get it again?'

'Why don't we think positively? What if we do get it?' Adam countered. They were now glaring at each other.

'What do you think, love?' Mum asked me.

'I don't know. Everything has gone wrong since the house sold to Betty five years ago. Nothing has gone to plan. So it's hard to believe that the dream could come true. But...' I trailed off.

'But what?' Mum nudged me.

I glanced at Kathleen, who was looking incredulous, then at Adam, who gave me an encouraging nod. 'What if that's because we are meant to have Dove House? What if things not working out was because this time it will?'

'I give up,' Kathleen said, throwing her hands in the air. 'You're all delusional.'

'Kathleen,' my dad said in a warning tone.

'I just don't understand why you'd put all your eggs in one basket,' she said, rubbing her baby bump.

I looked away. Kathleen had so much in her life, but that didn't make her any less tough on those who didn't have it all.

'Well, I've always believed you and Adam could do it,' Mum said, cheerfully. After all, I was a dreamer because she was. 'And I think you could be right that nothing else has worked out because this was meant to be all along. When I took you both to look round Dove House as kids, you adored it immediately. The two of you ran from room to room playing and laughing. You were so happy there,' she remembered fondly. 'You were away on a school trip,' she added to Kathleen. 'So you don't have that same connection that Adam and Lorna do.'

I had been about eight when Dove House had come on the market for the first time in my life, and Mum had taken us with her to look round. She hadn't had the money, of course, to make an offer, but she had told us what she would have loved to do to the house, and I had been able to picture her vision, even though I was young. I could see how happy you could be staying there, and when we'd made our own plans for the house five years ago, my memories were still there. When you walked inside, it felt like home. I wanted everyone to be able to feel that. It was what was missing at Glenmarshes Inn now; what I missed about the place. I knew that I could create that at Dove House. But it meant taking a big leap and I had spent a long time refusing to even take a little jump anywhere.

'Look, let's take a breather and have something to eat,' Mum said, reaching out to squeeze my shoulder. Thankfully the discussion was paused then as I helped Mum serve out the stew and mash and green beans to everyone. I followed her to the table with my food, once everyone was tucking in. I watched her sit down and smile at her family fondly. She had had five children, and my dad's taxi business was the priority as we had to live on the money earnt from it. There was no option of starting a bed and breakfast; they didn't have money to save. But when we talked about me and Adam doing it, she had told us how she had imagined Dove House could be as a place to stay, and Adam and I had fallen hard for the idea. It really would be a magical place for guests, but it would be a lot of work and would take a lot of money. It was a huge project, and I had no idea if we were up to doing it. What if Kathleen was right, and we should let our dream go?

'This is delicious,' my dad said as he tucked into the stew.

'How was work?' Hamish asked Adam. Hamish worked as a communications director for a big company in Inverness.

'Can you pass me the salt?' Kathleen asked.

'Ow, stop it!' Noah and Leo were fighting as usual, my mum's surprise twins when she thought her family was complete. I couldn't even imagine having five children. Even one seemed so out of reach for me. Another dream that was taking its time to come true. So far, I had been as unlucky in love as I had with my career. And I hated that it was getting me down, but it was really starting to.

'Would you call it Glendale Bed and Breakfast?' Hamish asked us then. His wife threw him an annoyed look at bringing it up again, but he kept his eyes on us. My sister had married a very easy-going man, in my opinion.

'No, we always said we'd call it Dove House Bed and Breakfast,' I said.

'I still think it sounds perfect,' Adam declared. He looked so happy tonight. I saw my mother smiling, but next to her Kathleen was frowning, looking concerned as she often did. I suppose if we had been more practical, like Kathleen was, we might have found somewhere over the past five years to turn into our B & B. I knew that maybe Adam would have been happy elsewhere – he was just a happy person – but I hadn't let myself even consider it. My heart had been broken not getting Dove House.

I wanted more from my job, and I still longed for someone special to build a life with, and both those things hadn't felt within reach for years. But now one of them was.

'Lorna, what do you think? Why don't I just get in touch with the estate agent's Monday morning and find out the guide price? That wouldn't hurt, would it? Then at least we would know where we stood. Whether we even have a chance.'

'I think that's sensible,' Mum agreed with him.

I nodded reluctantly and they beamed at me, while Kathleen sighed. Nerves fluttered in my stomach and I wasn't sure I'd be able to finish my dinner. What was I hoping for? That we could afford it, or not?

I had really tried to put Dove House out of my mind, but now it was on the market again, and I knew Adam was right that I would regret it if we didn't at least look into it. Maybe I had been close-minded with my dream and it had held me back, but what if both Mum and Adam were right and there had been a reason for it, after all? I would rather believe them than Kathleen, who seemed to think that we should forget all about Dove House. But she didn't know what it was like to want something as much as we wanted this. She didn't believe in destiny. And I had started to believe that it wasn't real either, but what if it was?

And Dove House had been meant for us all along…?

Under the table, I crossed my fingers.

Chapter Five

Getting ready for work on Monday morning was a mad rush. I overslept after tossing and turning for most of the night, thinking about everything, and had to run out of the door after the fastest shower I'd ever had. I threw on my work uniform, and not having time to have my usual coffee and bagel, I rushed out of the house pulling my coat on and shouting goodbye to my family as I dived into my old car.

It was a rainy morning as I set off for Glenmarshes Inn. I left the village and drove down winding country lanes through the beautiful Highlands. The serene drive didn't calm me down as much as it usually did. It was going be a nerve-racking morning waiting for Adam to call after he'd spoken to the estate agent, and on top of that, we had the annual general meeting of a large company to make sure ran smoothly. I knew my boss Chris would be like a headless chicken, but at least I'd be too busy to think about Dove House.

As I pulled down the lane to Glenmarshes Inn, I couldn't help but imagine I was driving up to my own hotel instead. The mock-Tudor style of Glenmarshes was nothing compared to how I knew Dove House could look once restored to its art deco glory. I knew that I wanted to make it a homely place to stay, which this Inn had once been. But I needed the chance to try to do it first. 'Please,' I whispered out loud. I had pushed away my dream for so long, but now I had a glimmer of hope again, it was finding its way back into my heart. I wasn't sure that I'd ever take the risk of leaving the Inn for anything other than Dove House. I needed that house to push me, otherwise

I might end up working here until I retired, and that was a sobering thought.

I parked and walked inside, heading to the staffroom. The Inn was busy with people arriving for the AGM. We had many more corporate guests now that we no longer attracted people looking for a cosy weekend away in the Highlands.

'Morning!' my friend, the Inn events manager, Grace, burst into the staffroom as I stowed my coat and bag and attached my name tag to my Inn uniform. 'I'm a bag of nerves for this conference today,' she said, looking harassed. 'I've been here since six a.m. trying to make sure everything is ready, but I'm still worried something will go wrong.'

'You always think of everything, don't worry,' I said. Grace was the most organised person I'd ever met. Events always ran smoothly on her watch, but still she was nervous about them every time. I looked at my phone and frowned. Nothing from Adam yet.

'Waiting on a man?' Grace asked excitedly as she went to the mirror and reapplied her lipstick.

'As you well know, there is no man to wait on,' I said, rolling my eyes. 'No, just waiting for my brother to call me.'

'Oh, how is Adam? I haven't seen him since your birthday drinks,' Grace asked, glancing at me in the mirror with a smile. She and Adam had got on really well that night, but Grace had been seeing someone at the time. Someone who had proven not to be the right person for her, unfortunately.

'Probably as nervous as I am right now. There's a property up for sale in my village.' I lowered my voice just in case Chris was about. 'It would be perfect for our bed and breakfast.'

Grace turned round from the mirror. 'That sounds more exciting than the man idea, to be honest.'

'True.' I shook my head. 'It's the place we tried to get last time.' I'd told Grace all about it when we became friends. 'We've never found anywhere we like as much, but I'm worried. We might not be able to afford it. And I don't think I can stand losing it again.'

'Well, I'll be crossing my fingers. You know that I think you're wasted here. You'd be perfect running your own place. When we first met we both said we didn't want to stay for more than two years, and look what's happened.' Grace grimaced.

'I know,' I agreed. 'I guess we both got too comfortable here.'

'Maybe we need to change that,' she replied pointedly. She checked the clock on the wall. 'I need to go otherwise Chris will kill me, but let's do lunch, okay? And you can tell me all about it!'

I chuckled as she hurried off in a cloud of blonde hair and perfume, wishing her energy would rub off on me this morning. I quickly poured myself a coffee and took a long gulp before I went to meet the housekeeping team as I did every morning. The team were all good at their jobs so I didn't have much to remind them of, but Chris had made it clear this conference had to go well so we needed to be on top of our game.

After the meeting, I started to walk up to the honeymoon suite to inspect it. It was booked tonight for the head of the company whose AGM they were having at the Inn, and I needed to make sure it looked perfect. It was the most expensive room in the Inn, so the appearance had to live up to the price tag. I passed by the large meeting room and saw Grace talking to a group of people in suits. They all seemed happy so far. My phone rang, vibrating in my pocket, and I ducked into the empty breakfast room in case Chris saw me, and answered the call from my brother, my pulse starting to race.

'Adam, what did they say about Dove House?' I asked urgently instead of saying 'hello'.

'It's offers over again, and they have the same guide price as last time. I mentioned all the extra work that was needed but the agent, Jenny, like I thought, said houses are really sought after in Glendale now, so it's in line with the market. She's right, although I didn't tell her that. With how the village is thriving, prices are much higher than they were five years ago. And so far,

Jenny said there are two interested parties,' Adam said matter-of-factly. He never sugar-coated anything. 'I spoke to Glen to see what he thought about the building work.' Glen was an old school friend of ours; Adam played rugby with him, and he worked for his father's building company. They'd quoted last time we tried to buy Dove House. 'He said the work would cost more because he now knows the house has a lot of damp to be treated, and last time the roof was okay but it needs repairing after that big storm last year.'

I sighed. 'So how are we looking moneywise?' I knew he would have costed it all before phoning me. Adam was the practical one in our pairing. I had the creative vision. Which was why we thought we'd always work well together. We just needed a chance to do so.

'Based on our current savings, how much I think we'd need to offer to outbid the other parties, and how much we need to spend on repairing and decorating the house, I think we're £20,000 short.' I slumped against a chair. This was what I'd been afraid of. 'I registered our interest and booked us in to look round after work today.'

'You did?'

'I thought maybe we could find someone to come on board, to invest or give us a loan.'

'If only we could ask Kathleen.' I knew Kathleen and Hamish had money to lend us, but my sister just didn't get why we wanted that house so much. 'Would the bank help us?'

'They didn't last time,' Adam reminded me. 'Let's think about what we can do and meet up there at six o'clock.'

'I...' I hesitated. I was remembering how upset I'd been when we found out Betty's offer had been accepted and not ours. If we were potentially £20,000 out, was there any point looking at the house again?

'Lorna, please. For me. I feel like we shouldn't give up this time,' Adam pleaded with me.

It was so hard saying no to my brother. 'Okay, I'll look round with you but I feel like it's pointless,' I admitted. I knew I shouldn't have got my hopes up.

'No,' Adam said. 'Don't think like that! Let's try everything we can before we think like that. Remember our dream and think positively, okay?'

I half sighed, half said, 'Okay.'

'I have to get back to work, but I'll see you later.'

I hung up. I didn't know how to feel. Adam had already worked out that we didn't have quite enough money, but he still thought that somehow we could pull it off. I trusted my brother, but I thought that sometimes we both needed to add a dash of reality to our big ideas. I thought about Kathleen; she would tell us not to bother even going tonight, which would usually make me want to do exactly that, but I had to wonder if she was right about this. I had agreed, though, not wanting to let Adam down, but I thought I might have to tell him we needed to let it go once we were there. Which I really wasn't looking forward to doing.

I walked out of the room, everything whirring around in my mind, and saw a man leaning against the wall looking at me. 'Oh, can I help?' I asked, forcing on a smile for a guest.

'No, just having a ten-minute break from the conference. I couldn't help... I'm sorry,' he said, somewhat flustered. He had a Scottish accent and wore a suit that didn't seem to quite fit him. Tall and lanky, I would have described him, with messy dark hair and glasses. He moved away from the wall. 'I heard you mention a Dove House?'

I thought it was a bit rude that he had eavesdropped but I had to be polite to guests. 'Yes, I was just talking to my brother, he's an estate agent. It's a property up for sale,' I said, starting to walk away. I needed to get to the honeymoon suite.

'Dove House is up for sale?' he repeated, walking with me.

'That's right,' I said, wondering why he was looking at me so oddly.

'Are you going to buy it?'

Wow, he was nosy. 'Well, it might not be possible, I don't know. It's been a dream of mine and my brother to own it, but…' I trailed off, wondering why I was telling this stranger so much.

He looked distracted for a moment but then met my gaze. I realised he had bright blue eyes behind his glasses. 'Don't give up on your dreams, you'll regret it if you do. Trust me,' he said with feeling before turning and going back into the conference room.

Huh. That was odd. I walked up to the bedrooms and thought about my call from Adam. I should just tell him we should walk away, but then I pictured me and Adam when we had been in that house as children and how it had felt like home somehow. I looked around the Inn and thought about how I would never have changed the decor like they had, how I no longer felt like I was working somewhere special; how I longed to leave but kept on turning up day after day, stuck in the familiarity of it all. How was I ever going to move my life forward if I kept hiding from change and opportunities?

That man downstairs was right about one thing – I didn't want to regret giving up on my dreams. I had, if I was honest, these past five years. Kathleen had made me realise that I had let go of my drive and determination. I had let life get me down. Well, I needed to stop that. I needed to take a leap. I needed to prove my sister and that little voice of doubt inside me wrong.

But what should I do?

We were short of the money that we would need to offer on Dove House. Adam had mentioned getting someone on board to help. There was no way I was going to ask Kathleen only to have her turn us down. And the bank hadn't liked the fact that neither of us was a homeowner last time we asked about a loan.

Suddenly it struck me. A way that we could make up the shortfall, maybe. But first I needed to ask someone what they thought.

I opened up a message and asked Anna if I could pick her up at Glendale Hall on my way home later.

Then I told myself to put it out of my mind, otherwise I was going to drive myself crazy, and I focused on the task in front of me, all the while hoping that one day instead of looking at the rooms here at the Inn, I'd be inspecting the rooms in my own bed and breakfast.

Chapter Six

I drove back from the Inn towards Glendale Hall that evening with butterflies in my stomach. I had spent more time at the Hall over the past year than ever before. I'd always known the family, but the owner, Beth Fraser, was a few years older than me so not in my friendship group. Once I became close to Anna, though, I was included in lots of things at the house as Anna lived there, working part-time as the housekeeper while she studied. Everyone at the Hall was really friendly despite the house being so grand. It had a warmth to it; you felt it when you walked in, and I longed to have a place of my own that had the same feel about it.

Anna was sitting on the doorstep waiting for me, wearing joggers with a leather jacket draped over her sweatshirt, sipping a takeaway coffee. She had clearly come back from a run. She loved to run. I had tried to join her a couple of times but running wasn't for me. Shopping was my cardio. I jumped out of my car and hurried up to the door. 'Thank you for meeting me,' I said. 'Adam is waiting for us at Dove House to look around. And we need your help.' I held out my hand and pulled her up.

'I'm intrigued. I'd love to see inside that house! Let's go.'

Once we were in my car heading to the property, I explained everything. 'My mum has always loved Dove House. She grew up in Glendale and she made friends with the family who lived there when she was a teenager. She said she used to love going there. But I don't know – something happened, and they ended up moving away, and she said she was left with the feeling that

33

she wished she could own it one day. She imagined turning it into a place for people to stay, people who would love it as much as she did. Anyway, time passed and she met my father and she soon fell pregnant with my older sister, then Adam and then me. And then the surprise that were the twins. She just didn't have the time or money to start a bed and breakfast.' I drove through the High Street feeling excitement rise up, knowing I was about to look around the house again. 'But when the house came up for sale when we were kids, Mum took me and Adam to look around it and I became as hooked as my mum. I understood why she loved it so much. It has that feeling when you walk in, you know?'

Anna nodded. 'Like Glendale Hall. That house is magic. Everyone loves it.'

'Yes. Dove House is like our Glendale Hall. Well, my sister doesn't really get why we love it so much, or my dad – he's too practical to be sentimental about anything. But Mum, Adam and me, we always dreamed that one day it would belong to our family. When I started my course in hotel management, I began to plan to turn it into a B & B with Adam, and we started saving, and when it finally came up for sale five years ago, we tried to get it. But as you know, we were outbid by Betty and her family. I got my job at the Inn and I've been settled there for years, and Adam became an estate agent and we let go of our dream. I suppose I thought it would never happen, but now it's up for sale again and... well, you know the rest.'

'Do you know why Betty is selling it?'

'I think she and her husband had a similar idea to us and were going to run it as a business, but he passed away and then she fell ill and it became too much for her. She moved out to live with her daughter.'

'It really sounds like it's the one that got away,' Anna said. 'Do you think you can make the highest offer this time?'

'That's what we're going to need your help with.'

She looked surprised. 'If I had the money...'

'No, it's okay, I know you don't, but thank you. I was thinking, though, that we both might know someone who does.' I pulled into the road and we drove up to the house. The large white wrought-iron gates styled like two sunbursts were slightly open so we could drive through. They were so distinctive – it always gave me a thrill to see them and all the other art deco features of the house.

Adam's car was parked in the driveway already and he was leaning against it waiting for us. Behind him, Dove House rose up in its glory and the striking front door, with its stained-glass panel showing a sunrise to match the gates, was also open ready to welcome us.

'It's like something out of a book,' Anna said, looking out of the car window. 'Izzy would love it.'

'I was hoping you'd say that,' I said as I parked. 'As I thought her mother might have the money we need.'

Anna turned to me and grinned. 'Beth does love helping women set up businesses.' Beth Fraser had invested a lot of money in the shops on the High Street. 'Like how she did with Emily.' Emily, Anna's sister-in-law, had lived in London but, like Beth, had returned to where they had grown up, and Beth had helped Emily open up her own bakery in the village alongside the other shops that were doing so well now.

I really hoped that Beth might be willing to invest in our B & B. I knew that she and Anna were good friends; Anna really trusted her opinion, and Beth's daughter, Izzy, was a bookworm and had her own library in the family home. So it was good to hear that Anna agreed with me that this house looked like something out of a book, as it might help persuade Beth to give us a loan.

I nodded. 'That's what I was hoping. Come on, let's look around.'

We climbed out and Adam unlocked the door with the keys the agent had given him. He had persuaded Jenny to let us tour by ourselves, and we stepped inside. I looked around, that familiar feeling settling over me that I was home. It was in a worse state than the last time we saw it. It had been empty since Betty had moved in with her daughter, and it felt unloved.

'Okay,' Adam said, straight to business. 'As we know, the roof needs repairing, there is a lot of damp that we need to treat, a couple of windows need replacing, Jenny said, and the house needs a new boiler. Beyond that, it needs decorating – plastering, painting, new flooring everywhere, and the art deco features need restoring,' he added, nodding to the spiral staircase that led you to the other floors. It could be a real centrepiece of the house, but we could see the paint was peeling.

'It needs a lot of TLC,' I agreed. The house had three floors, and the entrance hall had always been my favourite part. Light streamed in through the Crittall window. I loved the slimline steel frame and horizontal bars so distinctive of the era. The ceiling was high with coving and a dusty light fitting that I itched to change for something dazzling.

'I bet the art deco style could be a real selling point for the B & B,' Anna said. 'Let's see the rest.' She smiled and I knew she already understood why we loved this house.

We walked through into the reception rooms – a large lounge that ran the full length of the house and had floor-to-ceiling French windows that looked out on to the large overgrown garden. There was a grand dining room next door. 'I want to recreate the style of the era: lots of geometric prints, and go back to the original fireplaces,' I said, pointing to one in the dining room that had been boarded over.

Adam pointed up to the ceiling. 'There are cracks in here.'

'We need to get these carpets up and go back to the original hardwood floors,' I said, tapping my ankle boots on it.

'It could look stunning,' Anna said. 'How would you make it work as a B & B?'

'So, these two reception rooms would be for guests. Follow me.' I led Anna into the large kitchen which had a small room attached to the back of it. 'We thought these two rooms would be for us. We can make this' – I gestured to the room just off the kitchen – 'into a small living room, and the kitchen we can use to make breakfast for the guests and for us the rest of the time.'

'And how are you at cooking breakfasts?' Anna asked me with a grin. 'Do you need my expertise?'

I chuckled. 'I've grown up in a large family – breakfasts are definitely something I can do. The twins are always begging for my pancakes. I really enjoy cooking, but I don't have my own kitchen. My mum does most of it, so I'd be excited to have my own space to cook.'

'We thought we could use the downstairs toilet off here too, and guests can use the one near the hallway,' Adam continued, showing Anna.

'And how would you work out the bedrooms?' Anna asked.

'That's why this house is perfect. The second floor would be for guests – there are four bedrooms. And then on the third floor there are two bedrooms and two bathrooms.' I smiled at Adam. We had planned it out so many times. 'Adam and I would live up there.' Adam had his own flat, but he wouldn't be able to keep paying the rent on it if we took this on, and I'd be excited to move out of our family home. It had always made perfect sense to us that we'd live here and run it together.

'Lorna would look after the guests and I'd run the business side of it all,' Adam continued. 'But it's always been a big project, and it's even bigger now it's been neglected for so long.'

We showed Anna the rest of the house and I tried not to feel too excited as I looked in all the familiar rooms. The second floor was the largest with the four double-sized bedrooms and en-suite bathrooms. They all needed decorating, but the upstairs was in a better condition than the downstairs, I was relieved to see. Then we climbed the narrow staircase up to the third floor.

In one of the bedrooms, we looked out of the window at the excellent view of Glendale, the village all three of us loved.

We stood in silence for a moment, drinking it in, and then I turned to Anna.

'What do you think? Do you think Beth might help us out with the extra money we need? As an investment?'

'Beth is passionate about this village, and having a bed and breakfast here will only help the local economy. I know Hilltop have guests, but that's a way from the village and a very different vibe to what this will be. That's a farm out in the middle of nowhere. This will bring people into Glendale itself. And the house will be so wonderful once you two have worked your magic on it. I think you should ask her. I have a feeling she would be very much on board with it.'

I finally let inside the hope that had been circling my heart. I looked at my brother, whose smile was as wide as my own. At last, our dream felt within reach. We needed to put behind us what had happened before and focus on making this work. I didn't want another five years where I just sat back and let life pass me by. I needed to take control of my future. Starting with buying this house.

'There's no time like the present,' I said. 'Let's go and talk to Beth.'

Chapter Seven

A few minutes later, we drove through the large iron gates of Glendale Hall and over the gravel to park alongside the cars that belonged to the family. We climbed out and walked up to the large oak front door, which had ivy climbing over it. The Hall was a grand cream stone building but inside it wasn't intimidating. Beth had decorated it simply, with warmth, and there were lots of hints of her love of the outdoors throughout, such as vases of lavender and paintings of the stunning grounds hanging on the walls.

'They will all be in the kitchen. I left lasagnes in the Aga before we went to Dove House,' Anna said, leading the way. She was right – the family were finishing eating when we walked in and it was as chaotic a scene as dinner at our house. According to Anna, this was just a typical family evening meal, but the table was full and everyone seemed to be talking over one another.

'How's the family, Lorna?' Brodie, Anna's older brother and Glendale's minister asked me as he passed a basket of garlic bread down the table. My family always went to church on a Sunday, as did everyone at the Hall. There was always a good turnout; Brodie was a really popular minister.

'Fine, thanks. Actually, Adam and I...'

'Please take Elsie.' Emily, Brodie's wife, walked in behind us. She smiled. 'Hi, Lorna, Adam. She's just woken up,' she explained as she passed her youngest daughter to Brodie. She had two little girls, and yet somehow managed to run a bakery at the same time.

'Can you please pass the water?' Drew, Beth's husband who was a doctor at the hospital in Inverness, called out. Caroline, Beth's mother, handed him the jug.

'Where's Beth?' Anna asked the table. 'We need to speak to her.'

'Greenhouse,' Izzy, Beth and Drew's teenage daughter, called out, seemingly able to listen to what was going on around her as she read at the table with one hand, using the other to eat her lasagne.

Anna grinned at me. 'Come on, that's her happy place, so hopefully she'll be in a good mood.' We walked out of the back door and Anna led us across the lovely grounds of the Hall towards the greenhouse. It was dark now, but there were lights lining the side of the house casting a glow by which we could see and the greenhouse was lit up brightly.

'Shouldn't we have our business plan with us?' Adam asked worriedly.

'That can come later. Beth will respond to you guys talking about how much you want this house,' Anna replied. 'Trust me.'

Adam and I looked at one another. I gave him a reassuring smile. I trusted Anna knew how best to speak to Beth, but I understood his nerves. If she wouldn't help us I wasn't sure we could find the money elsewhere, and now I had let myself see inside the house again, I didn't think I could bear that.

We found Beth in the greenhouse repotting a plant, humming to herself, her thick wavy hair falling over her shoulders.

'Escaped the madness?'

Beth grinned as Anna stepped in and we followed her. 'Always a good idea. What can I do for you three?'

'These two have a business proposition for you.' Anna moved to the side as Beth looked at Adam and me.

Beth raised an eyebrow. 'I'm intrigued. Fire away,' she said, straightening up, dusting soil from her gloves.

I took a breath. 'We want to buy Dove House and turn it into a bed and breakfast. And we are looking for an investor.'

Beth glanced at Adam and then back at me. 'Why Dove House?' she asked.

I was surprised that was her first question, but was fired up by it instantly. 'We've loved that house since we were kids. Our mum always dreamed of owning it, and passed that dream on to us. I love that it's unique, the style of it, the shape and colour, the fact that it's hidden by all those trees. I always thought it was a house that a heroine in a book would live in. When I was younger, I used to imagine a princess was hidden there. What can I say? Adam says I've always been a hopeless romantic.' Adam chuckled under his breath. 'But now I see it as a business opportunity. Glendale needs a place for people to stay. The village is thriving, people want to come here. I just know they would fall in love with Glendale if they could stay and enjoy it for a few days. And Dove House is the only property as special as the village and that's up for sale. We want to restore its art deco features and run it as a family business, really looking after our guests, making it feel like a home from home. I've studied hotel management, and as you know, I work at Glenmarshes Inn, and I've always wanted my own hotel. I know I can create somewhere really special for people to stay. And Adam is perfect to run the business and the renovation project.' I stopped, running out of breath. I looked at Anna, who nodded in encouragement. 'We just need a little help to get it started.'

'How little?' Beth asked with a raised eyebrow.

Adam explained how much we thought we'd need to make the right offer on the house and have enough to renovate it, and how much we were short by. He told her when they wanted final offers in; it wasn't far away at all, so we needed to work out the money situation quickly. I watched Beth as she listened. She was canny; her face gave nothing away. I was sure that my fingertips were sweating.

'Let me talk to the family solicitor and I'll come and see the house with you on Wednesday.'

'I'll email you our business plan,' Adam said, looking relieved to be able to do that.

'Excellent,' Beth said, and then she turned to me and winked.

—

Adam came back home with me after seeing Beth so we could eat. Kathleen and Hamish were there and everyone was eating chicken and salad, so we plated up some and joined them at the table.

I felt a mixture of emotions. Seeing Dove House again had made everything clear to me. I had been too complacent these past few years, and I couldn't be like that any more. I wasn't happy in my job and I had been trying to ignore that. But I was anxious, too. Because now that my passion for Dove House was back, I was scared that something would get in our way again. I was trying to be positive like Adam, but it wasn't easy. Setbacks in life had made me wary and unsure and I didn't like that about myself. It wasn't who I wanted to be.

I wanted to go after my dreams.

'Beth seemed really open to our investment idea,' Adam was saying to our mum as he ate. 'She said she'd come to look at the house with us on Wednesday after she's spoken to her solicitor.'

'Investment idea?' Kathleen asked, looking at us in confusion. 'What's going on?'

'The guide price for the house is too high,' Adam said, glancing at me. I knew he was uneasy about telling her. 'Our savings won't cover it, not if we want to make sure we offer the highest bid, so we thought we'd go and see Beth Fraser and ask for a loan.'

'She's helped out so many Glendale businesses,' I added. 'And she knows that having a place for people to stay will be great for the local economy. I think it will really benefit the village, and I hope she will think so too.'

Kathleen shook her head. 'But if you needed money then why didn't you speak to me and Hamish first? We're family.'

I looked at her. 'You made it clear the other night that you don't think we should make an offer, so why would we?'

'Well, I was right, wasn't I? You can't afford it!' she cried. 'This loan… will you be able to pay it back? What if you can't make enough money with the bed and breakfast?'

'We do have a business plan,' Adam said drily. 'We have all the numbers sorted. Hamish even looked it over for us.'

'Did he?' she glared at her husband, who just shrugged.

'Why can't you just support us?' I asked my sister, my patience fading.

'Well, of course your sister does,' Mum said, throwing Kathleen a look.

'I think it's a strong business plan,' Hamish put in mildly. 'Beth is likely to give you fair terms, she's known for that.'

I nodded. 'Exactly.' Being honest, I was less good at the numbers and the planning but I trusted Adam had it all worked out; he knew what we could and couldn't afford. 'I know what it's like to run a hotel, what people are looking for. We will have plenty of guests, I know it.' It was one thing I was sure of. I knew when the Inn had been special and I was going to make sure Dove House was exactly that.

'I still think you need a plan B in case you don't get it again,' Kathleen continued stubbornly.

Mum cleared her throat. 'You're going to the bank tomorrow, aren't you?' she asked before we answered Kathleen, which was a relief.

'Yes, to get the mortgage agreed,' Adam said. 'We've organised the reports and surveys to be done this week, and noted our interest through our solicitor, so we're just waiting to see if Beth will come on board and then we can make our offer.' Anyone interested needed to make their best offer over the guide price by the closing date that was fast approaching. This was when it had all fallen apart before and Betty had won by making a

43

higher offer than us. I really didn't want that to happen again. Everything was riding on Beth giving us the loan and I just had to hope that she would come through for us.

'Money is going to be tight with the renovation,' Adam admitted, looking at me.

'I can do things on a budget,' I insisted, although I was hoping my vision for the place wouldn't be too hindered by lack of money. I wanted it to be perfect. 'Maybe we can do some of the decorating ourselves to keep costs down.'

'Maybe you should both keep working just in case,' Kathleen said. 'I worry that you're pouring all your savings into it, and losing out on an income too.'

'There's no way we could manage to work during the renovation,' Adam said. 'I'm giving up my flat, so we'll be saving on rent money.'

'I don't like the idea of you both leaving your secure jobs,' my sister continued. She looked at the family. 'Surely I'm not the only one who thinks this?'

I was getting frustrated now. 'This is what we want to do, Kathleen. I know you've never had ambitions for a career, you just wanted to marry Hamish and have a family, but we want to own and run a bed and breakfast. This is the time to go for it.' I couldn't help but remember what that man had said to me at the Inn. 'I don't want to regret not going after my dream a second time.' I knew I could easily stay on at the Inn for years, with nothing changing, but I knew that wouldn't make me happy.

'Nor do I,' Adam agreed. 'We're both single, we don't have any responsibilities. It's the right time.' I nodded along. Adam hadn't found his person either. When Anna had come to Glendale, he had thought that maybe they would get together but she had fallen for Cameron almost straight away. We could let ourselves feel down about our unlucky love lives or we could see it as the perfect time to start our business, as we could put all our energy into it.

'Well, don't use this as a substitute for not having a husband and family,' Kathleen said to me then. 'If you focus too much on it, you'll never have them.'

'God, can't you just say good luck and leave it at that?' I snapped, my patience gone. My sister thought her life was the best, but just because I was on a different path to her, I didn't see how my life was not as good as hers. I got up from the table and walked into the living room with my plate. I couldn't sit and eat with my sister any more. She thought everything I did was wrong, and I was fed up with it. I hated how she always ended up planting a seed of doubt in my mind when she was like this.

When we were little we fought a lot. She was older and liked to boss me around. She still did, to be honest, but now I tried not to let it end in shouting matches. What was the point? We were grown-ups now. Still, sometimes I wished I could wrestle her like I had back then. Especially tonight.

Mum came in. 'Your sister just worries about you.'

'She has a funny way of showing it,' I retorted.

'You're just very different people.'

'Tell me about it.' I looked at my mum. 'I feel like I can't be happy unless I try this one last time. I'll always regret it if I don't. Yes, it's a risk and a challenge and it'll be hard work, I know all of that, but this is what I've wanted for years.'

She nodded. 'I know, love. I want it for you. I've seen that you've lost some of your sparkle recently, and I've hated it. Your sister isn't a dreamer like we are, she just worries, but I know you'll work it all out.'

'I hope so,' I said, trying to shake off my sister's warnings. 'I would rather give it a go than regret not trying, like I have been doing.'

'You know we're all behind you. I'd better go back in.' She paused. 'Make it up with your sister, you both need each other.'

I didn't reply and she went back to the table. I felt like Kathleen should apologise to me but I knew she wouldn't, she never had. It wasn't in her nature. And tonight, I was too annoyed to reach out. She had a way of making me question everything and I was already trying hard not to do that.

By Wednesday, we'd know if we had enough money to make an offer and nothing that Kathleen or me could say would change that.

Chapter Eight

After work on Wednesday, Adam and I met up again at Dove House to tour it with Beth Fraser.

There were two cars in the driveway when we arrived. A woman was standing outside; Adam said she was the estate agent, Jenny, and the front door was open. I could see a man inside looking around. I tried not to let my heart sink, but it was hard to see someone else appraising what felt like our house already. Then I leaned forward to look at him more closely.

'I know that man,' I said in surprise to Adam as we climbed out of the car. Beth drove in then and parked next to us in her Range Rover. She came over to us and asked what was wrong. 'That man was at the Inn and heard me talking about Dove House being up for sale. And that I was worried we couldn't afford it. What if he's going to try to outbid us?' I asked. He had talked about going after my dreams, but maybe he had meant his own dreams and he was going to steal the house from us.

'Just follow my lead,' Beth said and started to walk over to Jenny. I looked at Adam but he simply shrugged and followed her. Steeling myself, I trailed after them, hoping this wouldn't put Beth off from helping us to secure the house.

Jenny led us into the hallway and started to spiel off facts about the house as Beth asked her questions. 'I can see it needs a lot of work,' Beth said loudly, her voice echoing around the hall. I turned to see the man I'd met at Glenmarshes Inn in the doorway looking up at the ceiling, but his head tilted and I knew he'd heard her. If it was possible, my heart sank even further. I watched him step a little bit closer. He was as tall and thin as I remembered, his glasses perched on his nose, and he wore another suit that was as ill-fitting as the first one I'd seen him in. This time, though, I noticed that he was younger than I had imagined the first time we met – the suit throwing me off, perhaps – he seemed to be only a couple of years older than me.

'Do the electrics need replacing? What about all this damp?' Beth was asking Jenny. She looked at Adam. 'The budget for repairs is going to be sky-high.'

Adam nodded. 'I wonder if a potential buyer would be better off just knocking it down and building something new.'

'One of the other interested parties might turn it into flats,' Jenny confirmed.

'Is the staircase structurally safe?' Beth asked, her voice sounding very loud in the empty space as she walked over to examine it.

I walked away, unable to bear it. Knock Dove House down? I would never want to see that. 'You were at my Inn,' I said to the man as he took a picture of the ceiling on his phone.

He looked startled to see me beside him; his attention had been on the others. 'Oh, uh, yes,' he said with a cough.

'When you asked me if Dove House was up for sale, I didn't know that you were interested in it yourself,' I said, trying not to sound as annoyed as I felt.

He turned a little pink and coughed again. 'I was surprised that it was… I had wanted to come here to see it, so when you said it was up for sale, I took it as a sign that I needed to come now. Before it was too late.'

I sighed. I had believed that Dove House coming up for sale again was a sign for me and Adam, and now it seemed someone else thought it was a sign for them.

'Are you all thinking of buying it?' the man asked, nodding to the others.

'It doesn't look like it,' I replied dully.

'Your husband doesn't like it?' he asked, nodding towards Adam.

'That's my brother. We wanted to turn it into a B & B. We have always dreamed of owning Dove House. Ever since my mother brought us here as kids. She's always loved this house. She knew one of the old owners and fell in love with it as a teenager. She knew it would make a perfect place for people to stay. But as you heard at the Inn, we can't afford it without Beth's help, and as she says, it needs a lot of work.' Then I realised I was telling this stranger way too much. 'Anyway, what about you?'

'I knew someone who used to live here too. Someone who wanted me to see it for myself. People do seem to fall in love with this house.' I caught a glimpse of pain behind those tortoiseshell glasses. I was struck by his blue eyes once more. They really were quite startling. Then he shook his head and seemed to remember that I too was just a stranger, and stepped away from me.

Jenny, the agent, Beth and Adam joined us then. 'I was just saying you could save on the heating costs if you insulated up in the loft. The former owner had it closed off and never went in there, but I had a look and once you clear everything out...' Jenny said.

The man next to me looked startled. 'There are still things in the loft?'

Jenny nodded. 'That's right, Mr Scott. Betty, who is selling the house, never used it so there are things from former owners but it wouldn't be a big job, and then you could insulate.' The man looked away, deep in thought. I wondered what was going through his mind. Had the loft put him off? If anything, I was curious myself as to what we'd find up there – maybe some original decor I could use. But then I remembered we needed Beth and she was examining the wall with a very critical eye.

'Look at this mould,' she said, calling me over.

My shoulders slumped. 'Coming,' I said. I glanced back at the man – Mr Scott, Jenny had called him. He was walking towards the door with Jenny following him. I wished I knew if he was going to make an offer on the house and for how much. Even if he had known someone who lived here, I didn't want to think about him buying it instead of us. It felt unfair when he only knew about it being up for sale because of me.

We toured the rest of the house, Beth pointing out everything that needed work, and I felt worse and worse. The mystery man from the Inn drove off halfway through our tour and we went upstairs alone while Jenny took a phone call.

Once we were on the second floor, Beth turned to me. 'Well, you weren't kidding, this place is fabulous.'

'Huh?' I stuttered, staring at her. 'But all you've done is talk about what's wrong with it.'

'Well, yes, that man was listening to us. I was trying to put him off!'

'We were trying to pretend we either aren't going to make an offer or it'll be a low one so he doesn't go in too high,' Adam added when he saw my confused expression.

'You were?'

'I'm glad you didn't realise, as you looked so crushed. It worked perfectly,' Adam added with a grin.

'I thought you were going to say no,' I said to Beth.

'I can see how you two could transform this place.' Beth walked into a bedroom. 'This could be such a great place to stay. But more importantly,' she added, looking at us, 'I believe in you, and I can see how much you both want this. I think we should meet with my solicitor and decide what you're going to offer. We can't let that guy get this house. It needs to stay in Glendale hands. Right?'

'Right,' Adam agreed. He nudged me.

I was still taken aback. 'Right. I mean, yes, definitely! Wow, Beth.' And then I ruined any pretence of keeping things professional and grabbed Beth, pulling her into a hug. 'I can't thank you enough for this!'

Thankfully, she laughed. 'Don't thank me, just make this the best B & B Glendale could ever hope for.'

'We will,' Adam said. 'Won't we, sis?'

I let Beth go and hoped she couldn't see the tears welling up in my eyes. 'I promise.'

'I'll speak to Jenny and see if that guy is interested – we need to know what we're up against,' Adam said and walked off with a look of determination.

'I hope he doesn't want it,' I said, biting my lip.

'What would he do with it?' Beth wondered.

I shrugged. 'No idea. He said he knew someone who lived here once.'

'Well, we'll make the best offer we can and hope that Glendale will work its magic and let us have it,' Beth said.

'You really think we can make this a great place to stay?'

'I think if you believe you can, then you can.'

I looked out of the window at the overgrown garden. It was going to be a big challenge, but one I had been yearning for. And I had fantasised about what I'd do with this house for years. 'I always imagined decorating this house for Christmas and having guests staying to enjoy the season. I pictured cooking the turkey in an Aga in the kitchen. Is that mad? I mean, there's no way Adam will let me have an Aga, we won't be able to afford one.'

'Christmas in Glendale is always magical! People would love to stay here for it.' Beth clapped her hands. 'If you do get this house, then we have an Aga! And my mum wants to buy a new one for the Hall, so why don't you have our old one? It works perfectly, really, there's just a couple of scratches and she no longer likes the green. I told her it was a waste but sometimes there's no arguing with my mother, and if it'll make her happy...' She shrugged.

'That would be amazing! I just wish we could get started right now. I have so many ideas. Adam thinks we could be ready for guests sometime in the New Year, if we get the keys quickly enough.'

'It looks empty. Betty must have cleared the house with her daughter before they put it on the market.'

I nodded. 'Jenny says the loft needs a clear-out, but the rest they've taken already. I can see myself here, I always have, but it's hard to believe it might actually happen. I was heartbroken when we lost the house to Betty five years ago, the last time it was up for sale,' I admitted.

'Well, if we can stop the council selling off the High Street to developers like we did a few years ago, we can certainly get you this house. Come on, let's go and find your brother and get the ball rolling.'

Beth had a reputation for being fearless, and she had achieved so much it was hard not to trust her that we could do this. Like my brother, Beth's enthusiasm was contagious. I followed her out and made a silent promise to the house that I'd be back very soon.

Chapter Nine

Everything moved quickly after we had toured the house with Beth. Her solicitor explained everything about her investment – Beth's terms were more than fair, as Hamish had told us they would be – and together we agreed on what we would offer to Betty.

'All that's left to do is to contact our solicitor and get him to make our offer,' Adam said after we had left the office and said goodbye to Beth and were driving back to the village.

'That sounds simple, but the thought terrifies me,' I admitted. Once we had made our offer, that would be it – no going back, no way to know if it would be enough. We still didn't know if the man we'd seen at the house was interested; all Jenny would say was that there were several parties that she thought would be making offers along with us. I looked at my brother. 'You're really sure about this, right?'

'Nothing has changed for me. I still love Dove House and think it will make a great place for people to stay. And I think we work really well as a team.' Adam parked outside our family home, took off his seat belt and spun round to face me. 'And we both know we are going nowhere at the moment. We need this challenge, this project… this adventure. You know that I believe we can do it.'

'I believe it too, but I'm so nervous.'

'That's natural. It's a big undertaking. Has Kathleen made you doubt the idea?'

'A little bit, and the fact that we didn't get it last time. It's hard to be optimistic.'

'I know, but look, neither of us knows what will happen, if we can do it, if it'll be a success. But neither of us is happy not trying it, are we? I say we go for it and throw everything at it. If it works, great. If it doesn't, we won't have any regrets.' Adam shrugged.

'It's that easy for you?' I asked with a smile.

'It's the furthest thing from easy, but you know, I have faith that everything will work out, that it'll all be okay in the end.'

'And if not, it's not the end,' I said with a smile.

'Exactly. I know you believe that too, really. Yes, it's been a tough few years, and we've had setbacks, but that will make it all the sweeter when we do it. Right?'

'Right,' I agreed. I did believe that. 'What if you meet someone and run off and leave me there all alone?' I asked then, all my worries coming out now.

Adam chuckled. 'I could say the same, but I know neither of us would do that. If we are lucky enough to fall in love, they will just become part of it all.' He held out his hand. 'Deal?'

'Deal,' I agreed, shaking his hand firmly. I looked over at our house. 'I wish I could talk to Betty and explain why this means so much to us,' I said.

Adam turned to me. 'Why don't you?'

'What do you mean?'

'I once sold a house to a woman who wrote a letter to the family selling it explaining why she wanted it, and they chose her over the person who made the highest offer because they knew she'd care for it like they had. Why don't we write to Betty and tell her why she should choose us to be the new owners? She must have loved Dove House too. Let's hope she wants it to go to someone who will restore it and not knock it down. To people from Glendale like her, you know? It's worth a try. This is our last shot, isn't it?'

I smiled. 'You're right. It's a good idea. Shall we write it together?'

'You know I'm no good with words. I trust you. You write it and email it to our solicitor to send along with our offer.'

'You're sure?'

Adam nodded. 'You've got this, Lorna.'

I sucked in a breath. 'Okay. I'll message you when it's done.' I climbed out and walked into the house, waving as Adam drove away. I was scared that he was trusting me with writing the letter, but I also knew he was right that we had to try. If we could get Betty to believe in our vision like Beth had, then maybe she wouldn't just focus on the highest offer if that wasn't ours. We might be able to persuade her to think with her heart and not her head.

I walked into the kitchen where Mum was making tea. 'Is there enough water in the kettle for me too?'

'Of course, love. How did it go?'

I explained that we were all ready to make our offer. 'Adam had an idea. He thinks we should write a letter to Betty explaining why we want the house so much. He thinks it might help, if someone does offer more than we can.'

Mum passed me a mug of tea and took a sip of hers. 'I think that sounds like a perfect idea. I know if we ever sold this house, I'd want it to go to a family who could be as happy here as we have been. Betty had big dreams for the house, but sadly couldn't make them happen. But you and Adam can. She needs to know that.'

I nodded and sipped my tea. 'How do you put dreams into words, though?' I looked over as she started chopping up carrots ready to make dinner. 'Why did you fall in love with Dove House?'

Mum paused and smiled. 'Whenever I walked through the front door, I was filled with this feeling of warmth and comfort. As you know, my father died when I was really young, and it was just me and my mum in our flat and she had to work so hard… That house felt like a dream to me. And the people. I loved them like my own family.' She sighed, sadness crossing her face. 'Unfortunately, it wasn't to be. I wasn't meant to become part of that family, but I was happy there for a time. And I still remember it fondly. I suppose that house became a symbol of a happy time for me, and I wanted other people to feel that happiness too. I wasn't able to do it there, but I hope I've done it here in this house. I've learnt that your home really isn't about the house, it's the people in it, and this has been a happy family home, hasn't it?'

'It has,' I replied. 'We would have been happy anywhere together. But I know what you mean. That's why I got so sad when they changed the Inn. It didn't feel like a home from home any more. But I think I can make Dove House like that. I want people to love to stay there and have that special happy memory like you have of your time there.'

She glanced across at me. 'And to also raise your own family there one day?'

'Who knows if that will ever happen, but I hope so,' I replied. I would love that. I still longed for a love like my mum had with my dad or Kathleen had with Hamish.

'I think your letter should just be from your heart. That will be enough.'

'I wish I had the same faith as you do.'

Mum stopped chopping then. 'You've got a bit lost recently, but now is your time to shine. I went through a stage of not believing in myself when I was younger. I thought when that family left Dove House I hadn't been good enough for them and their house and their life, I suppose. I think I felt that way until I met your father and I realised that I was good enough.'

'You did?' Mum had never told me that before. She always seemed so strong and confident to me.

'I did. Meeting your father made me believe again. And becoming your mother. I knew I was doing exactly what I was supposed to be doing and although I would have loved to have had a bed and breakfast, my family meant so much more to me. It was what I was meant to do. And when I saw how much you loved that house, I started to dream of it for you instead. And I think it was always meant for you and Adam, and not me. What I'm saying is, no one should ever make you feel like you can't do something or that you don't deserve something. Because you can and you do.'

'Thanks, Mum. I'm going to write the letter,' I said, gulping down the rest of my tea. 'Wish me luck.'

'Good luck!' Mum said as I left the kitchen and went up to my bedroom.

Sitting down on my bed, I picked up a notebook and pen, crossed my legs and stared at the blank page. I thought about what Mum said about not letting someone make you feel like you aren't worthy or that your dreams are impossible.

And I remembered then what my ex, Mark, had said to me once when we were together. When I told him I wanted to open my own bed and breakfast one day. He had actually rolled his eyes. *Your head is stuck in the clouds. You shouldn't give up your job at the Inn. You need to be practical. This is where you belong.*

I still was pissed off about that, but at the time I had been upset and I'd wondered if he was right. I hadn't stood up for myself; I'd nodded along with him. It was the same sometimes with Kathleen. She made me feel like maybe I should just be practical and stay at the Inn and not try to do the B & B project. She would never do anything like that. But she wasn't me. And nor was Mark.

I had to stop listening to their doubting voices and, like Adam and Mum said, have some faith in myself. I had to believe that I was good enough to make my dreams come true. And if I didn't quite believe it yet, I was going to pretend that I did. Fake it until you make it and all that.

I picked up my pen and started to write.

> *Dear Betty*
>   *When I first walked through the door of Dove House, I was a child. I thought I'd stepped into a house straight out of a fairy tale. Tall and grand and all white, it felt like somewhere a princess should live. My mother adored*

Dove House and she dreamed of owning it one day and turning it into a place for people to stay, but she was never able to do that.

She passed that dream on to my brother Adam and I.

When Dove House came up for sale in my early twenties, we bid for it, but you were the one who got the house. I watched as you and your family moved in and I was happy for you. I don't know if you saw me but I walked past when you were moving in and I saw you and your husband looking at the house in the front garden, arms around one another, smiling and looking so happy because you were home. And I knew the house was in safe hands. I could see you loved it as much as I did and I hoped that you and your family would be happy there.

Years later, here we are, Dove House is up for sale and for one last time my brother and I are trying to buy it again. I know that I'll always regret it if we don't try once more. That's why I wanted to write to you. To explain that Dove House somehow feels like our family home even though we've never lived there. It brings me comfort. When I walk past it, I smile. It has a warmth to it. Did you find that? When you walk through the door, you feel as if you've come home.

I want to feel that every day, but I also want other people to feel it too. Because my brother Adam and I don't just want it to be our home, but a home for anyone who needs warmth and comfort, or who might be lost — we want to help them be found. We want to restore Dove House in all its art deco glory and open it up as a bed and breakfast.

I've lived in Glendale all my life and I love it here. I want other people to be able to stay here and fall in love with our village and for Dove House to feel like a home from home for them.

I know that you planned to do something similar when you bought it, but sadly, it wasn't possible for you, which I'm so sorry about. I want to do it for me, my brother and my mother and all of my family, but also for you and your daughter and your husband. And also for all the families over the years that might come and stay with us there.

Owning Dove House has been a dream of mine for so long, and I have spent the past few years thinking that I need to stop dreaming and that it's never going to happen. But now I have one more chance to make it come true. I feel like you understand the dream my brother and I have because you had the same dream once. Let me and my brother make it come true now. Let us call Dove House home…

My brother and I would love you to come and stay with us at the House once it's restored and open for guests. Because we all deserve to see our dreams come true.

Love, Lorna

Before I could talk myself out of it, I typed the letter into an email along with our offer and sent it to our solicitor. I knew I had done all I could. I just had to hope it was enough.

I picked up my phone and sent a message to Adam telling him I'd sent it. And then I went over to the window to draw the curtains as it was now dark. I looked up at the night sky dotted with stars and made a wish on the brightest one.

Chapter Ten

The closing date for offers on Dove House passed, and Adam came round to spend the evening with me and the family as we waited for news from the estate agent, Jenny.

I was a nervous wreck. Adam seemed as calm as usual but he couldn't really sit still and kept getting up to make a drink or look out of the window or pull his phone out of his pocket to stare at the screen. I was relieved that Kathleen and Hamish had a midwife appointment and would be coming later, when hopefully we would know either way and could prepare ourselves for what she would have to say about it.

'Whatever happens, you'll be fine,' Mum said, after looking at us both anxiously for a few minutes.

'Absolutely,' Dad agreed, although they exchanged a concerned look.

'I'm bored. Can we watch a film?' Noah complained. Mum put one on for him and Leo, and the four of us went into the kitchen.

And then Adam's phone rang.

'Oh,' I gasped as Adam grabbed his phone and put it on speaker. Mum, Dad, me and Adam crowded round it as he placed his phone on the kitchen table.

'Hello? Jenny?'

'Hi, Adam,' she said brightly. I looked at Mum. Did her tone offer a clue, or was she always bubbly on the phone? 'How are you?'

'Uh, fine,' he mumbled. 'Is there news?'

'There is.' She cleared her throat. I wondered if I was going to scream. 'We've had all the bids in for Dove House, and Betty and her daughter have considered them very carefully. I have to tell you that yours was not the highest offer made...'

I sank into a chair and sighed. Mum put a hand on my shoulder.

'However, she loved the email that your sister sent and she really believes in your vision of turning the house into a bed and breakfast. It was what she and her husband had dreamed of doing. The highest offer, she felt, didn't have such a vision and she was worried they might knock the house down, which I think would break all our hearts, wouldn't it?'

Adam looked at me. 'So...'

'So,' Jenny said, 'I'm delighted to tell you Betty wants to sell Dove House to you and your sister!'

I did scream then. Mum clapped her hands in delight and my dad banged Adam on the back so hard Adam's cheer of delight turned into a splutter.

The twins ran in to see what the commotion was all about and began jumping up and down in excitement.

Jenny laughed down the phone amid the chaos. 'Congratulations!'

'Oh, thank you, Jenny,' I gasped as I jumped up and hugged my mum, who was already crying.

'Why don't you call me in the morning? Celebrate tonight,' I heard Jenny say as I turned to Adam.

'Thank you,' he said, hanging up the phone and reaching for me. He hugged me tightly. 'We did it, sis. Can you believe it?'

The back door opened and in walked my sister and Hamish. They both stopped short at the scene in front of them.

'We got it,' I said, letting go of Adam. 'We got Dove House!' Adam slung an arm around my shoulders and squeezed me as I beamed at Kathleen and Hamish.

'Well done,' he said, coming over.

'I hope you know what you've let yourselves in for,' Kathleen said, putting something down on the kitchen table.

I turned away from her, determined she wouldn't spoil this moment. 'We did it,' I said to Adam. 'We really did it.'

'I always knew we would,' he replied. I laughed, knowing that even my optimistic brother hadn't felt that way, but I would let him off because this was the best news.

'Oh, Kathleen, how was the scan?' Mum asked, turning to my sister suddenly. 'Can I see the photo?'

Kathleen shrugged. 'Sure, I have it here.' She glanced at me but I couldn't read the expression on her face.

I sat down again, feeling overwhelmed. My cheeks hurt from smiling and I sucked in two shaky breaths. It was what we had wanted for so long. I was so excited, but I knew this was only the first step.

We had a long journey ahead of us.

–

I handed my notice in at my next shift.

I went to see Chris, my boss, to tell him I was leaving to open my own bed and breakfast. He had been shocked. I supposed I'd never given him any idea that I was restless at work, but then again, he wasn't the type of manager to ever check in with his staff.

'I hope you know what you're letting yourself in for,' he said, echoing what Kathleen had said. I knew Chris was always saying the wrong thing, but that put a dampener on my excitement exactly as Kathleen had done. I was trying to hide my nerves and keep focused on how great it was that we had our dream property, but they were making it very hard. At least Adam was always on hand with encouragement. He had said we should quit our jobs straight away so that once we had the keys, we could start on the renovation.

'Shouldn't you wait and keep earning money for as long as possible?' Kathleen had asked.

'I need to be there on-site, as the project manager,' Adam had said. 'And there is so much to do. If we don't go all in, we won't be able to open for months. It's better to work as hard as we can and get the business up and running as soon as possible.'

'What if you run out of money?'

Adam and Kathleen had argued about it but I knew in my heart I wouldn't be able to focus on my job at the Inn. Dove House was my job now, even if it would be a while until we earned any money from it.

'How did it go?' Grace found me after I had met with Chris.

'I can't believe I've actually done it,' I admitted. It all felt rather surreal. 'I'm shaking.'

'Well, you can't take a break, I'm afraid, there's a man asking for you in reception. A very good-looking man. Have you been hiding a boyfriend from me?' she asked with a grin.

'I haven't had a date in two months,' I replied. 'I hope it isn't a guest complaining. I'll see you at lunch.' She waved me off and I walked into reception and stopped short in the doorway as I recognised the man pacing up and down in a dark suit. It was Mr Scott. Why was he here again? I hoped he wasn't going to kick off that me and Adam had got Dove House and he hadn't.

'Lorna,' he said, looking relieved to see me.

'You know my name?'

'It was on your name badge when we met. I remembered. Have you got a few minutes, please, to talk? Uh – in private.' He looked rather agitated.

'Okay,' I said in surprise. I led him into the lounge and over to a table in the corner. 'Have a seat. What can I do for you?' I asked, staying polite in case it was something to do with the Inn. I had met him first when he'd been here for a conference, after all. I didn't think it was about his stay, by the look on his face, and I hoped he wasn't going to beg me to sell him the house because that was definitely not going to happen.

'I'm not sure if I ever introduced myself… I'm Finlay. Finlay Scott,' he said, after a moment. 'I think I said, but honestly, the past month has been a bit of a blur. But I knew someone who lived at Dove House, which was why I came to look round.'

'And why you wanted to buy it?' I said, politeness fading as I guessed what he was going to say.

'No,' he said quickly. 'Although I did put in an offer because I panicked. When you said it was up for sale, I knew I'd better hurry to have a look at it. I had promised I would go to the house. And then Jenny started talking about the loft and I thought, hang on, maybe he was right? And how could I fulfil my promise if someone else bought it? So I made an offer but I didn't really want the house. I just didn't know what else to do,' he said all in a rush.

'Well, I'm sorry your offer wasn't accepted, but if you didn't really want the house...' I said, confused. 'Sorry, but why are you here?' I asked then, bluntly. I knew Chris wouldn't be happy if I didn't get back to work soon and I wasn't really sure what Finlay was talking about.

'He loved Dove House, he talked about it all the time, especially near the end. I promised him that I'd come here, and things weren't great between us for a long time so I needed to do what I'd promised him,' Finlay continued as if I hadn't spoken. He really was in a state. 'He asked me to find something but I told him there was no way it would still be there. But then Jenny said the loft hadn't been touched and I thought, what if it is? I'd promised him I'd make sure before he died. It was the last thing he ever asked of me.' I couldn't not feel sorry for him; his words were spoken with such emotion. Behind his glasses, his lovely eyes had heartbreak in them.

'Who asked you all this?' I couldn't help but wonder.

'My father,' he replied heavily. 'He passed away. And he was very upset at the end, thinking about whatever it was that he'd left there, that it might still be there. He kept telling me to go and find it and give it to the person who was meant to have it. That it could be in the loft. I thought he was crazy, but... what if it is there?'

My heart went out to him. 'What can I do, though?'

'I was hoping you'd let me look. In the loft. When you get the keys.'

It was a relief that he wasn't expecting me to give up the house to him or anything. I opened my mouth to say that would be okay but then I had a sudden thought. 'And I suppose this thing you say your father wanted you to find is some kind of heirloom?' I folded my arms across my chest. I assumed that he was after something worth a lot of money if he'd been willing to buy the house to find it, and I wasn't going to let him take it from us without a fight.

Finlay looked confused and then twigged what I meant. 'God, no. It's purely sentimental, I promise. Before he died, it was troubling him that he never knew what happened to it, and he wanted the person it was meant for to have it at last. It gave him peace to know that I was going to try to find it. That's all, I swear. But I'll show you as soon as I find it. Then you'll see,' he pleaded with me. 'We can look together. I could help you clear the loft out. It sounded like a big job, potentially. And if we find it then you can decide what happens to it. I promise!' He spoke urgently. Desperately even. The promise to his father clearly meant a lot to him. It seemed genuine.

'I'd have to check with my brother. We've bought it together,' I said after a moment.

'Of course, of course. Here.' He slid a business card across the table. 'My contact details. I'm heading back to Perth now, but if you could talk to your brother and let me know? Then when you get the keys, I could come back and help you clear the loft. It would mean the world to me. If you made a promise to your father, well… You understand, don't you? I need to do this.'

I looked at the card. He was an accountant. The business was called Scott Accountants Ltd. 'You worked with your father?'

'Yes. I left for a while but I'm back. We were having the company annual general meeting when I first came here to the Inn,' he said. He fiddled with his tie. I got a sense again that he didn't like wearing a suit. 'I need to take over running the company now, which was why I was here.' He smiled weakly.

There was more to this story, but I knew I needed to get on with work. 'Okay,' I said, pocketing the business card. 'Let me talk to Adam and I'll be in touch. I know that if I made my father a promise, I'd do all I could to keep it,' I admitted. 'If we can help, we will.' I wasn't sure if I could forgive myself if I just said no. I knew Adam would feel the same way. We'd grown up in Glendale where we tried to help one another, and only on Sunday the minister, Brodie, had talked at church about kindness. It seemed wrong to refuse Finlay this chance to do what his father had asked of him. And we had to clear the loft, it was true, and it could be a big job. If we did it together, it would be done faster, so it would be helpful for me and Adam, not just Finlay.

Finlay relaxed visibly. 'Thank you, Lorna. I can't thank you enough.' He smiled then, and it lifted his face. Grace had called him good-looking, but that smile of his would probably have made her say handsome.

I was a little wrong-footed for a moment, thinking about him being attractive. 'Yes, well, I'll talk to Adam,' I repeated, hoping I wasn't blushing. 'What will you do while we wait for the keys?'

'There is so much to do. I need to hit the ground running with my father's company and speak to our clients,' he said, looking worried again. 'And my father's house... my family home... there is so much there that needs sorting out.' He sighed. 'It's just me, I don't have any siblings. My uncle is coming to help, but there is a lot to process, you know?'

'I can only imagine. I'm sorry for your loss.'

'Oh,' he said, startled again. 'Yes, thank you. And I'm glad you got the house, Lorna, I really am.'

'That's very kind of you.' I stood up. 'I'd better get back to work. I'll be in touch then.' I paused. 'Look after yourself, won't you?'

He nodded. 'You too,' he added. I walked away but I couldn't help glance back before I left the lounge. Finlay was staring out of the window, lost in thought. I couldn't imagine losing my father like he had. And he was all alone. No siblings for support.

Adam and I could help him, though. That made me feel better.

I got on with my day, but Dove House and what Finlay and I might find in the loft wasn't far from my thoughts.

It was going to be a long wait for those keys.

Part Two

Chapter Eleven

It was the last day of September when I walked through the lobby area of Glenmarshes Inn, my shoes clip-clopping on the polished marble floor.

The nights were drawing in and the light was fading outside as my shift came to an end. It felt so surreal to be here for my last Friday shift as Housekeeping Manager. I had two days at work next week, and then I would be leaving. And I felt a real mixture of emotions. Relief, because I had been unhappy here for a long time, if I was honest with myself; trepidation, because the future suddenly felt uncertain after being so predictable for so long; and excitement for the challenge ahead.

While I worked out my notice, I spent as much time outside of work with Adam planning the renovation as I could, and it had been almost easy to keep my fear under check with so much to do. But soon I would be unemployed and starting this huge endeavour. Half of me wanted to grab Chris and beg for my job back, and the other half wanted to run out of the Inn jumping for joy. It was going to be interesting which half won out before it was time for me to leave.

I checked the clock on the wall. Grace had asked me to come into the lounge so I headed that way.

Pushing the door open, I was surprised that I couldn't hear the usual merriment inside, but when I opened it wide, I realised why.

'Surprise!' Grace yelled, and cheers surrounded me as I stepped into the lounge and saw a crowd of familiar faces raising glasses to me. I gasped as I took in the sight. Behind everyone was a table full of food and drinks and above them hung a banner that shone gold and said, 'GOOD LUCK, LORNA!'

'Guys, I can't believe this,' I said, walking over and smiling at the kind gesture. I felt dangerously close to welling up as Grace pulled me into a tight hug. 'You did all this?' I asked her.

She pulled back and grinned. 'I know it's not your final shift, but there was no way I was going to let you slip away to Glendale without a send-off.'

I laughed. 'You're the best,' I told her. 'But what did Chris say?'

She grimaced. 'He said we could do it tonight as long as it only lasts for an hour and no one slacks off,' she said. 'There are no corporate guests and it's nice and quiet, so he couldn't refuse. He'll probably keep checking the time, though.'

I rolled my eyes. 'Never mind, we have an hour to enjoy. I'm really grateful you did this.'

'Well, of course. You have no idea how much I'm going to miss you.' She gave me a squeeze. 'Come on, the whole gang is here,' Grace said, as we joined everyone else. She wasn't wrong. Most of the Inn staff had come along to wish me well, which was really lovely.

I had a glass of sparkling wine and then Chris found me. 'So, it's almost your last shift then,' he said a little awkwardly. For a hotel manager, he really wasn't good with people.

'It's crazy to think I leave next week. I will miss this place,' I said. And I knew I would. I did love my colleagues, and the place had taught me a lot about running hotels, and even though in the past two years the place had changed so much, when I first started I had loved it here. And I was still fond of the Inn. 'But I've always wanted to open my own bed and breakfast.'

He nodded and looked around to ensure we were alone. 'I will miss it, too. I'm being transferred to a bigger hotel and Alec is coming with me, so we need to find a new chef. Head office are transferring a manager here but there isn't anyone available to take over from Alec in the restaurant so they want me to find someone locally.'

I raised an eyebrow. 'That's a lot of change,' I replied. I hadn't thought Chris would ever leave, but maybe that explained why he had been so tough while he was here: he'd been working towards a promotion.

'Indeed. Finding a new chef isn't going to be easy, that's for sure.'

Inspiration struck. 'I might have the perfect person,' I said. 'One of my best friends has just got her chef's diploma and is looking for somewhere to work. She is an amazing cook,' I added, thinking of Anna. She wanted to have her own restaurant but needed more experience first. I also knew that Cameron's bosses had offered her work at the Hilltop Farm retreat, but she wanted to keep her relationship with Cameron separate from her job. And if Chris was leaving too, the Inn might well bounce back to the place it used to be.

Chris nodded. 'Get her to come and see me on Monday,' he said.

'Great, I will,' I said, so happy I could help Anna like she had helped me and Adam by taking us to see Beth.

'I wish you well, Lorna,' he said briskly, before walking off.

I chuckled under my breath. That was the closest thing to praise I'd ever had from him. I thought about his news that he and the chef were moving on. I always suspected that the chain would replace Chris with someone they already knew; they would never have promoted one of us, and that cemented I'd made the right choice to leave. I was going to be my own boss, finally. It was going to be hard, but I knew it was what I had to do.

Two of my housekeeping team came over to tell me how much they were going to miss me, which made me well up properly.

I was feeling quite emotional when Grace found me again and handed me another glass of bubbly. 'I already booked a taxi so you don't need to drive home. We need to toast Dove House.'

I clinked my glass against hers. 'I still can't quite believe it.'

Jenny, the estate agent, had told me and Adam that my letter had touched Betty's heart. There had been one offer that was higher than ours but not enough for her to choose them over us. That meant the world to me, and to say thank you, I was determined that she would be one of our first guests. I wondered who the higher bidder had been. Perhaps it had been Finlay Scott, but thankfully he wasn't too disappointed. I was over the moon that, finally, we had the house of our dreams. Well, tomorrow we would. Tonight I was going to drink another glass of bubbly and get ready to say goodbye to Glenmarshes Inn.

'I'm so proud of you,' Grace said. 'When I grow up, I want to be just like you.'

'You're a year older than me,' I reminded her.

'You know what I mean. Come on, I need a cupcake.' She pulled me over to the food table. 'I can't believe you're leaving me here alone,' she said as she grabbed us a cake. She pouted. 'The Inn is going to be dull without you. You won't forget about me out in Glendale, will you?'

'As if I ever could. You have to come and see the place as soon as possible. I can't wait to show you.'

'I'd love that,' she replied happily. 'You get the keys tomorrow, don't you? Make sure you send me a photo to document it.'

'The whole family are coming with me and Adam, so there will be a lot of photos. Even Kathleen said she'd come.'

'That's a turn-up for the books, isn't it?' Grace had met Kathleen a few times and thought she was grumpy. Kathleen was definitely not a 'let your hair down' kind of person, whereas Grace always was.

'She probably just wants to point out everything that's wrong with the place.'

'Well, don't let her bring you down! You've got the place you always wanted, and I think it's going to be brilliant. Of course, it's a project, but you can do it.'

I smiled. 'I hope so.' I finished the rest of my glass and Grace poured me another. 'I'd better not drink too much. Can't have a hangover for picking up the keys,' I said.

'We only have an hour – we need to make the most if it.'

'So, what are your plans for the renovation?' Clare, our receptionist, asked, joining us. I took a deep breath and filled her in on everything we wanted to do to the house, along with my decoration ideas. We had already spoken to the council. Betty and her husband had been granted permission to change the home into use as a business and they were honouring that for us. As we wanted to restore the features of the house and fixing everything that was in disrepair, and not looking to add to the building or change the structure, we hadn't needed to go through a formal planning permission process with them, they had been agreeable to what we wanted to do. 'Wow, it sounds like a real challenge,' she replied.

'It will be,' I agreed. There was so much to do, it felt like we had a mountain to climb.

'Here's to the challenge!' Grace raised her glass and I clinked mine against it and tried to tell myself not to panic about it yet, just focus on the fact that the house was ours and the rest would fall into place. It had to. This had been five years coming, but really, it had been twenty-three years in the making, ever since my mum first pointed out Dove House to me on that autumn walk when I was just a child.

Chapter Twelve

Despite my best efforts, I did have a slight headache after all the bubbly at the Inn when I walked to Dove House from home the following morning. Adam had offered to get the keys from the estate agent's in Glenmarshes and was going to drive and meet us at the house with them.

So me, my mum and dad, the twins, Kathleen and Hamish all set off together.

'My back hurts,' Kathleen grumbled as we walked towards the High Street.

I ignored her, refusing to let her affect my mood today. I looked up at the clear blue sky. It was a sunny, crisp morning marking the start of October. The leaves on the trees lining our walk were beginning to turn shades of gold and brown. I loved autumn, and the signs that everything was changing. I couldn't wait for the leaves to fall and crunch underfoot. To pick up conkers to pass on to Noah and Leo who always competed for the largest pile. To wear my cosiest jumpers and light my favourite scented candles. And to drink hot chocolate in my pumpkin-shaped mug.

I hoped that getting the keys to Dove House at the start of my favourite season was a good sign. That the change on the horizon would be a really good one.

'Let's get some hot drinks,' Hamish suggested, so we stopped off at Emily's Bakery to pick up teas and coffees and hot chocolate for the boys. The delicious smell of her baked goods made sure we all left with a tasty treat as well.

'So good,' Kathleen said, in a better mood as she ate her muffin. No one could be angry eating one of Emily's muffins, I bet.

My phone rang and I smiled as I answered Anna's call. 'Thanks for calling me back.'

'What's up? Aren't you picking up the keys today?'

'We're walking to Dove House now. I wanted to tell you that last night I had my leaving do at the Inn and I found out that my manager and the chef are both leaving. They really need to find a new chef, and my manager, Chris, agreed to see you about the job,' I told her down the phone.

'Are you serious?!' she squealed. I explained that he wanted to meet with her on Monday if she was happy to. 'That would be amazing. Wow, Lorna, thanks for thinking of me.'

'Just paying it forward. I wouldn't be picking up the keys to Dove House without you.'

'You'd have found a way, I'm sure,' she replied, as modest as ever. 'Should I be nervous of this Chris?'

'Are you ever nervous of anyone?' I replied with a smile. I wished I could be as feisty as Anna. 'He doesn't have the best people skills, but he's leaving, so I wouldn't worry. Just impress him with your cooking and you'll have him eating out of your hand. Pardon the pun.'

She snorted and I grinned down the phone. 'And it would be a good place to work?'

'You know I didn't like how it became more corporate now that it's part of a chain, but the staff are lovely and you'd get so much useful experience there.'

'And I will know that it's not forever. It's a stepping stone, like it was for you. Okay, I'm going to make some food to take to the Inn, so this Chris won't be able to refuse me the job. I have to go! Good luck with the keys. See you at the pub later.' She hung up and I chuckled. Anna was always full of energy. I had no doubt she'd knock Chris's socks off on Monday.

'Here we are,' I told Noah and Leo as we turned into the road. 'That is our new house,' I said, pointing ahead. You could

77

just make out the top floors, its white spire peeking above the tops of the trees. My heart lit up to see it. 'It's big, isn't it?'

'It's huge,' Leo said, staring. 'Does it have a ghost?'

He loved reading scary stories. 'I hope not, Adam and I will be living there soon.'

'Race you!' Noah cried, and charged off, Leo trying to catch up as always.

'Watch the road!' my mum yelled after them. She caught up with me and slipped an arm through mine. 'How are you feeling?'

'Freaking out just a little bit,' I admitted. I hadn't been able to eat the flapjack I'd got from the bakery but I sipped my coffee. 'You?'

'Jittery,' Mum agreed. She squeezed me. 'But very proud of you and Adam. I brought a pack of tissues as I am very likely to burst into tears when we go inside.'

'Me too,' I agreed. We were both the criers in the family. We reached the white gates, open already, and inside, Adam's car was parked and he was by the front door, pacing back and forth impatiently waiting for us.

'Adam!' The twins rushed up to him, Noah declaring he was the winner of the race with a cry of triumph. Leo kicked a stone on the driveway in annoyance.

Adam waved the keys as me and Mum approached. 'I got them. Let's go!'

'Shouldn't we say something?' I asked.

Adam sighed. 'Fine, but not a long speech, sis. I forgot my coat and I'm cold.'

'You never have a coat,' I replied. Adam was one of those men who still wore shorts in winter. I'd never understand it. I needed about five layers before I could leave the house once winter arrived. We lived in the Highlands, after all. I cleared my throat as the others reached us and we all gathered round the front door. 'The first time I walked into this house, I was just a child. But I knew I had walked into somewhere special. Adam and I have wanted to turn this house into a bed and breakfast for so many years, and that today, we actually have the keys. But I want to thank Mum for bringing us here all those years ago and making us believe that one day it could be ours.' I turned to my brother as my mother sniffed, fumbling for her tissues. 'I'm so excited to begin this journey with you, Adam.'

He held the keys out. 'Your letter got us this house. You do the honours, sis.'

I grinned and took the keys and unlocked the door, pushing it open and stepping inside. Sunlight streamed in through the window and pooled in the hallway and it felt like it was welcoming us in. I drank in the sight and smiled, feeling a lump rise in my throat. The house was finally ours. 'Here we are,' I said as my family filed in after me.

And then there was a loud crashing sound followed by splintering wood. I looked up and gasped, putting my arm up to stop anyone walking past me. Then we all watched in horror as the old light fitting fell from the ceiling and shattered on the floor. Dust and debris clouded our vision for a moment before it settled and the house became still again.

'Awesome,' Noah said, breaking the shocked silence.

'At least we had always planned to replace that light,' Adam said, trying to be cheerful as ever.

Dad chuckled while Mum tutted and I looked across at my sister Kathleen, who gave me a look that unmistakably said 'I told you so'.

I sucked in a breath and hoped that wasn't a bad omen or anything. Our surveys had found the house structurally sound, but I really hoped they hadn't missed anything because our budget was tight enough as it was; we couldn't afford for anything else to go on the renovation list.

Adam saw my face and cleared his throat. 'Who wants a tour?' he asked.

'Me!' the twin boys cried in unison, throwing their hands up in the air with enthusiasm.

Chapter Thirteen

Mum found me a while later in what was going to be my bedroom. The room was on the top floor of the house, looking out over the garden. I stood by the window and tried to picture what it would look like down there once the grass was cut and flowers planted and tables and chairs put out for guests to enjoy. I was able to visualise things easily but I knew the final image in my mind would be a long time coming, and I couldn't help but feel even more panicked about the work ahead after our dramatic entrance earlier.

'Penny for your thoughts?' she asked me gently.

I turned round and gave Mum a small smile. 'I was just thinking what I might bring from my room at home. I'll finally be able to have a bigger bed.'

'You could fit a king-size in here,' she agreed. 'Are you okay? You've been so quiet since that light fell down.'

'It was just a stark reminder that there is a lot to do in this house before we can get up and running as a business. It's such a big project. While we've been planning it, it's felt abstract, I suppose, but now we're here, it's real. The work is about to start. And it's all new. Neither of us has ever had a house before, let alone renovated one.'

'I know you overthink sometimes, like I do,' Mum said. 'But don't let your nerves get in the way of the plan. It's a sound one. Adam has your budget all worked out. Glen's builders have their timeline. There's no point in worrying about things that haven't happened yet, now is there?'

I nodded. I knew Mum was right. 'It's just that so much is riding on this. This is not only our home, but it's going to be our job, our source of income. I've waited so long for this. And now I'm here, it all feels so big, you know? Like this has to work out.'

'I know the last few years haven't gone to plan, but you need to look forward now. You've made this happen, and I know that you and Adam are up to this.' She joined me at the window and smiled at the garden. 'This place could look amazing. I know, don't forget – I've been in here when it was.'

'Tell me about how it was then,' I requested, never tiring of hearing about Dove House. My house now, I supposed, although it would take a while for that to properly sink in and for the house to really feel like that. After all, I'd still be going back to our family home later. This wasn't my bedroom yet.

'Well, the garden was perfectly kept. They had a gardener and he loved roses, so that space over there was a beautiful rose garden and there was an archway, I think, over there, and there used to be a lovely bird table near the house.' Mum turned back to the room. 'And this room belonged to the daughter of the family. She was younger than me. It was decorated all in pink – not your taste, I know, but it was really pretty. I envied her, I'll be honest.'

I saw the wistfulness in my mother's eyes as she remembered the house back then. She had always said that once she had felt happy here, almost part of the family, but that had been suddenly snatched away when they moved. I'd never really got the full story as to why. 'What happened to that family, Mum? Why did you stop coming here?' I asked, hoping that now we were in Dove House, she might tell me.

Mum turned to me and opened her mouth and then Kathleen walked in. 'There you are. Hamish needs to get to work, so I'm going with him. I have some things to do at home.'

'Of course, darling,' Mum said, smiling as if our conversation had never happened. 'We were just imagining what this could look like once it's your sister's room.'

'I hope you're getting the boiler sorted ASAP, it's freezing in here,' Kathleen replied, looking at me.

'A new one is being fitted next week.' The boiler would be the biggest expense, along with fixing the roof, but once both things were done, the house would be liveable again. I looked at my sister. 'You could say something positive about the house, you know.'

She sighed. 'It's a striking building, but it's going to take a lot to turn it into somewhere people will pay to stay. I just hope you both know what you've taken on.'

'No, we haven't thought about it at all. Don't treat us like kids! You know we have a plan. Adam's got it all sorted. You know what I think?' I snapped. 'That you can't stand this.'

'Please, can we not...' Mum started, seeing an argument brewing.

'Can't stand what?' Kathleen fired back, ignoring our mother.

'That we did it. That we made our dream come true. When you always thought we wouldn't do it. Well, watch us prove you wrong.'

'All I can say is good luck, because you're going to need it,' she flung back, spun round and stormed out of the room.

'Why can't she ever be happy for me?' I asked Mum.

'Of course she is. She's just tired and worried about the baby. It's her first, and it's a nervous time.'

I shook my head. Kathleen was like that before she became pregnant. 'You'd better go after her. I want to take some pictures,' I said, not wanting to talk about my sister any more. She was ruining picking-up-the-keys day as I had been afraid she would.

Mum left and I exhaled. Mum had been right about me feeling like my life had been waiting to start. Well, here it was. I couldn't let Kathleen bring me down. I pulled my phone out and took a video of the room. I wanted to film each room so that we could document them being transformed. I thought it would be great for the website we needed to set up for the B & B, and for social media too. I turned the camera on and took a selfie standing in the room.

Let the reno begin #DoveHousebedandbreakfast

I posted it on all my social media accounts and took a deep breath before walking out and heading back down the stairs to find my family. Adam had cleared away the broken light fitting, so thankfully the hall no longer looked like a disaster zone as I walked through to the kitchen.

'Good news and bad news,' Adam greeted me in there.

'Bad news first, always better to get it over with,' I replied, steeling myself.

'There's a patch of damp that wasn't on the survey,' Adam said, pointing. 'Good news is that Hamish is going to set up a website for us, so we don't need to pay someone to do that.'

I turned to our brother-in-law. 'That is definitely good news, thanks, Hamish. You'll have time?'

'It won't take long to get you started, and then you guys can update it. Leave it with me.' He glanced at the doorway as Kathleen called for him from the hallway. 'But, you know, maybe keep it between us. I have to go to work. It looks great, well done you two.' He hurried out with a wave.

'Kathleen really got lucky with that man,' I said.

'You're right there,' Adam agreed.

'So, are you going to call Glen and his dad about the extra damp?' The builders were due first thing on Monday to get started. I had two more shifts at Glenmarshes Inn, but Adam would be here project-managing from Monday, having had his last day as an estate agent yesterday.

'I'll give them a heads-up, yes. Let's hope it's the only extra patch, otherwise our budget is going to go quickly out of the window.'

'It's already tight,' I said. 'We need to have enough to decorate otherwise no one will want to stay here.'

'I'm trying to make the money go as far as I can,' Adam replied, a tiny hint of stress in his voice. 'No one can stay here if the building isn't safe and warm. That has to be our priority.'

I sighed. 'I know, I know. Oh, I'd better tell Finlay Scott we have the keys now.' Adam had agreed with me that we should let Finlay come and look at the loft with me, and when I had messaged him, Finlay had been relieved and grateful. I had said I'd let him know when we were at Dove House.

'It's going to be interesting what you might find up in the loft,' Adam said.

'I know, I wonder what his father wanted him to look for...' I started to say, then I broke off when I heard a noise behind him. 'What's that?' I walked to the back door where a scratching sound was coming from. 'God, I hope there are no rats,' I said anxiously. I opened the door and was greeted by a meow. A large tabby cat pushed past me, walking into the kitchen as if he owned the place, and flopped down on the kitchen floor and began washing.

'Um... who are you, then?' I asked, bending down. The cat was purring happily but he looked thin and his coat wasn't in the best condition. 'A stray?'

'Looks like it,' Adam said. He smiled. 'We always wanted a cat.' My dad was allergic so we'd never had pets growing up.

'Maybe we should take him to the vet?' The cat's ears pricked up, and he gave me a look of what I can only describe as disgust, got up and walked back out the door. 'Oh dear.'

Adam looked at the door. 'Long gone. We'll keep an eye out for him. Right then, we need to do some measuring...'

'And I want to try these paint samples in the hallway before we lose the light.' I'd feel better once we got to work. Adam had created a spreadsheet with everything that needed to be done and an estimated timeline, which kind of made my eyes swim when I looked at it. Adam was the logical numbers one in our team. I had a folder full of decor inspiration and a notebook with all my ideas in. The two different ways of

84

doing things summed us up, which was why I was hopeful we'd make a great team on this project, if we didn't get into too many budget disagreements. I knew if it came down to a choice between something practical or something pretty, we might need a mediator.

Mum, Dad and the twins left us to it shortly afterwards, and we got as much done as we could before the light started to fade outside. 'I like this green best,' I said, looking at the paint samples one more time. I wanted the hallway to be sage green with gold decor, to make a big impact on people when they walked through the door. 'It would match that velvet chaise longue I found on the second-hand website.'

'The greens all look the same,' Adam said, squinting at them. 'Whichever you think,' he added quickly when I glared at him. They were completely different shades! 'Anyway,' he went on, 'I just heard back from the window company and they'll be here on Monday evening to quote for restoring the windows and doors.'

'I'll come after I finish my last shift. It's so strange to think I won't be working at the Inn any more next week.'

'I've sold my last house, thank God,' Adam said. 'Oh, I handed my notice in on the flat too.'

I stared at my brother. 'Already? This is a building site.'

'I can sleep in a sleeping bag if it comes to it. It'll be better to be here to organise everything, and I can't afford rent with all my money going into this place. And before you suggest it, I'm not moving back home. There's no room. Don't look so worried, sis,' he said when he saw my face. 'The more time I have here, the better.'

'Well, then, I'm moving in too. We're in this together.' I stared at him hard when he looked like he was about to protest. 'But we'd better see if we can find some airbeds to borrow in the village – we don't need bad backs on top of everything.' I grabbed my bag from the staircase. 'Let's go to the pub, I need a drink.' Adam led the way out of the door but I paused before following and glanced back at the hallway. It had been a long day, and there were more things on the list to do than we thought, and now it looked like we'd be moving into a building site, but the beginning was always the hardest part. I had to remind myself of that.

I turned off the light and followed Adam out, but not before I saw a pair of green eyes glowing in the room. I chuckled as the cat hurried off, no doubt to curl up for the evening, and I closed the door behind me.

Chapter Fourteen

It was hard to concentrate on my final shift at Glenmarshes Inn. I moved around in a daze. I remembered when I had walked in on my first day, excited to start working in my first hotel and relieved that everyone had been friendly, and I had settled in quickly. It was hard to walk away from all that was familiar, but I had to keep telling myself I was leaving for something so much better.

'There you are, your friend is here,' Grace said when she spotted me.

We walked through into the lobby where Anna was looking most unlike herself, dressed in a black suit with her pink hair tied back away from her face. 'Good luck!' I said as we walked up to her. She was here to interview for the chef position and it felt like I was passing the baton of Glenmarshes Inn on to her. 'You've got this.'

She smiled. 'I hope so. I see what you mean about the chain-hotel vibe,' she said in a low voice. 'But as long as the kitchen is good...'

'Exactly. Focus on the restaurant and what you can learn there.' I realised then that I shouldn't feel so glum today because that was what I had done. I knew now that I'd stayed two years too long, that once the chain had taken over and I knew it wasn't for me I should have moved on. But I didn't want to dwell on that. This was a fresh start, a new chapter, all those clichés, and I intended to make the most of it and take everything I had learnt at the Inn along with me.

We directed Anna to the kitchen. 'I really hope she gets it,' I said to Grace after we had wished Anna good luck again. 'We need another Glendale resident working here after I go.'

'Come on, I need to show you something,' Grace said, her eyes lighting up with mischief.

'Why am I worried?' I asked as she pulled me along with her.

We walked up the stairs and she led me to the honeymoon suite and unlocked it. 'The couple in here just left,' she explained. 'And they didn't take anything with them, so...' She gestured to the fancy toiletries and the complimentary champagne in an ice bucket.

'We can't,' I protested, hovering in the doorway. 'Chris will kill us, you know how he is.'

'Come on, he's busy interviewing Anna,' Grace said. 'The housekeeping team are staying away for half an hour so we can toast your leaving. Don't worry, it's all sorted,' she said confidently.

I smiled and closed the door behind me. 'Okay, just for half an hour then,' I conceded. I mean, it was my last shift, and I had always wondered what it would be like to stay in the honeymoon suite.

Grace handed me one of the robes and we pulled them on over our clothes. Then we popped the champagne, filling up two glasses, and sat on the sofa together. 'I can't believe we're doing this.'

'We had to mark your last day in style,' Grace said. 'Make sure you put out nice hand cream like this for your guests,' she said, smelling the rose scent of the cream from the basket of toiletries the couple had left in the room. 'They looked so in love, the couple staying in here,' she added with a sigh.

I sipped the champagne. 'Well, you'd hope so, as they've just got married.'

'Will I ever stay in this suite?' Grace spread herself out over the sofa dramatically. 'Will you?'

'I always used to think I'd meet someone and find that fairy-tale love, but I've got to be honest, I've been losing hope on that. At least one life plan is coming along, now we're starting our renovation.'

'Exactly. And you've inspired me! I really do want my own events company, and I need to begin working towards it. You leaving has given me a little kick up the bum. I've been treading water.'

'I think we've both been guilty of that.' I lifted my glass. 'Here's to shaking things up.' We each took a sip of champagne. 'I wonder if we'll ever have a honeymoon couple at Dove House? I hope so, one day, it would be so cute.'

Grace rolled her eyes. 'You're way too much of a hopeless romantic. It annoys me when I see happy couples.'

'It annoys you?!' She shrugged and I laughed. 'I mean, I get it. Look at me – I've been single since Mark left. But maybe it's best that I'm single so I can focus on renovating.'

'Maybe everything happens for a reason.'

'I've really tried hard to believe that,' I replied. 'I do think that Mark wasn't my person. I'm just not sure who is.' We smiled at one another. Then my phone rang. 'It's Anna,' I said to Grace. I directed her to the honeymoon suite and a couple of minutes later she walked in.

'This looks fabulous,' she said, smiling at us. She unpinned her hair and shrugged out of her blazer. 'That's better,' she said, perching on the edge of the four-poster bed.

'Don't keep us in suspense!' I cried.

'How did it go?' Grace asked as she poured a glass of champagne for Anna.

'Really well. Chris has asked me to work with the current chef for his last two weeks as a trial on both sides, and then we shall see.' She grinned. 'The kitchen is amazing. It's just what I've been looking for. I get to work close to home and gain experience, and it's the kind of food that I'd want to cook at my own restaurant one day.'

I lifted my glass again. 'That is the best news, Anna, I'm so happy for you.'

'We're going to have so much fun with you working here,' Grace agreed.

I felt a pinch of envy that I was leaving just as one of my closest friends was starting work here, and Grace and Anna would be working together every day, but I knew that would fade once I started renovating Dove House. And I was over the moon that Anna would be getting to do what she had always wanted to. 'Here's to us three,' I said, taking a long sip of champagne as they echoed my toast and drank along with me.

'It's so sad that it's your last shift,' Grace said to me then. 'The end of an era.'

'All the fun I've had working here has mostly been down to you,' I said.

'Don't, or I might cry,' she warned. 'Lorna was so lovely to me when I started working here. It felt like we'd known each other forever.'

'It wouldn't have been the same here without you,' I agreed with a smile. 'I hope you'll really like it here,' I added to Anna.

'You were right that Chris lacks people skills, but he won't be here for much longer and the kitchen is so dreamy. Plus, the chef gets free rein on the menus – apparently head office don't really care about the food as long as the restaurant makes money. Which works for me,' Anna said. 'Hopefully I can learn a lot here.'

'Mostly to do things completely differently,' Grace said with a chuckle.

I nodded. 'I definitely know now what I want Dove House to be like and what I don't want it to be like.'

'I think people want that cosy, homely feel in a B & B,' Grace said. 'And it will fit in perfectly in your lovely village.'

'I'm really hoping people will want to stay in Glendale,' I replied.

'They will. Look at me, I never thought I'd settle anywhere,' Anna said. 'But Glendale got into my heart somehow.'

'I've always enjoyed coming to see you there,' Grace agreed. 'I can't wait to see what you do with the house, Lorna.'

'Come to look around whenever you can. Actually, you should before we start so you can see the transformation.'

Grace grinned. 'You're right, I'm too nosy to keep away, so I'm going to come this weekend and see it.'

I chuckled. 'Great.'

'I'll come too, and bring lunch. I want to practise some recipes,' Anna said, her eyes lighting up as they always did when she talked about food.

'I never turn down anything you make,' I replied. 'Ooh, I'll need your waffle recipe for the B & B. Pancakes I'm great with, but waffles...'

The door to the room opened suddenly, interrupting me. 'Chris is coming up,' Hazel, one of the housekeeping team, hissed at us.

'Time to go!' Grace trilled as we all jumped up and hurried to hide the fact that we'd been in there. Laughing, we ran out of the room, tore down the stairs, skidded around the corner and ducked into the dining room as Chris strode past us.

'That was close,' Grace said breathlessly as Anna leaned on my shoulder and I shook my head, my heart racing in my chest. She started laughing and we couldn't help but join in. I had to hand it to Grace — I'd never forget my last shift at the Inn, that was for sure.

Chapter Fifteen

Hamish found me on Monday evening, after Adam and I had spoken to the window company that were going to restore the Crittall windows for us, popping into Dove House on his way home from work. 'It's all go here,' he said as one of the builders walked past us carrying a huge piece of wood. The renovation had begun this morning and they were just finishing for the day.

'Adam is somehow keeping track of it all,' I said, feeling like I'd been a deer in headlights since I came in from my last shift at the Inn. 'I have no idea how.'

'How was your last day at the Inn?'

'Surreal. I had my leaving drinks on Friday, so it felt like I sort of just slipped away and then entered the madhouse,' I said, gesturing around me. I knew that I wasn't good with change. The past five years could have told anyone that. And I was feeling more than a little unsettled. I forced on a smile. 'How can I help, anyway? You're not here to put up scaffolding, are you?'

'Not my area of expertise, I'm afraid. This, however…' He pulled his laptop out of his bag. 'I wanted to show you what I've done on the website so far.'

'Let's go over here,' I suggested, showing him a fold-up table Mum and Dad had found in the garage for us to use until we could buy furniture. Adam was outside talking to Glen and his dad about the plan for tomorrow, so it was finally quiet in the house. It was like the calm after the storm. I had no idea what tomorrow would be like.

Hamish loaded up the site and showed me what would be the home page.

'I've used a photo of the house from a few years ago, and we can replace that with a new one once the renovation is complete. If people go to the website now, this is all they will see, with a small paragraph about Dove House coming soon, etcetera,' Hamish said, pointing. 'And I've added the wording you gave me...'

I read what people would see when they first clicked on DoveHouse.com:

> The property was built in 1929, and after lovingly restoring its art deco features, we are delighted to open the doors of what everyone in Glendale has affectionately called the house since it was built – Dove House – as the village's first bed and breakfast. Dove House is a home from home. Comforting and cosy, with rooms that will transport you back to a golden age in the picturesque village of Glendale. We have beautiful reception rooms, a lovely garden to relax in, and grand bedrooms each with their own bathroom that will make you feel like a character from an F. Scott Fitzgerald novel. It is the perfect place to stay to explore the Highlands.
>
> Families have lived at Dove House since it was built, and if you book a stay here, you will feel like you have joined our family. Whether you are here to enjoy a snowy Christmas or a lovely summer walk, Dove House will give you a warm welcome, and this special property will find a place in your heart as it has done for generations here in Glendale. We can't wait to meet you.

My heart lifted. I would want to stay here after reading that.

'And then just for us, we can click here and I'm building the booking page so it will look like this…' Hamish continued, showing me. It was simple and accessible. He had used photos that I'd taken around Glendale and added a page all about our village. And there was an area for me to document the renovation too. 'It's perfect. I can't thank you enough for this, Hamish.'

'It's really no problem.' He showed me how to log in and make edits myself, so that once things started to come together in the house I could add photos and descriptions on the website. He also demonstrated how to turn an edit page into a live one. 'At the moment we just have the holding page live,' he said, showing me where it indicated that in the website builder. 'I've also added your social media accounts here, so anything you post will appear on the website.' I had created accounts for Dove House and was updating them with the renovation project when there was anything to share that I thought people might be interested in. I'd also posted photos of the village on my accounts too – anything to start building a following – for people who might want to come and stay at Dove House when we were finally open. Beth had shared them on the Glendale pages, and we had a few local businesses and residents following us. Heather Fraser had a popular Instagram documenting her life owning two farms, and she had shared one of my posts on there too, which had been really helpful in starting us off.

'Great. This looks easy to use but I'll shout if I run into any issues,' I said, smiling at Hamish. 'It feels strange to have a website without a bed and breakfast yet, but I think getting people excited about this place as much as we can will only help.'

'And if they become invested in following the renovation journey, then they might want to come and stay to see the finished product for themselves.'

'That's what I said to Adam! So, you're off home now?'

'Yep. Kathleen will be wondering where I am,' he said, checking his watch.

'Would she be angry knowing you've helped us with this?' I asked. Hamish and Kathleen met through my dad, who had supplied transport for Hamish's company. I had been intrigued at how such opposites could attract after I had met him, but they seemed really solid.

He closed the laptop and stowed it away again. 'No, but she would probably have made me charge you.' He grinned, but I thought she likely would have.

'She really isn't on board with all this, is she?' I asked.

He hesitated, clearly not wanting to reveal any secrets. 'Kathleen is more sensitive about things than you realise. Although she might have something to say about what Adam told me – are you really going to live here with all this work going on?'

'That's the plan,' I said, biting my lip. Now I had seen the mess for myself, I was questioning the idea, but Adam was still very much in that 'it'll all be fine' mindset of his.

'Well, I admire you both, you know,' Hamish said when we reached the door. 'And Kathleen does too.'

I raised an eyebrow. 'It feels like she thinks we're crazy.'

'Well, that's a given.' He chuckled at my glare. 'Right, see you later.'

'Have a good evening. And thank you again, we really appreciate it.'

He waved his hand. 'You're family. And ask Kathleen if you need anything, okay? She'd never say, but she'd be thrilled if you asked her, I know it.'

I watched him walk out to his car and saw that Adam was waving the builders off for the night. I stood in the doorway, wondering if Hamish was right. I thought Kathleen didn't want to be any part of all this.

'First day down,' I said when Adam came over to me. My phone beeped with a message. 'Oh, it's Finlay. He's planning to come to Glendale next week, so we can make a start on the loft.'

Adam nodded. 'Good. It will help with heating costs once we get the loft insulated. The window quote was more than we thought, so I need to look at the budget again. I'm going to move in this weekend once the boiler has been installed, so at least there will be no more rent to pay. Are you still going to move in too?'

'You really think it would be okay?'

'Sure. Once the new boiler is in we will have heating and water, and I'll bring my toaster and microwave so we can have some hot food until we get the Aga from Glendale Hall.' He shrugged. 'Besides, I lived in worse when I went to uni.'

That didn't make me feel much better.

Chapter Sixteen

It was strange to leave my house and not drive to Glenmarshes Inn but walk to Dove House instead, my new job, essentially, though right now there was no salary for me or my brother, just things to pay out for. It was October now and Glendale was growing chillier by the day; summer felt like a distant memory. I was pleased I'd worn my camel teddy-bear coat with scarf and gloves, although with my hair up in its typical bun, I regretted not adding earmuffs to the mix. I carried a bag full of ideas and images that I was building up for the house, and I was excited to test some more paint samples today and to meet with the man who ran a flooring company nearby who was going to discuss restoring the wooden floors.

Adam was already at the house, turning up at the same time as the builders, so I was looking forward to catching up with him on the plans for their week's work. I was just thinking that I should have picked up some coffees on the way when I realised there was a woman standing outside the white gates of the house. Her arms were folded across her chest as she watched me approach. I crossed the road apprehensively. 'Hello, can I help you?'

'Lorna, is it?' she asked in a scornful tone. She was in her sixties, I guessed, with grey hair and was wearing a quilted coat and welly boots. 'That man over there told me to speak to you,' she added, pointing out my friend Glen who was putting up scaffolding at the side of the house.

'I'm Lorna, yes, how may I help you?' I asked again as politely as I could manage after her blunt greeting.

'How long is this work going to go on for? There is so much noise and dust already. I live there,' she said, pointing to the house directly opposite. 'And I really do not want to be inconvenienced by all of this.'

'Oh, well, it's lovely to meet a neighbour,' I said, smiling as politely as I could. 'I know most of the people in Glendale. I think I've seen you at church?'

She looked a bit taken aback by that. 'Yes, well, I go most Sundays – I'm Mrs Andrews.'

'I knew I recognised you. We are turning Dove House into Glendale's first bed and breakfast.'

'So I'll be disturbed by people coming and going all the time?' she looked horrified. 'Do you have permission to do this?'

I swallowed. 'Yes, the council have—'

'Oh, the council.' She tutted. 'They never think about how this kind of thing affects the rest of us.'

'But it will help the village if there is somewhere for people to stay—'

'I don't care about that,' she cut me off. 'I want peace and quiet at my time of life. Can you please make sure any disruption is kept to a minimum? Otherwise I will take this further.' And with that, she stormed off back towards her house.

'Mrs Andrews! Wait,' I called, but she refused to turn around. 'Well, that could have gone better,' I muttered under my breath. That was all we needed – the neighbours in uproar about the building work.

'Who was that?' Adam asked, coming out of the open front door when he heard my boots crunching on the gravel driveway. 'I saw from the window and thought I'd better stay out of the way.'

'A very put-out neighbour. She's not happy about the disruption our building work might cause her. Can you please tell Glen to be careful around her house? I thought everyone would be pleased there would finally be a place for people to stay in the village…' I trailed off, feeling a little foolish. 'We need the neighbours on our side.'

Adam nodded. 'I'll speak to Glen. We want the neighbours to recommend us, don't we?'

An idea came to mind. 'Maybe we could think of something to get them on board? A Glendale discount if anyone they know wants to stay?'

'That could work,' Adam agreed. 'Right, I'd better go. I need to ring the plumber,' Adam said, hurrying off again.

I sighed. I really hoped Mrs Andrews wasn't going to complain about our work. I walked through to what was going to be the dining room, planning to think about how a Glendale discount might work while I tested out my paint samples.

I almost screamed when I spotted something furry in the corner when I walked in. 'Oh, it's you, Tabby, making yourself at home again?' I asked the sleeping cat who opened one eye and looked at me. I vowed to pick up a cat basket at the shops later and try again to take him to the vet. It looked like he was becoming a fixture around the house.

The cat suddenly lifted his head and looked behind me. He leaned forward into a crouch and I turned around to see what had caught his attention. A tiny furry something scuttled past and I squealed as the cat jumped up and ran past me after whatever it was.

'I don't think I want to know,' I whispered to myself, rather relieved the cat was around. Deciding I'd leave him to it, I turned my attention to the walls and hoped whatever it was would leave before we moved in, otherwise I could see I wasn't going to get much sleep here.

Chapter Seventeen

The first week at Dove House flew past in a blur – the scaffolding was erected ready for the roof to be repaired and new tiles laid there. We started stripping wallpaper off the walls ready for plastering. I chased the cat until finally I caught him and took him to the vet and he was given a clean bill of health, so I bought cat food and made a bed for him and decided that I'd just keep on calling him Tabby.

The new boiler was put in, which was the main thing on the list for week one. Once that was sorted, Adam wanted to move in. I knew I didn't need to but we were a team and I wanted to be part of it all right alongside him.

I had always lived at home, and the thought of moving out was emotional. Not just for me but for my mum too.

'Are you sure you should be moving in just yet?' Mum asked me as she sat on my bed watching as I folded clothes into a suitcase on Friday evening.

'Adam has let his flat go. I feel bad that he'll be there and I won't. And we will be able to get more work done this way.' I looked up at her. 'But I'm leaving most of my things here until my bedroom there is habitable. I'll be back and forth all the time, I'm not moving in properly.' I liked the idea of doing it one step at a time.

She nodded. 'No, I know. I was so excited that you'd bought Dove House; I didn't think about the fact that it means you won't live here any more. Only the twins are left now. All my babies are moving on. You'll understand this feeling one day,' she said with a wistful sigh.

'No, don't, we can't cry!' I said, shaking my head. 'I'm not leaving for good. I'm only round the corner anyway.'

'But who will watch romantic films with me now?' Mum and I loved nothing more than curling up with a cheesy film and a hot chocolate on a winter evening. The happier the ending, the better.

'We can still watch them together,' I promised. I looked at my clothes. 'I think I need to buy a couple more hoodies.' I'd worn a smart uniform to work at the Inn, but while we were renovating, I needed to be comfy and warm as winter wasn't far away and even though we now had heating, we didn't have carpets and furniture, and the doors and windows would be open a lot while the work was being done.

'I'll order you a few from that website we found last year.' She pulled out her phone, looking happy to be helping.

I smiled. 'Thanks, Mum. I'm glad I have these.' I held up the fleece Christmas pyjamas that were in my stocking last year. 'They'll keep me nice and toasty even if they are a bit festive for October.'

Mum chuckled. 'And make sure you take your slippers and scarves. You don't want your neck getting cold.'

I added two to my case. I looked around my room. 'It will feel strange to be sleeping somewhere else. I know I stayed with Mark a lot when we were together and we've been on holiday, of course, but pretty much, I've slept in here every night since I was a child.' My lip trembled. 'Maybe I shouldn't go…'

'No, we're being silly,' Mum said firmly. 'You'll just be down the road. And I'm so proud of you and Adam. Of course you should be there. It's your home now.'

'This will always be my home too.' We looked at one another, both welling up.

Mum stood and came over to give me a tight hug. 'Of course it will be, love.' We smiled at one another and wiped our eyes. 'Do you have everything you need for now?' she asked briskly.

I picked up the fluffy brown bear who still sat on my bed. 'I can't not take Ted,' I said. Not the most original name, but

I'd had him since childhood and I knew Dove House wouldn't feel like home without him. I looked at the case and leaned over, huffing to get the zip done up. 'I think that's enough for now.' I looked at the family photo I had on my bedside table and picked it up and added it to the case. 'That'll help make it feel more like home. Did you ever sleep over at Dove House?'

Mum smiled. 'No, never, although I wished I could. I went to several parties there. They were always entertaining, and it felt so glamorous to me.' Then she sighed. 'But once the family moved away and put the house up for sale, I never went to anything else there. No one else liked to entertain as they had done.'

'Did you keep in touch with that family?'

'No, I didn't know their new address,' she replied. 'Anyway, enough of the past.' Mum nodded at me and looked around the room. 'Let's get the car packed up.'

I watched Mum carry one of my bags out. I knew my mum had been really upset that summer when the family left Glendale, but I wondered if there had been more to it and if one of the family in particular had broken her heart. She had never really spoken about her relationships before my dad, but maybe that was why her heart had always had a piece of it left at Dove House. It was strange sometimes to think of your parents as being young and having lives before you came along, but now I realised I didn't know much about my mother's past at all. I resolved to find out more from her but it was getting late and I said I'd meet Adam, so I picked up my other bag and followed her out.

'Who will play chess with me?' Noah pouted as he and Leo and my dad followed me and Mum outside where my things were stowed in my car and I was ready to leave.

'We can still play. I'll be back all the time, and you can come and hang out at Dove House with me too.' I ruffled his hair and nudged Leo. 'You don't get rid of your big sister, ever, okay?' It was hard to see my loud, playful, excitable brothers looking sad. 'I'm round the corner now, that's all.'

Noah nodded. 'Okay.'

'Can we come and see Tabby soon?' Leo asked.

'Come over on Sunday. Anna and Grace are coming tomorrow, but we could all have lunch together on Sunday after church and you can give Tabby a treat. He needs feeding up.'

'That sounds lovely,' Mum said, hiding her face from us all.

'Okay, you lot, don't make me cry again,' I warned them.

Dad gave me one of his bear hugs. 'We are so proud of you and Adam, love.'

'Oh, God.' I gave them all a quick hug and then hurried into my car. I set off, glancing in the rear-view mirror as they waved to me in the driveway, and even though I knew I was going to see them on Sunday, I let the tears fall down my cheeks. It was the end of an era. I was where I'd always wanted to be, but it was still hard to leave my childhood home.

At Dove House, Adam was there already and had lit the house up and put the heating on. In the kitchen, the radio was on and he was making us both a cup of tea when I walked in with my bags and my tear-stained face. 'Oh dear,' he said when he saw me. 'Sit down. We need shortbread too,' he said, grabbing the biscuit tin that Mum had given us.

I sat down at the fold-up table we'd put in the kitchen. We just had a kettle, toaster and a microwave and four plastic chairs at the moment, but the room was warm and cosy and seeing Adam made me feel better. Tabby walked in and meowed at us. 'You don't have the house to yourself any more,' I told him as he came over and brushed himself against me. He was around us more and more each day.

'Here we go.' Adam handed me a mug of tea and put the plate of shortbread down between us as he joined me at the table. 'I fed Tabby and I put the airbeds up in the lounge.' The lounge would be the last room to be renovated, so it was the room we'd picked to sleep in. 'It feels like we're back at summer camp, or something,' he said with a grin.

'Was it weird to leave your flat?'

'I guess, but it never really felt like home to me.'

'Really?' I was surprised. I thought he had loved moving out of home. I had often been jealous of his independent life.

'Sometimes it was a bit lonely.' He shrugged. 'And I never knew how to make it homely.'

'Well, no fear there, this will feel like our home in no time,' I promised us both as I took a sip of my tea.

Adam nodded. 'We did it, sis. And even though we're broke and already exhausted, I'm glad we did.'

I smiled. 'Me too.' I picked up a piece of shortbread. Mum made the best shortbread. I would have to ask her to make some for our future guests.

'Right, we'd better get an early night then, lots of do. What do you think, Tabby?'

He purred his agreement so we headed into the lounge and the cat followed us through the doorway. The bare light bulb hanging from the ceiling cast much-needed light. Adam had set up two airbeds in the big room with sleeping bags. It looked comfier than I had feared. 'You're right, this does feel like we're at camp,' I told Adam. 'Although I never liked camping.'

'It won't be for long,' Adam said confidently. 'Someone's happy, at least.'

I watched as Tabby curled up at the bottom of one of the sleeping bags. 'Shotgun that one, he can warm my feet,' I said, hurrying over.

'I'd better find an extra pair of socks then,' Adam said, shaking his head at the two of us and walking out to get his bag from the car.

'You're happy we're here, aren't you?' I asked the cat as I got into my PJs and snuggled into the sleeping bag. 'Keep an eye out for that mouse, okay?' I asked Tabby as I gave him a stroke. He yawned and stretched out sleepily, looking completely at home. I looked around the room and hoped we would feel that way soon too.

Adam came back in and switched off the light as he climbed into his sleeping bag.

All I could hear was Tabby purring at my feet. I smiled into the darkness as I looked up at the ceiling. 'Sweet dreams,' I whispered.

Chapter Eighteen

I walked out of the house when I heard the car pull into the driveway and waved as Grace parked up. Anna walked through the gates a moment later. It was exciting to have my friends here for the first time. Saturday morning had dawned dry and crisp – my favourite kind of day. I gave Grace a hug. 'I'm so happy you could come. You too, Anna,' I added as she joined us. 'Excuse how I look,' I added when I saw their outfits. 'I've been up since six a.m. with Adam stripping wallpaper, and I'm a right mess,' I said, gesturing to myself. My hair was in its usual bun but I was sure there were bits of wallpaper in it, I had no make-up on, I was wearing an oversized hoodie and leggings, which were covered in dust, and my nail polish had completely chipped.

'Shut up,' Grace said. 'You always look gorgeous, and this suits you, you are glowing.'

'Definitely,' Anna agreed. 'Look at the giddy smile on your face.' She wrapped her arm through mine. 'Show us what you've done so far, I can't wait to see. Oh, and I brought lunch, as promised,' she added, patting the bag hanging off her shoulder.

'You're a star. Okay, let's go. Just watch your step,' I said, gesturing for them both to come in. 'We slept here for the first time last night. Airbeds are surprisingly comfy and Tabby kept me warm.'

'Tabby?' Grace asked.

'Oh, yeah, I forgot to tell you guys – a cat has moved in.'

'Wow,' Grace said, looking around the hallway as I closed the front door behind us. 'I can see why you had to have this house, it's gorgeous. Please tell me you're putting a chandelier up there,' she said, pointing up to the ceiling.

'I really want one,' I said, smiling. 'But the ones I've found so far Adam says are too pricey, so I am on the hunt for a second-hand one.' I was determined to find the most spectacular one that I could.

'Are my ears burning?' Adam strolled in. 'Oh, hi there,' he said, smiling at Grace and Anna.

'Hi, Adam,' Grace said, turning around to look at him.

'How are you, Grace?' Adam asked as he walked up to her and gave her a kiss on the cheek.

She smiled. 'I was just saying, I can see why you fell in love with this place, it's amazing.'

'It really was love at first sight,' Adam replied, still looking at Grace.

I cleared my throat. 'Anyway, let me show you the progress so far everywhere, then we can have lunch, I'm so hungry,' I said, looking between the two of them. I turned to Anna, who was grinning.

'Sounds lovely,' Grace said, finally turning to me. 'Lead the way.'

'I'm off to the tile shop, as Glen wanted me to pick some samples, but I'll see you later,' Adam said and sloped off, his hands in his pockets.

'What was that?' Anna asked Grace, one eyebrow raised.

'What do you mean?'

Anna looked at me. 'You saw it, didn't you?'

'I saw it when they first met, but Grace had a boyfriend then. Now she doesn't,' I said with a grin.

'Oh, honestly,' Grace said, rolling her eyes, but she was smiling too. 'Are we doing this tour or not?'

Anna chuckled as I led the way to the lounge, thinking that I was definitely going to be talking to Adam about Grace later.

'That is too cute,' Anna said as we went into the kitchen to have lunch later. I looked at Tabby curled up in the corner, light streaming in from the kitchen window. I pulled out my phone to take a photo for the Dove House social media accounts, telling everyone we now had our very own cat. Maybe Tabby would become a favourite of our future guests.

'I'm sorry it's all so makeshift,' I apologised to them as I dished out the delicious-looking food Anna had brought for us to try.

'It's fun,' Anna said. 'I've lived in worse places, I can tell you that. Some of the pubs I used to live above.' She shuddered. 'God knows what I'll do when I have to leave Glendale Hall – nowhere can compare.'

'I don't think Beth will ever let you go,' I said, bringing the food over and going back for the hot drinks.

'But I guess when I need to stop the housekeeping there...' Anna trailed off. I understood that she didn't want to think about that just yet; I knew how hard it would be for her to leave the first place she had ever felt really settled in.

'This looks amazing,' I said when I sat down, looking at what Anna had made for us – bruschetta and olives, home-made hummus and pitta bread, roasted vegetables, cold lemon pasta and a rice salad.

'I need feedback on it all,' Anna said, gesturing for us to eat.

'Okay, now you have to tell me all about your first week at the Inn,' I said. Anna had wanted me to do the tour first, but now we had food and drinks and they had seen all our work in progress, I wanted to know how her week had gone and if the place was managing without me. I half hoped it wouldn't be, not that I would ever say that out loud.

Anna grinned. 'It's been so much fun! And my trial must be going well because Chris is letting me do Saturday-night dinner tonight and tomorrow, Sunday roast as head chef with Alec just there if I need him.'

'That's great news!'

'I'm so happy it's going so well,' Grace agreed. 'Have you tried this woman's lasagne? I had it for lunch yesterday and it was just too good.'

I nodded. 'I have, and I'm so pleased everyone will be able to taste it now.'

'I'm so excited to run the kitchen by myself. I get to write my own menus and just do what I've always wanted to for the weekend. And fingers crossed if it goes well enough they'll give me the job full-time.' Anna smiled. 'Glendale really can help you realise what you want out of life.'

'I need to come here more often then,' Grace said as she reached for more food. 'Anna, this is all ten out of ten.'

'You're welcome any time,' I assured her. 'It really is, Anna,' I added as I dipped my bread in the hummus. 'The thing about Glendale is not only can it help you realise what you want, and give you a start in the business world, but there is also a lot of matchmaking going on in this village,' I said slyly. 'Right, Anna?'

'I got so annoyed at Beth, my boss at the Hall,' she explained to Grace. 'Encouraging me and Cameron to get together as well as getting me to stay in Glendale.' She sighed. 'But annoyingly, she was right. Although it hasn't worked for Lorna yet.' She turned to me. 'Perhaps we need to rectify that.'

'I have my hands full with this place,' I replied. 'I told you, I need a break from dating disasters. I think one amazing thing to happen to me this autumn is more than enough.'

'And for me,' Anna agreed.

'Let's hope I'm next then,' Grace replied.

We heard the front door open and Adam call out that he was back. I yelled that we were in the kitchen.

'Relax, and let Glendale work its magic,' Anna told Grace confidently. Then she looked at me and winked.

Chapter Nineteen

'Did you look at the budget spreadsheet I emailed you?' Adam asked, walking into the kitchen the following morning as I made a cup of coffee.

It wasn't even light out, and I yawned as I added milk, hoping it would wake me up as we wanted to finish stripping the wallpaper before we went to church and then had the family over for lunch. 'Not yet, I'm half asleep.'

'Well, I know you're looking for paint, and I saw some of the samples you have. The brand you have, Lorna, is too expensive, you'll need so many pots.'

'But the colours are perfect for a period style,' I protested.

'Find the colour you like and see if you can get the DIY store to match it with a cheaper paint then,' Adam said as he sat down at the table with a cup of coffee.

I hadn't known you could do that. 'Okay, I'll try to see if that will work. See, I can compromise.'

'Hmmm.'

'And I thought we should offer a fifteen per cent discount for Glendale residents' friends and family. We could ask Beth to share it on the Glendale social media. And I looked into doing an advert in the local paper... it's not too pricey and would be good publicity for us.'

'Good idea,' he said and I smiled, glad I wasn't going to be told not to spend money on that. 'It's scary to think about people actually staying here, isn't it?'

'You're nervous? I don't believe it. You never seem worried about anything.'

Adam shook his head. 'Of course I am, but I try to do what scares me anyway and it usually works out. In business. Not so much in my personal life, as you know.'

I remembered how he had really liked Anna when she had first arrived in Glendale, but her attraction to Cameron had been undeniable. 'Speaking of personal lives... Grace is so lovely, isn't she?'

Adam raised an eyebrow. 'She seems so, yes. Why?'

I shrugged. 'I thought I sensed some chemistry between you... and you are both single now.'

My brother chuckled. 'Why do I feel like I'm being set up here? As you said, we have our hands full right now, don't we?'

I sighed as he walked out, not looking forward to stripping more wallpaper, but then I smiled thinking that I would definitely invite Grace back to the house soon.

–

Adam and I walked through the High Street towards the church. Glendale was looking lovely as autumn settled in and it was another sunny, crisp day. We were looking more presentable after a morning of stripping wallpaper, a very messy job I had discovered, but now the hallway walls were bare, ready for plastering and then painting. As we walked, we greeted others walking to the service – we knew pretty much everyone in the village; we couldn't not, having lived here all our lives. It was one of the things I loved most about Glendale, its community spirit.

'Morning, you two,' Anna joined us, arm in arm with Cameron. 'I'm heading to the Inn straight after church to do my first Sunday roast. Can you come?'

'The family are coming over,' I said regretfully. 'But definitely soon. I'd love to have one of your roasts. I bet it will go down a treat.'

'I hope so,' she said. 'Did you get your wallpaper done?'

I had moaned to her about it yesterday over WhatsApp. 'Finally. The next room we're leaving to the decorator,' I told my brother. 'Is that Emily?' I said, seeing a blonde woman waving to us from outside the church.

'How are my favourite nieces?' Anna cried when we reached Emily and her two daughters, bending down to greet them with a wide smile. Anna was a great auntie. I hoped I could be the same for Kathleen's baby when he or she arrived.

'I was going to ask if you had time to pop into the bakery for a chat soon, Lorna,' Emily said, smiling when she saw me and Adam.

'Watch out... Emily has her business face on,' Anna remarked, standing up.

Emily laughed at her sister-in-law. 'I don't have a business face! But yes, I was thinking you might need baked goods for your B & B, and as we supply to Hilltop Farm...'

'It's a great idea,' I agreed. I wanted to use local produce; I knew guests would love that. 'I'll come and have a chat as soon as I can.'

'Why are we all outside?' We turned to see Beth Fraser with her husband Drew, along with everyone who lived at Glendale Hall, walk up to the church too. 'The gang is all here,' she added as she waved to Heather and Rory, who had come from their farm outside the village, and their little boy who was walking with his grandfather. 'How's the B & B coming on, you two?'

'It's getting there. You should come and take a look,' Adam said.

'I'll come along soon,' Beth promised. 'And Izzy wants to see it too, don't you, Iz?' she asked her daughter.

'I heard it's like something out of an Agatha Christie book,' Izzy agreed excitedly.

I smiled. 'I hope it will be once we've restored it,' I said. 'Actually, I was thinking about creating a reading corner, and Anna tells me you have a reading room at the Hall.'

'Oh my God, you must!' Izzy cried. 'You'll have to come and see mine. Ooh, at the Halloween party.'

'Invites are on the way,' her mother said. 'I hope everyone in the village can come. I know we always do the Christmas trail, but we thought why not throw a Halloween party this year? Otherwise it's a long gap between the garden party and Christmas.'

'Some would say it's nice to have a break,' Caroline, Beth's mother, commented drily.

'But far less fun,' Beth said, her eyes twinkling.

'We'll be there,' I replied. I loved going to the Hall, and I was keen to get some inspiration from the house for the B & B.

'Oh, we'd better go in,' Emily said. 'Brodie will be waiting for us.'

'Let's see what my dear brother is going to teach us today,' Anna said with a grin. I knew that, really, she was proud of her brother, even though they couldn't be more different. She had told me she hadn't been to church for a long time before she came to Glendale, but now she supported Brodie, and I think she enjoyed his sermons as much as the rest of the village did really.

'Mum and Dad must be inside already,' Adam said to me.

'We'd better go and find them,' I said as we all filed into the pretty church. The sun streamed in through the stained-glass window as the worship band played music, and we joined our family in the pew we usually sat in. The Glendale Hall gang went to theirs further up, greeting the rest of the village on the way. At the front, Brodie stood ready, smiling at everyone.

I sat down next to Mum, pleased that Adam and I could relax for the rest of the day. It really had been a hectic first week at Dove House. The number of things we had to do seemed to have doubled and I couldn't help but let doubts creep in as to whether we could pull this off. Adam may not have been anxious but I was, enough for the both of us.

'Welcome, everyone,' Brodie said once the church was quiet. 'I've always enjoyed this time of year. October, the start of autumn. I love watching the leaves outside change colour and

I think autumn has some wonderful lessons for us. The biggest being that change doesn't have to be negative. I think we tend to think of change as something to fear, to worry about, to run or hide from, but nature doesn't do that. Nature embraces change and so should we. Change is inevitable. And autumn shows us that it can be beautiful too,' Brodie said. 'We just need to trust the process and know that after autumn and winter, spring will always come.'

I smiled at Brodie's words. I loved this idea. Autumn had always been my favourite season for that very reason. I knew I wasn't always great at embracing change in my life, but I had been given a second chance with Dove House and I needed to embrace all the change that was happening to me now. It was scary, Brodie was right about that. It felt like there was so much to do, and that we might never get it all done.

But hopefully, after this scary part, once we got through all the changes and hard work, wonderful things would be on the way. If things worked out then when spring came, Dove House would be open for people to come and stay, it would be mine and Adam's home, and all our hard work would have been worth it. It wasn't easy to always believe that our dream would come true, especially when we were right slap bang in the middle of so much chaos, but Brodie's words had helped.

I just needed to try to trust that everything would be okay in the end.

Chapter Twenty

The family came back to Dove House with us after church, and Mum heated up a macaroni cheese she'd made for everyone in the microwave, and we all ate on the floor in the lounge while the twins played with Tabby, apart from Kathleen who claimed one of the fold-up chairs along with Mum.

'I hope he doesn't have fleas,' Kathleen said, watching the boys pull string across the floor for the cat to chase.

'I got him checked out at the vet, of course,' I said, rolling my eyes. Honestly, sometimes she treated me like I was a child too. 'He's a sweetheart.'

'I can't believe you called him Tabby,' Kathleen said. 'It's a worse name than your teddy bear Ted.'

'It just stuck, what can I say?' I turned to Mum. 'This is really good,' I said, pointing to the pasta on my paper plate. I knew we'd only be offering breakfast in the future, but I hoped my cooking would be up to scratch. I had so many good cooks around me, I felt under pressure.

'I've brought extra and put it in the fridge. I don't want you two not eating properly without a full kitchen,' Mum replied.

'How's your back after sleeping on an airbed?' Dad asked Adam.

'I think it's more comfortable than my bed back at the flat, and the hot water is better here with the new boiler.'

I smiled. Adam made the best of everything. 'I would be fine sleeping here if Adam didn't snore so loudly.'

'I remember his snoring, I used to hear it from my room,' Kathleen said with a laugh. 'I can't believe you still snore like that.'

'Hey, I don't!' Adam protested.

'Even the cat was terrified by the noises you were making,' I joked. 'I've ordered earplugs from Amazon.'

'Lies, I tell you, lies!' Adam cried as we all laughed.

'How has the first week been?' Mum asked us.

'I think it's going pretty well. We had a neighbour complain about the work, but Lorna came up with a great idea to offer Glendale residents a friends-and-family discount when we open up.'

'Oh, great, you're offering discounts already,' Kathleen said drily.

'It's a really good idea,' Adam said. 'We need recommendations from locals.'

'I'm sure there are plenty of people who would prefer family to stay here than with them,' I replied, giving Kathleen a significant look.

'Someone is tackling the damp next week,' Adam said, moving things on. 'And we've booked in the plasterer and the windows to be replaced and organised the flooring for after the painting. We're going back to the original flooring downstairs and new carpets upstairs.'

'Beth is giving us the Aga at Glendale Hall once their one new arrives,' I added.

'She's so generous,' Mum said. 'Oh, we had our invite, by the way, to a Halloween party next Saturday.'

'I hope I can go but I'm struggling to fit into our car already,' Kathleen said.

'I can push you in a wheelbarrow if it comes to it,' Hamish joked, earning himself an unamused glare from my sister.

'Oh, I forgot,' Adam said. 'The dining table you wanted on eBay went to someone else.'

I sighed. 'Okay, I'd better go to the antiques place in Inverness soon and see if they have any furniture for us. We have a big house to fill.' I had a vision for each room, but I had no idea if I would be able to find what we needed to make the vision come to life at a reasonable price. Adam's budget for decor was really small, but he was resolute on that. I tried to remember what Brodie had said about embracing change and to trust the process, but my tension headache was beginning to reappear. It had been there most of the week. There seemed so much to do that I kept having a wobble about whether we'd be able to get everything looking how we wanted it to.

'It's lovely and warm now you have a new boiler,' Mum said cheerfully.

'Heating this house is going to be expensive, so we're going to insulate the loft once Lorna has cleared it all out.'

'Hopefully me and Finlay can do it quickly,' I agreed.

'Finlay?' Kathleen asked.

Oh dear. I hadn't really wanted to tell her about Finlay. I just had a feeling she wouldn't approve. 'He was trying to buy the house too, but he didn't really want it. He thinks there's something in the loft that belonged to his father. And his dad really wanted him to come to the house and see if it was still there, so we said he could help me clear out the loft and we can look for it.'

Kathleen stared at me. 'You're letting a stranger clear out the loft? What if he finds something with—'

'Kath,' I interrupted her. 'Obviously I thought of that. I'm not stupid.'

'It's something sentimental,' Adam said, giving me a look that said *don't start an argument*. 'And Lorna will be with him the whole time. We're trying to be kind. His father died and he made him promise beforehand that he'd come to Dove House. How could we say no to that?'

'I think that was lovely of you both,' Mum said. Kathleen glowered but stopped arguing. 'I would have done the same. I wonder what it could be that he's looking for? I really hope he finds it.'

'Me too,' I said. 'I could tell he's really upset about his dad. He'll be here tomorrow anyway. I'm intrigued about what's up there. I hope there are things we can use.'

'It's probably just junk, or the damp will have got to it,' my sister told me.

'Thanks, Kathleen. Way to go looking on the bright side of things.'

'I don't want you to get your hopes up, that's all,' she insisted.

'Trust me, with you here, I never do.'

'Tabby has a mouse!' Leo called out then and we all jumped up, the conversation thankfully forced to come to a halt although I wasn't particularly happy about the reason.

Still, at least we knew Tabby was a good catcher.

Chapter Twenty-One

Rain arrived on Monday morning, pelting Dove House from all angles. It meant work on the roof had to be paused, so it would be a lost day on that. The builders came inside instead and I was glad I had got up and dressed early.

Adam found me in the kitchen munching on toast after I'd fed Tabby. 'They're starting work on the plastering and the damp as they can't work on the roof,' he explained as he grabbed an apple. 'How are you feeling about going up in the loft?'

I checked the time. Finlay was due to arrive any minute. 'I mean, I'm hoping there won't be any spiders…' I shuddered at the thought. 'I am curious as to what will be up there, though. And if he can solve his mystery.'

Adam nodded. 'Are you sure you'll be okay? Up there with him alone, I mean.'

'I'll take my phone with me, and it's not like the house is empty. Besides, I think he needs friends right now. He looked so lost when he came to see me at the Inn. I can't imagine what he's going though, losing his dad, and he doesn't have any siblings. He didn't mention his mother…'

'Okay. Well, call me if you need me. I hope you do find what his father left here. But if not, I hope he won't be too disappointed.'

'Me too.' The doorbell rang and we both looked at one another. 'See you later then,' I said, heading off to answer the door.

'Hi there,' I said, opening it up to Finlay wearing a grey sweatshirt with the hood pulled up as the relentless rain beat down. 'Come in, come in,' I said quickly, as he was getting soaked. He stepped into the hall and I closed the door on the horrible weather. 'What a day. Not a great welcome to Glendale.'

Finlay shrugged. 'Autumn in Scotland,' he replied. He pushed his hood down and wiped the droplets from his glasses. He looked around. 'Work is starting already then.'

'It's all go here. Probably a good thing we'll be out of the way. Would you like a coffee to take up?'

'I'm fine, thanks. I had two at the Inn.'

'Okay, let's head up then. And how is my old workplace?' I asked as we walked up the stairs.

'It's fine. I prefer older places to stay, if I'm honest.'

I smiled at him. 'Me too. I'm so excited to decorate here, bring back all the Twenties features, turn back the clock to when it was built.'

'I can't wait to see it,' Finlay replied, giving me a smile back. He pushed up the sleeves of his hoodie. He looked much more comfortable in it than he did in his work suit, and somehow it made him look younger too.

We walked up to the third-floor landing where the entrance to the loft was, via a ladder that came down when you pulled the hatch. I opened it up, aware of Finlay close behind me. I could smell his spicy aftershave. 'Right, let's see what we're dealing with,' I said, and started to climb the ladder. When I reached the top, I pulled the light string hanging at the entrance to the loft and the space lit up. Finlay climbed up behind me and we stopped, looking around in shock. It was much bigger than I had expected and my mouth fell open.

'I didn't think it'd be so huge,' Finlay said.

'Me neither. No wonder Betty didn't get up here to sort it. It's going to be a bigger job than I thought.' I turned to him. 'But it might mean that what your dad left is still here.' There were boxes everywhere plus old, broken furniture, and everything was coated in dust. I could see cobwebs in the corner, which made me shiver.

'I hope so,' he said quietly. 'Where do we even start?' Finlay asked.

'I think begin at this end and work towards the back wall,' I replied, pushing my sleeves up. 'Let's look at each box and make three piles of things: stuff we need to throw, anything that can be donated or sold, which I doubt there will be, and anything we want to keep,' I said, feeling unsure that there would be anything of use up here. I stepped around a box. 'Is there anything I should be keeping an eye out for? I mean, do you know what you're looking for?' I asked.

Finlay had ducked behind me as he was so tall and there wouldn't be much space to sort, but I was loath to lug everything downstairs as things were in such chaos with the building work. He cleared his throat as if he was nervous. Perhaps he was. 'My father was adamant that there's something in this house of his and I'd know it when I saw it, and that I should give it to the person it was meant for. The person was really special to him.' He sighed. 'I'd never heard him say anyone was special to him before,' he added, in such a low voice I wasn't sure he had meant me to hear.

'Well, what's your father's name? I can keep an eye out then.'

'Thomas Scott,' he replied shortly, and I sensed that he didn't want to say any more. It was obviously painful for him to talk about, and I did understand, even if I was curious. Maybe he would open up eventually. 'I'll start with this box.'

'I'll take this one,' I said, sitting down cross-legged and pulling a large one towards me. We worked for a few minutes in silence. 'I think it's admirable that you're trying to find what your father wanted you to. I'd like to think I would do the same for my dad, but still,' I mused as I looked through a stack of old vinyl records. I wondered if I could find a record player up here; that would be fun to have in the lounge for guests. I kept the records just in case.

'If you knew our story, you might not think it was,' he replied as he stuck his head into his box. 'Are you close to your family?

I suppose you must be to be doing this place up with your brother.'

I nodded, although he couldn't see me; our backs were now facing one another. 'We are a close family,' I replied, while thinking about Kathleen and feeling unsure if that really was the case with her or not. 'Adam and I came to Dove House as children with our mother, and we've had the dream to turn it into a bed and breakfast for so long… and now we're here doing it. It's not going to be easy, though,' I added, looking at the loft again and shaking my head. 'But Adam is so optimistic, he won't let us not succeed.'

'You're not optimistic?'

'I guess that lately I haven't felt so positive about things. I suppose it's been hard, not being able to make our dream come true till now. And here we are, and I'm so excited and relieved, but I'm also really scared about whether we can pull it all off. Life knocks your confidence sometimes, doesn't it?'

'The estate agent, Jenny, she said the letter you wrote to the previous owner got you the house. You persuaded her to believe in your dream – that doesn't sound like someone who isn't optimistic to me.'

I stopped what I was doing. 'Thank you,' I said. 'That means a lot to me.'

Finlay turned round and met my eyes. 'Well, being here means a lot to me, so anything I can do to help, just let me know, okay?'

'I appreciate that,' I replied. I pulled out an old board game. 'My sister always used to win at Monopoly. It used to really bug me.'

'I've never played it.'

I gaped at him. 'We'll have to, one night. Christmas isn't far off – we always play board games for that.'

'Look at this.' He held up an old-fashioned telephone. 'Do you want to keep this? See if it works?'

'That would be perfect on the table in the hallway,' I agreed. 'I don't think we need to keep this, though.' I held up a broken lamp. 'It's amazing what people have left here through the years. Will you have to clear out your family home? Was it in Perth, did you say?'

'That's right. It's a big house, so there's a lot to go through. My uncle thought I was crazy to come to Glendale when there was so much to be done there and with the company, but... I need to do this, you know?' He looked over at me.

I nodded. 'I would too.'

He looked relieved that I understood. I carried on sorting through the box. I knew that if it was me in his shoes, I wouldn't be able to move on, so I really hoped I could help him find what he was looking for.

Chapter Twenty-Two

My stomach rumbled loudly in the loft later, so I pulled out my phone and checked the time. 'I think we deserve a lunch break,' I said, stretching out my arms. I felt stiff after leaning over boxes all morning and in desperate need of a break and something to eat and drink.

'I can't believe how many Christmas decorations are up here,' Finlay said, sitting upright. His boxes had mostly been filled with broken baubles and dusty angels, and pretty much all of it had gone into the rubbish pile apart from a small pretty gold tree that I thought would be perfect for the festive season.

'I'd rather that than all the magazines I had to go through,' I said. Someone had kept every issue of *Fishing Weekly* ever published, it felt like. 'Although I'm going to display these vintage *Vogue*s somehow. Come on, let's go downstairs and refuel,' I said, putting the magazines in a box that I had written 'keep' in Sharpie on. Finlay followed me downstairs and, in the kitchen, we found Adam and Beth Fraser.

'Hi Lorna, I was just checking that we could bring the Aga over on Wednesday, and I also wanted to give you these,' Beth said, waving two invitations. 'I know we sent them to your family home, but I wanted to make sure you two are coming to the Halloween party next Saturday, and that you know you can bring plus-ones,' Beth added, glancing curiously over my shoulder at Finlay.

'This is Finlay Scott,' I introduced, walking over to the fridge. They shook hands. 'He's helping me clear out the loft.'

'Rather you than me,' Beth said with a shudder.

'You won't believe how much is up there,' I said to them both. 'It's crazy what people have kept.'

'The one at the Hall really needs doing too,' Beth said with a sigh. 'I can't face it, though. Maybe I'll pay Izzy and Luke to do it for me.'

'We can't thank you enough. Not just for the Aga,' Adam said. 'We've sent the paperwork back to your solicitor,' he added. Beth was happy for us to not start paying back her loan until the B & B had been open for six months, which was so generous of her. She waved a hand. 'This will be great for the village.'

'Oh, speaking of…' I told her about Mrs Andrews and our idea for a Glendale discount.

'Brilliant idea. I can help you publicise that once you know when you're going to open. And don't let Mrs Andrews faze you. She'll come round in the end, once she sees how great this place looks.'

I wasn't one hundred per cent sure she would, but I hoped Beth was right about that. 'Are you sure you don't want to stay for lunch?' I asked her.

'My mother's in the car – we need to go shopping. I wish I could, but I can't back out now,' Beth said, looking terrified at the prospect. 'You'll come to the Halloween party, won't you?'

'We love your parties,' I said, pulling cans of Coke from the fridge. 'Thanks, Beth.' She gave us a cheerful wave and headed off. 'She helped us get this place,' I explained to Finlay as I handed him a can and tossed one to my brother.

'Wasn't she here when you looked around? I got the impression she didn't think it was worth investing in. Oh,' he said, realisation striking. 'She was trying to put me off. Crafty.'

'She's a brilliant businesswoman,' I replied with a laugh. 'Glendale wouldn't be what it is today without her. She really has helped it thrive again. It's probably back to how it was when your dad lived here. Everyone want a sandwich? Sit down, I'll make them,' I offered, pulling out whatever I could find in the fridge.

'Dad always said he missed Glendale a lot when his family moved away. He never came back, which was why he wanted me to. When it's not raining, I'd love to look around the village and see what it's like.'

'There must be someone here who knew your dad,' Adam said to Finlay. 'Most of us have lived here all our lives.'

'Maybe,' Finlay said. 'I don't think my father kept in touch with anyone after they left.'

I was about to ask why when I saw a drip coming from the ceiling. 'Uh-oh.'

Adam jumped up and put a bucket under it. 'We really need the roof fixed. I hope it stops raining soon! Glen said he and his dad will start extra early tomorrow – they can't do much more today in this weather. So I'll head out after this. I need to go to that bathroom tiling place that Dad suggested. They sometimes have cast-offs that they sell cheaply.'

'The tiles have to match, though,' I said, worried about what he might come back with.

'I know, I know. Oh, Kathleen and Mum said they're coming round tomorrow to take you to that antiques place.'

My heart sank. 'Why both of them?'

'Probably because I said you need someone to make sure you don't go over budget. And who better than our dear sister?' Adam grinned at my glare. 'You might need help carrying things anyway.'

'Well, she can't exactly help with that, can she?' I pointed out. 'My sister is pregnant,' I explained to Finlay.

I carried over three plates to the table and we tucked into our sandwiches.

'So, anything good in the loft?' Adam asked, aware I was annoyed about being chaperoned at the antiques shop.

'I've found a couple of things that we can keep. I'm hoping we can find a record player, as there are some good vinyl records up there. But there's a lot of junk. Finlay found a couple of boxes too damp to even look through, which is a shame. We can keep going for a bit. I think when it gets dark, we'll have to stop for the day — the light isn't very good as it is, especially with this rain.'

'You haven't spotted anything of your family's yet then?' Adam asked Finlay.

He shook his head. 'No, nothing. I just wish I knew what we were looking for.'

'Can I ask…' I said hesitantly, as I didn't want to upset him. 'What about your mother? She doesn't know anything about what it could be your father left here?'

He looked at me sadly. 'My mother passed away when I was a teenager. She had cancer. It's just been me and my father for a long time. My only family — my father's brother and sister — didn't know when I asked them about it. My uncle doesn't think I should bother looking for it. But I'm sure that's because he thinks I should be focused on my father's company.'

'You are currently running it?' Adam asked Finlay.

He nodded. 'It's an accountancy company,' Finlay said. 'I was an accountant there, but I had left a few months ago. When my father became ill, though, I came back to help out and the company has been left to me. My uncle is looking after things while I'm here. I don't think he really understands why I've come. He's like my dad was — very focused on work.'

'I didn't realise you no longer worked there,' I said. I wondered if that's why he had looked uncomfortable when we first met at the Inn for his father's company's annual general meeting.

'I had wanted to do something else,' he said quietly. 'But things don't always work out the way you want.'

Adam and I looked at one another. Finlay looked so despondent. I wondered what it was he had wanted to do, but then his phone rang, preventing me from asking.

'My uncle. I'd better take it. Excuse me.' He left as he answered his phone.

'Seems like the past few weeks have been difficult for him,' Adam said in a low voice.

'I can't imagine losing your father and then having to deal with his house and the business and everything all by yourself like he has to,' I agreed. My heart went out to him. He was clearly grieving, but there was more to it. He was very unhappy and I hated to see someone feeling like that.

'Me neither,' Adam said.

Finlay came back in. 'I have to head back to the Inn — my uncle needs me to join in a meeting virtually. When can I come back?'

'Tomorrow afternoon when I'm back from shopping?' I said. 'I can text you when I'm on my way.'

'Perfect. Thank you. Both of you. I'll see you tomorrow.' Finlay walked out in a hurry.

'He doesn't seem happy to be working for his dad's company again,' Adam said.

'I hope he's okay. His uncle doesn't sound very supportive. That must be hard. Especially if working for his dad's company isn't what he really wants to do.'

'It must be hard not to have support around you,' Adam agreed.

I smiled at my brother. 'We might be mad taking this leap, but at least we have each other.'

Adam chuckled. 'That's one way of looking at it.'

Chapter Twenty-Three

The following day, Mum and Kathleen picked me up from Dove House and we drove into Inverness to visit an antiques shop there together. Thankfully, the rain had eased and the builders were able to get back onto the roof, so I was leaving the house in good hands.

Mum asked me how clearing the loft was going.

'It's mostly rubbish so far, but I've found a couple of things I can make use of. We haven't found anything belonging to Finlay's father.'

'I still think you're nuts letting him look in the loft,' Kathleen informed me from the passenger seat. 'He could be dodgy.'

'He's not dodgy. He's grieving. His dad asked him to do this. I think it's lovely that he's keeping his word, actually.'

'I just think you should be careful. He is a stranger, after all.'

'We're opening a bed and breakfast. We're going to be surrounded by strangers.'

'I wish I could be up there too,' Kathleen said then. That surprised me. She looked at her bump. 'I'm starting to feel useless.'

'Don't be silly, you're doing a very important job,' Mum said. She looked at me in the rear-view mirror. 'I'd love to meet Finlay,' she said.

'Well, maybe you can all come over for dinner and I'll ask him to stay. Otherwise he'll just be eating alone at the Inn.'

'I bet he'd like that,' Mum said.

'You'll all like him, I know it,' I said.

Kathleen turned to look at me. 'You mean, he's good-looking.'

I felt myself blush annoyingly. 'That has nothing to do with it,' I replied shortly, but I knew that only made it sound worse.

'Fine, well, I'll see him over dinner and make up my own mind. Just don't fall in love with him or anything.'

'Yeah, right.' I rolled my eyes. 'You know I'm staying well clear of men while we get the B & B up and running.'

She snorted and I wished I had something to throw at her.

'Why don't we put the radio on?' Mum suggested, which I quickly agreed to.

I hated how my sister got my back up. She always seemed to think she knew better than me. I knew that Adam liked Finlay. He was quiet and kind and was clearly grieving for his father, so he needed our support. I admired him following his heart and coming to Glendale, even though his uncle clearly thought otherwise. I didn't say that to Kathleen. I wasn't sure she'd admire it the way I did. Sometimes I wondered if she even had a heart to follow. Thankfully the radio silenced her and the rest of the drive passed quickly, and we soon arrived in Inverness.

'So, how's the nursery coming?' Mum asked Kathleen after we had parked the car and all climbed out. It was dry today, thankfully, but the weather was getting chillier by the day and the light breeze scattered leaves in our path as we walked towards the antiques shop we'd come to look around.

'I'd love your help with where to put the cot, and if I need a chair,' Kathleen replied. 'I'm thinking if I get one, I won't end up using it. Maybe you could come round tomorrow?'

'I was going to look at Lorna's paint samples…'

'Oh, it's fine,' Kathleen said quickly.

'I can come after that, though. Did you decide on a paint colour?' Mum asked.

'It's hard to know what to do when we don't know if it's a boy or a girl,' Kathleen said. 'We're trying out neutral shades, but I keep wondering if I should call my midwife and get her to tell me what we're having.'

'I was surprised you didn't want to know,' I said. 'You're usually such a planner.' And that was putting it mildly. My sister was the ultimate organiser.

'Hamish really wanted it to be a surprise, and as he's letting me have my favourite names...'

'That's a nice compromise.'

Kathleen sighed. 'I am capable of it! I know you think I don't have a romantic bone in my body but I do, I just don't make it an everyday habit.'

'You can say that again,' I replied with a chuckle.

'Here we are,' Mum said, opening the door to the shop.

I beamed. It was a treasure trove. It went back seemingly for miles and was bursting to the brim with furniture and decor.

'How are we going to find anything in here?' Kathleen asked in a low voice.

'Unearthing the treasure is all part of the fun,' I told her, but she tutted at the disarray in front of us. 'Look for anything art deco, or anything we can repurpose,' I said, turning to the shelf next to me. 'Gold is good.'

'I hope we're getting lunch after this,' she muttered, but she turned to the opposite shelf and began looking.

'Don't you think the past seems like it would have been a happier experience, sometimes?' I asked, picking up a gold clock.

'Could you live without your iPhone or Netflix, though? You love your movies,' Kathleen replied.

I shook my head. She was so literal. 'This could look really good on the mantelpiece in the lounge,' I added, holding up the clock for them to see.

'I love it,' Mum said. 'What about this?' she held up a plate.

'There's a chip,' I pointed out. 'Well, to me the past just seems like it was more glamorous and romantic. I hope I can make Dove House feel like that to guests, anyway. Oh, I love this painting.'

'You can't afford it,' Kathleen said, leaning over to look at the price.

I sighed and put it back. 'I suppose you're right. But this mirror… wow.' We stood in front of an ornate gold mirror propped up on the floor. I was distracted momentarily by our reflections. Me with my hair up and wearing jeans, boots and a cosy jumper; Kathleen with her neat bob and baby bump covered in a smart wool dress; and our mother with her short, grey-tinged hair, wearing leggings and a long cardigan. We all had the same nose but we didn't look much alike to me.

Mum smiled. 'It's perfect.'

'Can you afford it?' Kathleen asked. 'I'll see if the seller will reduce it.' She stalked off with purpose. I shrugged. Let her ask. I had to have this mirror, and I was sure Adam would agree.

'He'll knock twenty quid off,' Kathleen called over then.

Okay, sometimes my sister did come through.

–

'I'm back,' I yelled into the hallway of Dove House. 'And I need manly assistance,' I hollered, my voice echoing around me.

'At your service,' Adam said, coming from the kitchen.

'I said manly, but you'll do,' I replied.

'Ha, ha, ha.' He followed me out to the car. 'So, how did you do?'

'It's a really good shop – we have to go back. The owner said he'll ring me if anything good comes in for us.' I opened the boot of my car. 'But I got a mirror, a clock, this dinner service and these two velvet chairs. The mirror is so heavy…'

'It all looks great,' Adam agreed. 'How much did you spend?'

'Not too much,' I fudged.

'Make sure you add it to the spreadsheet so you keep track. You can't go over the decor budget, Lorna.'

'I know! Kathleen kept reminding me, don't worry,' I said. 'How's everything gone this morning?' I asked as we picked up an end of the mirror each.

'Well, losing yesterday put the roof behind, but they're working hard on it and the plastering has started. The carpets are being taken up as we speak. When is Finlay coming?'

'He's on the way, so I'll be up in the loft all afternoon. Kathleen seems to think there's something dodgy about him, so I said we'd do a dinner for the family soon and they can meet him.'

'Do you think he knows more than he's telling us about what his dad wants him to find here?'

'Maybe, but maybe it's because it's just too personal, you know?'

Adam nodded. 'Let's have the family over when we can then. Okay then, on three...' We lifted the mirror between us and carried it inside.

'Wow,' I said as I tilted it up against the wall. 'It's going to look so good in the hallway.'

'We'd better cover it well for now. Oh, and we found some more damp, so they will need an extra few days to work on that, and I'll need to revise the budget and time spreadsheet again, and...'

I closed my eyes for a second trying to remember the giddy feeling of seeing the mirror in here and how amazing it was going to look when people walked in, and then I opened them to find Adam staring at me. 'I just needed to remind myself of the vision.'

'Hmmm, well, remind yourself of that in the loft while I open the spreadsheet. Give me the receipts from the shop and I'll add them in to the expenses.'

With a sigh, I handed them over. 'You're really taking the fun out of the shopping, you know that?'

'Good. This isn't shopping for fun, this is business.'

I rolled my eyes when he couldn't see. Thankfully, the doorbell rang then and I went over to let Finlay in so we could go back into the loft.

Chapter Twenty-Four

Finlay and I spent the afternoon up in the loft until daylight faded into night and it grew too dim to see clearly. Almost everything we found was unusable, apart from a record player that made me gasp with pleasure. There was still no sign of anything belonging to the Scott family.

Adam was still out; he'd messaged to say he was popping over for a drink with Cameron in the pub after the tile shop, if I didn't mind, and I could meet them if I wanted to. But I was tired and dusty and didn't feel like going out, so I told him to have fun without me. Then I asked Finlay if he wanted to have a drink before he went back to the Inn and he agreed, so we went downstairs together with Finlay carrying the record player. I told him to take it into the lounge and I brought in a glass of wine for me and a beer for him.

When I walked in, Finlay was staring out of the window into the garden although he couldn't have been able to see much out there.

'Are you okay?' I asked. He'd been pretty quiet in the loft this afternoon, and I could tell being here was making him think about his father.

He started and turned round. 'Sorry, I was miles away.'

'So I can see. I know you said you didn't want to talk about it, but I'm here if you do,' I said, going over to one of the fold-up chairs we had in there. I put his beer down and sat with my wine, watching him.

He came over and sat down beside me and took a sip of his drink. 'I was thinking about my father. He said he was so happy here. It's hard to picture. He hadn't seemed happy for a very long time.'

'I'm sorry to hear that. Why wasn't he, do you think?'

'I think he spent so many years just focused on work. After my mum passed away, he never found anyone else. I think he was lonely. He wasn't someone who entertained, who had people over. He didn't have friends, really, just colleagues, you know? He had his brother, my uncle, and his sister, but she emigrated. My uncle had his own business and was just as work-focused, but he sold it last year.' Finlay looked at me. 'We weren't close, my father and I.'

'Oh. I thought you were because you had come here,' I said, surprised he was trying so hard to live up to his promise if they hadn't been close.

'We were estranged before he fell ill, and he reached out to me. I came back to the family home to be with him.' He paused, searching for the right words. I couldn't imagine not being close to my family, so I understood why it hurt to talk about. 'I used to work for my father, as you know,' Finlay said. 'I went to university and took my accountancy exams because he wanted me to, and I joined the company because he wanted that. But it was never what I wanted.'

'What did you want to do?' I asked as I sipped my wine.

'I wanted to be a writer.' He saw me raise an eyebrow. 'Quite different, huh?' He laughed once, but I could tell it wasn't funny to him. 'I always wanted to write, but my father never encouraged it. If anything, he was pretty scornful of it. When I had finally worked up the guts to say I wanted a year off to work on my novel, he hit the roof. He told me I was mad, that he needed me at work, I was to take over the business one day, after all... He said I'd never make it as a writer, so why even bother trying? We had a pretty vicious row. Then my father told me to leave and not come back, so I did.'

'I'm so sorry,' I said. 'That must have been so hard.' I knew I would be heartbroken if I ever fell out with my parents.

'It was, but I was angry and stubborn too, I can't just blame him. I didn't want to be the one who reached out, I felt like he should instead.' He sighed. 'I stayed with a university friend and I started writing, working in a pub in the evenings to pay my way. And then suddenly my father called me and said he was ill. When I came home, I was shocked. I hadn't realised that he was… dying.'

'I can't even imagine,' I said. I reached out to touch his arm. 'I'm so glad you were able to be together at the end,' I said. He looked at my hand on his arm, so I took it away, embarrassed.

Finlay nodded. 'Thank you. Me too. But it wasn't easy. Neither of us was ever very good with our emotions. I didn't want to argue, so I didn't bring up my writing. He wanted to talk about the past. First of all, when I was a child with him and my mother and the happy times we had had.' Finlay sighed. 'And then about his childhood here in Glendale. And this house. Near the end, he told me that he had wanted something too, but he let his parents decide his path and he regretted letting them. He asked for my help. He said I should come to Dove House to see if there was something he left here all those years ago. As you know, I told him there wouldn't be but he became upset and so adamant that in the end I agreed. I promised I'd try to find whatever it was and give it to the person he had meant to have it. But he wouldn't tell me the full story. He said he wanted me to find out for myself. Maybe he thought I wouldn't come if I knew.'

I let his story sink in. I thought about how, when I had first seen Finlay, he had been wearing a suit that didn't seem to fit him, and now I understood why. It didn't fit him. He wanted to be a writer, not an accountant, but when we'd met he was at the Inn at a company meeting. 'And now you feel you need to take over the company like your dad wanted?'

He nodded. 'But I knew I had to try and find what my father wanted me to find first. It was the least I could do for him. After everything that happened between us.'

'You healed your estrangement. You made up in the end. The rest of it doesn't matter,' I said firmly.

'Maybe,' he replied quietly. Then he shook his head. 'Tell me... why did you always want this house?'

'It was my mother, really. She came here a lot as a teenager, and she loved the family who lived here and I think she hoped they would become her family too, but they left Glendale and I think she always wished things had turned out differently. She thought this house would make a wonderful bed and breakfast. That other people would love to be here like she had loved it. But then she met my dad and they had us kids. There are five of us.'

'Five? Wow.'

'Our family is pretty chaotic. So her dream of running a bed and breakfast faded, but she brought me and Adam here as kids and it felt like this special house, like somewhere I could be happy, and when I grew up, I saw its potential as a business too. Adam and I wanted to start a bed and breakfast together and Mum said this would be perfect, and once it was in our heads it was all we could think about. But we lost out buying it five years ago and, honestly, I thought the dream would never come true.'

'But here you are.'

I smiled. 'We were so lucky that Betty decided to sell it and then Beth helped us buy it, as you know. It's been a long time coming. I can't believe we're actually here. There's something about Dove House — it never really leaves you. Maybe that's how your dad felt.'

He nodded. 'I think so. I just hope I can find what he wanted me to. I need to do what I promised him I would.'

'Don't be too hard on yourself. Whatever he left here or lost, it might not be here any more but you've come and that's what he wanted for you. Maybe he thought this place would be good for you, too.'

'I hope so.' Finlay looked over at me and I felt a connection between us. I wasn't sure why or what it meant, but I had a feeling that Finlay felt it too.

'Let's see if this works.' I got up, unsure why but I needed some distance between us. We'd been together all day and there was something about looking into those blue eyes of his that made me nervous. I went over to the record player from the loft and picked up a vinyl and tried it out. The soothing voice of Billie Holiday filled the room. 'It works!'

'It sounds great,' Finlay said.

I turned around excitedly. 'Can you picture guests in here drinking a cocktail, sitting in velvet chairs and listening to jazz on a cosy autumn night just like this one?'

'I really can,' he replied, smiling at my enthusiasm. 'I'd love to see that.'

'You have to come back when we're open to see it all finished,' I said eagerly. 'I mean, if you want to.'

'I would love that.'

Chapter Twenty-Five

I enjoyed the colours of October as I walked to Emily's Bakery to get myself a coffee. I had been in the loft with Finlay all day and I really needed some fresh air. He had wanted to stay, so I said I'd go and get coffees for us and Adam. The leaves were changing all around the village now. Glendale was always attractive, but at this time of year it really did look beautiful draped in golds and oranges. Even though I was tired from the day, I felt a hundred times better for getting outside to see it.

'Hi Lorna, how's the building work going?' Emily greeted me as I walked in.

'Honestly, I'm not even sure. It looks like complete chaos, but apparently there's method in the madness,' I told her.

'A coffee, was it?'

'Three lattes, please. Me, Adam and Finlay need them.'

'Finlay? Oh, this is the man here to help you clear out the loft?'

I wasn't surprised she knew; Beth had probably told her. 'That's right. His family used to live at Dove House.' I noticed Emily's aunt Sally was sitting at one of the tables nursing a cup of tea. Sally lived in a cottage in the grounds of Glendale Hall. She had been the housekeeper before Anna, but had retired. I knew that she knew pretty much everything about Glendale. I turned to her as Emily made my coffee. 'I wonder if you knew his father – Thomas Scott?'

Sally thought for a moment. 'Oh, yes. That's right. The Scott family lived there for maybe five years. They moved away when the children were teenagers – there were three of them, I believe.'

'What were the family like, did you know them well?'

'Not that well, but Beth's grandmother was friends with Thomas's wife. They came to the Hall a fair bit. I think they moved to a bigger estate after a relative died and they inherited their house.'

That was interesting. Finlay had mentioned having to sort out his family home so I wondered if this was the estate they had inherited. I assumed then that they came from money, if his parents had been friendly with Beth's grandmother at Glendale Hall. Perhaps that was why his father had been so furious about him trying to be a writer; it didn't fit with the family legacy. 'I think Finlay is here to feel closer to his father. He passed away recently.'

'Oh, that's such a shame to hear,' Sally said with a sigh. 'Younger than me, too. I don't know, everyone I used to know seems to be disappearing.'

'Aunt Sally, you'll outlive us all,' Emily told her, handing me my coffees.

'I hope not,' Sally replied, indignantly. 'I hope this young man finds what he's looking for. Coming back to where you're from can bring up all kinds of feelings.'

'Definitely. There is so much up in the loft from previous people who lived in Dove House. It has seen a lot over the years, that house, I bet.'

'Like Glendale Hall,' Sally agreed. 'These old houses, it makes you wonder the stories they could tell, doesn't it?'

'I'm glad the vicarage isn't that old, that spooks me out,' Emily replied with a shudder. 'Poor Lorna won't sleep tonight now.'

'No, I like the fact that I'm sleeping somewhere with such a history – I hope I can discover more about everyone who lived there before me. And it's so exciting to think about who might come and stay and add to that history.'

'That's a lovely way of looking at it,' Sally said with a smile.

'It'll be so fun having people stay in the village,' Emily said. 'Good luck with it all, Lorna, we can't wait to see it restored.'

I thanked them both, and as more people came into the bakery, I left with my coffees. I thought about Thomas Scott and his family. It was strange to think that if they hadn't left Glendale, I might have grown up with Finlay. I understood why his father had missed Glendale. I didn't want to ever move away. And he had a link to Glendale Hall. I knew that Beth's grandmother had been instrumental in Beth running away, pregnant with Izzy, when she was only sixteen. But when her grandmother became gravely ill, she and Izzy came back and they had stayed there ever since.

Maybe Thomas Scott had thought he would come back one day, but obviously he never had. I felt a little bit sad that he hadn't been able to see Glendale one last time. But I was pleased that his son was here now.

Back at Dove House, I gave Adam his latte then I headed to the loft. I climbed the ladder and found Finlay up there on the floor surrounded by boxes, rooting through one with a look of deep concentration on his face. I wondered if he did know what he was looking for up here after all. Could I blame him if he did, but didn't want to tell me and Adam? 'Any luck?' I called up.

He looked startled to see me. 'No. I wonder if I'll ever find it.' He sighed and ran a hand through his hair.

'I saw someone today who remembers your father. Maybe you can talk to her about him and what his life was like in Glendale.'

Finlay looked at me sharply. 'What did you tell them about my father?'

I flinched at his tone. 'Nothing. I just knew that Sally has lived in Glendale all her life, and I thought she might have known him. She remembers him and his family being here. I know she'd be happy to talk to you about him. That's all. I haven't told anyone about this,' I said, gesturing to the loft.

'I just don't like people talking about my family.' Finlay stood up.

'People here mean well. No one is gossiping. People are just interested as your father used to live here,' I said. 'Here, I got you a coffee.'

Finlay sighed. 'I'm sorry. I've been cooped up here for too long, I think. I just feel really frustrated. Like I'm letting my father down somehow. Thank you for the coffee.'

'You can't think like that.'

'I walked away from his company, his home and him! And then he died. How can I not feel like I let him down? And now I can't even find the thing he most wanted before he...' He broke off, his voice catching.

'You need to give yourself a break. You're here like he asked you to be. You're doing all you can.'

'It just doesn't feel good enough.'

I wished I could think of a way to help him, he looked so distressed. 'Your father wouldn't want you to feel like this.'

'You didn't know him,' he snapped. 'I'm sorry. It's been a long week. I thought by now...'

'We still have the back wall to sort through, so there's hope,' I said, gesturing to the boxes we had yet to get to. It had been a much longer job than I had thought, but it had gone quickly doing it with Finlay and the week had flown by. I tried not to think about the fact that once we'd finished that last wall, he would be going back to Perth.

'My uncle needs me back this weekend,' Finlay said then. 'So, can you wait until Monday for me to come and finish it with you?'

'Of course. And have dinner with us afterwards, please?' I'd already asked the family to come over and I wanted everyone to meet Finlay.

'Sure. Thank you, Lorna. I'll see you Monday, then.'

It would feel strange not to have him here all weekend, I realised. 'Have a good weekend,' I said, giving him a wave.

He walked quickly past me as if desperate to get away. I looked around at the boxes once he had gone, and wondered how many secrets had been stored away up here. The boxes were like the secrets people stored in their hearts. Maybe they didn't want to be opened, but they needed to be.

I hoped Finlay could unlock his father's secret while he was here, otherwise I wasn't sure what he was going to do.

Chapter Twenty-Six

I had been looking forward to an easy weekend with the builders off and Finlay back in Perth. Adam had planned to drive to a builder's yard a couple of hours away as their supplies were cheaper, so I was going to see if I could get the paint colour I wanted colour-matched for a more affordable price.

But then I heard a commotion outside. With a heavy sigh, I slipped out of the front door to see what was happening. Adam was by his car ready to head off, waving and shouting at a lorry driving away from the house. I walked out into the driveway to see that the lorry had dropped off a huge skip, leaving it outside the gates, and it was taking up a lot of the road.

'This wasn't due until Monday, and they've just left it and driven off before I could stop them,' Adam said. 'What now?' he added when a car drove in through the gates. I sighed, seeing it was Kathleen's car. 'I'll phone the skip company.' He sighed and, dialling, put the phone to his ear. 'An answerphone saying no one is there because it's the weekend. Unbelievable!'

We walked over to look at the skip. Dove House was at the end of the road, but if anyone wanted to get to the last two houses opposite, they would struggle to get past it. 'That's Mrs Andrews' house,' I hissed just as the front door opened and she marched out.

'What's happening?' Kathleen said as she climbed out of her car to join us.

'Not now,' I said to her before I stepped forward and threw on a smile. 'Mrs Andrews, how lovely to see you again.'

'What is the meaning of this?' Mrs Andrews glared at the skip. 'My nephew is coming to see me for lunch – how will he get his car past?'

'I know, we're sorry, we just found it like this,' I said, trying to stay calm. 'It wasn't meant to arrive until Monday, so we weren't out here to watch where they left it.'

'Well, what are you going to do about it? Because I'll call the council and get—'

'No need,' Adam said hastily. 'We'll move it right now. Leave it with us, okay?'

'You have half an hour.' Mrs Andrews stormed off. Great. Adam and I looked at one another.

'How are you going to move a skip?' Kathleen asked.

I spun round. 'That's helpful, thank you. Can you wait inside, please?' I asked her. 'Why are you here anyway?'

Her face fell. 'I wanted to ask for your help with the nursery...'

'I can't right now, we need to fix this,' I said, feeling bad, but I really didn't have any idea how we could move the skip.

'Can we tow it?' Adam asked.

'Not with our cars. I know!' I pulled out my phone and rang Cameron. 'Please say you can get here with your truck and help us move a skip? Within half an hour?' I cried when he picked up the phone. Cameron was always calm in a crisis. He didn't ask questions, just said he'd get here.

'Okay, I think we can do this,' I said to Adam. 'Now, Kath, what...' I trailed off to see my sister back in her car. She drove past us, ignoring me waving my arms at her. 'Couldn't she see this was an emergency?'

'She'll be fine,' Adam said. But I wasn't so sure. I had a feeling my sister had been crying.

Cameron turned up in his truck from the farm with Anna in thirty minutes. Mrs Andrews came back out as we were moving it, tutted, but stayed to watch at least and not ring the council. Thankfully, Cameron was able to move the skip back so it covered our driveway and wasn't out in the road. Adam and I would have to put up with our cars being stuck in the driveway until Monday when we could get the company to move it.

'I hope there aren't going to be any more issues like this,' Mrs Andrews said.

'Me too,' I said under my breath as she walked away.

'Well, that was fun,' Anna said.

'You two are lifesavers,' I said to her and Cameron. 'Thank you so much!'

'She seemed to enjoy that,' Anna said. 'She's not a fan of yours, I take it?'

'She's not happy about the building work. I hope we don't have any more issues, or she's going to complain about us.'

'Coffee, everyone?' Adam suggested. We agreed and followed him inside.

I pulled out my phone to send a message to my sister. Now the crisis was over, I did feel bad about snapping at her but she could see our neighbour was having a kitten fit.

> Mrs Andrews is a nightmare! Cameron helped us move the skip, so all good here now. Do you want to come back later and we can talk about the nursery?

'So, where's Finlay?' Anna asked. Since Beth met him, Anna had sent me lots of messages asking for all the gossip on him. She had yet to bump into him at the Inn, which she wasn't impressed about.

'He went back to Perth for the weekend. He'll be back Monday. We think we have a couple more days of clearing up there to do. We haven't found anything of his father's yet.' I hadn't wanted to tell people too much about his search; I just said he was hoping to find something his father had left up there. 'I hope he'll be okay if we don't.'

Anna looked at me. 'I know that face, Lorna. You like this mystery man.'

I hoped I wasn't blushing. 'I just feel bad for him. He's lost his father, and Dove House and Glendale meant a lot to him. I know what that's like, you know? His dad never got to come back here like he has. It must be hard.'

'Facing your past is never easy,' Anna said with certainty. 'I think he came to stay at the right place – Glendale can fix anyone.'

'I hope so,' I replied. My phone vibrated and I looked to see what Kathleen had messaged back to me.

> It's fine. Mum is helping me. See you at church tomorrow.

'And it doesn't hurt that he's easy on the eye,' Anna said then as I put my phone away, glad Kathleen was sorting what she needed with Mum.

'He is?' Adam said, looking at us over his shoulder as we walked into the kitchen.

'How do you know?' I asked Anna. She had yet to meet him, after all.

'Beth said something about him looking like Clark Kent.'

I laughed. I could see why she'd said that. It was those blue eyes behind the glasses… 'Well, if he turns into Superman, I'll let you know.'

'Maybe he already has,' Anna said, dropping me a wink.

'I feel like I'm missing something,' Adam said.

'I always feel that way with these two,' Cameron observed.

'Speaking of,' Anna said, brightly, changing the subject, which I was very grateful for. 'Grace was running an event at the Inn last night, and she was saying she'd love to see the progress you guys are making with the B & B.'

I hid a smile. 'Why don't you both come over next week?'

Anna turned back to me. 'Oh, good, then I can meet Finlay!'

I really hadn't thought that through.

Chapter Twenty-Seven

On Monday, Finlay returned and we went back up to the loft. He was still quiet, and hadn't wanted to talk about his weekend much. He'd spent it with his uncle, he said. 'Talking through the company. I don't know a thing about running a business like my uncle does,' he had said once we were up in the loft.

'Is that what you want to do then?' I asked, wondering what had happened to his plan to be a writer.

'It's what my father would have wanted.'

'Really? But he talked about his regrets, too, and I'm sure he wouldn't want you—'

'Look at this,' he said, showing me old floor plans of the house.

I knew he wanted to change the subject so I didn't bring it up again, but it was frustrating that he wasn't thinking about what he wanted at all, only what he thought he should do now. I would have to try and talk to him again about it, I told myself.

In the evening, the family came round to eat with us and to meet Finlay. I left him cleaning up in the bathroom as the loft was very dusty, and went downstairs to greet the family once all the builders had left for the day.

'They've finished the plastering in the lounge,' Adam was saying as we opened the door and everyone came into the hallway. 'So, we can start painting. We're going with the warm cream in there, aren't we?'

'And wallpaper on the back wall to make a feature of it. I found a cream and gold fan design that's perfect.'

'Great, so we can... Hi, guys!'

'Oh, it's looking like a lot of work has been done,' Mum said, looking around at the plastered walls. I walked over to her while Adam took the others into the dining room to show them the paint samples and get their opinion.

'I need to find the perfect chandelier for in here,' I said, looking up at the empty light fitting. 'I can't wait until everything is ready for me to decorate.'

'It's going to look wonderful,' Mum replied.

'Come on, I can't wait for you to meet Finlay,' I said, leading Mum towards the lounge. 'We still haven't found anything that belongs to the Scott family up in the loft.'

'The Scott family?'

'That's right,' I said as we walked through the doorway. Finlay was standing by the French doors waiting for us.

Mum stopped suddenly and I almost walked into her. 'Mum?'

'What did you say his name was?' she asked, her voice barely above a whisper.

Finlay looked at her, and I saw the colour drain from my mum's face.

'This is Finlay Scott,' I said, wondering why my mum looked so shocked.

'His father?' she whispered.

'Thomas Scott,' I replied.

'Oh, my goodness, I didn't think I'd ever hear that name again,' she said, stepping forward almost as if she was in trance.

'You knew my father?' Finlay asked, in surprise.

'Did you, Mum?' I supposed that they had been similar ages, as me and Finlay were.

Mum nodded, still staring at Finlay. 'I knew your family. I spent a lot of time here with them.'

'They were the family?' I asked her. 'What a coincidence,' I said. 'They were the reason you fell in love with Dove House. Why we're here right now,' I said, smiling. It was nice to think things had come full circle.

Mum wasn't smiling, though. She looked sad. 'Lorna said Thomas had passed away?' she asked Finlay.

He nodded. 'Recently. That's why I'm here. He wanted me to come to Glendale and visit this house. It was his last request.'

'Did he?' She shook her head as if she didn't want to ask what she was about to but then she took a breath and carried on. 'Did he ever mention me?'

'What's your name?' Finlay asked, looking as confused as I felt.

'My name when he knew me was Amelia Kelly.'

Finlay did a double take. 'Amelia Kelly? You're Amelia Kelly...?' They both stared at one another.

Kathleen walked through the doorway then. 'What's happening?' she asked.

'You're the reason I'm here,' Finlay said after a moment. 'Before he died, Dad wanted me—'

'I'm sorry, I need some air,' Mum burst out before spinning round and rushing out of the room, leaving all of us staring after her.

Chapter Twenty-Eight

After a beat, I hurried out after Mum.

I heard Kathleen struggling to walk as fast as me with her baby bump, but I couldn't slow down, I was too confused by Mum running out like that. I saw her heading outside, so I went out of the kitchen door and found her in the garden just standing on the grass looking lost. 'Mum?' I said gently as I approached her. 'Are you okay?'

She sighed, wrapping her arms across her chest. She kept her face towards the horizon. 'Sorry for rushing out like that. It was just such a shock. Hearing Thomas's name again... seeing his son. And knowing that he's... gone.'

I saw the sadness in her eyes. 'Mum, were you and Thomas together?' Now that I thought about it, she had always been rather cagey about why she had never kept in touch with the family who had lived here, or what had happened that summer she had spent at Dove House as a teenager. I glanced back as Kathleen caught up with us. She stopped next to me and we looked at Mum as she thought about her answer.

'Thomas was my first love,' she confirmed. She turned to look at us, daughters by a different man to the one she was talking about. It was strange to see the hurt on her face caused by another man, not Dad. 'Maybe that's why I wanted this house so badly. I had been my happiest here. I had fallen in love for the first time, and for a minute I thought that I belonged here, that this would be my home,' Mum said, looking back at the house that seemed to be watching us. 'Until Thomas left me.'

'He was your boyfriend?' Finlay's father and my mother... I hadn't expected that his mystery would be linked to my past as well as his.

'We fell in love that summer. I spent so much time here with him.' She looked around the garden, remembering. 'But then his family moved away,' she said wistfully.

'I don't get it,' Kathleen said. 'Why did you still love this house? Why would you want it after he left you?' She looked confused and I didn't blame her. She wasn't romantic like me, but even I wasn't sure I'd want to be in the house where my heart had been broken.

'I don't know. I felt special when I was here. And I loved the summer that I spent here. And when they left, I felt like the house was waiting for me to come back. Maybe that sounds crazy, I don't know,' Mum said. 'That's why I was so happy when you bought this house with Adam. I know you always felt like this house was special too, and you both deserve to live somewhere special and be happy. I really want that for all of you,' she added to Kathleen.

'What happened? Why did you and Thomas not work out?' I asked.

'His parents didn't approve.' She gave a wry smile. 'An age-old story. I thought we could overcome it, I thought he'd come back for me one day. But he never did. After he left, I never heard from him. Time went on and my wounds healed and I met your father... Still, I always wondered if I'd ever see Thomas again. Seeing Finlay just now was like seeing a ghost. It was a shock. I'm sorry I ran out like that. He must think I'm so rude.'

'He'll understand.' I turned back to the house and saw Finlay was still there in the lounge looking out at us. I wondered how he felt. He clearly knew my mum's name. His dad must have told him about her.

'Sally said the family moved to an estate they inherited. That's when Thomas left and you broke up?'

'He said he'd write to me, that we'd make it work. They decided to move to break us up, that was clear, but we were both so confident, so sure, that it wouldn't happen. That they couldn't. Our love was too strong.' She shook her head. 'But once he left, he must have thought they were right. I never heard from any of them again.' She looked sad, but then turned to us. 'It wasn't meant to be. I wouldn't have you girls or Adam or the twins if it had, so all's well that ends well. We'd better go back inside now – the others will be missing us.'

'But…' I protested. I wanted to know so much more.

'Leave it, Lorna,' Kathleen said as Mum started to walk back to the house. 'She's upset,' she added quietly, so Mum wouldn't hear her. 'Give her time to process it all.'

I sighed, supposing my sister was right. I pushed down my questions and trailed after them. As I approached the lounge, my eyes met Finlay's and I wished I knew what he was thinking.

–

Dinner had a strange atmosphere to it. Adam and I had ordered pizzas and garlic bread and we all sat along a fold-up table on fold-up chairs to eat. Family dinners were usually lively and loud, and half the table was living up to that with Dad, Adam, the twins and Hamish talking and eating enthusiastically, whereas Mum was silent and Kathleen and I kept looking at her and at each other. Finlay's gaze was fixed on his plate and he barely ate anything.

I couldn't stand it any longer. 'So, can we just talk about the fact that Mum knew Finlay's dad,' I said, loudly, over everyone. Finlay's head snapped up and the others looked at me. 'His family used to own this house.'

'What a small world,' Hamish said. 'You knew them well, Amelia?'

'I spent a lot of time here a lot as a teenager. I was friends with Thomas's sister first, at school, then I got to know the whole family,' Mum said quietly. 'Is she and your uncle…?' She trailed off.

Finlay nodded. 'They are still with us. My uncle has been a big help since my father passed away,' he said, clearing his throat. 'My dad's sister lives abroad, so I don't really know her that well.'

'I thought you were here to find something in the loft?' Dad asked him then.

Finlay nodded. 'My dad said there was something of his here and he wanted me to find it and give it back to the person it was meant for. He didn't tell me what it was, I was honest about that,' he added, looking at me. 'But he did mention a girl... He said he had so many regrets about the girl he left behind. He said he had loved her very much. He told me your name in the end,' Finlay added to my mother. I could see her eyes shining with unshed tears as he talked about his father's last moments. I realised then what a shock it must have been for Finlay to lose his father as he had done. My mum seemed so young to me. But his father, the same age, had passed away. Goosebumps appeared under my jumper just thinking about it. 'He said that whatever it was he'd left here was meant for you. He told me your name, but obviously I realise now it's your maiden name. Which was why I didn't make any connection to Lorna or Adam.'

I wondered why Finlay hadn't mentioned the girl to me. I would have connected it to my mother straight away. Not that I supposed it would have helped with the search at all.

'Something meant for me?' Mum repeated. 'But what?'

'I don't know. He just said I would realise when I saw it. I have no idea if it's still here or not. He said that years later his parents told him they'd put it up in the loft. He didn't make a lot of sense at that point, but I think whatever it was, they took it and hid it so you never got it. And he wanted me to find it and give it to you.'

'After they moved to Perth, I never heard from him again,' Mum said. 'Thomas's parents never approved of me. His father practically threw me out of the house when they told me they were moving. It really hurt. And then Thomas never got in touch, never came back for me. I always wondered what had happened to him… I can't believe he thought of me at the end.'

'Maybe he wanted you to know once and for all why he didn't come back,' I suggested.

'I'll find out; I made him a promise,' Finlay said, determination back on his face.

'Maybe the past should be left alone. What can finding out do now? Your dad isn't here, and Mum moved on a long time ago,' Kathleen said. 'I don't want this to upset you, Mum.'

'I don't have to share it with you,' Finlay said quickly. 'I made Dad a promise, I have to try to fulfil it. I owe him that.'

'It's okay,' Mum assured Kathleen. 'As you say, it was a long time ago.' She smiled at Finlay. 'I understand you need to do this. Let's cross that bridge when we come to it.' She looked at my father, who nodded, understanding floating in the air between them. I wondered what it was like to feel that with someone. It must have been weird for my dad to know Mum loved Finlay's father before him, and that she had always wondered why he had never come back for her. But I knew my mum loved my dad and he knew it too, and that was what mattered, not what happened before they met.

Still, maybe my mum deserved closure. I wondered if she was about to get it at long last and how it might make her feel. It sounded like Finlay's dad died feeling regret, and I really didn't want my mother to feel that too. Things had suddenly become very complicated.

'I can keep looking then?' Finlay asked, but this time he was looking at me. 'And try to find what my father wanted me to?'

'If it's okay with my mum,' I replied. She nodded and Finlay looked relieved. I heard Kathleen tut under her breath but Leo and Noah noticed Tabby coming into the room now and wanted to give him some of the chicken on their pizza, so the conversation went back to normal. Yet I was sure that all of us were still wondering what Thomas Scott might have left behind here for my mother.

Chapter Twenty-Nine

The next morning, Adam and I had breakfast together. He was looking at his spreadsheet again, his brow creased. 'What's wrong?' I asked after he let out a sigh.

'The two bathrooms that need refitting are going to cost more than I first thought because they need new pipes, and we couldn't get the cheaper tiles. Things are getting tight. I think I'd better go out into the garden today and see what needs doing – maybe I can do some of the work myself so we don't need to find a gardener? That will save us quite a bit. And that chandelier you want is just too expensive. Can you keep hunting for a cheaper one?'

'I can try.' I was worried at having to cut the decor budget by much more. 'No one will want to stay here and pay what we need them to to recoup costs if we don't make it look good, though,' I reminded him.

'No one can stay full stop at the moment. We have to make sure the building is solid. We can't cut corners on things like the roof or the plumbing or plastering. I'm trying to get the best quotes for the work that I can.'

'I know,' I said quickly, seeing he was looking stressed. 'I'll keep looking.'

Adam nodded. 'And can you finish the loft soon? I know you've got to look through everything for Finlay, but it's taking much longer than we thought. If you were free to help out in other areas we could save on labour.'

'I'll be up there with him this morning and I'll try to finish, but if not, Finlay can carry on without me. This afternoon

Mum and I are going costume-shopping for the Halloween party. After that, I'll be able to do whatever else needs doing, okay?'

'Sorry to moan. There doesn't seem to be a day when we don't have any extra costs coming in or something causing more of a delay. Remind me never to renovate a house again.' He smiled, though, and I was relieved his good humour had returned.

'At least the new windows are being fitted and the plastering is almost done. We're getting there. And I'll look into more second-hand shops that I can buy from. Oh, and I got the paint mixed more cheaply using the colour-match service you told me about, so that's something.'

'Thank you. I just want us to try to keep on track to start the painting and decorating next month, and then we might still be able to open in the New Year. That feels very far away right now.' Adam got up when he heard noise outside. 'And another day begins. I'll go and say hello to the builders.'

I watched him go and hoped that nothing else was going to come up today; another setback and I wasn't sure what we'd be able to do. I exhaled. I was so grateful we had each other – I could never have done all this on my own. We had known that all the work was needed but somehow, before we started, it hadn't seemed as much as it did now that we were in the thick of it. I looked at Tabby finishing off his breakfast by the back door. 'Wish us luck, Tabby, we're going to need it.'

–

When Finlay arrived, we went back up to the loft and moved to the back wall to go through the remaining boxes. The contents of the rest we had either put in the skip or donated to charity, or I'd kept to use downstairs.

Sunlight streamed through the skylight as we worked.

'I hope your mum will be okay. She was so shocked. I mean, I was too when I realised she was my father's long-lost love.'

Finlay glanced at me a little self-consciously. 'Isn't it strange how we met, and then we find that out?'

'Really strange,' I replied. Did it explain the connection I felt to him? 'Mum never told me about your dad. I always knew she had loved her time with the family that used to live in this house, but I didn't know she had fallen in love here. I suppose some things you want to keep to yourself.'

'My dad had never mentioned her before. Even after my mother died. I'm still finding it hard to picture him young and in love – he's always been this rather formidable figure to me.' Finlay sighed next to me as he sifted through his box. 'Although maybe losing your mum made him that way.'

'I know my mum is happy with my dad, but it's weird to think that she did love someone else. And that she'd always wished she could live here. Maybe she thought by owning it she would get that happy ending she had dreamed of when she was a teenager, or that she could help other people get theirs. Always a romantic.' I smiled because I too hoped that Dove House would be my happy ending, and my brother's. And that it would bring other people happiness when they stayed here. So I knew why she had felt like that.

'My dad regretted how things ended between them. I think he saw your mum as the one that got away.' He sighed. 'It makes me feel bad for him, but also for my mother. I mean, was he ever happy with her? Did he also love her? But maybe not quite in the same way? I don't want to end up with regrets like that. Or be with someone that I'm not all in with, you know?'

I nodded vigorously. 'I feel the same.' We looked at one another and I felt that connection again. 'I suppose we all want a happy ending, but it doesn't always work out that way. It did for my mum, thankfully. But I'm sorry if it didn't for your father.'

'I have to believe that he did love my mum. I mean, we did have some happy times together. When she died, he became more distant, I suppose. I just wish he'd told me all this sooner.

Why did he wait until he was dying to let me get to know him? I felt so guilty that we stopped speaking, that I let him push me away; I should have tried to make things up with him. But it wasn't until he became so ill and reached out to me that I went back.'

'I understand. But you did make up, and that's what matters. He wouldn't want you to feel guilty, I'm sure of that,' I told him firmly. I moved to another box and opened it up. 'He would want you to be happy.'

Finlay shook his head. I could tell he wasn't sure whether to believe that. It must have been so hard to not have your father support what you wanted in life. My mum and dad had always supported me. 'My father put duty first, always. I need to be like that now.'

'But you said yourself that he regretted that at the end. He asked you to come back here. Surely it was because that was when he had been happy. He wanted you to see this house and to have a chance at that kind of happiness.'

I knew I didn't know him that well yet, but I couldn't imagine Finlay would be happy as a businessman running his father's company, wearing that suit day in and day out and living alone in their house in Perth.

'Or he didn't want me to make the same mistake he had done. Maybe following your heart just doesn't work.'

'You don't believe that,' I said confidently.

Finlay turned to meet my gaze. 'I wish I could see the world the way you do — you believe that everything will be okay in the end, that it all works out, that you should go after your dreams. And I used to as well. But since I tried to do that, everything has gone wrong.'

'I don't always believe that,' I protested. 'I've had a tough few years thinking I wasn't ever going to do what I wanted to do. I wasn't even sure about making our offer on Dove House. I didn't think after all this time that our dream could come true. Life can make you uncertain, can't it? But I always had a hope about this house. I'm glad I didn't give up on what I wanted. I'm glad that I still let myself hope. And I try to think that things will be okay in the end because otherwise why even get up in the morning?' I realised I had spoken more passionately than I had intended. Finlay was staring at me. I felt my cheeks flush. 'Did that make sense?'

'Perfect sense,' he whispered, then he started to get up. 'Lorna, I…' Then he stopped and looked down at what was in his hand. 'Oh my God.'

'What?'

'This is my father's handwriting.'

I scooted across the floor and leaned over Finlay's shoulder so I could see what he was holding. It was a letter.

Finlay turned to me; our faces were only an inch apart. My breath hitched at our sudden closeness. 'We've found it,' he said, in wonder.

'We did.' We were still looking at one another. I suddenly wished I could close the inch between us. Finlay's eyes flicked to my lips and I hoped he was wishing for the same thing.

But then he coughed and looked back down at the letter. I quickly looked at the letter instead, my heart thudding in my chest. That had been a charged moment. I knew we had both felt it. 'See?' Finlay broke the silence, pointing to his father's signature at the end of the long letter. It was faded with age but legible. Finlay found the front page of the letter then.

'It's addressed to my mum,' I said with a gasp.

Chapter Thirty

Finlay held his father's letter in his hands. 'This is it. This is what he wanted me to find, and why he said he wanted me to give it to the person it was meant for. It was a letter. To your mother.'

I could hardly believe it. It was still here after all these years. That Finlay's father had written to my mother and we had found it! I was relieved that Finlay had fulfilled his promise, and I was curious, but I was a little afraid as to what the letter was going to say. 'Do you want to read it on your own?' I asked, hoping he would want me to read it with him.

'We should read it together.'

'Read it to me,' I suggested. I crossed my legs as Finlay leaned against the wall and nodded.

He read his father's letter aloud.

'Dear Amelia, I'm writing this the night before we leave Glendale for Perth. I haven't seen you for two days. I think this is the longest time we've gone without speaking since the first day we kissed. I know that my father upset you and I wasn't strong enough to stand up to him. I let him make you leave, and it's haunted me ever since. I don't know what to do.

'My parents are watching me all the time. I haven't been able to come to your house. The telephone has been disconnected already. Everything is in boxes. The house feels so different. Not because we're packing up, but because you're not here. I think the house is missing you. I know I am. I need to speak to you but I don't know how. Tomorrow we'll be miles apart and I don't know how I'll bear it.

'I have a plan, though. I'm going to write this letter and ask the housekeeper to give it to you and then you'll know that it wasn't only your heart that broke when you left this house the other day, but mine too. I know how to mend them both. I'm putting money in this envelope for you. I want you to get the train to Edinburgh and meet me there. I'm going to take as much money from my parents as I can and we can start a new life together. In time, they'll forgive me and accept you – I know it – when they realise we are meant to be. I just need to show them how serious we are. We can't let them stop us.

'Meet me at the Royal Hotel on Saturday. I'll be there from ten in the morning. I can't wait to see you and hold you again. Just a few days more and we'll be together. Forever. I'll leave the phone number for our new house in case of an emergency but try not to ring me, just meet me at the hotel in case my family work out what we're doing and stop me somehow. I'll see you on Saturday, and after that, we will never be parted again. I promise.

'I will always love you. Thomas.'

Tears rolled down my cheeks after Finlay stopped reading, his voice catching on his father's name. The letter floated down onto his lap as he stared at me. I wiped my cheeks. 'He really loved her. He wanted them to run away from their families and be together. But my mother never knew!'

Finlay shook his head. 'His parents must have intercepted the letter from the housekeeper, and stored it up here with whatever else they didn't take with them when they moved, making sure Amelia never read it.'

'So she waited to hear from him and then had to assume he'd forgotten all about her in Perth.'

'And my dad must have gone to the hotel and she never turned up.'

'You said your grandparents admitted they took it, though. That's what he said when he asked you to come here, wasn't it?'

Finlay nodded. 'Yes, I didn't really understand what he meant but now I do. They took the letter so your mother never got it and they didn't tell him until years later. He must have always wondered why she didn't meet him that day. He assumed it was because she didn't feel the same way about him, I suppose. And then he realised she never got it, so he knew she must have always wondered why she'd never heard from him again. That she assumed he hadn't loved her. What a mess.'

I nodded. The story was so sad. 'I wonder why he didn't come back himself to talk to my mum once he found out what his parents had done,' I said, wrapping my arms across my chest.

'I wonder when they told him. Maybe it was only after my mother died. I don't think he would have wanted to hurt her memory. I know now that my parents weren't a true love match, but I think he felt loyalty, duty to my mother. He was fond of her. And I suppose by then so much time had passed. He didn't know if your mum was still here in Glendale, or if she would want to see him.' Finlay sighed. 'It's all so sad. I suppose at the end, Dad couldn't bear to leave it up here without your mother ever reading it. It was a regret for him that Amelia never knew that he had loved her, that he hadn't wanted to leave her. He wanted me to give her that closure. At last.'

I nodded. 'I suppose the things you didn't do are what you regret in the end. His parents were so cruel to hide his letter. Mum deserved to know that he wanted to be with her. Why were they so against them being together, I wonder? Because my mother didn't come from money?'

Finlay sighed. 'I think so. Your mum said they didn't approve, didn't she? My mum was the daughter of a family friend. My dad said their parents had brought them together. I'm sorry, Lorna.'

'You have nothing to be sorry for.'

'My family hurt yours,' he replied simply. We looked at one another. 'I don't understand my dad,' he said then.

'What do you mean?'

'His parents stopped him from being with the girl he loved because they cared more about money and reputation than happiness and love, but then my dad turned out the same way, and acted the same way towards me. Why did he do that?'

'Because he didn't know any better, I guess,' I said. I understood his anger towards his dad. It was worse because he couldn't ask him these questions. His father had revealed the story far too late for them to talk about it, for them to heal the past together. 'But telling you about this house and Glendale, asking you to come back and find this letter and tell my mother what happened back then, maybe that was his way of giving you his blessing. Of him realising that he should have done that a long time ago. That he does want you to follow your heart because he didn't, you know?'

'Or to warn me that if you do, it just ends in tears,' Finlay replied, his voice tinged with bitterness. 'I need some air. Show your mum the letter, keep it, I don't want it. I don't know why my father sent me here. What he thought this was going to achieve. My uncle was right all along. I should never have come here!' Finlay got up. 'I need to go, I'm sorry, Lorna. I need to think. I'll go back to the Inn,' he said and walked out before I could stop him. I picked up the letter and looked at it. A letter full of love. Urgent and heartfelt. Desperate, even. Thomas Scott longed to be with my mother but only now, decades later, after his death, had it been unearthed.

I wasn't sure how to feel about it myself, so I understood why it had shaken Finlay. What would my mum say? Should I even tell her we'd found it?

Maybe Finlay was right, and this letter should have remained up here hidden in a box coated with dust if all it was going to do was hurt people in the here and now.

Chapter Thirty-One

'Lorna!'

I walked into the hallway surprised to see Anna and Grace walk in through the front door. I had been in a daze since Finlay walked out, his father's letter to my mother in my pocket. 'What are you doing here?' I asked, confused.

'You said we should come round and see how things are going before we start work at the Inn. We're both on the afternoon shift,' Grace said, also looking confused.

'Oh, of course I did!' I cried. 'I'm sorry, it's been a crazy morning, to be honest.'

'Why crazy?' Adam asked, as he walked in behind them. 'Finlay's car has gone.'

'Like I said, it's been a morning. Let's go into the kitchen, I need a cuppa.'

'I bought sandwiches,' Adam said. 'I thought we could all have lunch.' He glanced at Grace, who smiled at him.

'At least someone remembered we were coming,' Anna said with a chuckle. She linked arms with me. 'Come on, tell us all about it.'

We went into the kitchen and Anna made us all tea while Adam plated up the food and Grace told me to sit down. I handed her the letter and she read it out to the others who joined us at the table for lunch.

'Wow. So, Finlay's dad wanted Mum to have it after all this time? I suppose it's nice to know he had loved her and had wanted to be with her. When you think how many years this has been lost! Thank goodness we have mobile phones now,' Adam said.

'It's so sad,' Grace agreed. 'Finlay's dad must have always wished that your mum knew how he had felt about her back then, to ask his son to find the letter after all this time.'

'I think Finlay is angry with his dad. His dad has never opened up to him. I think he feels like he never really knew him, you know?'

'I can imagine. It's always weird thinking about what your parents were like before you came along, but especially if they seem completely different now to who they used to be. Maybe losing this love kind of made him closed off. To protect himself from heartbreak again,' Anna said. 'We all know when you get hurt, it's so easy to want to avoid another situation where you could get hurt again.'

I nodded. 'I think that could be it. And his parents encouraged him to put family and duty first – they cared more about what kind of family his wife was from than whether he loved her. I'm so relieved that my mum found Dad. It seems like Thomas never really got his happy ending.'

'That's awful. No wonder Finlay is upset. I bet he wishes he could talk to his dad about it,' Grace said.

'I think he does. He has so many questions. It must be so hard,' I said. My heart really did go out to him.

'So how did the letter end up in the loft? Why didn't your mum ever get it?' Anna asked.

'Thomas's parents didn't approve, so they intercepted it. I guess the housekeeper told them about it and they were horrified he was planning to run away to be with Mum. So they hid the letter in the loft before they left Glendale.'

'They must have been awful people,' Grace said. 'To do that to your son. Ugh! And your mum got hurt too.'

'I think this Thomas sounds a bit of a coward. Why didn't he go to her house and talk to her instead of writing a letter that got lost? Why didn't he stand up to his parents? Why didn't he come back to Glendale when she didn't show up at the hotel? He didn't really fight for your mum, did he?' Anna asked.

'I know what you mean. I'd want someone to fight for me,' Grace agreed. I saw her look at Adam.

'Cameron fought for me,' Anna said, a little bit dreamily.

I rolled my eyes. 'I preferred you when you were cynical.'

She threw a crisp at me. 'Will you show the letter to your mum?'

'I don't want to upset her. But she deserves to know, doesn't she?' I looked at my brother for advice.

Adam nodded. 'You have to show it to her. She knows that Finlay was looking for something from Thomas. He wanted her to have it. We should honour that.'

'I would want to know,' I agreed. I sighed. 'I hope Finlay is okay. He just kind of ran out to go back to the Inn after we found it.'

'We can keep an eye out for him at the Inn, and we'll message you,' Anna said.

'Do we know what he looks like? Oh, Clare the receptionist will be able to point him out,' Grace said.

I had forgotten they hadn't met him. it seemed strange as I had spent so much time with him. 'Great, thanks. I'm off to find costumes for the party with Mum this afternoon, so I guess I'll show her the letter then.' I looked at it doubtfully.

'It'll be fine,' Adam reassured me.

—

After Grace and Anna had left for work, Adam went back into the garden to see what needed doing out there. I left Dove House and drove to Mum's to pick her up so we could go costume-shopping together for the Halloween party at Glendale Hall on Saturday night. I took Thomas Scott's letter along with me. Mum was upstairs when I let myself in. I wondered how she would feel reading the letter. I think what worried me most was that she'd somehow regret that she hadn't been able to be with Thomas, that she'd wish things had turned out differently for them. But I reminded myself that Mum loved my dad with all her heart. Still, I hoped she would be okay reading the letter.

'Help me choose a coat!' Mum called when I shouted I was there, so I went up to her room. I passed by my old bedroom and for a second I longed to go in, close the door, lie down on the familiar bed and not do what I knew I needed to. 'What's that?' I asked, turning from my bedroom and walking into Mum and Dad's room, which was at the front of the house.

'I don't know one which goes best,' Mum said, holding up two options – a short furry black coat and a longer black wool one. She had on leggings and a knitted dress and her trusty knee-high boots. I told her to go with the wool one. 'I'd better wear a scarf, it's so cold today. I hope we haven't left it too late to find outfits – I bet half of Glendale have been into the shop already.'

'It's come round so quickly,' I said, perching on the bed.

'Well, you've been so busy. What's wrong?' she asked, seeing my face.

'Before we go out, I need to tell you something. Maybe you should sit down too.'

'Are you ill?' she asked, sinking onto the bed.

'Oh, no, nothing like that, don't worry,' I said quickly. She exhaled with relief. 'It's just, Finlay and I have found what his dad wanted him to find in the loft. Thomas wanted Finlay to give it to you, but he let me take it and decide whether to show you. I wasn't sure if you'd want to read it or not, but...' I pulled out the letter. 'Thomas wrote this letter to you before he left Glendale.'

'Oh.' She looked at it. 'It explains why I never heard from him again?'

'Not exactly. It's a letter he wrote just before they moved to Perth. But his parents stopped it getting to you and it's been buried up in the loft ever since, which is why you didn't hear from him.' I held it out to her. 'I really hope it doesn't upset you too much, Mum.'

She took a breath and reached for it. 'It's so sad that he's gone. Only my age, and…'

'I know you didn't want to talk about you and Thomas after you met Finlay, but I'm here if you want to. After you've read this.'

'Okay.' Mum put it in her bedside drawer. 'Let's go out. I'll read it later.'

'You don't want to read it now?'

'I think I need to do it alone, love.' I nodded; I could understand that. 'How did Finlay feel, finding it?'

'I think he's still working that out. He left and went back to the Inn. He was upset and angry, I think. He didn't have a great relationship with his dad. In fact, his father basically threw him out when he said he wanted to leave the family business and become a writer. I think they did make up at the end but he feels guilty about the time they were estranged. Understandably.'

'He wants to be a writer? And Thomas didn't approve, I assume?'

'He thought Finlay should stay working for their accountancy company. I think he's left it to Finlay, and the family home. And I think Finlay feels like he should do what his father wanted. I hope he doesn't give up on his dream, though. I want him to be happy. I guess he doesn't know what to do.'

Mum sighed. 'It must be so hard not to be able to talk to his father about all of this. I'm glad he has you, love.'

'I'm not really sure what I can do.'

'You're being a good friend to him. I get a sense he hasn't really had that before. Come on, let's find us some costumes.'

I hoped Mum was right and that I could be there for Finlay, if he let me. But he had walked out before I could speak to him. Maybe, like Mum, he needed to process his dad's letter on his own for now. I just had to hope they would both talk to me when they were ready.

My phone beeped and I saw Anna had texted me.

> I saw Finlay walking in the Inn grounds. He was
> on the phone out there. Let's hope he's okay!
> Talk to you later xxx

I wondered if Finlay was telling his uncle about the letter or asking him about it. He might be able to tell Finlay more about his father, and that last summer they spent in Glendale with my mum. I hoped it might make him feel closer to his father.

I followed Mum out of the house and drove us to the costume shop in a town close to Glendale. It was well known in the area, and Mum was right — a lot of the costumes had already been hired or bought for Beth's party when we got there. We went through the rails side by side, looking for something to take our fancy.

'I haven't been to a costume party in years,' I said. I sighed. 'I'm not liking anything. Anna is going to wear the Thirties-style dress Beth bought her for the murder mystery weekend they all went on, and Adam has scrubs from that stag weekend.'

'What about this for your father?' Mum held up a gangster outfit. 'It might be a bit big, but if he wears a belt…'

'We can find him a hat too,' I said. 'I think he'll like it. Ooh, look…' I pulled out a ball gown. 'We were joking about me wanting to be a princess who lived in Dove House.' The dress was pink with lots of tulle and sparkles. 'This is a real Cinderella dress.' It was silly, I knew; I was a grown woman, but my childlike heart swelled.

'It's so pretty,' Mum said, fingering the skirt. 'You always wanted a dress like this. I think it's a sign. You have to get it.'

I held it against myself. I hadn't dressed up in so long. I was the queen of casual clothes, but this was a special dress. I couldn't walk away from it. 'I owe it to my younger self,' I agreed. 'What about you?'

'Look!' Mum held up a costume and I burst out laughing. 'Tabby would approve,' she said as I giggled. She put the cat outfit against her. 'It's purrrfect.'

'You didn't just say that,' I said, shaking my head. I put my dress over my arm and glanced at the Prince Charming outfit it was hanging with. For a second, Finlay flashed in my mind. But no: I was fine that there wouldn't be a prince by my side. I had always wanted a dress like this, so I was going to wear it and love every moment of it.

'Oh, I'll need to find some whiskers!' Mum said as we made our way to the till, and set me off laughing all over again.

Chapter Thirty-Two

The following day, the Glendale Hall Aga was delivered and installed. We had decided that the kitchen needed sprucing up, and as we didn't have the money for anyone to do it, I told Adam I would decorate it myself. Guests wouldn't be coming in here, so a new kitchen could wait until we had the money. Adam went to pick up the bathroom tiles he had finally found at a price that didn't make our eyes water. Outside, the builders were taking down the scaffolding as all the roof tiles were now fixed, and it was a relief that the biggest job was now completed. Inside, the plastering was being finished, so it made sense for me to stay in the kitchen out of the way.

Tabby was watching me, half asleep in his bed, and I had the radio on as I covered the walls in a pretty lemon shade to brighten it up, when I was startled by a tapping on the back door.

I turned round to see Finlay out there. I waved him inside. 'There was no answer round the front.'

I turned the radio down. 'There's a lot going on today.'

'I'm sorry I left like I did yesterday. I needed a moment, I guess, after finding the letter. And I wanted to talk to my uncle about it all. I wanted to come and find you today. I felt bad for just leaving you like that.'

'I understand. It was a shock finding that letter. Have a seat,' I said with a smile. It was good to see him here. After a week of having him with me every day, it had felt strange being here without him.

'That's a real spring shade,' he said as he sat down at the kitchen table.

'I thought it would make the room lighter, as it's pretty small.'

He reached down to give Tabby a stroke. 'I always wanted a cat growing up, but my dad wasn't keen on pets.'

'What's your family home like? In Perth?' I carried on painting as I asked him. I wanted to know what his life was like there.

'It's even bigger than Dove House. It's in the middle of nowhere. It was always my dad's pride and joy. He hadn't wanted to leave. We got nurses in so he could stay there until the end.'

'That must have meant a lot to him. You don't feel the same connection to the house, though?' I asked, turning round.

'I suppose I never quite felt like I belonged there. It was really hard when I left, but I felt... free.' Finlay sighed. 'And now I just don't know what to do.'

'You don't have to do anything right now. Take your time. You've had a lot to process.'

'My uncle thinks...' Finlay stopped speaking as someone came into the kitchen.

'I read the letter,' my mum said as she appeared in the doorway. She noticed Finlay then, and she smiled. 'Let me give it back to you.'

'I'm sorry you didn't get it when you were meant to,' Finlay said, taking it from her and looking at it in his hand. 'I keep wondering why he didn't come back to Glendale for you. I would have, if I really wanted to be with someone. And he obviously regretted not doing that at the end, because he wanted me to find this and give it to you.'

Mum sat down at the table. I put my paintbrush down and leaned against the counter to listen. 'Pride, I suspect. He thought I had rejected him, chosen not to come to the hotel as he had asked. To find me here would have meant me rejecting him face to face. But maybe deep down he didn't want to. He knew that for us to be together he would have had to leave his family, his home, all their money, everything he'd ever known, and that is not easy to do even if you do love someone.'

'And maybe once he found out that you hadn't got the letter, he realised too much time had passed. And there was my mother. I know he wouldn't have wanted to hurt her even after she passed away,' Finlay said, swallowing hard.

My mum nodded. 'I'm sure he loved your mother, Finlay, and that they were happy. And I married Lorna's father and built a life with him. A lot of time and life had gone by when he realised I had never received this letter. Perhaps he always wished he had told me about it. Which is why he asked you to come here. And I'm glad I know now that he did love me like I loved him. That's enough. What was meant to be was what happened,' Mum said. 'I'm so sorry you've lost him, Finlay. It sounds like at the end he realised what's truly important in life. I hope you can take comfort from that.'

Finlay sighed. 'I just feel so guilty that we didn't speak for those months. It's hard to take comfort in anything. But I'm glad that I found the letter like he wanted, and that you've read it. I just wish I could have done it sooner so I could have told him. Given him that peace. Why did he only ask me when it was too... too late?' He finished and I could see his eyes glistening with unshed tears. I hated to see him upset. I longed to reach for him but I wasn't sure if he wanted me to.

'Perhaps he thought he had time. We all think that, don't we? I'm sure it gave him peace to know you were going to come to Dove House. He knew you'd fulfil your promise.' Mum smiled at him kindly and then stood up. 'I'd better go. Kathleen is coming over. Thank you for letting me read the letter, Finlay. I hope it brings you comfort, in time. Just remember, your father loved you and like every parent, only wanted the best for you, I'm sure of that.'

'I think she's right,' I said after my mum had said goodbye and left. 'Your dad realised what matters in the end. I think he wanted to show you that. For you to see the place where he had been happy.' I went over to sit by him.

'I get it. Glendale and this house... I get why he loved it here.' He smiled at me. 'But I wish he had been happy when I knew him, that's what is so hard. We lost so much time. We weren't close. And we could have been. He could have let me understand him.'

'I know that he did it too late, but he did it in the end, Finlay. He let you in. I think he wanted you to find happiness.'

'And how do I do that?' He looked across at me. I hated to see the torment in his eyes.

'By living life the way you want to. He didn't. He let his parents decide for him. But you can be different,' I said. I reached out to touch his hand. When our skin connected, I felt the same warmth I had when I first looked into those blue eyes of his.

'I don't know,' Finlay said. 'My uncle wants me to come home. There's so much to sort out still at the house, and not to mention Dad's company. He understood that I had to come here, but now I've found Dad's letter, my uncle needs me back in Perth,' Finlay explained with a sigh. 'I suppose he's right. I can't hide here in Glendale forever, as much as I wish I could. I need to make decisions...'

'But are you really going to take over the company? To give up your dream of writing? And you said you felt you didn't belong in your family home.'

He moved his hand from under mine. 'It's just not simple any more. I can't be selfish. I have responsibilities. I have to deal with everything. There is only me now, after all.'

'It isn't selfish to dream. I believe that if there is something you want, you should try to make it happen. I don't think you should end your life with regrets and "what ifs", or that you should always be unhappy just to please other people. And I don't think you believe it either.'

'There are people relying on me. People who work for my dad, people who work at our house. I can't let everyone down. I need to step up now. You don't understand.'

'I do! I'm just trying to be supportive. I'm trying to show you that you don't have to do what your dad did or what your uncle thinks you should do – that you could be the man your father wanted to be.'

'You see the world through rose-tinted glasses.' I flinched at his tone. 'You have been encouraged to dream big. You have a supportive family. Your brother is here doing this with you. I don't have that, Lorna. I don't have anyone.'

I shook my head. I had thought he knew he had me. 'I thought we had a connection, Finlay. I thought that maybe your father and my mother brought us together somehow. That there was a reason you came here. I thought you felt it too. But I can see I was wrong.' I realised then that I had been hoping for a happy ending of our own, but I should have known that was impossible.

Finlay stood up, agitated. 'Do you have any idea how badly I've wanted to kiss you since we met?'

His question hung in the air. For a moment, I felt huge relief that he had felt our connection too. Then he started pacing. 'But how can I do that when I have no idea if I can be there for you? I don't want to leave you with a broken heart like my dad left your mum. I don't want to hurt myself thinking that this could be my shot at happiness and it isn't. I can't think about myself right now, or what I want. I tried that once. Look at how it turned out!' he said, bitterly. 'I decided I should go off and try to make my dreams come true and my father died. And yes, I feel guilty. Wouldn't you?'

'But your father would want you to be happy,' I said, feeling my voice tremble. I really didn't want to cry right now.

'You have no idea what he wanted. You didn't know him.' Finlay sighed. 'And I didn't know him either. But what I do know is that I have to go home. I can't run away again. I need to face up to my responsibilities.'

I hated to see how much guilt he felt about his father. That he thought he didn't deserve to have what he wanted. But I understood too. He was upset and angry and grieving. And he had a lot on his shoulders right now. He did have to deal with everything. I just hoped he wouldn't lose sight of himself in the process. I nodded. 'You have to do what you think is right,' I said, even though it was tearing my heart in two.

Finlay's chest sagged. 'I do,' he said. 'I'm sorry, Lorna. I can't thank you enough. You and your family, for letting me be here. For helping me to find the letter. For letting me fulfil my promise to my father. I can see why he loved Glendale and his time here at Dove House, and why he missed it and why he thought about it at the end. You're lucky to call this place home.'

I nodded. He was right about that. I thought he would regret letting go of his dreams, but I knew that he needed to do this. I could only wish him well and hope that he would be okay in the end. 'Good luck, Finlay.'

He looked around. 'I'm glad that Dove House belongs to you now. I hope you'll be happy here.' There was nothing left to say. He looked at me for one last time and then Finlay walked out of the back door. Out of my life.

I sank into my chair again and wished he would have the same hope of happiness for himself.

Chapter Thirty-Three

'Earth to Lorna!'

I looked up from my sandwich to see Adam frowning across the kitchen table at me. It was Friday, and I had stumbled through the past couple of days since Finlay left and I could see Adam was getting frustrated with me. 'Sorry, what?' I was thinking for the one millionth time about what Finlay had said to me before he walked out. *Do you have any idea how badly I've wanted to kiss you since we met?* It was like an earworm I'd never shake from my mind.

'I said, you almost ordered two hundred rolls of wallpaper instead of twenty!' He showed me the online order. 'Good job you couldn't find your credit card and had to wait for me.' He sighed. 'There – all fixed and ordered.'

'I'm sorry.'

'Look, why don't you go and see Mum? Drop round what she needs for her costume tomorrow. Take the afternoon off. I need to be out in the garden as it's dry and the plastering is being finished inside, so there's not much you can do here. Maybe getting out of the house will do you good.'

'Thanks, Adam.'

'And put that order in for the two chandeliers – I don't think you'll find ones any cheaper, and we can make a cut somewhere else. I know you think they will look the best,' he added.

I smiled. 'You must be worried about me. They will look perfect, I know it!' I got up and went round the table to ruffle his hair. 'Thanks, big brother.'

'I'm sorry Finlay had to go,' he added softly.

'I know, me too, but it was for the best,' I said, forcing myself to sound brighter. 'He has so much to sort out. I just wish he didn't feel like he can't do what he wants, you know? I just want him to be happy.'

'I'm sure he knows that, and wants that for you too. He'll work it all out. And maybe he'll come back to see this house finished one day.'

I hated how much I hoped that would be the case. I nodded. 'Okay, I'll see you later.'

'At least we have the Halloween party to look forward to, right?'

I smiled. 'Right.' I walked out, not wanting to admit I wasn't in a party mood at all. I headed into the lounge to grab my coat and the cat face-painting kit I had ordered for my mum. I smiled at Tabby curled up on my sleeping bag again. It was a grey day, and he didn't want to go outside. 'I don't blame you,' I said, giving him a stroke before I left. I glanced behind me. The room was empty of builders. I went to my pillow and pulled out what I had tucked underneath.

I wasn't sure if Finlay had left it before or after our conversation in the kitchen, but on my sleeping bag when I went to bed that night was Thomas's letter to my mother. I wasn't sure why he had left it for me. I touched it with my fingertips and sighed before putting it back under my pillow.

Leaving Dove House, I walked round to my mum's house and tried to sort through my tangled thoughts. Part of me wished Finlay had kissed me, but the other part was relieved that he hadn't because if it hurt this much with him gone, I couldn't imagine how much it would have hurt after his kiss. Dove House just felt like something was missing and I was annoyed at myself for feeling like that as he'd only been here a couple of weeks. I wished I knew how he had felt walking back into his family home in Perth. Happy to be home? Or did he still feel like he didn't belong there? I wished I could ask him, but he clearly didn't want me to get in touch.

Walking in through the front door, I called out for Mum. She was in the living room having a cup of tea. 'I brought the face-painting kit for tomorrow,' I explained.

'Come and sit for a bit,' Mum said, smiling. 'Do you want tea? The kettle's full.'

'I'm fine,' I said, sitting down in the armchair.

'Are you sure, love? You look a bit tired. How are things at the house?'

'On track, I think. Adam said I can order the chandeliers I sent you a picture of even though they are a bit pricey. So that's a relief.'

'They looked lovely.' Mum was peering at me. 'You're not sleeping? Is it house stress? Is it… Finlay?'

'I just keep thinking about what he said,' I admitted. 'About me seeing the world through rose-tinted glasses. I don't understand why he couldn't see that his dad asked him to come to Glendale because he didn't want him to be like he was, you know? That he wanted him to follow his dreams.'

Kathleen walked in then from the kitchen with a cup of tea. My heart sank. I hadn't realised she was here. 'You have to be practical in life, sometimes. He can't just walk away from everything that easily,' she said, sitting down in the armchair with difficulty thanks to her bump.

'I know,' I said. 'But he feels so guilty about arguing with his father, and he's not thinking clearly.'

'Maybe not,' Mum said. 'Thomas was very different to me. I knew that even though we were young. We had grown up very differently. I was full of dreams of the future, but Thomas had it all planned out for him – to follow in his father's footsteps. I think that when Finlay told Thomas he wanted something different, he couldn't understand and lashed out. But when he became ill, he thought about it, thought back, and started to wonder how his life might have been if he hadn't done what his own father had wanted. I think asking Finlay to come to Glendale and find his letter was to show him that Thomas had once tried to put love and happiness first. It hadn't worked out for him, but he wanted it to for Finlay.'

'That's what I wanted him to realise,' I agreed. 'But he thinks the opposite. That Thomas was trying to warn him not to follow his heart.'

'Sometimes you have to think about other things as well,' Kathleen argued. 'Life is tough. You have to do things you don't want to. I think he's being sensible going home to deal with everything, and just because it isn't his dream job, he can still be happy working at his father's company. Just because it wouldn't suit you...'

'It doesn't suit Finlay,' I insisted.

'You don't know that for sure. You've only just met him,' Kathleen replied with a smirk that said, as always, that she knew better than me.

'I know that Finlay walked away from his old life for a reason,' I said. I looked at Mum. 'Why did Thomas live a life he didn't want, and then expect Finlay to do the same?'

'Habits are hard to break. I think when you've lived a safe life, something different is scary. He was worried Finlay would get hurt, or fail, and he wanted him to have security. That was important to him. It's hard as a parent. You want to protect your children, keep them safe, stop them from making the same mistakes you did. But that's how you learn and grow in life, it's how you find the right path for you. So you have to let them do that.'

'Maybe you think because Mum and Thomas didn't have a happy ending that you and Finlay can instead,' Kathleen said. 'But life isn't a fairy tale, sis. Sometimes there isn't a happy ending.'

I stared at her, my eyes welling up. How did she always know what to say to make me feel worse? Because part of me had wondered exactly that. Hoped for exactly that. That we had met for a reason. That Mum and Thomas hadn't been meant for one another because me and Finlay had. I felt stupid. 'Oh,

I know that, don't worry,' I said bitterly. I stood up. 'I know there's no chance of a happy ending for us. I know that you think I don't deserve one. Well, maybe I never will have one. At least you'll be there saying you told me so, if that's the case.'

Kathleen's mouth fell open. Before I could break down and cry in front of my sister, I bolted from the room. I could hear my mum calling after me and her saying something to Kathleen, who snapped back, but I couldn't bear to stay to listen to any more.

I left the house and thought maybe Finlay and my sister were right – that I had always seen the world through rose-tinted glasses. But I needed to stop, because it certainly wasn't working for me.

Chapter Thirty-Four

It was the night of the Halloween party at Glendale Hall. I didn't want to go, but I'd hired my Cinderella costume and I was dying to wear it, plus Beth had been so good to us, I didn't want to let her down. I asked Anna if I could get ready with her as Dove House was still such a mess, and then I wouldn't have to spend the night with my family.

'Your room is giving me lots of my ideas for mine,' I said as I put my make-up on in front of the full-length mirror, while behind me Anna curled her pink hair, sitting on her four-poster bed.

'Glendale Hall has ruined me! How can I ever live anywhere as lovely as this again?' she asked with a grin. 'I can't wait to see how you decorate Dove House. How's progress?'

'Slow but steady. The loft is being insulated,' I said, trying not to think about Finlay, but it was impossible – he was part of that loft now. 'The roof and plastering are all done, and the damp has been treated, so we can start wallpapering and painting and then all the flooring will be done. The wooden floor is being restored and carpets will be laid upstairs. Adam is working on the garden, too. I sometimes wonder if it will ever be finished.'

'You've already done so much, and I know you want to get it open as soon as possible, but sometimes things take the time they need to take.'

'It's true,' I agreed. 'I'm more impatient about it than Adam is, but I think that's because I can do more once the building work is finished, and at the moment he's leading on the project. I have been starting to buy things, and it's so exciting shopping for furniture and decor pieces, it's hard not to get carried away and stay on-budget!'

'I bet. Now that I'm working at the Inn, and still doing part-time here, I'm trying to save money, but it's hard, especially when I see something I want to buy.' She laughed. 'I'm done, so let me do your hair. And no, you can't wear it in a bun with that dress,' she added when she saw I was about to protest. She held up her curling tongs. 'Let's go, Lorna.'

'Okay, okay,' I replied with a laugh. I did want to live up to the dress, so I let Anna turn my hair into lovely curls, which she let fall over my shoulder. She pinned hers back in waves and then we pulled on our dresses. Anna's long plunging silver gown and mine, which I still loved, the gorgeous pink tulle gown. Anna added a pearl clip to her hair and I put on a silver tiara I'd found in a charity shop, and once ready, we stood side by side in front of her bedroom mirror.

'You look gorgeous,' we both said at the exactly the same time. We smiled at one another in the mirror. Honestly, I felt like the main character in a movie and I let myself do a twirl. Why not? I wanted to enjoy every minute of wearing this dress tonight. Tomorrow I'd be back in my oldest, warmest clothes to work on the house, so I knew I needed to make the most of being dressed up.

'Let's go,' Anna said, grabbing her clutch bag. I followed her downstairs where I was amazed all over again at the effort Beth put into her events at the Hall. She already outdid herself every year with their Christmas trail in the grounds, but she hadn't gone in half-hearted to the Hall's first Halloween party. Trailing down the staircase were giant cobwebs complete with spiders, and a LED pumpkin stood on each step as Anna and I descended into the grand hallway that was already filling up with people.

I looked around in wonder. Music streamed in from the drawing room where a DJ was playing Halloween classics. Servers weaved in and out of guests wearing skeleton outfits carrying trays of drinks served in goblet-style glasses. LED pumpkins lined the room, and the ceiling was covered in another spiderweb complete with plastic spiders that made me shudder. By the front door was a huge coffin with a skeleton inside greeting partygoers, and on the table by the door to the drawing room was an array of spooky-themed cakes and sweets.

'I don't know how she does it,' Anna said when she saw my face.

'She's amazing,' I agreed.

'Oh, there's Izzy, she wants to show you her reading room!' Anna called out to Beth's daughter and she led us to her cosy snug. We stepped in and I smiled to see the armchairs and cushions and throws, and the wall of colour-coded books making a pretty rainbow.

'I like the armchairs with the reading lamps. I would love to make a corner like that in the lounge at Dove House,' I said. 'I bet you love curling up in here.'

'It's my favourite room in the house,' Izzy said happily.

'I kind of want to stay in here right now,' I admitted. I asked Izzy if I could take a photo for inspiration and then we reluctantly left and headed back towards the party.

'It'll be fine,' Anna said to me. She knew I was worried about seeing Kathleen. I had told her about our argument. 'Let's get something to drink.'

'I'm on board with that,' I said.

We weaved through people into the drawing room and Izzy went off to find her friend Luke. In there, we found Cameron, who was wearing a suit to match Anna's dress, and my brother, dressed as a surgeon. They had glasses of punch for us, and I took a really long gulp. I looked around at the familiar faces. I tried not to wish that Finlay was here.

'There you are!' Kathleen appeared. I looked away, wondering how to escape. She had tried to call me earlier but I had declined it. She and Hamish were dressed as Gomez and Morticia from *The Addams Family*, and my mum in her cat outfit and my dad as a gangster were behind them. 'I can barely breathe in this dress,' she said, gesturing to her bump which looked as if it might topple her over.

'You look lovely,' Mum said, looking at my dress. 'People keep stepping on my tail,' she added, glaring at someone walking past her.

'You guys are wearing fabulous costumes!' Beth Fraser cried, greeting us. She was dressed as Mary Poppins, and gave us all a little curtsy. 'Enjoy yourselves!' She twirled off to greet more people, in her element hosting the party. I hoped I'd be as good a hostess at the B & B.

Kathleen turned to Hamish. 'Let's carve pumpkins, then I can sit down,' she said, pointing to the kitchen where everything was set up for people to do just that.

'Are you feeling okay?' Hamish asked her.

'I'll be fine!' They disappeared into the crowd.

'There's Grace,' Adam said. 'I'll get her a drink.'

I looked enquiringly at Anna when my brother went off. 'I thought she'd enjoy the party, and Adam doesn't have a date,' she said, leaning closer to me. 'So…'

I shook my head with a laugh. 'Such a matchmaker! Hi Grace,' I said as she found us. 'That's a fabulous outfit,' I added. She was dressed as Catwoman and looked amazing.

'You look like a princess!' she replied, giving me a hug, then thanking Anna for inviting her. Adam reappeared with a drink for her and I was sure I caught a spark between them as they said hello and he showed her some of the decor behind us. Anna turned to me with a look that said, 'I told you so!' Cameron asked her to dance, so they left us and then Mum and Dad went to greet some of their friends.

Suddenly I felt like a third wheel with Grace and Adam. 'I'm going to look at the Halloween display in the garden,' I told them. I grabbed another glass of punch and drank it in one go. And then I went off, glad I had boots on under my dress. The tulle hid them perfectly and heels were never my friends. I walked through the kitchen, where the pumpkin-carving was in full swing, and out of the French doors into the stunning Glendale Hall garden.

It had been suitably dressed for the occasion. They had pumpkin lanterns all along the side of the house and leading the way to the Halloween display they had erected near to a large tree. The music could be heard dimly as I stepped over to the display Beth and her family had created. People were looking at it and taking photos or strolling around the garden, as it was such a lovely night for October. The sky above was clear, so the stars and the moon glittered down on us. I always loved seeing the garden here; I knew it was Beth's pride and joy. I hoped that we'd be able to create a lovely outside space at Dove House, although neither of us had Beth's green fingers.

I looked at the creepy scarecrow they had fixed over the display of hay and pumpkins. Two huge skeletons stood either side and more cobwebs and spiders hung over the top. On the other side was a witch figure looking as if she was about to cast a spell on us. I knew that Beth's events would be a draw for guests at the bed and breakfast. I took a picture for our social media. I hoped people would be excited to come to things like this in Glendale. I knew for sure that the Christmas trail here would be popular.

With my phone in my hand, I had a weak moment. I searched for Finlay Scott. I shouldn't have been surprised that, if he had any social media accounts, they were private. I supposed I couldn't imagine him posting about his life. He was used to a quiet life. I wobbled even more, and found myself looking up my ex-boyfriend, Mark. After I had seen his engagement announcement, I had tried to stay away from his accounts, but now I looked, and saw a photo of him and his fiancée posing with her engagement ring held up to the camera. I sighed and stowed my phone away quickly. What was the point? I didn't miss Mark. I missed Finlay. And I longed for a love of my own, not what my ex had with someone else.

Perching on one of the hay bales, I looked back at the beautiful Glendale Hall all lit up and full of life and laughter.

I hoped Dove House would soon be like that too, but I was feeling unsure. My confidence in my dream felt shaky.

People told me that I wasn't realistic enough. Mark. Finlay. My sister.

What if they were right?

What if something went wrong and we couldn't open as we wanted to at Hogmanay? What if our dream was just too big? I sighed to myself. I had put my dream on hold for so long, and now that it was on the horizon, I was starting to worry that I just wasn't good enough to make it happen.

I knew I hadn't been focused enough the past couple of days and Adam had been frustrated. The business and money side of things just came naturally to him but not to me; I wanted to make this perfect place for people to come to stay but the decor budget was shrinking each week and I was worried people just wouldn't want to come if I couldn't turn it into the vision that I'd had in my head for so long. If I couldn't make it what I had dreamed of.

I felt lost. And if I was honest, a little bit lonely too.

Looking up at the starry sky, I send out a plea to the universe to give me back my hope, because it was fading fast.

And then suddenly, the silence around me was shattered.

A wailing sound floated across the garden. I turned to the house. That was weird. And then I heard it again. It sounded like an animal in pain.

People around me turned to the house as well to see where the noise was coming from.

I frowned. Somehow the sound was strangely familiar.

'Lorna!' Hamish appeared in the doorway of the kitchen. His usual calm demeanour had disappeared as he frantically waved at me. 'Kathleen has gone into labour!'

Chapter Thirty-Five

I rushed into the kitchen, following Hamish, to find my sister clutching the kitchen table, crying out in agony.

'I'll get Drew,' Beth said when she saw what the commotion was about and ran off to find her husband who was thankfully the doctor we needed right now.

'Have you called an ambulance?' I asked Hamish.

'The floor,' Kathleen gasped, so Hamish and I helped her to sit on the floor, crouching down there with her.

'There's been a big car accident – said it might take an hour to get here, so we should drive to the hospital ourselves,' Hamish said, his face pale with worry. 'She's four weeks early,' he added, looking over at me.

'Lorna,' she gasped. 'I'm so... sorry.'

My heart squeezed. 'Me too, me too. It's okay, it's okay,' I said, grabbing her hand. It was clammy.

'What do we do?' Kathleen asked us, her eyes wide with panic.

I wasn't used to having to be the calm one. I clasped her hand tightly and felt her squeeze back. 'It's going to be fine. Drew is an excellent doctor, he'll know what to do,' I said. I saw Adam behind Hamish then. 'Get Mum, please,' I told him. 'Try to breathe,' I said to my sister, who was panting. 'Hamish, do the breathing with her,' I said sharply as he looked on helplessly.

'Oh, right, yes.' He knelt beside her and took her other hand in his. 'Like we practised, Kath...' And he did it with her.

I looked around. People were watching. I stood up. 'Can we have some privacy, please?' I called out, then I breathed a sigh of relief as Beth strode in, her husband right behind her.

She clapped her hands once loudly. 'All of you, out now!' she barked and everyone hastily dispersed.

I moved to make room so Drew could get down on the floor beside my sister with his bag. Thank goodness Beth had married a doctor! 'It's okay, don't worry,' he said. 'Now, can you move?'

'No!' Kathleen cried. 'It hurts so much! Here's another one!'

'The contractions are coming really close,' Hamish said, looking panicked.

'Okay,' Drew said as he pulled on surgical gloves. Kathleen cried out again. 'Yes, they are close. Are you happy for me to examine you, see what's happening?'

'Just help me,' she pleaded.

Drew nodded.

I held Kathleen tightly while Drew examined her. I couldn't believe this was happening. My sister looked terrified. 'Drew knows what he's doing, you're in safe hands,' I told her. 'Everything will be okay.'

'Right,' Drew said. 'The baby is coming. There's no time to get you to the hospital,' he said, still calm. 'We're going to have to deliver the baby here at the Hall.' We all looked at one another in astonishment.

'What's happening?' Mum came in. It was kind of ridiculous to see her worried face through the cat costume. I realised we must all look just as strange.

'She's in labour,' Hamish said, his face pale.

'Oh my,' Mum said, rushing over.

'We could carry you,' Drew said then to Kathleen. 'Upstairs?'

Kathleen shook her head. 'I can't! I can't!'

'It's going to be okay,' Drew said soothingly. 'Kathleen, who do you want here with you?' he asked her quietly.

'Hamish. Mum,' Kathleen said. Then she gasped in pain. 'And Lorna.'

'Me?' I repeated in surprise. She squeezed my hand. 'I'm not going anywhere,' I promised.

'Right, if we're staying here, then let's get Kathleen more comfortable,' Drew said. He got up and turned to Beth. 'We need cushions and blankets, and I need iced water and a flannel.'

'And please tell my husband and Adam what's happening,' Mum added.

'I'll be back,' Beth said with a capable nod and hurried out, closing the kitchen door behind her and shutting out the noise of the party to a muffle, leaving Drew, Mum, Kathleen, Hamish and me.

'It's too soon,' Kathleen said as she panted. 'Will the baby be okay?' she asked Drew.

'Everything will be fine,' he replied.

'Please, God,' she moaned as another contraction came.

'You can do this,' Hamish said. His face had gone deathly white.

'You can,' I agreed. 'It's going to be fine.' I sent out a silent prayer that I was telling the truth.

Beth returned then with everything Drew had asked for, her mother Caroline passing things through as well. I saw Adam and Dad outside the door looking worried.

'We'll stay by the door if you need anything,' Beth said to her husband before walking back out.

'Right, let's get you more comfortable,' Drew said, holding out a cushion.

It felt better having a task. Hamish and I helped Kathleen settle onto the cushions. I wrapped a blanket over her shoulders but she shrugged it off as she was too hot, so I loosened her costume and Drew passed my mum the iced water bowl and a flannel and she held it against Kathleen's forehead. Drew put a blanket on his lap. For the baby, I realised. It was hard to believe this was actually happening.

'I wanted an epidural,' Kathleen said as she cried out in pain.

'I didn't have one,' Mum said. 'You can do this. We're all with you.'

Drew parted Kathleen's propped-up legs. 'I can see the head,' he said. 'This is happening right now. It's time to push. The baby is ready to come out.'

'Now?' Hamish repeated, looking at Drew in horror.

'I can't,' Kathleen cried out.

'Of course you can,' Mum said to her.

'Squeeze our hands as tight as you need. Your baby is ready,' I told my sister. I felt panicked, but I knew I couldn't let her see that. I glared at Hamish, who nodded quickly.

'You can do this,' he reassured her, pushing his hair from his face.

Drew nodded at us. 'Okay, on three, Kathleen,' Drew instructed. 'And then push down as hard as you can. Keep breathing, okay? Ready... one, two, three.'

A guttural cry from my sister echoed through the kitchen and she crushed my fingers in hers. I bit my lip as pain shot through me but I knew it was nothing to what she was going through.

'Brilliant,' Drew encouraged her. 'Can you go again?' Kathleen managed to nod. 'Okay, one, two, three...'

'Almost there,' I said to Kathleen.

'Keep going,' Mum encouraged as she mopped her brow again.

'Do you want to come down here?' Drew asked Hamish. Hamish frantically shook his head.

I shook my head. Men. 'I will,' I said.

'Okay, we're going to go again, Kathleen. One more push should do it,' Drew said as my eyes widened to see a pair of shoulders. 'Here.' He handed me the blanket. 'I'll guide the baby out and you wrap this around it.' I nodded, unable to speak. Drew counted down again and my sister gave one final wail and a push and suddenly the baby was in his hands. He guided the baby out gently and handed it to me.

'Is it okay?' Kathleen gasped as she half collapsed on Mum and Hamish. They held her steady as the beautiful sound of a baby's cry filled the room.

'It's a boy,' I cried as I took him from Drew. Drew tucked the blanket around him as I looked down at the squirming pink bundle. I couldn't believe it. My nephew had arrived. In the most dramatic way possible. 'He's perfect.'

'Really?' Kathleen asked, breathlessly.

'Here.' I held the baby out to my sister, whose eyes filled with tears as she held him in her hands.

'You did it,' Hamish said. 'He really is perfect.' He leaned down and kissed the baby and then my sister.

'My first grandchild,' Mum said, her eyes full of tears.

'Who wants to cut the cord?' Drew asked with a grin. Once Drew had sorted everything and cleaned the baby, he tucked a blanket around my sister's legs and phoned the hospital to arrange bringing them in to be checked over.

'We're dying out here,' Dad called through the closed door.

I got up to let Dad, Adam and Beth into the kitchen.

'It's a boy,' Kathleen told them, her eyes shining with tears.

Beth looked at Drew and they smiled at one another as he wiped his brow. 'This house really has seen it all now,' she said with a laugh.

'Thank you,' Kathleen said, holding her son tightly to her. 'Thank you all.'

I felt a tear roll down my cheek.

Chapter Thirty-Six

Adam and I returned to Dove House at dawn, weary but full of joy. We left mother and baby being checked out at the hospital, but despite the dramatic and early arrival, they both seemed remarkably well. 'We won't forget the first Halloween party at the Hall,' Adam said as we walked in, the sky behind us turning an inky blue.

'I still can't believe it. Kathleen had everything planned down to a T, and then that happens. Thank goodness they're both fine. They looked so happy when we left them, didn't they?' I smiled, thinking back to the way Kathleen and Hamish were looking at their baby boy.

'It was so sweet,' Adam agreed.

'By the way, we need to talk about you at the party before the dramatic birth, you and Grace...' I said, nudging him.

'I don't know what you mean,' he replied, closing the front door behind us.

'Adam, I'm not blind! You like one another, don't you?'

He blushed a little. 'She's lovely, but I don't know what she thinks. And after Anna...'

'Just invite her out for a drink! Don't get ahead of yourself,' I said. I could tell by the way he had made her smile that she would definitely be up for a drink. And the fact that I texted her myself at the hospital to make sure. But I wasn't about to tell my brother that.

'You're so bossy,' he grumbled, but he smiled and I knew he would do it. 'What about you? Are you going to get in touch with Finlay?'

'I don't think there's any point.' Adam seemed about to protest. 'I'll just have to wait a bit longer for my person,' I added with a shrug. I hoped Finlay was finding his way. And that I would find mine too.

'Coffee? I don't think I can sleep,' Adam said.

I nodded. 'Me neither.' We walked towards the kitchen. 'What's that noise?' I wondered, hearing a gushing sound.

Adam cried out and turned on the kitchen light. We both looked in horror to see the kitchen floor flooded in water two inches deep. Water was also seeping across the floor towards what would be our living room and coming towards us out into the corridor towards the reception rooms.

'What's happened?' I cried in horror.

Water appeared to be gushing from below the sink. 'I'll look and turn the water off,' Adam said, rushing over to the sink where the water appeared to be coming from. He opened up the cupboard underneath while I hurried out to find some supplies to help.

I returned with two buckets and a pile of towels and stepped into the kitchen, thankful I had boots on as I stood in the water.

'Okay, I've turned off the water,' Adam said. 'It looks like the pipe rusted with age. Pass me a bucket.'

Adam started to scoop up water while I put the towels down across the doorway to try to stop the flow of water out from the kitchen.

'All over the new paintwork,' I said, looking at the damp seeping up my freshly painted wall. I supposed at least the new kitchen table and chairs I'd ordered hadn't arrived from the online shop. 'Oh no,' I added, pointing as I turned around. 'The rug!' I cried, rushing to it.

'It's ruined,' I said, holding up the soggy rug I had propped up in the corner ready to go into the dining room. It had been a steal at a second-hand furniture shop. 'What are we going to do?'

'Let's get as much water out as we can. I'll ring our insurance company to see what's covered. See if we can get an emergency plumber out for the pipe. I'll ring Glen, too. We'll need a dehumidifier to dry these rooms out… that'll be more money,' Adam said, shaking his head.

'And more delays,' I muttered, my heart sinking.

We worked in silence trying to scoop the water out in the buckets and into the garden. I focused on the task but my ears were ringing. It had felt like we had been getting there. But now we had this big setback. What if we couldn't open in the New Year? What if we ran out of money to decorate? I didn't want to voice my fears aloud as I could see by the look on Adam's face that he was thinking the exact same thing as me.

–

Dove House was a hive of activity by the time late morning came around. Exhausted after trying to get as much water out as possible, I walked through the front door to add our rug to the skip. It was ruined. I heaved it in with a groan.

'Lorna, I know you don't need any more bad news today, but…' Glen, our builder, called over and pointed. There was a group gathered by the front gate. What now, I wondered as I hurried over to them.

'Mrs Andrews says the plumber scraped her car,' Adam said when I joined the group. My unflappable brother was red in the face.

'I told you if there was one more thing, I was going to call the council…'

'No, please, we can sort this,' I said quickly. 'Is there much damage? What happened?' I asked everyone, trying not to panic.

'You know what?' Adam said, throwing up his hands. 'Call them. The whole day is a mess anyway.' And he stalked off.

'Well, what a rude young man,' Mrs Andrews said, putting her hands on her hips.

'I was nowhere near her car,' the plumber appealed to me then.

'I saw you,' Mrs Andrews snapped at him. 'I can't take this any more!' she spun round and marched back towards her house.

'Lorna?'

'What?' I cried, turning round to see one of our builders, Mike.

'The fittings for the final bathroom are going to be two weeks late, I'm afraid.'

I closed my eyes. 'Anything else?' I asked.

'You didn't plan a deep clean into the budget,' Glen said, reappearing. 'I did mention it, but it got left off the list. So once the work is all finished, you'll need to get it professionally cleaned before you can open, what with the dust and the—'

'Leave it with me,' I said, walking away before another problem came up. I went inside and found Adam sitting with his head in his hands. 'Adam, you shouldn't have spoken to Mrs Andrews like that! What if she goes to the council and...' I trailed off at the anguished look on his face.

'We can't afford it,' he said, looking up. 'The budget...' He gestured to his laptop beside him. 'It's out of control. I shouldn't have let you order those chandeliers!'

'So, it's all my fault?' I snapped at him.

'I didn't say that,' he said, wearily. 'But even with the insurance covering the pipe, we still need to spend out more on labour to sort out the damp and we'll need to repaint two of the kitchen walls. We need to hire a dehumidifier to dry out the kitchen and living room before we can even do that. It's all extra work and money and delays to us opening,' he said. He sounded as despondent as I felt. My brother didn't often admit defeat. 'I don't know what we're going to do.'

My fears had been realised. We were running out of money. We couldn't start on the painting yet, now that the flood damage needed sorting first. We might have the council round at any minute to close us down anyway!

All our plans had gone wrong, and Adam was right: I didn't know what we were going to do either.

I had no idea what to say. 'I need to get out of here,' I said and I walked out of the French doors and into the garden, the cold of the first day of November greeting me. I walked as far away from the house as I could and then I couldn't help it. I released the tears that had been building since we'd walked into the kitchen early this morning. It didn't help that we hadn't slept after the Halloween party. I was exhausted and I had to cry it all out.

I turned around to look at Dove House behind me. Our dream was becoming a nightmare. I thought of Finlay's family, of Betty, of the owners before them. Had anyone been happy living there? Maybe my mum and Adam and me had fallen for a house that instead of being a fairy tale, was going to turn out to be a curse.

Chapter Thirty-Seven

We went round to Kathleen's house the following evening. She wanted everyone to see the baby, now that she felt recovered from the dramatic birth. Adam and I hadn't spoken about Dove House since our terse words, and we walked over to Kathleen and Hamish's in silence, neither of us seeming keen to break it.

We found the whole family in their cosy living room with Kathleen on the sofa looking tired but happy holding her sleeping baby. 'They are doing great,' Hamish said as he led Adam and I inside. Mum and Dad and the twins were there too, and everyone looked so happy. Adam looked at me and I knew what he was thinking – we shouldn't tell them what was going on. It would spoil the mood. Unfortunately, neither of us was very good at hiding our feelings. I saw Mum looking at us enquiringly. I looked away.

'It still feels like a dream,' Kathleen said when we'd sat down. 'I can't believe Drew Fraser had to deliver my baby.' I had never seen my sister look so contented.

'Thank goodness he was there,' Mum said. 'I am so proud of you. All of you.'

'I wish we'd been there,' Leo said, annoyed. 'We always miss all the good things.'

'Trust me, this is better,' Kathleen said, ruffling his hair with a laugh.

'So, you two, any idea of a name?' Dad asked them.

Hamish perched next to my sister and they smiled at one another. 'Yes. Everyone, meet Drew Ferguson-Donald,' he said.

Hamish and Kathleen had used both their surnames when they got married.

'We had to name him after the person who helped bring him into the world,' Kathleen added.

'That's lovely,' I said. It was such a good idea.

'It's perfect,' Mum agreed.

'Did you see the update I made to the website?' Hamish asked me and Adam.

'Uh, no, it's been a full-on couple of days,' Adam muttered, looking at me.

I picked at an invisible thread on my jeans to avoid meeting his eyes.

'You and Adam are quiet,' Leo said. Sometimes the twins were scarily observant.

'Has something happened?' Mum prodded.

'Can I hold my nephew?' I asked before Adam could answer. I went over and Kathleen readily handed baby Drew over but she was looking at me trying to work out what was going on. I didn't meet her gaze. I didn't want her to say, 'I told you so.' I cuddled Drew to me. He didn't wake up and was warm and snuggled in my arms. I smiled. This was definitely helping me to forget our troubles.

Adam sighed heavily. 'We've had a flood at the house.'

'Oh no!' Mum cried. 'Is anything damaged?'

'It's all ruined,' I said. 'We should never have bought that house.' Adam looked at me in shock. 'You said yourself the budget is out of control,' I told him.

'Tell us what happened,' Dad said.

I couldn't stand to hear it all. I wandered out into the kitchen with the baby, rocking him gently. I remembered holding the twins like this when they were born and I was a teenager. 'Welcome to the family,' I whispered as I went into the kitchen, glad to be alone. My sister's house was small and cosy, decorated in neutral shades, and I knew she was really proud of it. I leaned against the counter and reached out to touch baby Drew's tiny fingers. I sighed, hoping one day I would be able to be a mother too.

Kathleen came in. 'Let me show you the nursery,' she said. I was relieved she didn't mention Dove House. I followed her upstairs to the baby's room. She had gone for an all-neutral room up here too, with cute cuddly toys on the window seat, a pretty mobile hanging over the cot, and a rocking chair in the corner with a bookshelf above it filled with classic children's books.

'Oh, it's lovely,' I said, looking around, holding Drew tightly to me. I hadn't seen it finished. It was warm and light and cosy. I felt guilty then that I hadn't helped her when she'd asked for my opinion on the decor; I had been too focused on what I was doing at the house. She had done a wonderful job.

She smiled, pleased. 'Thank you,' she said, sitting down in the rocking chair. She held out her arms and I gave her the baby. 'I want to talk to you,' she said.

'It's been a long couple of days for all of us,' I said, not wanting another argument.

'I know, and I'm sorry. I wanted to thank you – the way you helped me at the Hall. I still can't believe it happened!'

'You would do the same for me,' I replied, surprised.

'I would, but you didn't have to after the way I spoke to you, the way I've been with you lately... I'm sorry, Lorna. I think... no, I know I've been too hard on you and it's been unfair. Mum told me that I was making you doubt yourself and Hamish told me I was being childish. Holding my baby in my arms, I realise they were right. I've been so petty. And it's ridiculous. You're my sister and I love you. I want you to be happy, to have everything you want.' She touched her face and shook her head. 'I keep crying.'

I was taken aback. She had never said anything half as heart-felt to me before. 'Well, thank you. But maybe you were right about Dove House.'

She ignored me. 'I told myself it was because I didn't want to see you hurt again if you didn't get the house, and when you did, I told myself I was just trying to make sure you didn't let your vision run away with you and kept on top of all the practical things. But it wasn't. It was because I was jealous.'

Frowning, I stepped closer. 'Jealous? Of me?'

'Yes. You and Adam. And the fact that you're doing this together and doing it so well. I kind of felt... left out. It sounds so pathetic and childish. But you two are this great team and I felt left out. And it's silly because I have baby Drew, and I couldn't help with the building work or anything, but I suppose I kind of wished you'd asked me to be part of it all. Even if I couldn't. Does that even make sense?' She bit her lip and I saw a tear roll down her cheek. I passed her a tissue.

'Wow. I'm sorry you felt like that. I didn't know you'd ever want to do anything like that. I mean, you had that office job but then you met Hamish, and after you got married, you gave it up...'

She nodded and blew her nose. 'I hated the job. I thought after we got married, I'd find out what I really wanted to do, but then I got pregnant. I guess I was jealous that you had this clear dream and you were making it happen. I felt like all I'd be was a wife and mother, and even though that's what I've always dreamed of, I felt like it wasn't good enough, maybe.'

'But I envy you for having a husband and a baby,' I said in wonder. 'Wow, talk about comparison being the thief of joy.' I sat down on the floor beside the chair. 'Why do we always want what we don't have? I should have been here for you more. I didn't help with the nursery. I was so caught up with Dove House. I'm sorry. I think we did leave you out, without meaning to.'

'No, I knew how hard you were working, I shouldn't have asked...'

'I always want you to ask if you want my help!' I protested.

Kathleen smiled. 'Well, me too.'

'And there's no need to feel left out. You are our big sister – me and Adam will always need you, okay? We are better than a team. We're family,' I said firmly.

She nodded. 'I know, I know.' She held out her arms and I scooted over and she leaned down to hug me with one arm, the other holding the baby. 'Can you forgive me?'

'Can you forgive *me*?' I countered. We smiled at one another. 'I'm scared that you were right all along. We're in trouble. We're running out of money. This flood will set us back. I don't know when we'll be able to open. Me and Adam had an argument. We never argue! It's all getting too much,' I admitted in a rush. I knew she was going to say we should give it all up.

'Well, that doesn't sound like my sister talking,' she said instead. 'I know I'm always telling you to be more practical like me, but the truth is, I admire your dreams and how you and Adam always look on the bright side. It used to irritate me how optimistic Adam was, but now I feel sad seeing you both so down and so anxious. When I saw how happy you both were the day you got the keys, I didn't doubt that you could do it. Both of you. I'm so sorry if I made you think otherwise.'

'You said Finlay was right about me seeing the world through rose-tinted glasses.'

'Only because I wish that I could sometimes! And I'm sure he does too. You shouldn't give up your dream just because you've hit some hurdles. I'm surprised you're even considering it. That's not like you at all.'

I gaped at her. I'd never seen her this supportive. 'Really?' I bit my lip. 'Do you think we can really do this? Finish and open up Dove House? What if I haven't been realistic enough? What if we have dreamed too big?' I poured my fears out to my older sister.

'No such thing,' she replied. 'And you have me in your corner. We're going to sort it all out, I promise.'

'You have me in your corner too, you know that, right?' I had a feeling I would be needing her more than she needed me.

She nodded. 'So, there isn't anything we can't do, okay?'

Adam appeared in the doorway. 'Kathleen is right,' he said to me. 'I'm sorry for yesterday. We will work out what we can do. You don't really regret buying the house, do you?'

'I don't want to,' I said. I was just so worried we'd hit a wall we couldn't get through.

'We'll sort everything. Together,' Kathleen said.

I really wanted to believe her.

Part Three

Chapter Thirty-Eight

Mum and Kathleen came to the house the next day to help us, with baby Drew asleep in his pram. Dad and Hamish were at work and the twins were at school. Adam and I were really grateful to have their input, and we took them first into the kitchen to see the flood damage.

'We have a dehumidifier in here and in what will be our living room,' I said. 'We'll need to redecorate in here. And thankfully we hadn't started the living room yet, so that's still to do. But that's only once it's dried out, and we don't know how long we will need to wait for that. They have fixed the water pipe, at least.'

'And the water didn't damage the Aga,' Adam added. 'Out here we will need to redo this wall,' he said, pointing to where the water had reached the corridor. 'It's all added time and costs.'

'While the builders sort all this, can you and Adam get on with something else?' Mum asked.

'We can't decorate downstairs yet,' I replied dully. 'Glen said they need to deal with the damage first, plus they need to finish the final guest bathroom as the fittings arrived late.'

'What about your bedrooms?' Mum suggested.

Adam looked at me. 'We could decorate our rooms,' he said. 'The plastering is finished, so we can paint them and get the carpet fitter to start with them and order our furniture. Obviously we wanted the downstairs and guest bedrooms sorted first so we can open, but our rooms still need doing. We could just swap the plans around.'

'Exactly.' Kathleen beamed at him. 'Then you're still doing the work that's needed, just in a different order. And creating a home will make all the difference in the world to you both – you'll have so much more energy and spirit to get the bed and breakfast parts finished after that. It's mad to still be in sleeping bags in the lounge.'

I couldn't deny my sister had a point. 'It would be nice to have my own room again. But what about the budget?' I asked. 'We hardly have anything left to decorate, and surely we need to put all of it into the downstairs? We can't afford to do our rooms. Maybe I should just come back home,' I said.

'Let's go through the budget and see what there is left,' Kathleen suggested. 'I will need a coffee, though.' They departed into the lounge and I made us all a coffee and joined them, poring over Adam's laptop and spreadsheets with baby Drew asleep in his pram and Tabby curled up on my sleeping bag, opening one eye now and again to see what everyone was doing.

'I've costed all the new things that we need not covered by insurance, and the extra time and labour,' Adam was explaining. 'Glen reminded us that we'll need a deep clean after all the work is finished, so if we still want to open for New Year, this is the money we will need.'

'You're short by five thousand pounds?' Kathleen checked. 'And that's tight for decor and furniture?' she asked me.

'I will have to get everything second-hand, definitely,' I said, wondering if that would even be possible.

'We have a mirror that would work,' Mum said. 'You can have anything from the house that you like.'

I smiled. 'Well, thank you, but I don't think that's enough. We can't afford to decorate everything, so there's no way we can still open in the New Year. And if we can't earn money, then…' I trailed off. I had no idea how Dove House could ever turn a profit.

'Let me talk to Hamish about something.' Kathleen got up and left the room.

'You could do the downstairs painting and decorating yourselves, couldn't you? We could all help, that would save money,' Mum said.

Adam nodded. 'That is an idea. I think we'd still need wall-papering professionally done, but the paintwork we could do.' He updated the spreadsheet.

'That's not enough,' I said with a sigh. 'Maybe we should both get a job for six months and do the work slowly and then open up after that? Maybe it was too much of a gamble to give up working for the reno, after all.' I looked at my sister, who had just returned. 'I think you were right. I should have stayed at the Inn.'

'Would Beth be happy to wait for you to start repaying the loan?' Mum asked.

'She's already given us six months' grace,' I replied. I didn't want to get a job at another hotel, but maybe it was the most sensible idea we'd had. 'I think we should stop the work, push it back till we have some more money and maybe we can open for next Christmas?'

'No,' Kathleen said. We all looked at her. 'Let me and Hamish give you some money. We can give you a couple of thousand so you can decorate. We can all find things as cheaply as possible. Then you can still open in the New Year.'

'We can't take your money,' Adam said quickly.

'You're family. And we have it. We were talking about doing an extension, but that's not something we need to do right now. Let us give it to you. I really want to be a part of this. Please,' she said, urgently.

'But...' I started.

'We'd have to pay you back,' Adam said, firmly. 'And I'm not sure we'd make enough to be able to do that as we have to pay Beth back too. Maybe Lorna is right — we should get jobs and put the B & B on hold.' He looked as disappointed as me about the idea.

Kathleen sat down and thought for a moment. 'We have more money. Savings that we were planning to invest. Why

211

don't I invest in Dove House? Then you wouldn't need to do it on a budget. Or pay me back. We could be partners. I'd have to be a sleeping partner for now, as I have my hands full, but once the business grows and baby Drew is older, maybe I could come on board. I understand if you just want it to be the two of you, and we have no idea if this will be profitable, so to give me a percentage might be asking too much—'

I looked at Adam, who nodded once. 'We'd love you to be part of it,' I interrupted her. 'We should have done this from the beginning. I have no idea how long it will be until we make a profit, though,' I warned her.

'The money doesn't matter. You can give me two per cent, or something. I can wait until you make a profit. As long as it takes. Would I really be part of it all?' Kathleen asked. I could see by the smile on her face that she wanted this very much.

'We'd love you to be,' Adam said. 'Do you need to speak to Hamish again? We'll have to work the figures out, draw up paperwork, make it official... Currently it's fifty-fifty between me and Lorna, so we'd need to work out how much you want to put in, and then your share...'

Kathleen wasn't even listening. 'I'm so excited! I have so many ideas about how to bring guests in, too. We can definitely turn a profit quickly, I'm sure of it. You can leave all the marketing to me. That's something I can easily do at home with the baby.'

'That sounds great,' I said. It had always been hard to say no to my sister, so I had no doubt she could be good at that side of the business.

'Oh, loves,' Mum said, dabbing her eyes with a tissue. 'You three make such a great team.'

'Oh, Mum,' I said, choking up myself.

'To us,' Adam said, raising his coffee cup.

We all lifted ours and I felt like a huge weight had been lifted off my shoulders. We had a chance to really do this now. With Kathleen on board, I had hope again that we could turn our vision into a reality. Then I had a thought. 'Oh, what about Mrs Andrews? She was threatening to complain to the council. What do we do about her?'

'If I can get through giving birth on the kitchen floor of Glendale Hall dressed as Morticia Addams, we can definitely deal with Mrs Andrews,' she replied.

I chuckled. 'You're always going to bring that up, aren't you?'

'Probably,' she admitted. 'Let's plan how we can win her round.'

'And I'll make a new spreadsheet,' Adam said.

Chapter Thirty-Nine

We used the Glendale grapevine to find out that Mrs Andrews doted on her grandchildren, so armed with a carrot cake from Emily's Bakery and baby Drew, Kathleen and I went over to her house on Wednesday afternoon to try to talk to her.

'Yes?' She peered out of her front door suspiciously after we rang the bell.

'Mrs Andrews, I don't think we've met. I'm Kathleen, Lorna's sister. I've just had a baby. I wanted you to meet him. And we've brought a cake. Shall we have a cup of tea with it?' And somehow Kathleen manoeuvred around Mrs Andrews into the hallway and handed her the cake. Mrs Andrews stepped back in surprise as I quickly followed, pushing the pram, and closed the door behind me.

'Oh, well, I suppose so,' she said, looking down at the baby with a smile.

'Emily bakes the best cakes, doesn't she?' I said brightly.

'Through here?' Kathleen called as she walked into the kitchen. We all followed her. 'Sit down, I'll put the kettle on.'

Mrs Andrews sank into one of the chairs at her round pine table, for once lost for words. I lifted baby Drew out of the pram as he stirred. 'Oh, what a bonny boy,' she said, looking at him.

'Would you like to hold him?' I passed him over to her as Kathleen made tea. I jumped up and cut three slices of the cake for us. Kathleen dropped me a wink as we joined Mrs Andrews at the table. 'Kath, tell Mrs Andrews about the birth.'

Kathleen told her about giving birth at the Hall and how everyone jumped in to help. 'But that's what I love so much about Glendale, the community spirit here. Don't you, Mrs Andrews?'

Mrs Andrews was making faces at the baby. 'Yes, that's true, dear. My late husband and I didn't have much money but our friends and family all came together to help us get married. Someone made my dress and took the photographs for us, and we picked wild flowers, and the Glendale Arms let us have a reception there and we only had to pay for our drinks.' She beamed down at the baby as she thought back fondly to her wedding day, so I seized the opportunity.

I took a breath. 'Mrs Andrews, we came over to say how sorry we are that the work on Dove House has been disruptive. I really didn't want to cause you any inconvenience. We want our bed and breakfast to be the heart of the community. So, we are going to offer a discount for Glendale friends and family.'

She sighed. 'I see what you're doing.' She took a bite of the cake as she jiggled Drew in her arms. 'But I suppose you're right. It would be nice to have a place for people to stay in the village.'

'We are hoping to get all the building work finished really soon, and then we will just be decorating. We're hoping to open for Hogmanay.'

Mrs Andrews raised an eyebrow. 'I'm due to have my sister stay here then. She has a rather beastly dog...'

'We are allowing dogs,' I said quickly.

'How about this?' Kathleen said, leaning forward. 'We let your sister stay for free. We were only talking yesterday about how we'd like to have a couple of guests to give us feedback before we open officially.' I gaped at her; that was news to me. 'It would be so helpful, so we can iron out any issues, and it means your sister won't have to stay here,' she added brightly.

Huh? Actually, that was a very good idea, I had to admit. I nodded along. 'We would feel so much happier opening up if we knew things were just right.'

'My sister is very particular,' Mrs Andrews said. I tried not to laugh and saw Kathleen swallow hard too. We had no doubt about that. She nodded. 'Okay, then. I won't complain any more, and I'll tell my sister she'll be staying with you at New Year.'

I let out a puff of air. 'We can't thank you enough, Mrs Andrews.'

She passed the baby back to Kathleen. 'He really is a lovely baby.'

'As good as gold,' she agreed.

I took a big bite of carrot cake and mentally ticked one thing off our to-do list.

After we had finished up our tea and cake, we walked back to Dove House, where we saw an unfamiliar car in the driveway. Adam was talking to a man on the doorstep. 'I hope this isn't another problem to deal with,' I said to my sister as we hurried over.

'Ah. Lorna, this is...'

The man turned round. 'Jack Smith. I work for the *Inverness Times* and I've heard all about your renovation project. I would love to do a story on how you're restoring Dove House. It looks to be right up our street. Local readers will love it. Glendale is always popular in our paper, and if people can come and stay here soon, it's a big scoop for us,' he said eagerly.

'Wow, that sounds great,' I said, smiling. Free publicity was just what we needed right now.

'How did you find out about us?' Adam asked him.

'My friend hasn't stopped talking about Dove House since he saw it. Told me I needed to get over here and see what you're doing for myself. I'm glad I did. We can be the first local paper on this story.'

'Who is your friend?' Kathleen asked as she laid Drew back in his pram.

'Finlay Scott,' Jack replied.

I took a step backwards as Adam and Kathleen looked at me. Finlay sent him here? I hadn't heard from him since he left for Perth, but this meant he hadn't forgotten Dove House.

Or me, my heart whispered.

'So, can I have a look around?' Jack asked.

'Come on in,' Adam replied.

–

Jack Smith spent a couple of hours with us looking round and asking us questions, and said he'd come back at the end of the week with his photographer to finish off the feature piece that would run in the *Inverness Times* the following week. He was really enthusiastic about Dove House. 'Finlay was right about how special this house is,' he said as I showed him out. Adam had left us to talk to Glen and Kathleen had gone home to feed Drew.

'How is Finlay?' I asked, trying not to sound too eager.

'Busy. I keep trying to get him to meet me for a drink. But he has his hands full.'

'With his father's company?' I asked, burning with curiosity.

'And that house. It's huge, have you seen it? And he's rattling around in there on his own.'

'How did you two become friends?'

'I met him at university. We both took a creative writing class. I keep telling him he shouldn't give up on it. He's a great writer. Well, thank you again. I'll see you Friday.'

'Thanks, Jack.' I leaned against the door frame as he walked out to his car, thinking about Finlay. I didn't like to think of him alone in his big family home. I hoped he was okay. I pulled out my phone. I had to thank him for doing this.

Hi, Finlay. How are things? It's been chaotic
here. In fact, I was worried we might not be able
to finish what we started. But it feels like things
are moving forward again. And then your friend
Jack Smith turned up! I can't thank you enough
for sending him to Dove House. The publicity will
be amazing for us. I hope we can do this now.
And I hope that things are working out for you
too. All the best, Lorna

I added a kiss then deleted it, then added it again then deleted it
again. Finally I sent it without a kiss, feeling that was probably
for the best.

I put my phone in my pocket and walked back into the house
feeling so much better for having contacted him. I had missed
talking to him. I would always remember him fondly. I hoped
by sending Jack here it meant that he felt the same about me.
I didn't want to lose him completely from my life, but if that's
what he wanted, I would have to accept it.

Chapter Forty

I stood in the doorway of what was going to be my bedroom with the new paint I'd just been out to buy. Mum had said that when the room had been Thomas Scott's sister's it had been completely pink, and that wasn't my taste, but I thought a pretty vintage, almost Parisian style would be really lovely. It would be a space that would make me happy (and hopefully sleep well in, too!) and as my room at our family house was pretty small, I was excited to have a large room to work with.

I was thankful we'd stripped all the wallpaper in one go so the room was ready for painting and decorating. I put the new paint tins down and opened up the lid of the first one. I had found a really pretty cream colour to paint three walls, and then I was going to put up wallpaper on the wall that would be behind my bed, and I'd found a lovely floral design online and ordered that. I'd also found the bed of my dreams, with an ornate cream and gold bed frame, that I was waiting to be delivered. And I had chosen a cream carpet from the company that were going to carpet the upstairs once all the painting was finished.

'We have Mum's mirror.'

I turned round to see Kathleen and Hamish behind me holding a dressing-table mirror and looking puffed from carrying it up to the third floor. 'Where's the baby?'

'Mum is looking after him downstairs. We have an hour until I need to go down and feed him. How can we help?'

'You really didn't need to come today, you've got your hands full,' I said, touched that they were here.

'We want to help. Hamish, put that over there and see if you can give Adam a hand with his room. What do you want me to do, Lorna?'

'Well, if you're sure...' I said with a smile. I wasn't sure if she should be painting. 'Tell you what. That mirror is really pretty. I need to find a dressing table to put it on. All I've ordered so far is a bed. Could you have a look online for me?'

'I don't need a sitting-down job,' she protested.

'It would be a really big help,' I insisted. I gestured to my tablet. 'And you should take it easy, whatever you say. You've just had a baby. Mind you, you look glowing. I need your secret!'

She chuckled. 'I wish, but actually Drew hasn't been sleeping too badly and Hamish is a big help.' She sat down on the floor with my tablet. 'I'm really loving every moment. Even being up here for an hour, I miss him so much.'

'I always knew you'd be a great mum,' I said as I started painting the wall next to her.

'You did?'

'You tried to mother me enough growing up,' I said with a laugh. 'We can't thank you and Hamish enough for stepping in.' Adam and Kathleen had sorted her partnership and she had transferred the money we needed to make the house what we always wanted, and I hoped she knew how grateful we both were.

'I'm so excited to be part of it. And Hamish is happy that I'm happy.' She looked at the room. 'You'll feel so much better when this room is decorated and you can move in officially.'

'I think we sort of focused so much on the B & B we forgot about that we'll be living here ourselves. I tried to help Adam with his decor but he wants to do it himself.'

She grinned at me. 'Let's hope he doesn't paint it black like he did when he was fifteen. It gave me a headache being in his room.'

'Me too!'

'This is really pretty.' Kathleen held up the tablet. 'And there are two matching bedside tables. It's quite reasonable, and they'll deliver this week. No point ordering things that'll take months, as you want to move in.'

I had a look and nodded. 'Go for it, I think they will work really well with my new bed.'

Adam and Hamish came in then. 'We're nipping out to the DIY store for paint.'

'I hope it's not black,' Kathleen told him.

Adam grinned. 'I learnt my lesson on that, don't worry. No, I'm doing dark green and cream. I saw the samples you left out strategically for me,' he said to me. His phone beeped. 'Oh, and I'll be out later. I'm going for a drink.'

'With Grace?' I asked when I saw his smile became broader.

'With Grace. Need anything? Okay, bye,' he said, hurrying off before I could reply, Hamish following him with a grin.

I let out a sigh before I went back to painting.

'I heard that,' Kathleen said. 'What's up?'

'Nothing...'

'*Please*,' she scoffed.

'Fine. It's just that I'm really happy Adam and Grace are hanging out, but it makes me think about Finlay, that's all. I wonder what he's doing?'

'Did he reply to your message?'

I shook my head. 'Not yet. His reporter friend said he was super-busy. I hope he's okay. Do you think I shouldn't have said what I said? That he should follow his dreams and not live his father's life? Maybe it was too harsh. He's grieving, and he has a lot of responsibilities.'

'You were only trying to encourage him to think about his own happiness, too. That's not a bad thing. We all need that reminder sometimes.'

I nodded. 'I hate that he feels guilty about his father. I really don't think Thomas would have wanted that. He fell in love with Mum, and she is the kindest woman. I think he wanted Finlay to know that for a reason.'

'You really care about him, don't you?' she asked me then. I looked at her, wondering if she was going to tell me off for it, but she just looked interested.

'It's crazy though, isn't it? To like the son of the man Mum was in love with.'

Kathleen shook her head. 'I think you're overthinking it. You liked him as soon as he arrived, I could see that, and he seemed to really like you. It doesn't matter what happened in the past. If you want to be together, that's all that counts.'

I sighed. 'He told me he wanted to kiss me, but then he didn't. He left.'

'I think he just needs time.'

'I know. And it's not as if I haven't got enough going on right now,' I said with a laugh. Dove House was my priority. Just like Finlay was focusing on his life in Perth. But I suppose I did hope that Kathleen was right and that maybe I would hear from him again. In time.

'Okay, you have a dressing table and bedside tables on their way,' Kathleen said. 'What about some pictures for the wall over there? What vibe do you fancy?'

'Parisian,' I replied. 'To match the decor. Something dreamy and inspiring. And romantic.'

'Would I find anything else for you?' Kathleen chuckled. 'I remember the look you gave me when I said I'd bought most of my furniture and decor from IKEA.'

'We have different tastes, that's all,' I said. 'Life would be boring if we were all the same.' I turned round, wanting to help her as she was helping me. 'Let me come round later and make you dinner, then you can relax this evening.'

'I said I'm fine,' she protested.

I gave her a stern look. 'Let me return the favour for all this. Besides, Adam is going out with Grace, and I'll be alone. I'm really just gatecrashing your family.'

'You're never a gatecrasher. But let's all get a takeaway, it'll be more fun. What about this?' She held up a picture of a watering can.

'That's definitely not romantic,' I told her firmly.

Chapter Forty-One

Adam and I spent the rest of the week finishing off decorating our bedrooms, and on Saturday they were done and we were ready for the carpets to be fitted on Monday. Adam went to play rugby as usual and I met up with Grace, eager to see how her date with my brother had gone. I hadn't seen her since the Halloween party, and I was looking forward to catching up.

We met at our favourite café in Inverness and ordered coffees and pastries before going home decor shopping. 'I needed these,' I said as we settled in at our table with our treats. 'It's so lovely to see you. How are you? How's the Inn? Any gossip for me?'

'The new manager has started. A woman too! And we really like her. I hope she's going to give the place a new lease of life,' Grace replied. 'And the restaurant is fully booked all month – everyone is loving Anna's menu.'

'I knew they would. I need to book in for a meal myself when I can,' I said.

'I'm still thinking about my future. What with Anna planning her own restaurant and you and Adam creating your own business, I really need to give myself a kick up the backside and do something about my own dreams.'

'Make it your New Year's resolution. Start planning, and in the new year, go for it – I think you'd be great at running your own business, if that's what you want.'

Grace took a bite of her pastry. 'Thank you. I really admire what you guys are doing. Adam is so excited about Dove House;

I love hearing him talk about it.' She looked across the table at me.

'Did he tell you about all the dramas?'

She nodded. 'I'm so sorry you had to go through all that. Renovation is so stressful! I'm glad that grumpy Kathleen stepped up to help you both.' She grinned. 'I suppose I might have to change my nickname for her now.'

'Definitely grateful to my sister. She has been a real godsend. And I didn't think I'd be saying that! So, you and Adam had a lovely date? He was very coy about it.'

She smiled and I caught a trace of a blush on her cheeks. 'He's so sweet. And supportive of me. It's a bit of a revelation after my dating history.'

I nodded. I had met her ex-boyfriend. 'You and my brother both deserve happiness, so I'm really pleased.'

'I love his positivity,' she said.

'I'm always trying to be more like Adam. He just believes things will work out. We had a wobble after our kitchen flood and I wondered if we should walk away, but Adam and my family convinced me we could do it. And I'm feeling a lot more positive about it all now.'

'I'm glad. I never doubted you could do it, both of you. I can't wait to see it all finished! You said you had a reporter with you yesterday?'

I told her about Jack Smith coming back with a photographer. 'The article will be out next week. We decided to open up the booking form on the website, in case people reading it want to book. That's a scary thought when it's not all finished yet, but my sister had a great idea – she invited our neighbour's sister to stay for free to give us feedback and leave a review on the website. We're also going to give Glendale residents a discount for friends and family. The reporter loved that idea.'

'Ooh, that is a great idea. And Finlay was the one who told the reporter about Dove House? That was sweet of him, wasn't it?' She raised an eyebrow.

I smiled. 'It was. I hope he's doing okay.'

'It's a shame he had to go when he did. Timing is a weird one, isn't it? To think I met Adam ages ago... but I do think things happen when they are right for you.'

'I hope so. I just wish sometimes you knew what was going to happen in the future, do you know what I mean?' I asked her.

'But then there wouldn't be much point in living or looking forward to things or taking risks, would there?' Grace replied. 'If you believe that ultimately what's meant to be will be, that helps.'

I nodded. 'So everything will work out for all of us in the end?'

She smiled. 'Exactly. Now we've got the heavy stuff out of the way, what shops shall we go to? You need home decor and I need a new winter coat.'

I had definitely missed spending time with Grace.

—

When I got back from Inverness, the light was fading and Adam was back and watching a renovation YouTube video on his laptop in the kitchen. 'Did you have fun? How was Grace?' He smiled when he said her name, which was pretty cute to see.

'We did. I really enjoyed it.' I sat down next to him and kicked off my boots. 'I found these gorgeous mirror trays for my room, on sale, and I bought a couple of home-styling books in the second-hand bookshop. Grace got her new coat, and she found a lovely scarf to go with it, too, so we did well,' I replied. 'Speaking of Grace, are you going to see her again?'

'We're having dinner next week,' Adam said. 'You know, I liked Anna when she first came to Glendale, but I realise now that I tried to make her like me, and if you have a connection, it shouldn't be that hard. With Grace, it's, I don't know, easy. We get on so well, and I'm not second-guessing it. I'm just enjoying it. Does that make sense?'

I nodded. 'I think it's great. You've both been looking for someone special. I couldn't think of two people who deserve it more.' I felt emotional all of a sudden.

He grinned. 'Don't cry again, this isn't one of your romcoms.'

'Doesn't mean I can't wish for a happy ending for you and Grace.'

'Okay, I'll let you imagine that. I might give her a call. I wanted to ask her where she wants to go next week. Oh, Jack Smith emailed the photo he's going to use with his article. It looks great.' He passed me his laptop and disappeared to speak to Grace. I looked at the picture. It was of me and Adam outside the front door, one arm in the air, grinning like loons. Kathleen was just off to the side, smiling at us. We all looked excited and happy and behind us, Dove House looked like a welcoming place to stay. I felt bad that I had considered it a cursed house when everything seemed to be going wrong. Maybe there hadn't always been happy endings here, but I knew there had been happiness. Like every house, it had seen love and loss. I hoped over the next few years it would see a lot more love.

Listening to Adam talk about Grace made me think of Finlay, naturally. And seeing the photo of us that was going to be in the newspaper because of him. I had felt a connection to him, and it had felt easy, like Adam said, but then life had got in the way of anything happening between us.

I sighed. I was so excited that maybe Adam and Grace might find their happy ever after; so thrilled that Kathleen had her family, and of course that my other Glendale friends had found the love they hadn't even known they had been looking for, like Anna and Cameron. But I would be lying if I didn't admit that I still wished I could find it for myself.

That one day I would have my own happy ending.

Chapter Forty-Two

On Sunday morning, Adam and I walked to church together. It was bitterly cold outside, so we wrapped ourselves in about five different layers to walk there.

Outside the village church, Beth greeted us warmly and asked how things were going, so I gave her an update. Adam went over to talk to Cameron as Anna joined me and Beth.

'I'm so happy it's all going so well,' Beth said. 'Oh, Heather!' she called out, seeing her friend. 'She wanted a word with you,' she added to me.

'Lorna, I wondered if you wanted to come out to our farm next week,' Heather said. 'Anna said you might want some produce for your B & B once it's up and running, and I know you're speaking with Emily about providing the baked goods. But we can help with anything else you might need for the breakfasts.'

'Mates rates, obviously,' Beth added with a grin.

'Everyone is a friend according to you,' Heather said with a laugh. 'But yes, we are always happy to help a new business out.'

'That would be great, thank you,' I said. 'I can come out to Fraser Farm.'

'I'll come too, I love seeing the farm,' Anna said. She turned behind us to Emily. 'Emily, my brother is waving at you,' she said, gesturing to the church.

'Oh, I need to start the Sunday school,' Emily said, hurrying off.

'I never thought my friend would marry a minister and start running the Sunday school,' Beth said with a chuckle. 'I suppose we'd better take our pews too.' Drew appeared and she took his arm, giving us a wave as they walked off together.

'I need to talk to you,' Anna said to me once we were alone. 'Can we go and see Heather on Tuesday? I've got the morning off, and we can talk on the way. I'll pick you up.'

'Works for me,' I agreed, curious as to what my friend wanted to talk about. We followed the others inside and I joined my family, and Anna sat down in her usual Glendale Hall pew opposite us.—

I sank into the pew, glad to be having a rest today. It had been a hectic week. But I was so happy to have worked on making myself a lovely bedroom at Dove House. I was excited to sleep in there once the carpet was fitted and my bed arrived. It had been a good reminder that Dove House was our home, not just our business. And with Kathleen as our partner now, the business side was back on track and we all felt far more optimistic that we could get everything done.

'It's so easy to worry, isn't it?' Brodie addressed the church. I looked up, instantly alert. 'There are so many things in our daily lives that we struggle with or get stressed about, and it's tempting during those times to focus on the difficult situation we find ourselves in. It's hard not to feel alone in our worries. It's easy to let go of faith. But faith is a gift to help us during times like these,' Brodie said. 'It's so hard to have faith when it's something you can't see. You just have to believe. We like things we can hold in our hands, don't we? Faith is not tangible. You can't see it or hold it, and that makes it hard to reach for in difficult times. You want something you can really trust to cling onto. But what if you were able to trust that everything would be okay? What if you could let go of your worries?'

I found myself nodding along. I really had lost a bit of faith lately, and I wasn't sure I had even realised it. I had let my worries take over. I had lost hope that I could make my dream come true. I was so grateful that my family made sure they helped me to get it back. Brodie was talking about something I could really relate to, as he so often did.

'We need faith in God, of course, but we also need faith in ourselves that we can get through the tough times, and faith that we're not alone in those times either, that we always have each other. It always sounds so easy, doesn't it? Faith. Such a small word, but such a big idea. And if you're worried about something, it can be the first thing you lose. But this week, let's try to keep our faith and reach for it when we need it the most. Let's pray together to help us do just that...'

I looked around after Brodie's prayer and I knew I had to be grateful for all the people with me in the church – they were all on our side. They all wanted me and Adam to make our dream come true. We weren't alone. And we could do it with their help and, of course, our faith.

I had been worried that I had let myself be too much of a dreamer. That I needed to be more realistic. That I needed to take my rose-tinted glasses off.

But maybe all I had really needed was to believe that things would all work out how they were supposed to in the end.

–

A 1920s gem in the middle of Glendale... The dynamic brother and sister duo, Adam and Lorna Ferguson, with the help of older sister Kathleen Ferguson-Donald, are restoring the white three-storey property known locally as Dove House into Glendale's first bed and breakfast, where they want guests to feel like they are staying in a home from home.

'It's brilliant publicity,' Kathleen said. Everyone had come over to Dove House on their way to work or school to read our article in the *Inverness Times* as soon as it arrived on the doorstep. 'Look, they put Tabby in!'

'Aw,' I said, looking at the picture of Tabby curled up by the Aga in the kitchen. 'And they included our website and social media links. And the discount for Glendale residents... this is so helpful.'

'I love the part when you say you came here as children,' Mum said as she read it. 'And how you wanted this house for so long. Everyone will love that.'

'And the fact that you worked at the Inn,' Dad added, to me. 'So they can see you have experience.'

'It's a really positive piece,' Hamish agreed.

My phone rang and my pulse skipped when I saw Finlay's name on the screen. 'I'll just take this,' I said, leaving the room hastily. 'Hi,' I said, answering a little bit breathlessly.

'Lorna, it's me... Finlay,' he replied, rather nervously. 'I just got my copy of the paper and read the article. Wow.'

'I know! We're all reading it now. Jack has been so lovely! Thank you again for giving him the idea,' I replied, beaming down the phone.

'I got your message. I was so pleased he came round. It's great publicity for you. How's it all going? It mentioned there was a flood but that it's all dried out now.'

I nodded, although he couldn't see. 'There have been a few setbacks, and I wasn't sure if we could recover, to be honest, but yes, the builders are in there right now sorting it all out and Adam and I have been decorating our rooms while we had that delay. I can almost move in properly.'

'Oh, that's great,' he said. 'Even from these photos, I can see you've done so much since I was there.' He coughed. 'I haven't stopped thinking about our conversation the day I left,' he said then.

'You haven't?' I paced around the hallway.

'I took all my worries and stress and guilt, well, everything, out on you. You were only trying to look out for me, to make sure I was doing what was best for me, and I acted appallingly. I would never forgive myself if you lost even a tiny bit of your positivity or your ambition or your determination. I've never met anyone like you, Lorna. You have so much self-belief, and you work so hard to make your dreams come true and you just want everyone to be happy. And I didn't listen.' He said it all quickly and then paused, out of breath.

'If you had seen me after Halloween when the kitchen flooded... I was ready to give up on it all for a moment. But I understand. I did just want you to be happy, and I know I should have been more understanding about everything you had to deal with. I have my family, and so much support, and you have to do so much on your own. And I hate that. I wish I could help. I'm sorry for what I said too.'

'Well, I appreciate that but really, it's okay. I've kept replaying your words over and over about what you said about my dad... that he sent me to Glendale and wanted me to find his letter so I could see that he did regret how he'd lived his life, and to show me that I should follow my heart. I felt so guilty, so lost, I suppose, but I think you were right. I think that's why he wanted me to come to Dove House. He left things here in Perth, paperwork, letters, that make me believe that too. You were right, Lorna. I think he did want me to live the life that I wanted.'

I smiled. 'Well, I'm pleased. You deserve that, Finlay.' I didn't dare ask what it was that he wanted, but I hoped he would find it. I really did.

'I want to tell you about what I've been doing,' he said then. He sounded a little shy. 'And to show you something. I thought you might like it for Dove House. But maybe not. It's fine if that's the case.'

'Of course, I'd love to see it. And to hear all about what you've been doing.' My family came out into the hallway then, ready to leave. 'Um...'

'It's okay, you need to go,' he said. 'We can talk another time.'

I thought about how I had all this support around me but Finlay didn't. I thought about what his reporter friend had said about him rattling around in his house all alone. And that he had realised he could do what he wanted, and he wanted to tell me all about it. And to show me something for Dove House. 'I do, but I'd love to come and see you,' I said. 'Let me come to Perth.'

I could hear his smile down the phone. 'I would love that.'

Chapter Forty-Three

Anna drove us to Heather and Rory's farm on Tuesday morning
as we had arranged. It was another bitingly cold day, so we wore
our warmest coats and were nursing takeaway coffees, prepared
for it to feel even colder on Fraser Farm as it was outside the
village in the middle of countryside perched up on a hill.

'So, I have a few decisions to make and I wanted to ask your
opinion,' Anna said once we had driven away from Glendale.

'Fire away,' I said, sipping my coffee and leaning back in the
car seat.

'Well, the new manager at the Inn has offered me a full-time
job there as chef.'

'Oh, Anna.' I twisted round to look at her as she smiled.
'That's amazing news!'

She nodded. 'I know, I can't quite believe it. I think it's a
great place to gain experience for my own restaurant one day.
She's pretty much going to give me free rein, but she wants me
to work full-time, so do lunch and dinner with Wednesday and
Sunday night off, so it's going to be hard work. But I'm ready
for it, you know?'

'You'll be great,' I said. 'I'm so happy for you. Hang on,
though, what do you need my opinion on? You're not sure
whether to accept?'

'Well, it's not about the job, I'm really excited for the challenge and I know I can save up there for my own place one
day. It's the perfect solution, really, but it means that I can't do
any housekeeping work at Glendale Hall. I won't be able to
manage it. Beth has been lovely about me studying around the

234

job and doing this trial at the Inn, but now I'll be working there full-time, I can't be Glendale Hall's housekeeper any more.'

'No, that's true,' I agreed. 'She will be supportive, though, I'm sure.'

'Oh, I know she will, but I don't only work at Glendale Hall, do I?'

'Ah.' The penny dropped. Anna also lived there too. 'She will need the room for a housekeeper, do you mean?'

'Exactly. I know Beth won't throw me out or anything, but I can't in good conscience stay there if I'm not working. They need a live-in housekeeper. I'll need to move out. Which sucks, because I love it there, but it leads to another dilemma. I can rent a flat near the Inn or...'

'You could move in with Cameron,' I finished for her. Her boyfriend lived at Hilltop Farm, which he managed for Heather and Rory, and I knew Anna stayed in his cabin a lot but that was different to officially moving in. 'He can't really not live on the farm, can he?'

Anna shook her head. 'No. He has a lot of early starts, he needs to be on-site and it's not too bad a commute to Glen-marshes, really, only a bit further than Glendale Hall. But I've never lived with a boyfriend and it scares me, I'll be honest.'

'I understand. It's a big step. I haven't either, but you and Cameron feel like forever.' I had sensed their attraction as soon as Anna first arrived in Glendale. He and Anna brought out the best in one another. That's what I wanted in a partner. Someone who could inspire me and who I could inspire. Before Anna settled in Glendale, she had flitted from job to job and place to place, and it was a big deal for her to start training to be a chef and make a life in our village. And now this would be a real commitment, so I understood her hesitation.

'I know, it feels like forever to me, but I've never wanted the whole husband and two-point-four children thing. My brother has that with Emily, and I'm happy as aunt and godmother, but I just don't see myself with a family of my own. Cameron has always said the same, but what if he changes his mind when I move in and wants all that?'

'I think you'll have to talk to him about that, but if you see your life with Cameron then moving in just makes logistical sense,' I said, giving a practical viewpoint as I knew she wasn't as romantic as I was. I admired how independent Anna was, and that she knew what she wanted from life. It would be boring if we all wanted the same thing anyway.

Anna chuckled. 'You're right, it does. And I'd save even more money not having to pay rent. The cabin comes with the job, and I know Heather and Rory would be fine if I moved in. They've always wanted me to take on a chef's job at Hilltop, but I don't want Cameron and me working and living together. And there's not as much scope there to experiment like there will be at the Inn. I really am excited about working there.'

'Just talk to Cameron, but I think it sounds like the perfect plan to me. And you love it at Hilltop, all the running and fresh air.' I shook my head. I wasn't a runner like Anna, but I did love the countryside so I understood why a farm would be a lovely place to live. 'I can see you living there.'

'So can I,' she admitted. 'But God, can you imagine how many people are going to ask us if we're getting married if I move into the cabin?' She shuddered, and I laughed.

'As you're always telling me, it doesn't matter what anyone else thinks if you're happy, and I know that you and Cameron are.'

'Thanks, Lorna. I knew you were the right person to ask.'

Chapter Forty-Four

We approached Fraser Farm then, and Anna drove down the gravel driveway towards the red-brick farmhouse, passing horses grazing in the paddock. High up on the hill behind the farm, I could see the Highland cows they bred there. Anna parked outside the farmhouse and we climbed out, the wind whipping around us instantly as the door opened, and Heather appeared with her dog and her little boy, waving in welcome.

'You made it,' Heather said as we walked over. 'Let's have breakfast before I show you round, Lorna. I'm excited you've come out here.'

'Me too,' I said, smiling as Darcy, their sheepdog, circled my legs. I patted him hello. 'Hello Harry,' I greeted her little boy.

'Harry!' It was Angus, Cameron's uncle, who helped out on the farm. 'We need you!' he called from near the paddock with Luke, the young man who worked there too and who was good friends with Izzy, Beth's daughter. Harry rushed off as Heather told us to come inside out of the cold, which I was grateful for as it really was freezing.

'So, how is all the work coming on?' Heather asked me as she served up eggs and bacon for us at the table in the kitchen. There was crusty toasted bread, orange juice, tea and coffee, and a basket of baked goods from Emily's Bakery too.

'This looks amazing,' I said. I was so looking forward to making my first breakfast at the B & B. I would definitely do all of this and more. No one would go hungry on my watch.

'Thank you, but Anna is the breakfast queen, not me,' Heather said. 'Remember when you taught Cameron how to make breakfast for Hilltop guests?'

'It was annoying that he looked so good in an apron,' Anna said, buttering a slice of toast. She grinned. 'I think he enjoys cooking now and again when I let him. Which I will have to do more of soon.' She saw Heather's raised eyebrow. 'I need to tell Beth later, but Glenmarshes Inn have offered me the full-time chef job.'

'Oh, Anna! That's brilliant news. Honestly, I'm so happy for you and proud and... Emily is going to cry when you tell her, I bet.'

Anna smiled. 'I agree. She and Brodie are going to be over the moon. It's down to all of you that this has happened, though. I would never have gone after my dreams of being a chef if it wasn't for everyone in Glendale. What is it about this place? Look at all of us, living our dreams.'

'I'm trying, not quite there yet,' I said, tucking into the delicious food with gusto.

Anna waved her hand. 'Come on, you're almost there! I have no doubt Dove House Bed and Breakfast will be a huge success. Look at the newspaper article! Everyone in the village is talking about it. And look at you, with two farms and thriving businesses,' she added to Heather. 'And there was a time when you weren't sure if this was the life for you.'

'It's true,' Heather agreed when I looked at her in surprise. Heather always seemed the perfect farmer's wife to me. 'I went from being a librarian to managing two farms. It's challenging, but I really do love it. And I know you put it all down to Glendale, Anna, but you were the one who took the opportunity to chase after your dreams, and I'm so thrilled it's all worked out for you. Oh, so you'll be living at Hilltop now, will you?'

Anna's mouth fell open. 'How did you...'

'Come on, it was only a matter of time, and you can't be Glendale Hall's housekeeper any more. God, Beth is going to be crushed. She'll have to find someone else. I don't envy you telling her.'

'Thanks,' Anna said drily.

'This is so good,' I said, pointing to the breakfast. 'We definitely need your produce at the bed and breakfast. I really want everything to be local that can be. I think guests will love that.'

'Lovely,' Heather said. 'I always think that's the biggest selling point of Glendale, and the reason I'll always love living here – we all help each other out and we're all in it together, right?'

'Adam and I have been so grateful for all the support we've had so far. We definitely couldn't have done this alone! Let's just hope people will want to come and stay with us.'

'The guests that come to Hilltop want a real retreat, but I know so many people who've come to the village for the day who wanted to stay for longer, and it's so well positioned to go on to Inverness or Loch Ness,' Heather said. 'You'll be booked up in no time.'

'Especially after that article and your discount,' Anna agreed. 'Emily said Brodie might take advantage of it for a night away from the girls,' she added with a chuckle.

'And there are so many events at the Hall now, too, that our guests could go to,' I said. 'I thought as well if Beth has any weddings and guests need somewhere to stay, we'd be perfect for that.' Beth held weddings at the Hall in summer and I was sure she'd pass on our details to anyone who needed a bed for the night.

'Perfect,' Anna said.

We finished breakfast and I had a lovely time chatting with Heather and Anna about all our business plans. They were both so enthusiastic and inspiring that I felt fired up about Dove House afterwards.

'Come on, let me show you around before you head off,' Heather said after we had cleared everything away. We put our coats and gloves and scarves back on and Heather led the way. Anna had been there many times, but I hadn't and I loved seeing all the animals and how the place worked. I wasn't sure I'd like living in the middle of nowhere, especially in winter, but Heather looked good on it, that was for sure.

We walked up the hill to see the cows and we leaned on the gate to greet the fluffy Highland herd.

'I'll email you what we can offer then,' Heather said as we wandered back down to the farmhouse and our car.

'Please do. And thank you for a wonderful morning. It's lovely out here.'

Heather gave us both a hug and we climbed into Anna's car. 'She does give family life a good name,' Anna commented as we waved and watched Heather head off to find her son.

'I hope I can have this one day,' I said a little bit wistfully. I looked at Anna as she started the car. 'I heard from Finlay. He rang when he read that article. He said he wants to tell me all about his plans for the future, so I suggested that I go and see him.'

'That sounds promising,' she said as she drove us out of the farm.

'I think he really could do with a friend.'

'Or something more,' she said with a meaningful look.

I shook my head, unsure. 'But you think I'm right to go?'

'I do. You're always telling me that if things are meant to work out then they will, and I think you're right, but sometimes you have to give fate a helping hand.'

'Throwing my advice back at me,' I said with a laugh. 'I do want to see him again. And find out what he's doing in Perth. I really enjoyed getting to know him. If we are only destined to be friends, then that's fine.'

'As you say, you can find out when you see him. You'll know how you feel then. And so will he.'

'I will always wonder "what if" if I don't go,' I mused out loud.

'Exactly. And you know from all those romcoms you like and make me watch – it's not over till it's over.'

'You always say they are so unrealistic!'

'Well, they are, you don't get happy endings in life, do you? But if you get a chance to be happy in life, then I think you should take it.'

I thought about the fact that I had told Finlay the exact same thing. I wanted to see him again. And I couldn't help but hope that he was looking forward to seeing me too.

Chapter Forty-Five

Completing my bedroom at Dove House helped to take my mind off my upcoming trip to see Finlay. The carpet was laid and my bed had been delivered, so I was able to add the finishing touches of pictures on the walls and blinds at the window. And then it was ready for me to move in. But first, I had to go back to our family home and collect more of my things from there. Mum and Kathleen with baby Drew came up with me to my old bedroom to give me a hand, and it was surreal to be packing up after so many years sleeping in there, so that I could make Dove House my home.

'Last time, I knew that I wasn't completely moving out. I knew I'd be in a sleeping bag and I left most of my things here. But now...' I trailed off, feeling sad – it was the end of an era. I opened the wardrobe to see most of my clothes still there. I'd been living in old, cosy clothes but that wasn't going to be for much longer.

'I remember my last night here,' Kathleen said as she sat down on the bed with the baby. 'It felt so weird to think it wasn't my home any more.'

'What nonsense,' Mum said, carrying in two plastic storage boxes. 'This will always be your home, even if you move out and have you own family. This house is always here for you, as I am.'

'God, Mum, I can't cry yet,' I said, feeling a lump rise in my throat at her words. 'I don't know how people move far away from home – I couldn't imagine not being close to you guys.'

'Some people don't get on with their families. Hamish hardly sees his,' Kathleen said. 'I think that's why he loves being with all of us so much.'

'We are lucky,' Mum said, smiling at us. 'Now, what else do you want to take?'

'I have a new frame for that print,' I said, pointing to the picture of Glendale hanging above the bed. We'd found it at a craft fair; it showed the village years ago covered in snow, and I'd always loved it. 'Adam said we should hang it so guests can see it, but I don't think I can part with it and it doesn't fit the art deco vibe of the rest of the artwork I've bought.'

Kathleen yawned. 'Drew didn't sleep at all last night, and now he's napping all morning,' she explained, shaking her head. 'Hamish walked him around the village at six a.m. He goes back to work on Monday, and I'm a bit worried about being on my own with the baby,' she said. I looked at Mum in surprise over the coat I was taking off the hanger. Kathleen never admitted she was nervous.

'Of course you are, but you'll be fine,' Mum reassured her. 'You're such a natural with him, and you're not alone. You have us nearby, like Lorna says. I can always have him, you know that.'

'I still can't believe you had five kids to look after at one point,' I said in wonder.

'Nor me,' Kathleen said. 'Did you ever sleep?'

'Not for about ten years,' Mum said, laughing. 'When I realised I was pregnant again after you three, I dreaded telling your father, and then we found out they were twins! He almost fainted. But he rallied straight away when I started crying in panic. That's the way it's always worked. We've always stayed calm for the other one, so we've got through it all. If I had a bad day, he'd step in, or if he needed to get out, I'd send him to the pub so we both had some breathing space when we needed it.'

Kathleen nodded. 'Hamish is being really helpful like that.'

I folded up a jumper, and hoped I'd find a partner like they both had that I could be a team with. I thought about Finlay then. I was getting butterflies about seeing him the following day. I had no idea how I would feel seeing him, or how he would feel seeing me. My mum talking about my dad made me wonder if Finlay's dad would have handled being a father to five as well. Somehow, I thought not. She had found the right partner to journey through life with. And they'd raised a lovely family together. Mum was right — we were lucky.

'You don't want this, do you?' Kathleen asked, holding up a denim crop top I must have worn as a teenager.

'It's not as bad as this,' I replied, showing them a gold miniskirt. We all laughed and added them to the charity-shop pile.

'When were you going to tell us about the fact you're going to Perth?' Kathleen asked after a moment. I looked at her. 'Adam let it slip.'

I sighed. I had wanted to keep it quiet until I got back as I had no idea what was going to happen. 'Finlay wants to show me something that he wants me to have for Dove House. And he's been making decisions about the future that he wants to tell me about. And his reporter friend, the one who wrote the article for us, mentioned he was lonely so I thought I'd go and see him. Be a friend.'

'I think that's lovely,' Mum said. 'I'm sure he will appreciate you coming.'

'Just don't let him change your plans,' Kathleen said. When I frowned, she elaborated. 'His dad wanted Mum to give up everything for him and run away from Glendale. I just hope his son doesn't ask the same thing of you.'

'He wouldn't,' I said. 'He knows my life is here. But I don't want him to end up with regrets, like Thomas did.'

'He'll find his own way,' Mum said, confidently.

My phone rang and I said hello to Adam, hoping something hadn't gone wrong in my absence. 'What's up?'

'We just had a booking come in. Our first booking!'

'Oh my God,' I said, just as excitedly as Adam. 'When for? Who is it?'

'It's a group of friends who read the article about us and are planning a tour of the Highlands. They've booked all four rooms for the weekend at the end of January.'

'Oh, that's such great news!' Mum and Kathleen were trying to find out what was going on. 'We have our first booking,' I told them.

'Oh, congratulations!' Mum cried as Kathleen gave me a double thumbs up.

'All thanks to that article,' I added, feeling so grateful to Finlay and Jack Smith. 'Let's hope we get even more. We can't not get it all done now.'

'We will,' Adam said fiercely. 'See you in a bit.'

I hung up and carried on packing, feeling much more positive than I had a couple of weeks ago. There was still a great deal to be done downstairs at the house, but now we had our first booking. 'I'm so happy Finlay told his reporter friend about the house.'

'Me too,' Mum said. 'You know, he will probably have found it hard to forget all about Dove House and Glendale. Thomas was right to send him here. I think in time it will make him see he needs to go after his dreams like you're doing. You may have inspired him more than you realise.'

'I hope so. I know how easy it is to let fear and setbacks make you want to give up. I almost did, at Halloween. I had you guys to make sure I didn't. But Finlay doesn't.'

'He has you,' Mum reminded me.

I saw Mum smiling. 'What?'

'I was just thinking that you both want each other's dreams to come true. Perhaps you might find you have similar dreams, that's all.'

Kathleen sighed. 'I told her not to go falling in love with him.'

I would have thrown a cushion at her but my nephew was in her arms so instead I glared at her. 'I can't win. You tell me I should find someone, then you tell me not to.'

'When it comes to love, things work themselves out,' Mum said.

'This isn't love!' I protested, and they exchanged an amused look, so I decided to get on with packing and ignore them both. But Finlay's words came back to me as they seemed to do at the most inconvenient times.

Do you have any idea how badly I've wanted to kiss you since we met?

Chapter Forty-Six

'Well, I think we're done,' I said, surveying my new bedroom with Mum and Adam once we had moved all my things into my new room later in the day. I smiled, relieved that seeing it had chased away some of the sadness I felt at officially leaving my family home. 'I love it.' My bedroom at Dove House was cream with one wallpapered wall of maroon-coloured butter-flies. It looked so pretty, and I was already excited to sleep in there tonight. My new bed looked ornate but the mattress was so comfortable. I had found a maroon duvet cover and a velvet chair to match. I had a dressing table and mirror for the first time. My clothes were in my upcycled second-hand wardrobe and there was a soft fur rug on the pale carpet. Pictures brightened up the walls and on my bedside tables stood two gold lamps. Light streamed in through the windows in the roof. It was the room I'd always wanted.

'It looks lovely,' Mum said. 'Yours does too, Adam.' Adam had finished his earlier and all his things were in there. The two bathrooms up here on the third floor would need decorating at some point, but they were fine for us now.

'I'll be so happy not to be in a sleeping bag tonight,' I said, smiling at the cat bed I'd added to the room for Tabby. I hoped he'd sleep in here, too, tonight. 'It feels more real now,' I said with relief. It had been a great idea to decorate our rooms. Now Dove House felt like our home, and it would be easier to finish the rest of the house now that I had my own space here, and I could see how fabulous this house would be once the decorating was complete. This room looked nothing like it had when we first bought Dove House. 'How's everything downstairs?' I asked Adam.

'The kitchen is done and the new table and chairs are in place. The corridor looks great, so the wallpapering and painting can start at long last. We can decorate our living room, too, now that it's dried out. Things are back on track, I hope.'

'And now we have our first booking, and Kathleen is putting an advert in the local paper, so hopefully that will help. She is also talking to printers about making leaflets to put through doors and to ask shops to have on their counters. It feels like Dove House could actually happen.'

Adam shook his head. 'Of course it will. I never had any doubt.' I raised both eyebrows. 'Well, there was a moment, but you know, I always had faith we could do it.' He looked at my room and nodded. 'You're going to make the bed and breakfast look amazing,' he added.

'I'm going to try,' I replied, pleased. 'And I've found a company who'll supply toiletries at a reduced price, so we'll have lovely hand wash and cream in all the bathrooms.' I knew from the Inn that the finishing touches were so important to get right.

'I'm proud of you both for putting the delays behind you and working on these rooms. I can't wait to see the rest of the house. And the garden, too, when it's all finished. I think things will move really quickly from now on and you'll be open in no time,' Mum said.

It did feel as though we had turned a corner.

'Hear that, sis?' Adam said. He held up his hand and high-fived me, and Mum chuckled at us. 'Right, I need to get ready as I'm going to the Inn to pick up Grace.' He hurried out, but not before I saw his blush.

'He really likes your friend, doesn't he?' Mum asked me.

I smiled. 'It's so sweet. When I was younger, I would have been mortified if one of my friends liked my brother, and vice versa, but now I think it's perfect. If they do become a couple, I'll get to be with my favourite people all the time.'

'Grace seems lovely. And I know Adam would love to settle down. What did I tell you about Dove House? It's special. And it will be for you too,' Mum added, looking at me. 'How are you feeling about seeing Finlay?'

'A bit apprehensive,' I admitted. Part of me hoped our connection was still there, but that also scared me because what would we do about it? Had Finlay missed me? I knew I had missed him, but I also knew that we hadn't known each other for long. Maybe going to his house would end up being the last time I saw him.

'That's only natural. Just trust that whatever happens is the right thing, for both of you.'

'I'll try. How about we treat ourselves to a glass of wine to celebrate a job well done?' I suggested, smiling again at my room.

'I'm not going to argue with that,' Mum agreed. 'Can we watch that new romcom on Netflix too?'

'That is a fabulous idea.'

–

Later, I pulled a pair of pyjamas on, lit my new scented candle which emitted a lovely rose scent throughout my room, and climbed into my beautiful new bed. I heard a small meow and I looked down to see Tabby on the floor looking up at me hopefully. 'I bought you your own bed,' I said as he jumped up and curled up against my legs. 'Or you could just get fur all over my new bedding,' I said, shaking my head. But I reached out to stroke him and he rolled over, purring so I could rub his belly. 'I guess I don't have much choice in the matter, do I?' I smiled; it was nice to have the company. I looked at my bedside table, where I had put Thomas Scott's letter to my mother. Finlay had left it here when he went back to Perth, but I thought I should take it with me in case he wanted it. I wasn't sure why he had left it. Something to remember him by? Because he planned to come back for it? Either way, I thought he should have it. It was his father's, after all.

I picked it up now and read it again while Tabby slept peacefully against me.

> *We will never be parted again. I promise.*
> *I will always love you*

Thomas had been so in love, so sure and certain that he would love my mother forever and that they would have a life together, but fate had other plans. I wondered if, had my mum met him as he'd wanted, they would have been happy. My romantic nature pictured the young lovers meeting up at that hotel and running off and living happily ever after, but my head wasn't so sure. They would have been running away from their homes, their families, their lives, with no plans, no money, nowhere to go. How long before the love would begin to fade under the stress of it all? How long before they started to resent each other?

Thomas's father had thought of my mother at the end, but that was because he'd never had closure. He had always wondered 'what if'. Perhaps his dissatisfaction with his life had made him think it all led back to that moment, to my mum not getting his letter. But there was no way to know if they would have got through all those obstacles and been happy. I think that Thomas would have missed his old life too much.

Folding up the letter, I put it back on my bedside table, turned off my lamp and lay down in bed, Tabby curling himself around me.

I was curious to see that life for myself tomorrow, and find out if Finlay was happy or not. That was all I wanted for him. I didn't want him to regret things as his father had. And I wanted the same for myself too.

Part Four

Chapter Forty-Seven

It was the first of December when I set off from Glendale to Perth to see Finlay. It had been a month since he had left, which didn't seem possible. I thought back to when I had first seen him at the Inn, and how much had changed since then. It had been a crazy time since we'd got the keys to Dove House, but I was hopeful that things were coming together now, that all the hard work was paying off.

It was a two-hour trip to Finlay's house, so I let the satnav guide me and played my favourite music, enjoying the winter sunshine streaming into the car as I drove through Scotland. The house was on the outskirts of the city and down a twisting lane, and when I drove through the gates, I understood why Thomas had never left. The house was huge, not quite as large as Glendale Hall but not far off: an elegant Victorian house with what looked like a lot of land behind it.

Finlay came out of the front door as I parked and I smiled as soon as I saw him. He looked far more relaxed than when I had last seen him as he lifted a hand in greeting. I turned off the engine. He wore his glasses as usual; his hair was slightly longer and he wore jeans and a black shirt and he had stubble across his chin, which I had to admit looked good on him. I was relieved he wasn't wearing a suit. This look was so much more his style.

I adjusted my camel scarf and buttoned up my teddy-bear coat as I climbed out of the car. 'Hello stranger.'

'Lorna,' he said, warmly. We stood facing each other a little awkwardly before he laughed and gave me a kiss on the cheek.

'Thank you for coming. Let me show you inside. Was the journey okay? Do you want a coffee?'

'Yes, to both,' I replied, following him through the door. Inside, the house was warm, a log fire was burning in the hallway, and it was decorated in rich greens and blues although it clearly needed updating. Finlay held out his arms and I slipped out of my coat. Underneath, I had on a cosy jumper and my warmest leggings.

Finlay showed me the drawing room and dining room, then led me into the kitchen to make us coffees. 'It's a lovely house. It's very quiet,' I said, looking out at the landscaped garden from the kitchen.

'Not for much longer. Let's go into the study,' Finlay said. He carried our two coffees and I followed him through to a small, cosy room. This room felt more like Finlay to me with its big armchairs, a wall of bookshelves and another crackling log fire making it nice and toasty.

'I love this room,' I said, sitting down as he handed me a coffee cup.

'It's where I spend most of my time,' he admitted, gesturing to his laptop on the coffee table. 'It was always my favourite. Much less intimidating than the other rooms.'

'Are you here alone then?' I asked. It was a big house to live in by yourself. I assumed there was someone looking after it like at Glendale Hall.

'I am now. My uncle moved in for a bit when I came back from Glendale, and we still had dad's housekeeper and cook and his nurse, but everyone has left.'

'Oh.' I sipped my coffee, dying to know why. 'Your reporter friend mentioned you were rattling around in here.'

'Ah, Jack. Jack's a good friend. I think I've read his article about ten times. Whenever I miss Dove House.' He looked over his mug at me and smiled. I felt my cheeks warm up.

'I'm so grateful to you both. We've had our first booking, and they said the article was the reason they got in touch.'

Finlay broke into a happy smile. 'I'm so pleased. I know they will love their stay.'

'I hope so. It was really kind of you to do that for us.'

He looked at me seriously. 'It was the least I could do after I walked out like I did. I wanted to do something to help if I could. To return the favour. For you helping me.'

'Well, you really didn't need to. I was happy to help you find the letter. But I appreciate you telling Jack about us.'

'How's it all going? Have you managed to fix all the flood damage? Things are on track now?'

I told Finlay about the progress we had made and how Kathleen had stepped in to help. 'So, the next job is painting and decorating, and then we can furnish the house. I've been dreaming about furniture, I swear. Now that our sister is on board, we have been able to invest in some better pieces and really follow the art deco style that I wanted. She was a real lifesaver. And we even managed to get our neighbour onside.'

Finlay laughed when I explained about Mrs Andrews. 'I bet she'll end up loving the place. I'm so glad things are okay now. I can't wait to see how it all turns out.'

It was good to hear him laugh. 'So, what about you? How has it been back here?' I asked, a little fearfully.

He nodded. 'It's been good. There was a lot to sort out. We cleared the house. I went through all my father's things. And my uncle and I talked a lot about what to do here, and with the company. We talked through the letters my father had left for us. And his will. And it was hard. Really hard. But I think once we'd made some decisions, we both felt better. It was a relief to both of us.'

'I'm glad, I really am. I hope you'll be happy here,' I told him, sincerely. He looked lighter and more at peace than when he'd left Glendale, so I could see he felt good about his decision, which was a relief.

'Oh, no, I'm not staying,' he said quickly.

'You're not?' I asked, wondering where he would go.

'I wasn't sure at first what to do when I came back. I thought that my father wanted me to take over everything, but we found letters… he'd been corresponding with a school who wanted to move into this house. And it made me realise that he had been planning for me not staying here. He's left everything to me in his will, and the controlling share of the company, but he said if I didn't want to take over from him, that his brother, my uncle should. My uncle hadn't said anything as he had assumed I wanted it, but when I admitted I didn't, he told me that he was happy to take over. I will keep shares in the company and sit on the board and attend those meetings, but my uncle is the new managing director. And I knew I didn't want to stay here in this house. I've never felt like I belonged here, and the school still want it so I've sold it to them. They are keeping our staff, so I've given them a holiday before I need to move out and the school moves in, as it's going to be a big change.'

I took a minute to take all of that in. 'I'm so pleased you're doing what you want.'

'It's all thanks to you. I told you that. You made me realise my father wanted me to be happy.'

I smiled, pleased. 'Does that mean you're writing again?'

'I am. A story just came to me, and I couldn't get it out of my head. I've been working on it any spare minute I've had.'

'That's so great. What's the story about?' I sipped the coffee, comfy in the armchair across from his. He'd made it just how I liked it. He looked so much better than when he had left Glendale. The month back in Perth had obviously been good for him. I knew how much sorting things out could help you. He was definitely so much more positive, and I was pleased that he thought I'd helped him to feel that way. He hadn't forgotten about me, as I had feared.

'It's about Dove House.'

Chapter Forty-Eight

'Dove House?' I repeated in surprise.

'When I came back to Perth, I couldn't stop thinking about Dove House. It really is an inspiring place. And I thought what a good setting it would be for a novel.'

'I've always thought it was like something out of a book,' I agreed.

'Exactly. When I first saw it, I remembered how Elizabeth Bennet feels when she first sees Pemberley.'

My mouth fell open. 'You've read *Pride and Prejudice*?'

'Of course! I love that book.'

'Me too.' We grinned at one another. I had never met a man who loved that book. I hoped I wasn't about to swoon. 'So, if you set it there, does that mean you're writing about your dad?'

Finlay nodded. 'I thought our parents deserved their story to be told. I'm writing about them as teenagers, falling in love at Dove House, and my dad's family's story. Obviously, I want it to be a novel so I'm not sticking to the facts, but it's inspired by what happened. I thought it would be a fitting tribute to my father... what do you think?'

It sounded like the perfect idea to a hopeless romantic like me. 'I love it. But what will you do about the ending?' I preferred to read stories with happy endings, and Thomas and my mother certainly hadn't had that.

'Leave that one with me,' he said, giving me a wink.

I chuckled. I liked Finlay like this – relaxed and a little bit flirty. It was clear that making plans for the future had really helped him. And he said I had too, which made me happy.

'Come on, let me show you the rest of the house,' Finlay suggested.

'You know I love looking around houses,' I agreed.

We left our coffee cups and Finlay took me round. The decor was very traditional and the house needed updating; Thomas had clearly not been able to keep up with it in his later years, but there were some wonderful pieces. I loved the artwork on the walls and the antiques dotted throughout. Finlay planned to keep some of his father's favourites.

When we reached his father's room, I could see a hint of sadness in his eyes as he looked at the photograph on the dressing table. 'My parents' wedding day,' he said, gesturing to it. I went to his side to look at it. His father had been a very handsome man. Finlay did look like him but when I looked at his mother, I could see he had inherited her eyes and smile. She looked so happy in her white dress; Thomas was standing more formally beside her. 'I hope he did love my mum,' Finlay said then. 'I know not in the way he loved...' he trailed off. I understood.

'I'm sure he did. Perhaps, like you say, not that kind of giddy young love he felt with my mum. And his parents brought them together, so maybe they didn't exactly choose one another, but you were a family. Your father never contacted my mum, and I think that was out of loyalty to your mother.'

Finlay looked at me. 'I think you're right. He was a man of loyalty and family and duty. I suppose at the end, he just wanted to make sure Amelia knew that he had loved her. He was unable to tell your mother while he was alive but he could tell her through that letter. Through me.'

'I can understand that at the end you want to tell everyone who meant something to you that they did,' I agreed. We looked at one another. I looked at his bright blue eyes behind his glasses and I felt the connection between us again. It was a relief that it was still there, but it scared me. Could Finlay feel it too?

Finlay looked as if he was going to say something, but he stepped back. 'Are you hungry? Let's have some lunch.'

–

Light streamed into Finlay's kitchen as he served us the cottage pie he had made.

'I didn't know you could cook,' I said as we tucked into it with soft jazz music playing in the background. 'This is delicious.'

'I had to learn when I left here,' he explained. 'Our cook kept telling me to let her make my meals when I came back. I find cooking relaxing.'

'Me too. I'm going to start trying out some breakfast recipes ready for when we open, offer some special things along with a traditional menu, maybe.'

'Sounds like it will be delicious. So, how are your family? How is Kathleen doing?'

'Oh, I haven't told you!' I launched into the story of how baby Drew came into the world.

'Wow, what a night!' Finlay cried. 'I'm glad they are both doing well after that. And you said Kathleen's going to be part of the bed and breakfast?'

'I like how it's a real family business now.' I looked across the table. 'Oh, Finlay…'

'No, it's fine,' he said, shaking his head. 'I love your family and the way you all support each other… I know none of you take it for granted.'

'We don't,' I said softly.

'I thought of you all a lot,' he admitted, looking down at his bowl. 'I've never had the kind of family you have, Lorna. Like you said, it's really quiet here in comparison.'

'It's never quiet with us around, that's for sure,' I replied, lightly. I knew he didn't want pity; he was just being honest. 'Everyone has been asking about you,' I said, wanting to know that we hadn't forgotten him. 'Everyone wants to know how you are. We've all missed you.'

Finlay looked up and smiled. 'Well, I've missed you too. I kept wanting to get in touch, but I knew I needed to be sure of what I wanted. You were right. It feels good to follow my heart.' He held my gaze. 'I never thought I'd be writing a love story, but here I am.'

'I bet you're good at it,' I said, without thinking. 'I meant… um…' I trailed off, embarrassed, but he just smiled. I had a feeling that Finlay could do romance very well. I cleared my throat. 'I'd love to read some of it. You have to let me see my house on the page!'

It was his turn to look embarrassed then. 'Okay, maybe you can look at the first chapter and tell me what you think. It's when the main character sees Dove House for the first time.' Finlay got up and went out into the study, returning with some pages of printed paper. 'It needs editing, though, I warn you,' he said when he passed it over.

'I could never write, so it'll be impressive to me even if that's the case.' I carried on eating while I read the first chapter and Finlay instantly transported me away from his Perth family home to Dove House in all its art deco glory. He had set it in the Twenties, which I hadn't expected, and the past rose up off the paper and wrapped itself around me. I pictured the main character – a charming, handsome teenager arriving at his new home, his family ready to socialise and make their mark on the small Scottish village they had moved to. And a party was planned for the Saturday night, a party I was sure his future love would be attending. 'I love that you've set it in the Twenties,' I said when I'd read it.

'Your art deco restoration made me think of it,' Finlay said, pleased.

'You describe that feeling when you catch a glimpse of Dove House for the first time so well. The feeling that you've arrived somewhere you're going to belong. I thought that when Mum took me and Adam to look round when we were little, and that feeling never left me.'

'I knew it was somewhere special when I looked around too. I understood why it had never left my father, why he thought about it still. I think part of him always belonged to Dove House. Like you and your family.' He looked wistful.

'You'll find somewhere you belong, too,' I said. 'It's a great start to the book – I'd want to read on if I picked it up off a shelf. You're really talented.'

'I'm glad you like it. I wanted to ask you something about it, but let me show you first why I wanted you to come here. I hope it's something you want to take back home with you…' Finlay got up and held out his hand to me. I took it, enjoying the warmth of his skin against mine. He led us out of the kitchen and into the formal drawing room.

I took in the room. It was like the rest of the grand house – elegant and rich in history and decorated tastefully – but it lacked something. Romance, perhaps? It wasn't a romantic house. Not like Dove House with its spire and windows and art deco features, and its glamorous, distinctive white facade. And it didn't feel like a family home like Glendale Hall with its cosy warmth, filled with the people that loved it fiercely.

I had always felt at home with my family, but I knew that Dove House was where my heart had always been and now that I had my room on the third floor, I felt settled and excited for my future there. And I could see a family with me there too, one day, and Adam with us and his own family. It would be loud and chaotic and fun and full of love.

'Lorna?'

'Sorry, I was miles away,' I said, blushing a little at my fantasy. I really needed to learn that there was a time and a place for my daydreaming.

Finlay walked over to the corner where an old writing desk stood. 'This is what I thought would be perfect for Dove House, if you'd like it. I want it to go somewhere special.' He reached out and ran his fingertips across it. 'This was where my dad wrote the letter to your mum. It seemed fitting for you to have it at Dove House.'

I joined him there and looked at it. It was polished walnut and looked nearly as old as the house itself. 'It's beautiful,' I said, thinking it would fit perfectly by the window in the lounge at Dove House. 'Are you sure? It's crazy to think your father wrote this here.' I took the letter out of my handbag and laid it on the desk. 'A love letter that never got to the woman it was addressed to for thirty-five years.'

'I'm glad I was able to fulfil my promise to my father by finding it,' Finlay said, looking at it. 'I really didn't know what I was going to find in Glendale.' He looked up at me then and I felt the piercing gaze of those blue eyes. 'I'm glad I got to know my father better, as he was back when he knew your mum, and that at the end that's the man he wanted to be. That's what gave me the courage to finally sell this place and to tell everyone I wasn't going to run the company as they thought I might. You were right; I think sending me to Glendale to find this letter was like my father giving me his blessing to do that.'

I smiled. 'He knew your dreams weren't his. He would want you to go after your dreams, I know he would.'

'Thank you. For that and so much more. I have something to ask you, but I'll completely understand if you say no...'

I leaned against the desk. 'Uh-oh,' I replied with a laugh.

He grinned. 'As you've just read, the book I'm writing is going to be a love story. To youth and romance, to the Twenties, to Glendale and most of all to Dove House... it really did inspire me when I was there. I know that technically I can write anywhere, but honestly, I know that being at the house again would really help me with this story. I would love to be able to do some writing there. I wondered what you thought about me coming back to Glendale? I thought I could take a room at the Inn for the Christmas holiday, and maybe I could come to Dove House in the daytime to work on the book?' Finlay looked down at his feet nervously as if he wasn't sure he would be welcome. 'Just for the book,' he added, quietly. 'Nothing more, of course.'

I looked at him. He was worried that I wouldn't want him there. I touched the letter from his father to my mother on the desk. Perhaps it was strange that I felt connected to the son of the man my mother once loved, but I knew that she believed they were never meant to be. Maybe they were meant to lead us to one another. What if we were the ones who had been meant to meet all along? 'Of course you can,' I said. 'When?'

Finlay's face lit up. 'I was thinking in a week or so. The school isn't moving in until early next year, so there is time to sort things. I would love to spend Christmas in Glendale.'

'I'd love you to,' I told him. 'I want you to write this book and be inspired by Dove House and Glendale and be happy and...' I trailed off as he stepped closer.

'You know that I told you I had wanted to kiss you from the first moment we met?' Finlay whispered as he stood just an inch from me, looking down at me like there was no one else in the world but me. In that moment, I felt exactly the same way about him.

'Yes?' I managed to choke out.

'I wondered if you wanted to kiss me too?' he asked, playfully, reaching out with his fingertip to touch my mouth.

I let out a little sigh. I met his gaze and wondered if he could hear my heart beating. I was sure that he must have been able to, it was beating so hard inside my chest. 'I wanted to the moment I walked in,' I admitted in a whisper.

I had barely finished the sentence when Finlay leaned down and closed the gap between us and kissed me. His touch was so gentle that I wondered if I had imagined it but then he kissed me again, and pulled me closer. I wrapped my arms around him as his hand rested on the small of my back. This kiss was deep and full of longing and I never wanted it to end.

With a sigh, Finlay leaned back to look at me. His happy smile reflected my own. 'I left my father's letter with you so you'd know that I left a piece of my heart at Dove House.'

'I didn't know that, but you have a piece of my heart too.'

'I want all of it,' he said, fiercely, kissing me again. I was sure that I could become addicted to his kisses. I held on tightly to him, not wanting for us to be parted again. 'You changed everything when I met you, Lorna.'

'That might be the most romantic thing a man has ever said to me.'

'I'd better think of some more romantic things to tell you then.'

'I can't wait.' I reached for Finlay this time and gave him another kiss.

When we parted, he reached out to tuck a stray hair from my bun behind my ear. 'I'm happy I got to kiss you finally. I missed you as soon as I left, is that crazy?'

I shook my head. 'The house felt different without you.'

'I can't wait to come back.'

I was happy that he was coming back too. He held out his hand and I put mine in his, enjoying the warmth of his skin. 'So, what now?'

'I want to get to know you, Lorna. Everything about you,' he said, squeezing my hand.

'I want that too,' I replied. 'I'm a bit scared,' I blurted out then. There was something about Finlay that made me honest. I wanted to tell him everything, even if it was embarrassing. I wanted to fall in love, I wanted to get married and have a family, to find my happy ending, but it also terrified me.

Finlay smiled. 'Me too. But I'd rather be scared than not try for what I want. I think you feel like that too.'

I nodded. He was right about that. Finlay wanted to be a writer. He was giving up his big house and secure corporate life for that dream. He was following his heart. I had done just the same in taking on Dove House. Our dreams were scary because they were big. 'It's less scary now I know you'll be part of it all. I thought maybe that when you came back here, you would want to go back to your old life, you know?'

'I know you did, but I had walked away from that already. Losing my father made me question so many things and confused things for a bit, but coming back here just cemented it for me. I don't want my father's life. I need to live my own life.'

'You will.' I knew Finlay was a different man to his father. And I wasn't my mother. We could write our own story. And maybe, just maybe, we could do it together.

Chapter Forty-Nine

Arriving back at Dove House felt a little bit like a dream. I couldn't really remember the drive back – it was one of those times when you just find yourself home without remembering how you got there. My mind had been whirring the whole journey about what Finlay had said and how he was coming back to Glendale for Christmas. He'd be staying at Glenmarshes Inn, but he'd be at Dove House every day.

I'd be able to see him every day.

And my heart was happy about that.

I had been trying to focus on our renovations and building our business, but Finlay had come into my life unexpectedly and I knew that if I didn't see where this might lead I would regret it. But I was slightly worried about what Adam was going to say.

Taking a deep breath, I grabbed my bag and left my car, hurrying inside. I remembered Finlay's description of seeing the house, in the book he was writing, and his words echoed around me as I stepped into the hallway. The house was quiet, the builders all having left for the day, and now that everything was in place for painting and decorating, it felt more like home than ever before.

And then the smell of something delicious hit me and I smiled.

'I'm back,' I said, walking into the kitchen where Adam was taking something out of the Aga and Tabby was eating his dinner by the back door. 'Ooh, what have you got?'

'Pizza. There's enough for you too. I also bought a bottle of wine.' He looked at me over his shoulder. 'I thought you might need to talk.'

'Yeah, I guess I do,' I said, surprised at his insight. 'Wine sounds good first, though.' I poured us both a glass and kicked off my shoes. 'It's good to be home. I missed it even though I was only away the day.'

'Well, I have some good news we might want to toast.' Adam came over with the pizza and two plates. Once seated, he lifted his wine glass. 'We are ready to decorate on Monday. The painting team are coming first thing and the wooden floors are being restored next week. It's time to start the finishing stages.'

'That is definitely something to toast!' We clinked glasses and tucked in. Even though I'd had cottage pie for lunch, I'd had a long drive and now the butterflies that had been in my stomach had gone, I was hungry. 'I can't believe we're finally ready for this part. I need to start buying more furniture and decor. I'd better go to the second-hand shop tomorrow. I wonder if Grace and Anna might want to come, make a day of it.'

'That sounds like a good plan, but first of all, how about you tell me what happened today?' Adam said. 'I've been thinking about you all day. You're not too upset, are you?'

'I'm not upset, no. Oh, you thought I'd find Finlay settled in Perth?'

'Did he ask you to move there?' Adam said, alarmed. 'Because I can't do this without you, and—'

'Adam!' I cried out. 'What happened to your optimism?'

'Well, Kathleen said you might have gone and done something stupid like fall in love with Finlay, and then I got worried that maybe you'd give up on all this for love.'

'No way,' I said firmly. 'Never. This is it, for life. I don't want it to sound like a prison sentence,' I added with a chuckle. 'But we're in this together forever, right?'

'Until we're old and grey,' he confirmed. 'Our kids can take over then. So, you won't be seeing Finlay again?'

'Well…' I began. 'I have news on that front. He doesn't want to stay in Perth. He wants to write, like he's always dreamed of doing. His uncle is going to run the family business and he's selling their home, to a local school. And wait until you hear about the book he's started writing…' I told Adam all about it.

'I mean, it makes for a good story, doesn't it? I hope Mum won't mind.'

'Hmm… I'd better check with her,' I agreed. 'But it's going to be a novel. He's setting it in the Twenties and they will be fictional characters, just based on his dad and our mum and their love story. I hope he changes the ending. But anyway, he was so inspired by being here that he wants to write the book and set it at Dove House. And he wants to know if it's okay if he comes here to write it.'

'Oh. Wow. Well, yeah, I think so, don't you? I mean, would he stay here too?'

'No, he's going to stay at Glenmarshes Inn and then write here. He'll probably come in the next week or so.'

'So, Kathleen was right about you falling in love with him then?'

I spluttered on my wine. Honestly, my siblings! 'No!' I cried, but it sounded rather hysterical so I tried again. 'It's early days. I don't know him well at all. We'll see what happens…' I trailed off, my cheeks burning.

'I think it's great he's coming back,' Adam said.

'Really?'

'Yes! He supports you and your dream, he did right from the start, and he knows this is where you want to be, so he's coming to be with you.'

'To write his book,' I amended.

Adam scoffed. 'He could write that anywhere, and you both know that. I'm pleased for you, sis. Finlay seems like a decent bloke, and I think he could make you happy. You already make him happy, that's obvious.'

God, was I going to cry again? I jumped up and kissed him on the cheek. 'You're the best brother a girl could ask for.'

'Shut up,' he muttered, but he blushed and I could see he was pleased. 'Eat your pizza, it's from M&S.'

I went back to my seat. 'It's the best meal I've ever eaten,' I declared. Adam rolled his eyes.

—

I invited Grace and Anna to come shopping with me on Saturday and they were both free in the morning, so we drove off to a second-hand shop I hadn't been to before, an hour away from Glendale. The morning was chilly, with a frost still covering the ground and a bitter wind, but we warmed up in the car with takeaway coffees and the heating on high, and catching up.

'We need all the details,' Grace said from the back as I drove with Anna beside me in the passenger seat. 'Was it really dreamy seeing Finlay again?'

'Now we can tell you that when we saw him at the Inn, we both agreed Beth was right about him looking like Clark Kent,' Anna said with a grin.

'How was the kiss?' Grace added.

'Tell us everything!' Anna agreed.

I laughed. 'Okay, okay!' I'd briefly given them a synopsis in my message of what had happened with Finlay, but now I filled in the gaps. 'You know me, I've been happy being single, but I always wanted that happy ever after. I don't know, seeing Finlay made me think that maybe I could have found my person. And it's scary, but exciting! I can't wait for him to come back to Glendale and see what happens. Really get to know one another.'

'Get to know one another.' Anna raised her eyebrows as we giggled. 'I get it. Commitment scares the hell out of me. But when you know, you know. I think I knew Cameron was going to change everything when I first met him. I bet you felt the same with Finlay. And what about you, Grace? How are things with Adam? Do you feel that way too?'

Grace smiled. 'I think I might feel that way too!' She blushed. 'God, don't tell him, Lorna, I mean, he hasn't said how he feels, and...'

'It's okay,' I reassured her. 'I would never say anything you didn't want me to. Adam is so laid-back, he'll tell you how he feels when he realises he hasn't. But he probably thinks you already know, knowing my brother. I hope everything works out for all of us.'

'Speaking of. I have decided to go for it. You're looking at the new full-time chef at Glenmarshes Inn.' We both cheered Anna and she laughed. 'Thanks. You guys gave me the confidence to say yes. Oh, and me and Grace can keep an eye on Finlay while he's staying there, make sure he's good enough for you.'

'I don't think he knows what he's let himself in for,' I replied, but it was sweet of her to look out for me.

'And,' Anna continued, 'I'm moving into the cabin at Hilltop with Cameron. Which I am freaked out about, but I'm trying to keep calm...'

'Does that mean we might hear wedding bells soon?' Grace asked her with a teasing smile.

Anna shook her head firmly. 'I have never wanted to get married. It has nothing to do with how I feel about Cameron, he knows that and he's fine with it. We are in love and we are happy, and that will always be enough.'

'I think that's wonderful,' Grace said.

'I love your independent spirit,' I agreed. She had been a breath of fresh air since she arrived in Glendale.

Anna grinned at us. 'I will be sad to leave the Hall, though. Beth has started getting the Christmas trail ready. I can't wait to see what she does this year.'

'It's always so magical,' I agreed. I exhaled. 'What a crazy couple of months. So many changes on the way. Do you need help moving out, Anna?'

'I think I'll be fine, but Beth wants to throw me goodbye drinks, so you definitely both have to come to that. Glendale

Hall was like my sanctuary – I might actually cry and you know me, I don't cry.'

'It'll always be there for you,' I reassured her. 'And it's not like you won't see any of them again. You're part of the family now.' We pulled up to the shop then. 'I felt so strange leaving home, but I knew it was time for the next chapter. It's time for you now.'

Anna nodded. 'You're right. And I'm so excited about it.' She looked back at Grace. 'It'll be your turn in the New Year, I bet. Come on then, let's spend Lorna's money.'

'I don't need asking twice!' Grace jumped out as I shook my head at them, but I was pleased that my friends were happy. And I was excited for the rest of the month too – finishing the house and Finlay coming back. And then it would be time for Christmas, which always brought the promise of magic with it.

Chapter Fifty

The weather took a decidedly wintry turn the following week, with gentle snowflakes falling as Adam and I supervised the painting and decorating. The cold made me want to huddle in Dove House but I had to furnish it, so I went out second-hand furniture-shopping often with Mum or Kathleen and the baby or all of them, and then spent my evenings in, sourcing things online, making sure I kept a careful track of my spending. We certainly didn't want to creep towards going over the new budget. I had even worked out how to use Adam's spreadsheet.

The walls were being painted, curtains and blinds were being hung, and slowly things began to take shape.

And then as Christmas approached, Finlay arrived. He'd checked into the Inn and then came on to Dove House with his father's writing desk and his laptop. He found us painting what was going to be our own living room, off the kitchen. 'Wow, this place has come on so much since I was last here,' he said, looking around in wonder.

'It's good to see you,' Adam said, dropping his brush and giving Finlay a welcome handshake.

'Can you give me a hand with the desk?' he asked Adam, and then turned to me. 'Where do you want it, Lorna?'

'I'll come too,' I said, my cheeks turning a little pink at seeing him again. I wasn't sure if Finlay was going to kiss me, but Adam steered him out before he even had a chance. I dropped my brush and followed them out into the driveway where the desk was crammed into Finlay's car.

'It's a lovely piece,' Adam said when Finlay had opened the car. He'd managed to prop it across the boot and the back seat, and together they manoeuvred it out and carried it into the lounge where I pointed to the corner by the window. The room was painted now, and we were going to add panelling to the walls next.

'It fits perfectly there,' I said as they jostled it into position. It felt right to have something of Finlay's family in the house again, and I saw the smile on Finlay's face and knew that he felt the same.

'This room is really taking shape,' Adam said. 'Thanks, Finlay. Are you all settled at the Inn?'

'I am. And I've booked in there for dinner tonight. I wondered if you wanted to join me, Lorna? Your friend is the chef, isn't she?'

'Anna,' I confirmed with a nod. I could feel my cheeks were flushed again – how embarrassing. 'I'd love to. Are you going to do some writing here, today?'

'If that's okay? I thought maybe I'd set up in the hall out of the way. I want to have a walk around the garden, too, get the feel of it out there.'

'Whatever you need,' Adam said, walking back to the living room to carry on painting.

I looked at Finlay. 'We'll go back to the Inn later then?'

He smiled. 'Perfect. You have a bit…' He reached out and wiped a speck of paint off my nose, then he walked off out into the hallway. I shook my head; he had somehow made that feel incredibly sexy. I coughed and joined my brother, feeling excited at the thought of our first official date tonight.

Thank goodness painting didn't require too much brain-power, as I found myself daydreaming as I worked.

We kept painting until the light dimmed, which was happening earlier and earlier, and then we had to admit defeat.

'I need a shower,' I declared, looking down at myself, plastered with paint. 'We've almost done the first coat,' I said, surveying the room.

273

'It's looking great. You'd better get ready for your date,' Adam said with a smirk.

'You're not seeing Grace tonight?' I fired back with a raised eyebrow.

'Not tonight,' he replied, not rising to my bait. 'Just have fun, sis,' he added. 'You deserve it.'

'Thanks, Adam.'

I hurried upstairs to get ready, having a hot shower as my shoulder ached from painting, and then I got changed in my room, pulling on a black wool dress. It was strange to think this would be my first actual date with Finlay. I knew it was silly to be nervous, but I was, a little bit. I really liked this man, and he had made a pretty big move coming back to Glendale. Standing in front of the mirror after I'd done my make-up, I pulled on my coat and a pair of boots as it was freezing, and added some nude lipstick. Taking a calming breath, I went downstairs to find Finlay in the hallway on a fold-up chair, his laptop open, writing away. I paused, taking it in. He really looked like a writer with his focused expression, his glasses, and his shirtsleeves rolled up. It was a good look on him.

'Oh, hi,' he said, noticing me then. He closed the laptop. 'Sorry, I was miles away... You look lovely. Are you ready?'

'I am, thank you. So, writing is going well then?' I asked as he gathered his things and slipped into his dark grey coat.

'I think it is. I already feel more inspired just being here. Thinking about all the people who have lived in this house and what happened to them. If only the walls could talk.'

'I know, I would love to know everyone's stories.'

'Right then, let's go.' Finlay placed a hand on the small of my back as I walked towards the door. He opened it for me and I called out goodbye to Adam, before following Finlay out to his car.

It was dark outside now and the clear, cold sky was dotted with thousands of sparkling stars, and in the middle was a brilliant crescent moon shining down on us. 'I can feel snow in the air,' I said as Finlay opened the car door for me and I climbed in.

'You can feel snow?' His eyes twinkled as he joined me on the driver's side.

'Definitely. I love snow. It reminds me of being a kid, waking up on Christmas morning and rushing to my window to see if it was a white Christmas or not.'

'Actually, I remember doing that too,' he admitted as we set off for Glenmarshes. Now that Christmas was approaching, decorations were starting to pop up in the High Street. The shops always went all out, inspired by Beth and her Christmas trail at Glendale Hall, and there was always a large tree that was lit up in the middle of the village.

'I can't wait to decorate the bed and breakfast,' I said. 'I'm not sure if we can this year, as everything is still being finished off but next year, I'm going to go all out. I love the festive season, don't you?'

'Well, my family have never really been that big on Christmas. My father wasn't one for decorating or dressing up as Santa or anything. We always had a fantastic Christmas dinner, but we never had lots of family round.'

'Well, this year you will,' I said, without thinking. 'My family go big at Christmas, I'll warn you now.'

Finlay looked across at me. 'You'd really want me to be part of it?'

'Oh, I mean, of course. Only if you want to, though,' I babbled, unsure if he would or not. Was it strange that I was automatically thinking he would be part of things this year?

'I'd love that,' he replied, reassuring me. I leaned back in my seat and smiled.

'Maybe we can get a tree for the house. We always get a real tree in my family, so maybe we can get one for Dove House at the same time. Honestly, December is flying past. It's almost time for the trail at the Hall.' I hoped Finlay might want to come and see it with me. It was always one of my most looked forward to nights of the year – going to Glendale Hall and walking the trail with a hot chocolate, wrapped up in lots of layers, seeing everyone I loved there too. 'You were right to come at this time of year. You're going to have so much to include in your book. It really is my favourite season – well, apart from autumn. Ooh, I don't know – autumn or Christmas? I can't decide which I love the best.'

Finlay chuckled. 'I never thought about having a favourite season before.'

'I love the leaves changing in autumn, the promise of new beginnings, but the pretty lights and snow and cosy nights in of Christmas are so special too. You wait – I think you might have a favourite season after your stay in Glendale.'

Finlay looked across at me. 'I can't wait to find out,' he replied softly.

Chapter Fifty-One

We approached Glenmarshes Inn and I sat up in my seat to look out of the window. The Inn was decorated for Christmas, and the approach to my former place of employment was a beautiful one. The whole front of the house twinkled with fairy lights. Finlay parked the car and we got out and walked through the main door into the lobby, where a traditional huge artificial tree, decorated in red and gold, sparkled in welcome. I was glad I was getting to see it again this year; I would have missed it otherwise.

We walked through to the restaurant where a pianist was playing soft Christmas carols and candles flickered on each table. I smiled and waved to the staff I knew as we were shown to our table. It was strange to be a paying customer now, but I definitely preferred it. 'What do you think of the Inn?' I asked when we were left with menus to look at.

'I think it's a shame the inside doesn't match the outside. I expected it to be cosy and homely, but I'm glad the restaurant has that vibe. And I hear the food is delicious.'

'With Anna as the chef now, it will be,' I said. 'The Inn used to be exactly how you described. I think when they changed it after the chain took over was when I fell out of love with it.'

'That's why I think Dove House is going to do well. You know what your guests will want.'

'I hope so. Wow, Anna has really changed the menu,' I said, glancing over it. There were still the traditional gastropub offerings, but a sprinkle of her Italian cooking was mixed in. 'I can't wait to try the new dishes.'

We ordered our food and a bottle of wine and I texted Anna to tell her we were here, so hopefully she might have a moment to say hello during our meal.

'I feel as if I did everything backwards,' Finlay said once we were alone with our drinks.

'What do you mean?'

'I should have taken you out sooner,' he replied. He reached out and touched my hand on the table. 'I was just so focused on my father when I came to Glendale, and meeting you was so unexpected, I didn't really know what to do.'

'It was confusing for both of us,' I reassured him. 'And you're still grieving. I understand if this is all too much, too soon. As we said, let's just see what happens. We don't need to rush or label anything. I'm just happy that you're here.'

'Me too.' He smiled across at me. 'Tell me about your family. You all seem so close and part of each other's lives. As an only child, I can't really imagine it.'

'We are close. I mean, we get on each other's nerves at times, but mainly we do get on really well. My mum and dad knew they'd have more than one child but they didn't expect the twins to come along. Kathleen is the eldest and the most sensible of us all: she's practical, a real planner and has always wanted a family of her own. Adam is the optimist. He would always be there for you if you needed him, and I guess we're the most similar in that we're both dreamers... and the twins are boisterous and fun and a real handful most of the time,' I said, laughing. 'Mum is our rock. She holds it all together and she can handle anything. She gives the best advice, too... and my dad is quiet and a thinker. He doesn't say much but when he does, he'll blow your mind. He's such a hard worker, and he cares about us all. They're a real partnership.' I looked at Finlay. 'Oh. I didn't mean to be insensitive...'

He shook his head. 'You weren't. I think we both know my dad and your mum wanted different things from life, and were too different maybe to ever work. I know my dad could never have coped with five kids! I can't even imagine it. I love it that you have this family behind you. I can see what a support they are.'

'They really are. They've backed me and Adam all along. And Kathleen has been amazing. We couldn't have done it without her. What about your uncle? You're not close to him?'

'He's very similar to my father, but I've got to know him better these past few weeks and I think we are going to spend more time together. He has been really supportive.'

The waiter brought our starters over then, and we both cooed at the attractive, delicious-smelling food on our plates.

'What were you like when you were young?' I asked curiously as I started to eat my bruschetta and Finlay tucked into his truffle pasta.

'Quiet,' Finlay said. 'Studious. I loved school and I studied like mad. I was a real bookworm, and I suppose I didn't have loads of friends. I kept to myself a lot and maybe I still do, if I'm honest.'

I nodded. I sensed that about him. Maybe that's why we were drawn to one another. Opposites attracting? But there were similarities too. Our big dreams, our hopes for the future, the determination to forge our own path, and that romantic streak we both had. 'It'll be hard to keep that up in Glendale,' I warned him. 'It's a real community – we help each other out and get involved in each other's lives.'

'I love that,' he replied. 'And you know your optimism is already rubbing off on me.'

I laughed. 'Well, I'm glad. We all need to be more positive. Life can be so draining if we let it. I want to see the best in it if I possibly can. Anna!' I finished, beaming as my friend slipped out of the kitchen and came over to our table. 'This is Finlay,' I said, feeling a little bit shy as I introduced them officially for the first time. After they had shaken hands, Anna dropped me a wink when he couldn't see. I felt myself flush and hoped neither of them would notice. I gestured to our empty plates. 'The starters were amazing. I love that you're doing Italian food here now.'

'It really was delicious,' Finlay agreed.

Anna smiled warmly. 'Well, I'm glad you enjoyed it. Your mains are almost ready, so I thought I'd duck out to say hello. It's good to meet you, Finlay. I hope you enjoy your stay at the Inn.'

'I think I will,' he replied, looking over at me.

I couldn't help but smile. 'And how about you? How are you feeling about your move? Anna is leaving Glendale Hall to work here full-time, and live at Hilltop Farm with her boyfriend,' I quickly explained to Finlay.

'Excited. But sad to be leaving. I do love that house and everyone there. Beth is panicking, although she's pretending to me that she isn't,' Anna said with a sigh. 'I wish I knew someone who could take over as housekeeper. It really is a brilliant job for someone.'

'Beth understands,' I said to Anna. 'She wants you to go after your dreams.'

Anna nodded. 'Oh, you must both come over on Friday night! We're mixing the trail switch-on with my goodbye drinks. Everyone will be there! Okay, I'd better go otherwise no one will have anything to eat tonight. Enjoy the rest of your meal!' Anna dashed off again, always a bundle of energy.

'The trail switch-on?' Finlay enquired when we were alone again.

'The Christmas trail I told you about at Glendale Hall. There's always a grand switch-on of the lights, and it sounds like a goodbye party for Anna is happening at the same time. It should be a fun night. It's so magical.'

'I can't wait to see it,' he replied. Our main courses arrived and we tucked in eagerly. The whole meal was delicious. We ended up sharing a dessert as we were so full, but wanted to try Anna's chocolate speciality, and then we had two coffees to finish the meal off.

'Wow, that was amazing,' I said as we sipped them, the candle in the centre of the table almost burnt down completely as we'd savoured our meal for so long. I was having a really lovely time and hoped Finlay was too.

'Anna is a brilliant chef. I will be spoilt living here, for sure,' he replied. 'It's been a lovely evening.'

'It has,' I agreed, happily. 'Will you come back to write tomorrow?'

'If that's okay? I was thinking, shall I speak to your mum about my book? I wouldn't want to do anything she didn't approve of.'

I was touched that he had thought of her. 'I haven't said anything to her about it. I think she would appreciate that. We're going there for Sunday lunch after church — it's always the more the merrier,' I said.

'Count me in,' he agreed instantly. 'Although I haven't been to church since I was a child.'

'Oh, I didn't mean...'

'If it's important to you, it's important to me.' He took my hand in his.

'Brodie is unlike any minister you've met,' I promised him, smiling at our entwined hands. 'Be careful though, I might get used to you being here.'

'I hope so.' He picked up my hand and kissed it. 'I've never been so sure before in my life that this is where I'm meant to be.'

I smiled. It was exactly how I felt in that moment too.

Chapter Fifty-Two

It was the most enjoyable week we'd had since we'd received the keys to Dove House. The house was full of tradespeople working on it, and Adam was finishing the painting in our living room while I ran here, there and everywhere to buy the final pieces of furniture and decor. In the background, Finlay was working on his novel and giving us a helping hand if we needed him to. Every night, we'd eat together either with Adam at the house or I'd go back to the Inn with Finlay and we'd enjoy another tasty meal cooked by Anna. It felt as if we had been doing this forever somehow. I don't think I'd ever met a man I found it so easy to be with before. I was still so focused on the house, but Finlay didn't hold me back at all; if anything, he spurred me on.

'Grace and I wondered if you two wanted to eat with us and go to the trail and Anna's leaving drinks together on Friday?' Adam asked me later in the week, as we sanded down a table we'd found on eBay that we were going to paint for the lounge.

'I feel like I've been really restrained with you two, but I need the gossip. Is it serious?' I asked, peering over the table to where my brother was. Adam was always whistling, and he and Grace were forever on the phone or messaging or seeing one another.

Adam stopped sanding to look at me. 'I love her,' he said simply. 'I told her at the weekend and she said she loves me. I think I might have found my person, Lorna.'

'Oh, that's so lovely,' I gasped. 'I'm so happy for you both. Two of my favourite people...' I trailed off, feeling like I might cry. Adam gave me a warning look so I shook it off. 'Finlay and I will definitely come with you.'

'Good, I'm glad. Grace wasn't sure if you'd want to. Double dating feels like something we did as teenagers, but I think it will be fun.' He started sanding again. 'I like Finlay, you know. I like you two together. You complement each other, I think.'

'I think so too,' I agreed with a smile. 'Wait. Is Grace going to move in here?' I asked, my voice rising with excitement. How cool would it be to live with one of my best friends? 'Ooh, does she want to work for the B & B?'

Adam grinned. 'Slow down! No, she's going to set up an events company. And she wants to do that first. Then maybe we will... there's no rush for us.'

I smiled. They were both easy-going people. 'Well, I think that's great. I know you haven't had it easy when it comes to love... Me neither, let's face it. So this is perfect.'

'It's funny, isn't it? I thought I was in love before, but now I know I wasn't at all.'

I was starting to feel the same way myself. When I thought about my ex, Mark, I realised we hadn't been what I thought we were at all. What my mum said about love working out for the best made sense now. I hadn't been meant to be with him. But with Finlay...

I told myself to stop daydreaming and focus on the task in hand.

'What are you two having a deep chat about?' Finlay poked his head round the door. He was smiling, but I wondered what he would think if he had known what we'd been talking about.

'The Glendale Christmas trail,' Adam replied. 'We're double dating like we're in an American teen movie. What's that one you've seen a million times?'

'*Clueless*,' I said promptly.

'*Clueless* is a classic,' Finlay agreed.

'Yes!' I cried. 'See?' I said to Adam, who rolled his eyes at my movie choices all the time. I looked over my shoulder and smiled at Finlay. Good taste in films was very important in the person you were dating, after all.

'Anyway, I came to tell you,' Finlay said, remembering his reason for coming in. 'Glen wanted you to see – the dining room is all painted.'

'Ooh!' I jumped up and Adam hurried after me. The three of us went into the dining room and stood looking at the freshly painted walls. 'It looks perfect,' I declared. 'Once the wood flooring is down and the table is in...'

'The carpets are all fitted on the second floor,' Glen called out from behind us.

We went out again and upstairs to the guest floor where the smell of new carpets greeted us. We padded back and forth on them and it was amazing how cosy and comfortable they made the rooms. They were almost ready as bedrooms for people to sleep in. All we needed was the furniture and beds. It was all feeling rather real now.

'We're getting there,' Glen said, cheerfully.

'You've done such a great job,' I told him.

'I love it so far,' Adam agreed.

I looked at Finlay, who was standing in one of the rooms looking rather wistful. Glen and Adam went out talking, but I stayed and put a hand on his shoulder. 'Are you okay?'

'This was his room,' Finlay explained. 'My dad's room. My uncle told me.'

I looked around and tried to picture Finlay's father in here as a teenager. I wondered if he'd ever have guessed his son would be here one day in this very room, writing his story for the world to read. Somehow I thought maybe he had hoped for it – sending Finlay here as his last wish because he knew this house could inspire his son as it had once inspired him. Maybe he even thought it might bring love into his life like it had for him. 'He was happy here. It would make him happy to know that you are,' I said. 'I mean, I hope you are.'

'I'm loving writing this story. And being here is helping so much, not just to write it but I guess to get to know my father and feel closer to him.' He turned to me. 'And you know that I love spending time with you...' He leaned down and kissed me gently.

'I'm glad you're here,' I replied when he pulled away. I explained then about Adam's suggestion. 'What do you think?'

'I'm excited to see this trail I've heard so much about. I'm kind of nervous to get to know all your friends and family – I hope they like me. I hope your mum is okay with this... with us,' he added, biting his lip, which was a sexy move.

'She knows you're here, and she's happy you're back.' I hadn't really told her that we were seeing each other, but I think she guessed he wasn't only here to write. But this weekend felt like a bit of an official statement, so I knew what he meant. She didn't know what his book was about yet. Finlay had wanted to talk to her about it himself. 'It'll be okay,' I reassured him, although I was a little nervous myself. I wanted everyone to like him, and for everyone to get on so Finlay would want to stay. I leaned against his chest and he wrapped his arms around me. Finlay holding me felt just right. 'I'll be right there with you.'

He held me tighter and I lost track of how long we stood there with one another.

Chapter Fifty-Three

Friday arrived, and Finlay stayed at the Inn to write while Adam and I checked the work that had been done over the week. Real progress had been made, and all the painting would be completed the next week. Then we could put the furniture and decor in place. Finally, the finishing line was in sight. We were in good spirits as we drove to Glenmarshes Inn to meet Finlay and Grace. It was a chilly night, but dry, and looking good for the opening of the Glendale Hall Christmas trail.

'I was thinking – we have Mrs Andrews' sister coming for Hogmanay as a practice-run weekend but it would be useful to have a few more guests,' I said as we drove. 'Then we can ask them to write reviews and tell us if we need to change anything before we open properly in January.'

'It would make me feel better to really know that we have everything in place. Who else did you have in mind?'

'I think we should invite Betty and her daughter. She was so lovely letting us have the house, and I did say in my letter that we wanted her to come and stay – which means she'll be our first guest,' I suggested as the Inn came into view with its lovely twinkling lights.

'I think she'd love that. It's a great idea.'

'It feels so surreal that people have actually booked in to come and stay with us,' I said. It had been something we had talked about for so many years, and now we'd be opening up soon. 'I really hope people like it.'

'We'll do our best to make people feel at home, won't we? Right…' Adam parked the car and turned off the engine. 'Ready?'

I smiled. I was looking forward to the night. 'Let's go.' We walked into the Inn and towards the restaurant, where Finlay and Grace were waiting for us. Grace had been working but had changed into a skirt and blouse with a coat over her arm for later, and Finlay was in black jeans and a black shirt. Adam gave Grace a big hug when he saw her and Finlay leaned in to kiss me on the cheek. I breathed in the smell of his aftershave and enjoyed the feel of his arm on the small of my back. 'We missed you at the house today,' I said.

'It was strange not being there,' he replied. 'You look gorgeous,' he added, taking in my cream jumper and brown trousers. 'Anna said she made sure the best table was saved for us.' We went inside, and saw that Anna had reserved us the table by the window, a round one with lit candles on it and a pretty festive centrepiece with holly and pine cones. She wasn't working tonight, of course – the new manager had let her have tonight off instead of her usual Wednesday as it was a special celebration at Glendale.

'It looks so festive,' I said, smiling at the restaurant. In the corner stood the Christmas tree and the pianist was playing again tonight.

'Anna is doing a Christmas menu too,' Grace added as we all sat down. 'She wants our feedback on it, so basically we all have to order the three courses,' she added with a chuckle.

'Fine with me,' Finlay replied affably. The menu did look delicious – pâté to start, then a turkey dinner followed by Christmas pudding, so we all ordered it and glasses of wine for me and Grace and a beer for Finlay. Adam had a Coke, as he was going to drive us to the Hall after the meal.

'We were thinking we'd invite guests to stay for free at the bed and breakfast when we open, so they can review us, basically,' I told Grace and Finlay after our drinks had arrived.

'We already have our neighbour Mrs Andrews' sister booked in, and I wanted to ask Betty, who sold us Dove House. I think it would be lovely for her to see what we've done and treat her to a stay to thank her for selling us the house.'

'That's a great idea. If you need anyone else, I bet my uncle and his wife would come – I know he'd love to see his old home again,' Finlay suggested.

I looked at Adam, who nodded. 'That would be perfect. I know I'll be far less stressed if we've had people help us make sure we've got everything right,' I told Finlay. 'It'll be over New Year, if everything else goes smoothly.' I held up crossed fingers.

'It will,' Adam said, confidently. 'Next Christmas, we'll be doing all this.' He gestured to the decor around us.

'And hopefully I won't be here,' Grace added in a low voice in case any staff overheard her. 'I've decided to hand in my notice before I break for Christmas. I want to start working on my events business in the new year. A fresh start, and all that. You guys have inspired me,' she said to us. 'And you, Finlay, and Anna as well. I need to try to do what I've always wanted, like you're all doing.'

'You should talk to Beth tonight,' I suggested. 'She does weddings in the summer at the Hall and organises all the events there.'

'That's a good idea. I wonder if she needs help,' Grace mused.

'I think she always needs help, from what Anna says. She's always taking on too much.'

Our starters arrived and we tucked in eagerly. As always when it came to Anna's food, it was delicious and got us excited for Christmas dinner. We enjoyed our meal. The four of us got on easily. Grace and Adam seemed so at ease with one another. I wasn't quite there with Finlay; we kept looking at one another and smiling, and halfway through the meal his leg brushed against mine and I felt warmth travel up my body. There seemed to be electricity in the air between us. I wondered if he could feel it too.

'I can't wait to see this famous trail,' Finlay said as we ate our Christmas pudding and had coffee.

'It's pretty magical and romantic,' Grace said. She glanced at my brother. 'There have been a lot of marriage proposals there. Right, Lorna?'

I chuckled. 'Drew proposed to Beth and Heather proposed to Rory there,' I confirmed. 'It definitely is magical.' I glanced at Finlay, who was looking over at me. I bit my lip. 'We should get going in a minute.' We finished our meal and headed to Adam's car. It was colder now, but the sky was still clear, perfect for the trail, and I was glad I had my warm coat to wear over my outfit.

Finlay sat with me in the back and took my hand in his. I couldn't see his face in the dimly lit car as we drove back to Glendale, but I hoped he was smiling like I was. We reached Glendale Hall, and we had to park down the road as so many people were arriving there for the opening of the trail. The trail was really popular, and everyone in the village liked to come to the launch and be the first people to see it for the year. And Anna's leaving party had encouraged even more villagers to come tonight.

We walked into the Hall, which was a hive of activity. In the kitchen we found Anna and all the family with a table laden with drinks and Christmas baked goods that looked like Emily's creations. People had spilled outside into the garden with their drinks, chatting and waiting for the festivities to begin.

'There you are!' Anna cried when she saw us, rushing over. 'How crazy is this? I've never seen the Hall so crowded.'

'My cat is hiding in my room,' Izzy said as she squeezed past us. 'Mum!' she called out, searching for Beth, who was nowhere to be seen.

'I've had too much mulled wine already,' Anna continued, gesturing for us to pick up cups of it from the table. 'How was the Christmas menu at the Inn? I was stressed you'd be eating it without me there.'

'Delicious,' I told her, to agreement from the others. 'We're so full. How is the move going?'

'Everything is packed and boxed up. We're taking it all over in the morning,' Anna said as Cameron appeared beside her and wrapped an arm around her waist. She grinned up at him. 'This one has complained more than once that I've got too much stuff. I told him it's his fault; I used to travel light with two suitcases but now I'm all settled in Glendale, I keep buying things.'

'I can't grumble about that,' Cameron said, pulling her closer. 'But four leather jackets are too much for anyone.'

Anna laughed. 'Come on, let's go outside and see what time we're starting the trail.' She looked around the kitchen a little wistfully. 'I'll really miss cooking in here.'

'The cabin at Hilltop has a tiny kitchen compared to this one,' I explained to Finlay as we followed them outside.

'I would say most kitchens are – this place is huge,' Finlay replied, taking my hand in his again as we stepped into the gorgeous grounds of the Hall.

'Does it remind you of your house in Perth?'

'A little bit, but we never had this many people there even when my mother was alive,' Finlay said, his eyes widening at the whole of Glendale assembling in the garden. 'Is it always like this?'

'For the trail, yes,' I confirmed. 'I told you that you'd have a favourite season after this. Let's go to the front.' I pulled him along and we reached the front of the group. Beth gestured for everyone to walk across to the start of the trail so we joined Adam, Grace, Anna and Cameron and walked over to the banner that hung between two trees with a light-up Santa on one side and a snowman on the other. I had walked this trail for a few years now, but I was even more excited than usual as this was the first time I'd be walking it holding the hand of a man that I was fast falling for.

Chapter Fifty-Four

'Here we are again,' Beth said as she called for quiet. She stood by the banner with everyone from the Hall, who I knew all pitched in each Christmas to make the trail come together for her. 'This is our favourite time of the year, and it's so lovely to see so many of you here to celebrate it with us. I really hope you enjoy this year's trail and that it brings you as much joy as it does us! Izzy...' She gestured to her daughter, who walked over to the ribbon tied between the two trees. Her friend Luke was with her and together they cut the ribbon with a large pair of scissors to a big cheer from the crowd.

'Glendale really is unique,' Finlay said, smiling at me as everyone started walking through the trees to see the trail.

'It really is,' I agreed as we followed the others, just as a snowflake danced in front of my eyes. I looked up. 'I knew it...' I said softly.

Finlay looked up too. 'Let me guess... it's even more magical in the snow,' he said, his eyes twinkling.

'You're learning,' I replied with a laugh. We walked along, looking at the spectacular fairy lights that lined the way. There was a group of light-up reindeer and stars hanging from wire that they had suspended above the trail so that when you looked up it felt like the sky was right above your head. The snowflakes were gentle and feather-like as Finlay and I walked towards the grotto at the end, which had a giant sleigh inside and was decorated like Santa's workshop.

'Ho, ho, ho!' a voice cried, and the crowd parted as Santa himself walked through to go and sit in the sleigh. I recognised the husband of Beth's mother – John – behind the white beard. We left the kids to enjoy it and carried on walking past more fairy lights until we came to a stop like everyone else had, and looked in amazement at what was there.

'Beth,' I said, shaking my head, as I took in an actual ice rink in the middle of the garden. 'She has to top it every year.' We walked to the edge and watched as two staff members started handing out ice skates to anyone who wanted a go. In the middle of the rink was a giant Christmas tree covered in twinkling lights. We leaned against the edge and watched people step onto the ice. 'This is like a fairy tale,' I said in wonder.

'I understand now what you meant about this being magical,' Finlay agreed. He moved closer so our arms were touching. 'I think you're right. This might be becoming my favourite season.'

'Oh my God,' Grace said behind us.

'How is this even possible?' I asked Anna, who had joined us.

'It's a mobile synthetic ice rink, but how good does it look? Beth convinced a few local businesses to help out with the cost to hire it for two weeks,' she replied, pointing to the advertising next to the rink. 'Even comes with staff and skates for people. How cool?'

'It's brilliant,' I replied, still unable to believe Glendale Hall had its own ice rink.

'Who's coming on the ice then?' Anna asked us.

'Come on.' To my surprise, Finlay grabbed my hand and tugged me after Anna, who was pulling Cameron over.

'What do you think?' Beth asked at the edge of the rink. She had a huge smile on her face. She lived for things like this.

'You've outdone yourself,' I replied. 'Beth, this is my friend Grace. I think you met briefly at the Halloween party... she is the amazing events manager at Glenmarshes Inn, and she's looking to start up on her own.'

Beth's head turned happily in Grace's direction. 'We need to talk! Can you come round next week?'

I left them arranging a meeting and took Finlay's hand as we stepped out onto the ice. It was a decent-sized rink, and everyone was gleeful that Glendale now had one. 'I haven't done this since I was a kid,' I admitted as I moved gingerly. 'I might well be Bambi on ice,' I warned Finlay.

He helped me easily, looking immediately at home. 'I had lessons growing up,' he explained to my enquiring look. 'I had lessons in pretty much everything. Until I put my foot down and was allowed to spend most of my time reading, but I enjoyed ice skating and playing the piano so I've sort of kept them up through the years. Here,' he said, taking my hand. We started skating and Finlay supported me easily as we circled the rink, which was a good size even with everyone clamouring to try it. Snowflakes fluttered around us. It really was a pretty perfect moment, as if it had been lifted from a Christmas card.

'This is already the best Christmas,' Finlay said as we leaned against the side for a minute to catch our breath. 'Thank you. For this. For everything.'

'It's lovely to have someone to share it all with,' I replied. I reached up and kissed him. 'Want to come back to Dove House?' I asked. 'While everyone else is here?'

Finlay looked at me and caught my meaning. 'I'd love to.' We left the rink and slipped off out of the garden and started walking back to the village. It was chilly, but we were well wrapped up and we strolled, happily taking in the quiet snowy night.

'My dad talked about Christmas in Glendale,' Finlay said suddenly, after a minute of silence. 'He remembered it fondly. He said they'd had a large tree at Dove House and that they threw a Christmas Eve party with half the village attending.'

'It sounds wonderful. We should get a tree like he had.' I looked at Finlay. 'I'm sorry he can't be here with you to see it.'

'Me too. I think he'd be happy that I'm here now.'

'Good. I'm happy you're here now.'

He looked at me. 'Lorna, I feel like you're giving me so much,' he blurted out.

'What do you mean?' I asked as we walked down the High Street towards Dove House.

'Letting me be here with you and your family and friends, letting me experience this Christmas magic and inspiring me to write, letting me write at Dove House...' He trailed off. 'Not to mention encouraging me to follow my dreams.'

'You have helped me too,' I said. 'You got your friend to write about the bed and breakfast – we already have a booking from that. And talking to you about following your heart made me realise that I had been scared that I couldn't do what I wanted. But I needed to stop worrying and just make sure that I made my dreams come true.' I looked at him shyly. 'And I've never met anyone that makes me feel like you do. Like I can do anything.'

'I feel exactly the same,' he replied, as the house came into view. Finlay stopped and turned me towards him. 'I want you to have everything you want and dream of. You deserve it all,' he said, reaching out to brush a hair back from my face.

'That,' I said with a smile.

'What?'

'Your words. I've never met anyone with such a way with words before. You make me feel special.'

'You are special,' he said, softly, and then he kissed me. This kiss felt different to our others. In fact, it felt different to every kiss I'd ever had before in my life. I wrapped my arms around Finlay as he pulled me closer, deepening our kiss, and I knew I'd never get tired of kissing him. I felt his touch warm my whole body, which was pretty amazing considering we were outside in Scotland in December. 'Let's go inside,' Finlay said into my ear then, and I nodded.

We walked into Dove House and, holding his hand, I led Finlay upstairs in the darkness to my bedroom, the moonlight shining through the window as I turned to him.

'I think I dreamed of you most of all,' Finlay whispered. I shivered because I felt like I'd dreamed of him too. He leaned down to kiss me and I knew I'd never forget our first night together.

Chapter Fifty-Five

'Good morning.'

I opened my eyes to see Finlay walking back into my bedroom carrying a tray. 'What's this?' I asked, sitting up sleepily. I arched an eyebrow at him.

'Breakfast,' he replied, coming back to my bed with it.

'Well, this is a treat,' I said, smiling as he put the tray down between us. He'd made us both a coffee, brought up orange juice, and there was a plate of warmed croissants and jam, and toast and marmalade too, plus a bowl of berries. 'I could get used to this,' I warned him.

'Good,' he replied, leaning in to kiss me. 'I hope you do. And wait until you see what happened in the night.' He jumped back up and went over to the window, pulling back the curtains. The sun was only just rising but I could see there had been a heavy fall of snow during the night. For the first time, the Dove House garden was coated in fluffy white snow and it looked even better than I had imagined. I exhaled. 'So pretty. Wow.' I handed him my phone. 'Please take a photo for our social media. Who wouldn't want to stay and look out at that?'

'It's picture-perfect,' Finlay agreed. He came back to bed afterwards and we helped ourselves to breakfast. 'I love your room,' he said, looking around as he ate a croissant. 'I couldn't see it last night. It's lovely. Very you.'

'You think?' I said, pleased that he knew what 'very me' was.

Finlay turned to me. 'Definitely. You've put your stamp everywhere. I think people will love it here. It feels so special, but homely too. I loved staying here last night,' he added a little huskily.

'I enjoyed that too,' I replied, smiling into my coffee. 'Are you ready for your first Ferguson family dinner today?'

'Doing my best not to get too nervous about it. I know I've met them all, but then I was just a guy desperately searching through your loft. And now...' he trailed off, unsure what to say. 'Your boyfriend? If that's what you want.'

I nodded happily. It very much was. 'They will love you, don't worry. Are you sure you want to come to church too?'

'Why not? I want to experience all of Glendale.'

I wondered if that was because he'd only be here for Christmas, or if he might be thinking about staying for longer. I hoped so, but it felt too soon to have that conversation. 'Great. Well, I'll finish this and get ready.' I knew I couldn't stop smiling and I was pleased that neither could Finlay.

—

Glendale looked like a perfect Christmas card when we left church later that morning. The wintry sunshine had melted the snow a little so it wasn't too difficult to walk in now, and I loved how pretty and peaceful it made the village look.

'So, how was it?' I asked Finlay as we fell into step behind my family to walk back home after the service. Brodie had been talking about how Christmas brings with it hope, and how we should embrace hope during this season and not let the stresses of Christmas get in the way of remembering why we celebrate it in the first place. I felt hopeful for the last couple of weeks of December. I loved this time of year, and things were working so well with our house, plus I was so excited for our first family Christmas with baby Drew. And, of course, I had Finlay to share it with.

'I have never seen a service so popular,' Finlay replied as we walked side by side, wrapped up against the cold. 'I haven't been for a long time, but I don't remember hearing such a lively and personal sermon.'

I nodded. I liked how Brodie often talked about his own life – his past, his family, his life with Emily and their children – he always made his sermons relatable. 'He's the best minister we've had. He often seems to talk about things that are on my mind or that I'm worried about.'

Finlay took my hand in his. 'I liked what he was saying about hope. Things do seem so much brighter, don't they?'

'They do,' I agreed. We walked down the road towards my family home and it was so pretty, dusted with snow. 'There is always hope.'

'You have really shown me that.' We smiled at one another. 'I was thinking about how I felt a connection with you when we first met. I wondered if it was just because of the love story in our past, but I don't think it's that at all. I think it's our view on life that connects us. When we met, neither of us were happy where we were, and we had both thought that we needed to give up on our dreams.'

I nodded. 'You're right. I saw you and thought you looked uncomfortable in what you were wearing, where you were…'

'And I could see how much you wanted to buy Dove House. When the estate agent told me that Betty hadn't accepted my offer, I just knew she had accepted yours and I was pleased for you.'

'And now we're both following our heart.'

'This is our story now. The past doesn't matter. What matters is you and me and our future. Our… happy ending?' Finlay asked.

I shook my head. 'No ending, please.' I loved a happy ending in films and books, but life wasn't like that. 'Just happy days.'

'Happy days,' Finlay echoed. 'That sounds perfect to me,' he said as we walked together into the house I had grown up in.

Chapter Fifty-Six

Sunday lunch at my family's house was its usual noisy affair. The table was crammed with the family and food, and I glanced at Finlay to see how he was handling it but he seemed relaxed about it all.

'Here.' Kathleen passed me baby Drew. 'Let me eat a bit of food,' she said. Her plate was untouched as she'd been feeding him.

'Sure.' I cradled baby Drew on my lap and smiled down at his wide blue eyes which blinked with sleepiness until they closed. 'How can you possibly sleep through this noise?' I asked him as the twins were shouting over one another to tell Adam about their football game at school on Friday.

'He can sleep through anything, like his dad,' Hamish said proudly from opposite me.

'I had to practically kick him out of bed last night when baby Drew was crying, he can never hear it,' Kathleen replied with an eye-roll as she tucked into her dinner. 'So not helpful when it comes to husbands, but babies, I fully support.'

I smiled. 'Definitely a good trait in this family,' I said. Baby Drew was fast asleep in my arms now. I knew he'd probably be fine if I put him down in his pram but I was enjoying holding him too much. I glanced up then to see Finlay watching me. I wondered how he felt about having a family one day. I knew it was too soon to even think about that, but I couldn't help it. There was something about us that felt like it was going to be for the long haul.

I watched as Mum got up and went into the kitchen and Finlay slipped out after her.

Kathleen followed my gaze and saw it too. She leaned closer to me. 'Come and help me put baby Drew down,' she said, standing up. I followed her out with the baby into the lounge where his pram was. I wondered if I was about to get a lecture from my big sister, but I saw that she was smiling. 'I'm happy for you.'

'You are?' I was still a bit taken aback when Kathleen was nice to me.

'Why do you look so surprised? I think he's good for you. You're good for each other.' She took her son from me. 'Go into the kitchen, I know you're dying to.'

I paused before I left. 'Why did you think we're good for one another?' I didn't see any point in pretending that I hadn't. I thought it was pretty obvious to everyone by now.

Kathleen put baby Drew carefully in his pram. 'He's just as much of a hopeless romantic as you are,' she replied.

'Or I just always fancied being with Clark Kent,' I said, laughing as she waved me off, shaking her head at me. I went into the kitchen where Finlay and my mother were talking as they got the dessert ready. 'Everything okay?' I asked tentatively, hovering in the doorway.

'Finlay was just telling me about his book,' Mum said over her shoulder as she made custard. I walked over and saw that he was dishing up sticky toffee pudding into bowls for everyone. 'I said he'd better do me justice.' Her eyes twinkled so I knew she was okay with it.

'It's only going to be based on you both, my characters are already becoming their own people,' Finlay said.

'I hope you're giving them a happy ending. I only enjoy books with a happy ending,' Mum said.

'Like mother, like daughter,' I chuckled.

Finlay grinned. 'I can't possibly share how it ends. You'll hopefully read it one day for yourselves. Honestly, Mrs

Ferguson… sorry, Amelia,' he corrected himself at my mum's raised eyebrow. 'I can't thank you enough for today. For welcoming me into your home like you have. You've been so kind to me. And the fact that you're happy with me telling your story… thank you.'

'Well, there's no need…' Mum began.

'No, you have been lovely, and you didn't need to be, with your history with my family. Not just my dad leaving and you not hearing from him, but finding out that my grandparents hid his letter from you. I would understand if you thought badly of my family, and of me.'

'I would never think badly of you, or your father, or your family. I was hurt at the time, but I grew to understand why things happened the way they did. It's all in the past now. I'm glad that I read your father's letter and that he wanted to make peace with it all. Most of all, though, I'm glad that he sent you to Glendale. And that he wanted you to follow your heart. It's all I've ever wanted for Lorna, and I can see how happy you are making each other. That's what matters now.' She smiled at us both. 'Right then, let's feed these monsters,' she said, pouring the custard into a jug.

Finlay nodded and carried out portions of dessert to the family.

'Are you really okay with it all?' I checked with mum when we were alone.

'I just want you to be happy, you know that,' she replied.

'I am,' I said.

'Then it's all working out exactly as it was meant to.' She gave me a kiss as she passed by me carrying the custard. I watched her go and wondered if she was right and fate had had its plan all along for us. It was kind of comforting to think that. It was strange that Kathleen saw it too, even before I did, that Finlay was going to be special to me. And Finlay and I had certainly felt a connection early on.

But I knew that even if fate was at work for us, it didn't mean the road was going to be smooth and easy. Life had a way of throwing obstacles in your path, but my mum and dad had shown me that if you handled them together, then you could get through anything. And I really hoped that was what me and Finlay would do too.

Chapter Fifty-Seven

December was rolling past as we worked long days at the house, trying to get everything ready for our New Year guests. The painting was finished, so we could start furnishing the house. Beds were delivered. We found a sofa and another chaise longue, and we started to hang paintings on the wall. It was coming together quickly now.

We'd been busy all day in different parts of the house when Adam found me as the light began to dim outside. The days were getting shorter as we approached Christmas and the weather was cold and snowy most days, but Dove House always felt cosy to me and I hoped it would to everyone who stayed here too.

'My shoulders are killing me. We need a break,' Adam said. 'How about we go and find a tree?'

'I don't need asking twice to do that,' I said, happily. I knew that by the time anyone stayed here, Christmas would pretty much be over, but I didn't want to miss out on having a tree in our new home even for one year, and I was pleased Adam agreed. 'Are there any left at the Hall?' We were leaving it a bit late as the trees there were really popular.

'I had a word with Beth and she kept one for us,' he said.

'She really is a star,' I marvelled.

We pulled on coats and shoes and Adam drove us over to Glendale Hall. Once we'd parked, we walked around the side of the house and into the garden, and we could see the lights of the trail sparkling and sounds of merriment coming from the ice rink. Snow crunched under our feet as we walked past it all towards the trees at the other side of the grounds. They sold some each year and used them for the family, but it wasn't a huge tree farm or anything, so we didn't always get one from the Hall. But I was happy our first one would be – it felt fitting as we owed so much to Beth.

'Next week, I reckon we'll have everything done,' I said as we walked over to the trees where I could see John the gardener and Drew waiting for us. 'I've written to Betty and her daughter to invite them, and Mrs Andrews' sister and her husband and dog are booked in. Finlay's uncle and his wife have said yes too, so we should have all the bedrooms occupied for New Year.'

'I think it's a great idea – throw ourselves in at the deep end and then we'll know what we need to work on when we have paying guests.' Adam grinned. 'We're almost there – can you believe it?'

'What a crazy few months,' I said. 'Thank you for not letting me lose faith. Not just during the building work, but waiting for Dove House. I don't think I would even have tried to it buy this time if I'd been on my own. I needed the push from you.'

'Well, I couldn't have renovated the house without your vision, so as we've always said, we work as a team and we will make this business successful together.'

I nodded. 'We will. Is this for us?' I asked as we approached Drew and John, who stood by a large tree.

'What do you think?' Drew asked.

'It will look so good in the hallway,' I said, looking up at it happily. It was huge and would almost reach the ceiling. John started chopping it down with Drew supervising and Adam helping to hold it. I thought back to one of the first trees we got from the Hall. I had been much smaller than I was now and was in awe of it, and I felt the same way now watching the tree topple to the ground. Adam and Drew carried it back to Adam's car and strapped it to the roof.

'That's a good one,' Beth said, stepping out into the driveway as they fixed it to the car.

'Thanks for keeping one for us,' I said to her. 'It's the perfect finishing touch to the house.'

'You're almost ready to open then?'

I told her the plan to have guests for New Year to test us out. 'And then we can officially open in January. Three months' work, and we're almost there.'

'I can't wait to see it.'

'I can't wait to show you.' Spontaneously, I gave her a hug. 'Thank you again, Beth. We couldn't have done it without you.'

She waved off my praise as usual. 'Enjoy your tree, both of you!' Drew joined her and wrapped an arm around her. They seemed such a strong couple. They waved us off and we left Glendale Hall with our first Christmas tree, a tradition I hoped we'd continue for many years to come.

Back at home, I was surprised to see cars in the driveway although it was too dark to see them clearly, which made me make a mental note to look into lighting out here. 'I thought all the workers had left for the day?'

'They have.' Adam had a smug look on his face. 'Come on.'

Wondering what was going on, I climbed out of the car and followed him through the front door. I stopped in surprise when I realised the hallway was full of our family and I broke into a happy smile. Adam had invited everyone to come over to watch our first tree go up – Mum, Dad, the twins, Kathleen and her family, Grace and Finlay. It was so lovely seeing those two there and feeling like they were part of our family now too.

'I thought I was the sentimental one,' I told Adam with a laugh.

'You rub off on me. Right, let's get the tree inside.'

The tree looked as good as I imagined in the hallway, stretching up to the ceiling. Mum had brought some spare decorations from home and Adam had bought lights, so we all decorated the tree together with Christmas music playing on the radio. Kathleen brought out mulled wine for us and shortbread for the kids.

'Watch out,' I called as I watched a tail suddenly disappear under the tree. 'Get the Dreamies!' We managed to persuade Tabby to come out with his treats, but then he ran off with a bauble.

'Why is there always a drama?' Kathleen cried as Leo and Noah ran after the cat and knocked over a glass of wine.

'Watch the new floor!' I cried in a panic.

Hamish dropped to his knees with a tea towel. 'It's fine,' he assured me as he dabbed at it.

'Chaos,' I said to Finlay in despair.

'But look,' he said and pointed at the tree. I turned round. It was so lovely and sparkly next to the front door. I thought back to the little girl who had been so taken with this house and wondered what she'd say if she could see this now. 'Wow,' I whispered.

'Lorna, Adam, come here.' Mum waved us over to her. I left Finlay and walked over. 'I have a house-warming present for you both,' she said, handing us a gold-wrapped box.

'Mum, you didn't need to,' I said, as Adam gestured for me to open it.

I opened the present and took a breath as I saw that it was a photo of me, Adam and Mum right here at Dove House the first time we looked around the house together. 'Oh, Mum,' I said, feeling myself well up. What a night. We'd put up our first Christmas tree and now we had this photo to remind us of how long we had wanted to live here. 'It's the perfect gift.'

'It really is, Mum.' Adam pulled her into a tight hug as I wiped away the tear rolling down my cheek. 'It should go right here. Dad!' I called Dad over and he hung it for us above the table in the hallway so it was the first thing you saw when you came into the house. I stood staring at it on the wall, thinking it looked as though it had always been meant to hang there.

'Thank you for showing us this house back then,' I said to Mum. 'It's like you knew that this would happen.'

'Life has a funny way of working out,' she replied.

Kathleen came over to us. 'I wish I had been there that day too,' she said.

'Are you okay with us having it here?' I checked, hoping she no longer felt jealous of me and Adam.

She smiled. 'Of course! It has to be here. This is your home. I'm just excited to be part of it all, in a small way. It's something for Drew too, and your children one day.'

'I hope so,' I agreed. I wrapped an arm around her. 'I'm so happy you're part of the team now.'

'You should be – I got those leaflets printed half price, so we can distribute them around the village once we're officially open,' she replied.

'Of course you did!' I shook my head as she hurried over to the twins to stop them eating any more shortbread. I smiled at my family. Hamish was holding baby Drew; Dad was straightening the picture according to Mum's instructions; Adam and Grace were talking in the corner, his arms around her; and Finlay was putting the final bauble on the tree.

I knew that really it didn't matter what house we were in as long as we were together. A house wasn't a home – it was the people in it that made it a home, after all. But Dove House was somehow always meant to be our home.

And here we were.

Part Five

Chapter Fifty-Eight

It was the week before Christmas when I walked through Dove House alone. I had asked Adam to go and pick up Kathleen, and before she got here I rushed around finishing off a few things that I wasn't completely satisfied with. I added a rug to the lounge, as something had felt like it was missing, and I swapped two pictures around between that room and the dining room.

In one of the guest rooms, I added the new cushions I'd found online that had arrived yesterday, as the bed looked too empty, and in one of the bathrooms I rearranged the towels and soaps and took away the bath mat as I didn't like how it looked.

Then I walked through each room, switching on the lights as I went, checking that things were now in the right place. I checked each guest room and bathroom, and then I went into the hallway feeling like everything was exactly how I had pictured it. Finally.

Adam opened the front door, Kathleen behind him. 'We're both here. Now will you tell me what's going on?' he asked me as they walked inside.

I looked at them both and broke into a wide smile. 'It's done. It's finished. We're ready!'

'Huh?' Adam asked.

'Dove House is finished,' I said slowly and clearly.

'Finished?' he repeated.

'You've really done it?' Kathleen asked, her eyes widening. 'Okay, this was good enough to leave Drew and Hamish at home, you were right. Show us, then!' she said impatiently.

'Okay, first the hallway,' I said grandly, gesturing around. Above us the new chandelier sparkled, and off to one side was a console table with a large lamp and a vase of flowers from the local florist, and above it the picture of us here as children. To the side, I had created a reading nook inspired by Glendale Hall with a window seat and bookcase next to it, a lamp hanging over it and lots of cosy cushions. The oak floor had been restored and varnished, and at the back stood the wide spiral staircase leading up to the other floors, which had been fixed and now stood gleaming. 'Does it feel welcoming?'

'It's stunning,' Kathleen said. 'I think guests will be thrilled walking into this.'

I beamed happily. 'Let's start upstairs. Come on!' I hurried off up the staircase and they eagerly followed me to the guest floor. I cleared my throat and made sure I had their attention. 'Okay, let me show you the second floor in all its glory...' I led them into the bedrooms and bathrooms and my heart swelled as they marvelled at how they looked. Each one was decorated in as close to the art deco style as I could get them within our budget, and each one had its own colour scheme.

'These tiles look like marble,' I said, so pleased with the effect we had created in the bathrooms without spending a fortune. I'd added the fancy toiletries I had sourced for a discounted price. I also put out scented candles that Beth had given us for free as they advertised the Glendale Hall shop, so the bathrooms had a luxury touch. Each bedroom had a statement painting on the wall from the era which I loved, and the beds were king-size with pretty duvets and cushions and I had found what felt to me like the most comfortable pillows, so I was really hopeful that our guests would have a good night's sleep. The rooms still had a slight smell to them of fresh paint and new carpet, but also lavender, thanks to the reed diffusers that I had put in one corner of each room.

'Lorna, they are beautiful,' Adam said. 'Perfect for the era, but also comfortable and cosy. I have no doubt people will enjoy sleeping here.'

'They look so good, sis, I could never have decorated like this. It looks like something out of a magazine,' Kathleen agreed.

I beamed at them. 'Let me show you the downstairs,' I said, hurrying off. They followed me down the restored staircase into the hallway with its spectacular light fitting and restored oak floor. The huge ornate mirror was a real statement too when you walked in through the door. We went into the lounge next, where armchairs and a chaise longue looked stylish and inviting, and in the corner Finlay's father's writing desk stood proudly. The gold curtains at the French windows looked luxurious, and the green decor was striking but also calming somehow. We had quirky lamps in here and art deco clocks and fine paintings. In the corner, we'd set up a gold bar cart that we were going to fill with drinks, and next to it was the piano we had found on eBay of all places, which Adam had varnished to perfection.

'So classy,' Adam declared. 'I can picture people having cocktails in here before they go out for the night. Or curling up for the afternoon on a snowy day,' he said, gesturing to the restored fireplace that I couldn't wait to light.

We walked through into the dining room, where there was one large mahogany table. We had tried to find smaller tables, but we'd spotted this in a second-hand furniture shop and knew it would look stunning, and people might enjoy having breakfast together. If not, they could have it in their rooms. There was a sideboard for breakfast things complete with decorative china inside that I'd found in a charity shop. We had added a grandfather clock in here, and on the mantelpiece over the restored fireplace were a couple of ceramic figurines from the era. The floor was shiny wood and above the table was another stunning gold light.

Then we went into the downstairs cloakroom, which I'd decorated in pretty pink complete with a flamingo lamp in the corner and another ornate gold mirror above the sink. This room smelt of the fresh pink roses I'd added in a vase.

'And to the last rooms,' I said, leading them into the kitchen, which we hadn't changed but knew we wanted to update one day.

Then Adam said we had to go into the garden as we were doing the full tour, so he opened the back door and, shivering, we stepped outside. The lawn, thick with frost, was mown and green underneath its white covering and the trees had been trimmed and we'd added some patio furniture alongside the house, but we'd have to wait until spring to add the colourful flowers we wanted.

'Okay,' I said, too cold to stay out there, and I ducked back into the warm kitchen. 'The last room.' We walked through the kitchen into the adjoining room, which we'd be using as our living room. It had been full of rubbish while we were decorating, but now it was clear and complete with two comfy sofas, a large TV on the wall and a coffee table with decor books and a candle. This room was white and black, and I'd added black-and-white prints from old movies on the walls. 'What do you think?'

'That I want to watch a film in here right now,' Adam said. 'It's perfect, Lorna. Honestly, I can't quite believe how this house looks.'

'Me neither,' Kathleen agreed. 'You've made it so stylish, but it's so cosy and homely too. Congratulations, you two – you did it!'

Adam and I looked at her. 'The three of us did it,' I said. 'We couldn't have done it without you, Kath.'

'I was glad to help, you know that,' she said, happily.

'It's ready,' Adam said, and a smile spread across my face. And then Adam grabbed me and picked me up, spinning me round as I cried out laughing and telling him to put me down. When he finally did, he tried to do the same with Kathleen, who backed away quickly. She let me give her a hug, though.

'I can't quite believe it,' I said. There was a meow behind me and I saw Tabby coming in to see what all the commotion was about. I picked him up. 'How are you going to feel about people coming to stay here, eh, Tabby?' He purred in response so I took that as his agreement that Dove House was ready to open for business.

'Okay, you know what we need to arrange now?' Adam said.

'A house-warming party,' the three of us said in unison.

Chapter Fifty-Nine

I was waiting for Finlay to come over from the Inn to see the finished house, when my phone rang. I didn't recognise the number, but I was used to that now, what with all the tradespeople we were dealing with. 'Hello?'

'Lorna?' a male voice said.

'Speaking? How can I help?'

'It's me. Uh… Mark.'

I froze. 'Mark?' It had been two years, so I didn't recognise his voice for a minute. Why was he getting in touch after all this time?

'I've been at Glenmarshes Inn for a company meeting so we could all meet the new manager and see what head office want us to do next year in our hotels, and I bumped into Grace. She told me all about your bed and breakfast.'

I bet she had, I thought to myself. She had been furious when Mark had transferred to a new hotel and left me behind. Obviously now I knew it was all for the best. I remembered then all the times he had been dismissive of my dream. 'Yes, it's all ready to open up in January. How can I help you?' I added stiffly, still confused why he was calling me.

'Oh, right, yes,' he said, a little wrong-footed by my tone. He cleared his throat. 'Well, head office want us to try to make our hotels more personal. To go back to how some of them were before the takeover, a more homely, cosy vibe, and I know that's the kind of thing you always liked. I thought I could take you out for dinner and pick your brains?'

My eyebrows rose high on my forehead. So, my ex-boyfriend who had pretty much mocked me for wanting to open a cosy B & B, who hadn't understood why I didn't like the chain takeover, who had left me to run a large city hotel, who was corporate through and through, now wanted to pick *my* brains? I almost laughed, but I held it in. 'I seem to remember you telling me that "my head was stuck in the clouds". That I needed to be *"practical"*. That I had no chance with opening my own place, and that I belonged at the Inn?'

There was a short uncomfortable silence. 'Well, that was a long time ago, and you were only talking about your own place, and you hadn't done anything about it.'

'Well, no, because you made me think I couldn't!'

'Look, let me buy you dinner and we can put all that behind us. Can't we? Start again?'

I was confused. 'I thought you were engaged?' It was funny how seeing that Facebook status in September had sent me on a spiral, and now I felt nothing when I said those words. Mark was firmly in the past in all areas of my life. Business and personal.

'It didn't work out,' he admitted.

'I'm sorry to hear that, but Mark, we ended for a reason. We want different things from life.' I had been meant to find Finlay, I was sure of that.

'What about the hotel?' he said then.

I shook my head. 'I can't help you. I've got my own business to focus on now. I wish you all the best,' I said to him before saying goodbye. I exhaled. I was so happy that I hadn't let him stop me going after my dream. It had taken longer than I had planned, but thankfully there was no expiry date on dreams.

There was a knock at the door. 'It's good to see you,' I said to Finlay when I opened it. He leaned in to kiss me and the phone call faded from my thoughts. Finlay was my future now. 'Let me give you the grand tour!'

-

Later, Finlay and I sat in the lounge. I watched him and smiled. He was on the floor next to me going through a box of photographs. He had brought them with him to the Inn from his family home in Perth to sort through. They were of his father and his father's brother and sister, taken when they were children, and he was hoping to find one of them that featured Dove House.

He noticed me watching him, and smiled. 'I still can't believe how amazing this house looks, Lorna. It's incredible how you've restored it. I'm going to have to rewrite the first chapter of my book because my imagination was nowhere near as good as yours.'

'I'm so happy you like it. I hope the house likes it.' I grinned. 'Do I sound mad?'

'No more than usual.' He fake-yelped when I nudged him. 'I think the house is happy right now, don't you?'

'I think so too.'

'Oh, look.'

I scooted over as he held out a photo. 'It's the back garden,' I said. Thomas was with his sister on the grass, Dove House behind them. 'They look so happy.'

Finlay looked through the next couple. 'Isn't that...?'

We bent our heads over this one, taken in the lounge, and saw his father and my mother standing there, the fireplace we'd now restored behind them, Thomas's brother and sister off to the side. Thomas was looking at my mother, who was looking at the camera. I could see the love in his eyes. Mum was so young and so pretty and her smile lit up the room, as it still did. She was so lovely. I knew why Thomas had fallen for her that summer.

'It's so sad, seeing how happy they look in this picture. If only my dad had had the courage to fight for what he wanted. I'm not saying for Amelia – I think things have worked out just right,' Finlay said, smiling at me. 'But in his life in general. I wish I knew if he had been happy at all.'

'He was happy with you and your mother, I'm sure of it,' I insisted. 'And you should be too.' I took his hand in mine. 'He wanted you to have love in your life. He's looking down on you right now, and I know that he's so proud and happy. Your mum is too, I can feel it.'

Finlay leaned in to kiss me. 'How did I get this lucky to find you?'

'Well, I feel the same.'

'I want to remember my dad like this,' Finlay said then, holding the photo in his hand. He looked at me. 'I want to be like he was here in this photo.'

'You already are,' I reassured him. 'You know how to love, Finlay. And you know that's what matters most in life.' I leaned my head on his shoulder.

'You showed me that,' he said softly. He put the photo down and looked around the room. 'I wonder how many love stories this house has seen.'

'I hope it will see a whole lot more.'

'Are we too sentimental?' He chuckled.

'No such thing.' I looked at the other photo he had pulled out. 'Oh, look. There's a summer house,' I said, pointing to an outbuilding in the garden to the edge of the picture. 'It's so lovely. I wonder who took it down,' I said. 'That's an idea for the future, either as a separate guest house for people to rent or somewhere for me and Adam to move into so we can use our floor for guests, or if we have a family...' I trailed off, a little embarrassed.

'I agree, it would be great,' he replied, looking at the photo unfazed. 'Always good to think about future opportunities.' He looked up at me and winked.

I laughed. 'Very true. So, fancy a coffee?'

'Always.'

'Let's go to Emily's Bakery.'

We left the house five minutes later wrapped up against the cold and strolled towards the High Street. It was decorated for

Christmas now; everything was lit up and festive and the shops were celebrating the season with treats like gingerbread men and mulled wine and chutney. The large tree in the centre of the village was twinkling and swaying gently in the breeze.

I checked my watch and was pleased to see we were right on time, so when Finlay opened the door to Emily's Bakery for me, I saw Sally was already there seated at her usual table with tea and cake as I had arranged with her. There was a delicious smell in the air as we entered the warm bakery, and Emily gave us a cheerful wave as we walked in.

'Finlay, this is Sally,' I said, steering him to her table. 'Do you remember me telling you that she knew your father and his family when they lived here?'

'Ah, Finlay, it's good to see you. Would you like to join me?'

He smiled. 'Yes, thank you.' Finlay sat down as I went over to Emily and ordered us both coffees and some of her delicious pastries. When I returned with our goodies, Sally was talking animatedly to Finlay, who was absorbed in her stories of the past.

'So, they were well known in the village?'

'Of course. Your grandparents were very well known in the community. We weren't friends, of course, as I was the housekeeper at Glendale Hall. But I remember them coming to the Hall a lot and I was invited to some of the Dove House parties. It was always full of people, full of life back then. It was kept beautifully by your family, and it's been a real shame to see the house fall into disrepair the last few years.' Sally smiled at me. 'I can't wait to see what you've done to the house at your party.'

'What was my dad like back then? I find it hard to imagine him as a young man,' Finlay said, thanking me as he took his coffee and sipped it. It was lovely to see him learning more about his family. I lived around people who had known my family forever; we'd always lived in Glendale, after all. But Finlay hadn't had that, and he had so many questions, so I was glad he could ask Sally some of them.

'He was very handsome – all the girls in the village loved him. He was very chatty, always talking to people. As I said, their house was busy and full of life. His brother was quieter and more serious, but Thomas was more outgoing, I remember. And their sister was a shy girl, she took after their father. He was a man of few words, but their mother was the life and soul of entertaining. She was very beautiful and vivacious. I always thought your father took after her.'

'It's hard to picture my father like that,' Finlay said. 'He was very serious around me, growing up, and we never really entertained or threw parties. He changed a lot once he left Glendale, I think.'

'That's a shame,' Sally said. 'He wasn't happy when they moved away, I gather.'

'No, he had to leave Lorna's mum. His parents, my grandparents, didn't approve of them being together. I still don't fully understand that, to be honest.'

'Back then, appearance and reputation were more important than it is today. Margaret Mackenzie – Beth's grandmother who passed away a few years ago – was the head of the family at Glendale Hall and had that same mindset. It's hard for you to put yourselves in their shoes.'

Finlay nodded. 'I think my father wished he had acted differently at the end, but I suppose how he grew up, and his family, made that difficult for him.'

They talked more about Glendale back when Sally was growing up, Finlay asking questions to help with writing his book, and we finished our coffee and pastries without realising it. Sally was so interesting to talk to about the past, but once she'd finished her tea, she needed to go home, so we left her, grateful that she'd taken the time to talk to us.

'That was interesting what she said about Beth's grandmother being similar to my grandparents,' Finlay said when we left the bakery to walk back home.

'Anna told me the story. Her grandmother forced Beth to run away when she was sixteen and pregnant with Izzy, and she stayed in London for ten years. But she came back when her grandmother became ill. And I think they healed their estrangement. Her grandmother left the estate to her. Look at Beth now! She's practically running the whole village – she didn't let what happened in the past affect her. She's her own woman. Like you're your own man. You're not your father. Like Beth, you've chosen a different path.'

Finlay nodded. 'And for a while, he hated that. But you're right, I think he realised in the end that I needed to do it, I needed to make my own way in the world. I do wish he was around to see me do just that.'

'He's still with you,' I promised. 'I believe that.'

Finlay smiled at me. 'You make me believe in things that I never thought I would. Somehow you make me feel like anything is possible.'

'Well, good. Because it really is.'

Chapter Sixty

Before I knew it, it was the night of our house-warming party.

I looked at myself in my full-length mirror as I applied red lipstick. I rarely wore it but it felt like a red lipstick night. I was wearing a long gold dress with heels for the special occasion, too. Christmas was only a couple of days away but everyone had said yes to our invitations, eager to see Dove House and get into the festive spirit. We'd ordered a lot of drinks and nibbles, and Grace had found us a DJ to provide the music. I skipped out of my room and went downstairs, where everything was ready. We'd hung gold and silver balloons all around the downstairs, and the Christmas tree was lit up and sparkling.

'All ready?' Adam asked as I came down the stairs. He was wearing a suit for the occasion, a rare occurrence for him, and looked a little uncomfortable in it. 'Why do I feel nervous?'

'We just want people to like what we've done,' I said. Most of Glendale would be here tonight and some of them had seen Dove House through all its incarnations, and we both wanted them to think we'd done a good job with our renovations. The doorbell rang and we looked at one another. 'Here we go,' I said as I opened it and my chest sagged with relief. 'It's just Kathleen,' I said to Adam hovering behind me.

'Oh, charming,' she replied as she stepped through with Hamish. 'I was going to say you look nice.'

'We're just a bit anxious,' I explained. 'You both look lovely,' I added, to try to smooth things over. My sister did look lovely in her blue dress and Hamish was handsome in his suit.

'I feel the same,' she said. 'Baby Drew is with a babysitter for the first time. We might only last an hour.'

'We're just glad you're here,' I said, understanding why she might want to leave early. Behind us in the lounge, the DJ put on some music. The party was starting.

'Come on, you need a drink,' Hamish said to my sister.

'Good idea. Enjoy yourselves!' I told them as the doorbell rang again. It was a snowy night, so I hadn't wanted to leave the door open, but we might need to once the house filled up.

'I'm just popping in,' Mrs Andrews, our neighbour said, looking around as she walked inside. I could see her curiosity to look at all the work we had done.

'That's fine, Mrs Andrews,' I said, smiling at Adam. 'Adam, help Mrs Andrews find a drink,' I suggested, hoping she'd be even more amenable once she'd had one of the cocktails we'd made.

'Come on through,' Adam said, steering her firmly after Kathleen and Hamish.

'Oh, you've restored the staircase, and that chandelier...' Mrs Andrews trailed off, rendered speechless, it seemed. I grinned. Wonders would never cease. I was relieved she had come round, and hoped her sister would be happy staying here soon.

'You look gorgeous,' Finlay said behind me as he walked in.

I took in his dark jeans and shirt. He definitely wasn't a suit guy, and I was fine with that; he looked gorgeous too tonight. 'Very handsome,' I said as he kissed me hello.

'Let me get you a drink,' he suggested.

'That would be great,' I agreed as the doorbell rang again. For the next half hour, I greeted our guests, and Dove House was full for the first time in years. Everyone from Glendale Hall was there as well as Mum and Dad – the twins were with friends for the night – our minister Brodie and Emily, and Anna and Cameron, who came with Heather and Rory. Some of my colleagues from the Inn had come along with Grace, plus our friends from school and everyone who had worked on the house with us, and other businesses in the village. So many familiar faces. It was surreal to have them all here to help us celebrate the house being finished.

Eventually, I was able to leave the front door and walk into the lounge where most people had gathered with cocktails. The French doors had been opened now that the house was full and everyone was warm, and some people were out in the garden drinking and chatting, the wintry weather not putting them off enjoying the starry night. Adam was taking people upstairs and showing them round, and I saw Mrs Andrews right at the front of the group. Finlay was standing with my family chatting happily, which was lovely to see.

I was about to join them when I saw Beth, who gestured me over. She led me out into the kitchen which was quiet and where Tabby was curled up in his bed, trying to ignore all the commotion in the rest of the house. 'I just wanted to say wow,' Beth said once we were alone. 'This place is amazing! Adam just showed me upstairs,' she said. 'Lorna, I can't believe what you and Adam and Kathleen have done, it's so gorgeous. I know people are going to love staying here.'

'I'm so happy you like it,' I replied, smiling. This was high praise from the owner of Glendale Hall. 'I really want people staying here to feel how special this house is and to be inspired by it.'

'Well, you've succeeded in doing that,' Beth assured me. 'Glendale needed a place for people to stay, and this is just perfect. Actually, I'm wondering if I need to hire you to refurbish Glendale Hall one day,' she added with a laugh.

'And we can't thank you enough for investing so we could get this house to begin with, you know that!'

She waved a hand. 'It was a pleasure. You know I think this will be brilliant for the community. It's turned out even better than I thought!' She gave me a hug. 'You deserve every success.'

–

The party was in full swing when Finlay asked me to dance. The DJ was mixing party songs with some slower ones as couples twirled around the lounge. There was a *Great Gatsby* vibe to the night, with everyone dressed to the nines, the art deco backdrop and cocktails being sipped as people swayed to the music, laughter filling the room. I was so happy that everyone appeared to be enjoying themselves and that people kept calling out compliments to me and Adam about how the house looked. The house had never felt so much like home to me as it did that night. As Finlay took me in his arms and I leaned against him, I wondered how it could possibly get much better than this.

'What a night,' I said into his ear as a romantic song swirled around us. Finlay was a good dancer, strong and steady, and I felt safe in his arms. 'I never want to forget it.'

'I know what you mean,' he agreed. Finlay kissed me, and for a moment the room faded away, and it felt like it was just the two of us dancing in the house that meant so much to us, and when we parted and the room came back into focus, I knew that I had nothing to be scared of when it came to us. I had faith in us. This was the real thing.

The sound of someone tapping a glass could be heard then and the music was turned down low. We drew apart as we turned to see Adam at the top of the room waiting for quiet. 'Lorna,' he called, beckoning me to join him. Finlay gave my hand a squeeze as I walked over to my brother, all eyes drawn to us. I tried to pull Kathleen up too, but she shook her head resolutely.

'This is your moment,' she told me. I smiled at her and joined my brother alone.

'Time for the dreaded speech,' Adam said to laughter as I stood next to him. 'No, seriously, nothing dreaded at all about welcoming all our family and friends and neighbours into our home tonight. As you know, we've worked hard over the past three months to restore Dove House to its original glory and get it ready to open up as a bed and breakfast. We can't wait to welcome visitors to our wonderful village, but tonight, we're happy to be sharing it with all of you,' Adam said, raising his glass to the room. 'And we couldn't have done it without you either. So many of you helped make this happen, either lending your expertise or things you didn't need any more,' he said with a smile over at Beth, and then at Glen and his father who had done all the building work. 'Or went shopping with my sister,' he added to another chuckle from everyone. 'Most of all, we'd like to thank our family, wouldn't we, Lorna?'

I nodded. 'We first came here when we were little with our mother,' I said, finding Mum in the room, her face shining with happiness. 'I was swept up by the dream of one day being able to call Dove House my home. My mother had loved this house since she came here as a teenager, and my brother and I always knew it was the perfect place to turn into our dream business. It's thanks to our family that we're here now. Our wonderful parents, who have supported us every step of the way and taught us to always dream big, and our sister Kathleen... without her, we'd never have been able to do it,' I said, smiling over at her. She hid her face and I knew tears had got her. 'It really is going to be a family business, which we always wanted, and we hope that everyone who comes to stay here feels like part of that family. Thank you, to everyone who is here tonight to celebrate with us. As Adam said, we really couldn't have done it without you!' I looked around the room as I raised my glass, smiling at all the people I loved. 'So, here's to Dove House, and Christmas, and faith, hope and love, and dreaming big – but most of all, to family!'

'To family!' everyone chorused and joined in my toast.

Adam threw an arm around my shoulder and squeezed me. I looked at him and laughed. It had been a long journey since that day we looked around as kids and our dream started to take shape, but here we were – we had done it. Together.

Chapter Sixty-One

As the night drew on, I stepped outside into the garden with my drink, spotting Anna out there with Beth, Emily and Heather. The coolness of the night hit my warm cheeks instantly. But it was clear and dry and the fresh air was welcome as it was so warm inside. 'Are you having a good time?' I asked them as I joined the group. I loved how close these three women were. I didn't know the other three as well as I did Anna – they were older and so busy with their families and businesses – but I liked them all and knew they would always be there if I needed them.

'The best,' Anna said. 'I can't get over how lovely this house is, Lorna,' she raised her cocktail glass. 'You and your family have created such a beautiful home and place to stay.'

'You'll be booked up in no time by the sounds of it,' Beth agreed. 'I just knew this was the right thing to do.'

'Always so modest,' Anna said with a grin.

'I know you think I'm always poking my nose in and being bossy...' Beth said with a good-natured shrug. 'But guys, I'm always right, aren't I? I mean, look at you all, I knew you'd make your lives in Glendale and be happy here, didn't I?'

They all grinned at one another. 'Fine,' Anna said, begrudgingly. 'Adam's speech was so sweet. Kathleen looked like she was going to cry.'

'I know! I didn't think my sister was the sentimental sort, but I think we've rubbed off on her. I'm so happy she came on board with the B & B.' I smiled, thinking how proud I was that it was all ours.

'That's so lovely,' Emily said. 'I loved what you said in your speech about family. I always think of Glendale as one big family.'

'It can be pretty dysfunctional,' Beth said with a laugh. 'But we wouldn't have it any other way. It's crazy to think that I lived for so long in London. It feels like that was a different woman. Now I can't imagine living anywhere other than Glendale.'

'Me neither,' Emily agreed.

'We've all been on a pretty big journey the past few years,' Heather said. 'I'm a farmer's wife now, and Anna is a chef!'

'I'm proud of us all,' Emily said. 'I wonder what the future holds for the women of Glendale?'

'I wonder,' Beth said. She gestured over and we looked to where she was pointing. Her daughter Izzy, her auburn hair shining in the night light, was with her friend Luke and they were walking across the garden holding hands, the stars above twinkling down on them.

'So cute,' Heather said. 'I knew they'd be close the day I introduced them and they started talking about books. Both such bookworms!'

'They're always in Izzy's reading room,' Beth agreed.

'Is that what the kids are calling it nowadays?' Anna joked.

'Come on, they're only young,' Beth tittered at her. 'Mind you, I did have her when I was sixteen... I'd better keep an eye on them,' she said with a shake of her head. 'Izzy has big plans for uni and she wants to be a writer. I think she'll do it. That girl has always been wiser than her mother. And Luke will support her. He worships the ground she walks on, doesn't he?'

'Always has,' Heather agreed.

I watched Izzy and Luke laughing together. I thought about my mum and Finlay's dad and how they might have done something similar when they were teenagers here, but then the image changed to me and Finlay and I imagined us strolling out here together.

And I knew that life wasn't about looking back or thinking about what might have been, but living for today and being hopeful for the future. And following your heart. I looked at the women with me. We had all done that, and I hoped we would keep on doing just that.

'You have each inspired me,' I said to them, 'to go after my dreams – so thank you.'

'You got me the job at the Inn,' Anna said. 'I should be thanking you!'

'I don't think we need to keep saying thank you,' Beth said. 'We all pay it forward, and that's what matters.'

'With that in mind,' Emily said, 'let's give Beth her Christmas present now...' She pulled out an envelope. 'Open it!' she said eagerly to Beth, who gave her a questioning look.

I leaned closer to see as I wasn't sure what it was although the others were smiling smugly at one another.

Beth opened the piece of paper and read it aloud. 'Your Glendale Hall garden has won the Chelsea Flower Show Best Amateur Garden. Congratulations – enclosed are four tickets to this year's show, with travel and accommodation included. A special award commending your winning garden will be posted out to you.' Beth looked at her friends. 'You submitted my garden! I can't believe it!' Gardening was Beth's passion and Glendale Hall's grounds were amazing. 'You guys!' She pulled them to her and they drew me into the group hug, too.

'What are you all doing?' Izzy called out when she and Luke saw us huddled together.

'Just being grateful for each other,' her mother called out. 'Want to join the hug?'

Izzy made a swift exit as we all laughed.

Chapter Sixty-Two

I closed the front door after Mum and Dad had left with Beth and Drew Fraser, the final partygoers to leave, and I turned around. Balloons floated around the hallway as well as streamers from party poppers, and empty drink bottles and glasses stood on every surface. Quiet music played from Adam's laptop, which we had used once the DJ had finished. The clock in the hallway struck two a.m., echoing around the now empty house. 'What a party,' I said to Adam and Finlay when I walked through the hallway into the lounge. Adam was locking the French doors and Finlay was collecting up glasses.

'I'm exhausted,' Adam said. He yawned. 'Shall we clear up in the morning? I need to sleep.'

'Sounds like a plan to me,' I replied. 'Good night.'

'Sleep well.' Adam gave us a cheerful wave before he headed up the stairs. Grace had to work at the Inn tomorrow and had left early, but I had seen them dancing happily together and I knew she was joining us for our family Christmas, so they wouldn't be away from one another for long.

'It was such a good night,' Finlay said when we were alone. 'How about one more dance before we go to bed?'

'Hang on.' I bent down and pulled off my heels and scooped my hair up into a messy bun. 'That's better,' I said as I took his hand and moved into the centre of the lounge.

Finlay smiled. 'If it's possible, you look even more beautiful now.' He took my hands and drew me to him as we swayed slowly to the soft romantic music still playing. We hardly moved, but held each other close, the remnants of the party scattered around us, the room quiet and empty. It was a still moment after such a hectic night, and I was happy I was spending it with Finlay.

'Lorna,' he said after a moment, looking down at me. 'You know that I've fallen in love with you, don't you? I want to look after you and be with you, and make you smile every day if I can. I want to live my life with you by my side.'

My breath hitched. 'Stay with me,' I said in a fierce whisper. 'Here. Move in to Dove House. Don't go back to the Inn. I want to wake up with you every day.'

Finlay's face lit up. 'Really? I would love to be here with you. Would Adam mind?'

'I'll speak to him, but I don't think so. I bet Grace will move in too, soon. We always saw our families being here one day. Why wait to start? And maybe, like you said, we could one day build that summer house in the grounds...'

'It's funny. When I walked in here, I felt like this place was going to mean something to me,' Finlay said with a smile. 'I had no idea it would mean this.' He leaned down and kissed me. 'I don't want to ruin the romantic declarations, but I have to pay my way and...'

I put a finger on his lip. 'It's okay, I know. We'll sort it all out. But right now, I'm just happy you want to be with me.'

'Always,' he said.

'And I love you too, by the way,' I added with a smile.

He picked me up and twirled me around, making me laugh. 'Come on, let's go to bed,' he said as he put me gently down.

I didn't need asking twice. 'Sounds good to me.' It was funny. I had been nervous of starting what felt like something so big with Finlay, but now we were here, in this moment, I didn't feel scared, just excited. I wanted our life together to start straight away. I didn't want to wait. Yes, it was early days, and probably everyone would think we had moved a bit quickly, but it felt right to be with him and I didn't want to pretend otherwise.

He felt like my partner. Like we were a team. And I wanted him with me every day.

We held hands as we walked upstairs, Finlay holding my shoes in his other hand, and we smiled at one another. It was weird to know that only he knew how I felt, as he felt the same way. Like we were in on this secret together. And I hoped it was a secret we'd share for a very long time.

–

I woke up before Adam and Finlay, so I went softly downstairs and decided to make a big breakfast for the three of us. I was tired but I had too much excitement to sleep. It felt like the start of something special right now. Our bed and breakfast was going to open soon, something we had wanted and worked for for so long, and I had fallen in love for the first time, something I had always hoped for. It felt like there was so much to look forward to that I just wanted to get up and enjoy it. I saw that there was a thick frost again outside as I went into the kitchen, and greeted and fed Tabby, who looked happy to have the house back to himself this morning.

I made myself a coffee and started to cook bacon as I sipped it, enjoying the warmth as I padded around the kitchen in my cosy mule slippers. I put the radio on quietly and hummed along as I started making scrambled eggs. It was a simple thing – making breakfast in my home – but it felt so good. I had dreamed so long about living here and now here I was, and I intended to make the most of it.

'You're cheerful today,' Adam said, walking in. 'I have such a headache. How are you not hung-over?' he grumbled as he half fell into a chair at the table.

'I didn't drink that much; I was too busy mingling, I think. I'm making a big breakfast, that will help. Pour yourself a coffee while you wait,' I said as I put bread into the toaster and turned over the tomatoes I was grilling.

'Are you trying to butter me up for something?' Adam asked a little suspiciously as he watched me.

'No! Oh, well, actually...' I turned round. 'How would you feel if Finlay didn't go back to the Inn, but moved in here with us? Honestly, if you think it's—'

Adam held a hand up to stop me. 'I would never be against anything that makes you this happy. If it's what you want?'

I nodded. 'It really is.'

Adam smiled. 'Good, then I'm all for it. He'd better treat you right though, that's all I'm saying.'

'I promise,' Finlay said, walking in at that very moment. 'And I definitely want to pay towards the mortgage and help out with any more renovations that might be needed. I want to contribute to this house, and help you both look after it. Obviously, the bed and breakfast is all you two, but I want to do anything I can.'

'That's really appreciated,' Adam said.

'Okay, this smells amazing.'

'Sit down. It's ready.' I dished up three plates of eggs, bacon and grilled tomatoes and carried over a stack of toast. 'So, what about Grace?' I asked my brother as we tucked in eagerly.

'What about Grace?'

'Do you think she might move in here someday soon?' I asked, buttering my toast and looking at my brother. He was such a closed book sometimes, and I knew I wore my heart on my sleeve.

'She's focused on her business. I mean, I hope so, one day, but until then I'll just be a gooseberry.' He grinned, and I knew he didn't really mind. 'Maybe Kathleen will want to move Hamish and baby Drew in too,' he joked.

'I'm glad she's on board with the bed and breakfast, but there are limits,' I replied, remembering how my sister and I would bicker growing up. 'Mum did always see our family here in this house though, didn't she? I guess she was right all along, that we do belong here.' I looked at Finlay. 'And you, of course.'

'I think my dad thought so too. It's funny how life works out, isn't it?'

'I told you,' Adam said as he tucked into his food. 'You just need a little faith.'

Chapter Sixty-Three

It felt impossible that it could be Christmas, but I woke up on 25 December feeling that same feeling I had when I was a child, of excitement for the day. We had spent the days before getting the house ready for our guests who were due on New Year's Eve, and were looking forward to a couple of days off to celebrate before we had to make the final preparations for our first visitors. We'd had such a busy few months, and so much had changed, and I was so excited for the family traditions that we followed every Christmas. But with one difference this year. I opened my eyes and smiled at Finlay on the pillow next to me.

'Merry Christmas,' I said when he opened his eyes too.

'Merry Christmas to you too.' He nodded towards the end of the bed. 'Looks like Santa has been.'

I looked and chuckled at the presents that now sat there. 'Oh, wow, he was very quiet,' I said. I gave him a kiss. 'You didn't need to do this,' I said.

'What do you mean? I had nothing to do with it. It was all Father Christmas.' He sat up as I pulled the presents to me and put them on my lap. 'You were obviously on the good list this year.'

'Well, I should think so too,' I replied with a grin. I opened the first beautifully wrapped present. 'It feels like a book,' I said as I tore off the red and gold paper. I was wrong. It was a print of one of the photos that were taken by the *Inverness Times* for their article. I unwrapped the others and saw that there were four in total of the house, taken while we were renovating.

'So you can always remember the journey,' Finlay said.

'They are beautiful. So thoughtful! Thank you.' I gave him a kiss.

'I know you said you wished you could have them up on the walls.'

'I don't even remember saying that! But they are going to look amazing.'

'I remember everything,' he replied.

This man really did have a way with words. I leaned in for another kiss, this time a lingering one that I didn't want to end.

'There's more,' Finlay said when we had parted. 'When Jack sent them to me, he said he'd love to do a follow-up article now the work is finished, and he'll be in touch after Christmas.'

'Wow, that would be amazing. Thank you! As we're doing gifts now...' I reached under the bed and pulled out his present. I heaved it onto the bed. 'I hope you like it.'

'What is it?' He looked at the large package curiously. He tore off the wrapping paper. 'Oh, Lorna,' he gasped when it fell away to reveal a vintage typewriter.

'You might not want to write on it, but when I saw it, it just had your name on it somehow.'

'I can't wait to use it,' he said, stroking it. 'This is amazing. I've always wanted one. Thank you, Lorna, it's perfect. Just like you.'

'No one is perfect!' I protested with a laugh.

'I think you are.' Finlay wrapped an arm around me. I hoped we would have many more Christmases together like this. 'Breakfast in bed?'

'No, I'll make us coffees, you get ready. We're running late already,' I said, hopping out of bed. I pulled back the curtains and looked out. 'Oh wow, a white Christmas!' Finlay climbed out of bed too and looked out beside me.

'Dove House looks perfect in the snow,' he said.

I smiled, in full agreement. I loved it when we had a white Christmas in Glendale, and this year the weather had come through and it had snowed during the night. I couldn't wait to see the village looking like a winter wonderland. I went downstairs while Finlay went into the bathroom. I found Adam in the kitchen drinking a cup of coffee. 'Merry Christmas! Are you okay?' I asked, seeing his furrowed brow.

'Just a bit nervous,' he admitted as I poured myself a cup of coffee and joined him at the table. 'I know you're always telling me I'm optimistic, but right now, I don't feel that way at all. I feel like my faith might be deserting me.'

'What are you worried about?' I asked, thinking that everything was on track with the house and suddenly anxious something had gone wrong overnight. 'Another pipe hasn't burst, has it?'

'No, it's not the house. It's Grace...'

'Adam, what's wrong?' I asked.

He reached into his pocket and slid something small across the table towards me. It was a tiny box covered in blue velvet. I opened it and let out a little gasp as I looked down at the sparkling diamond ring inside. 'I was going to propose, and now I'm wondering if it's actually a good idea.'

'Oh, Adam, what a beautiful ring.' I looked at my brother. 'Did you choose this yourself?' I was surprised he hadn't asked my opinion; it was a stunning ring. 'Why didn't you tell me you were planning to propose?'

'It was a spur-of-the-moment thing. Grace said the other day she had always thought Christmas was such a lovely time to get engaged, and I suddenly thought I don't want to wait for a whole year to ask her if that's her perfect time. So I went to the jeweller's and I saw this ring and I don't know, it looked like it would suit her. Then I got scared and decided if I didn't tell anyone, I wouldn't have to do it. What shall I do?'

I'd never seen my brother so unsure. It was usually him advising me. 'It's such a lovely ring, I know she'll love it and she'll think it's so romantic you have chosen the time of year she would love. I've seen you two together, I think you're a perfect fit. But it's really about what you want, it's your heart you need to follow. You're always telling me that, right?'

Adam nodded slowly. 'I know it's right, but I haven't had the best luck when it comes to love. Sometimes I worry that I feel so sure, does that make sense? Like how is it this good?'

My mind went instantly to Finlay. 'I know what you mean. But if you feel that way then you should embrace it. Not many people ever feel that sure that it's right. And if you know Grace is the one, then why wait? I know that it was really soon to ask Finlay to move in, but I knew it was what I wanted. And this is what you want, isn't it?'

'It really is,' Adam said. He smiled. 'You're right. I know that I want to marry Grace. And I want to give her the proposal she deserves. Will you help me?'

'Of course I will!'

Chapter Sixty-Four

Glendale really did look like a winter wonderland as me, Adam and Finlay walked from Dove House to my parents' later that morning.

Mum opened the door to us with a wide smile. Like me and Adam, she was wearing a snuggly Christmas jumper. Grace and Finlay weren't in on the tradition yet, but next year, Adam and I had vowed they would be joining us. 'Merry Christmas!'

'Merry Christmas, Mum! We have to do something,' I said, yanking Adam inside with me. Mum and Finlay watched us with amused looks on our faces as we hurried into the living room before Grace joined us for lunch.

'What's going on?' Dad asked as he walked in with the twins behind him looking cute in their jumpers.

'All will be revealed,' I said, shielding Adam as he went to the Christmas tree. 'So, what did Santa bring you?'

'The best presents ever!' Leo and Noah took me out into the garden to show me their shiny new bikes.

'Oh, cool,' I said. 'You must have been really good boys.'

'That's debatable,' my mum said behind us. 'A drink, Lorna? Join me on the wine? I mean, it's early, but it is Christmas...'

'Definitely. Let's go inside, it's freezing. We can play after lunch with these two,' I said to the boys, shivering. It had started to snow gently so they didn't protest too much, and we went back into the warm house where we all got drinks and went into the living room to open presents. Kathleen, Hamish and baby Drew arrived, and then Grace, and the room was full of laughter and high spirits and everyone I loved.

Mum had made a special dinner as usual, and the table was crowded and lively as we tucked into turkey with all the trimmings, pulled our crackers and put on the paper hats and told each other the same jokes that came with them every year, and then we had Christmas pudding. Dad poured too much brandy on it and almost caused a small fire as he did every year, and then we went back into the living room with coffees and Christmas cake, full and sleepy and extremely happy.

'Before we play any games,' Adam said as the twins started to head to their toys and the adults sank into the sofas, groaning. He reached for Grace's hand and, surprised, she followed him to the Christmas tree. 'I wanted to give Grace her present,' he said, gesturing to the ornament he had hung on the tree earlier. It was a red and gold bauble. 'Merry Christmas,' he said as she reached for it.

'It's so pretty,' she said, reaching for it and taking it off the tree. 'I love it.'

'It opens...'

Grace opened the bauble and then gasped when she saw the ring inside. Adam got down on one knee and my family gasped too, although I just smiled, knowing the plan. Grace's face lit up as Adam took her hand and looked up at her with eyes full of love.

'Grace, I knew as soon as I kissed you that you and me were the perfect fit. You are the woman I want to spend the rest of my life with and build a life and a family with, and hopefully grow old with. I love you so much. Will you marry me?'

Grace's eyes were full of tears as she nodded. 'Yes. I love you,' she said as Adam jumped up and pulled her into his arms with happiness.

'Oh my! Congratulations!' Mum cried as everyone clapped and the twins cheered enthusiastically.

I looked at Finlay across the room and he smiled, and I knew that he was thinking the same thing – that one day that would be us too.

'I'm not sure we have anything sparkly left after celebrating Dove House and baby Drew,' Dad said, frowning. 'I didn't think there would be something else so soon.'

'It's been a pretty special Christmas,' Kathleen said, looking at her husband and baby and then at the rest of us.

'I can make us all a hot chocolate. It doesn't matter what we have, just that we toast to Adam and Grace,' I said, getting up with a smile seeing everyone I loved so happy.

–

We had a lovely time at our family home, and we didn't leave until well into the night when we spilled out into the snow with waves and shouts of 'Merry Christmas' echoing behind us as we walked back to Dove House. The newly engaged couple were arm in arm, beaming from ear to ear in front of me and Finlay, holding hands as we enjoyed the quiet walk back in the snow.

'I've never had a Christmas like this,' Finlay said. 'I can't thank your family enough for welcoming me like they have.' I had heard my mum say quietly to Finlay earlier that he was part of the family now, and I know that had meant the world to him.

I squeezed his hand. 'I hope we have many more Christmases like this one.'

'We will,' he promised.

'Look,' Grace said from in front, pointing up to the sky. We stopped and looked up. The sky was an inky blue and clear, so we could see all the stars and the moon was shining bright. Then we saw what she had seen. A twinkling light moving above us.

'A shooting star,' I said in wonder. 'Wow.'

'I've never seen one before,' Finlay said as we watched it streak across the sky.

'Make a wish,' Adam called out.

'Is that a thing?' I asked, but I knew that we had all made a wish. Just in case.

'It makes you remember how small we really are in the universe when you look up,' Grace said as we started walking again. 'Do you really think there is something up there waiting for us?'

'I always have,' Adam said, forever solid in his faith.

'I hope so,' Grace said.

'I want to believe,' Finlay said. 'But it isn't easy, is it?'

I shook my head. 'Nothing worthwhile ever is... But moments like this make me sure that we're never alone.'

'It's a comforting thought,' Finlay said. 'As is the idea that everything works out in the end.'

'That I can believe in,' Grace said, holding up her ring, which sparkled in the night light.

'Me too,' Finlay agreed, and Adam looked back and smiled at me as our lovely house appeared in front of us looking magical dusted in snow, welcoming all of us home.

Chapter Sixty-Five

We had a magical Christmas, and then it was time to celebrate Hogmanay. I was awake at the crack of dawn on New Year's Eve, making sure the house looked as perfect as I could possibly make it. Betty and her daughter, Mrs Andrews' sister and her husband, along with Finlay's uncle and his wife were staying with us for two nights to give the bed and breakfast a trial run. I had that Christmas morning feeling all over again – I was nervous but excited, and just hoped they would all enjoy their stay.

The next week, Jack Smith was coming back to do another article now that we were open. Beth had shared the news and the residents' discount on all the Glendale social media accounts, and Kathleen had put a leaflet pretty much everywhere in the village and had paid for an advert in the local paper, so bookings were coming through and we hoped, with some reviews from our guests, we'd get even more soon. It would take time to spread the word, but Glendale was a popular place so I hoped it would happen quickly. I knew our friends in the village would tell anyone who even mentioned about staying where they could come.

I stood at the window looking out through the steel-framed windows as snow fell lightly on the grass in front of Dove House.

'What are you thinking about?' Finlay asked softly, appearing behind me then.

'I just can't believe we're about to greet our first guests.'

'How do you feel?'

'Anxious, excited… exhausted. But so happy we did this.'

'You and Adam are doing such an amazing job. People are going to love it here. Just like I love it here.'

'And what about you? How do you feel about your book?'

Finlay wrapped an arm around my waist. 'I have news – the first draft is done.'

'Oh, wow, that's so exciting!' I kissed him. 'Can I read it all now?' Finlay hadn't let me read any more than the few pages I'd read back at his home in Perth, and I was dying to see where he had taken the story.

'Let me read it through first, but then you can. I need all the feedback I can get before I send it out to literary agents,' he said, looking nervous.

'I'm so proud of you,' I said. 'What did you decide to do about the ending?'

'I gave them the one they deserved.'

'Perfect.' I leaned in for another kiss.

'Lorna! Ugh, you two,' Adam said, appearing in the doorway. He rolled his eyes. 'Put each other down, would you?'

'Aw, leave them alone,' Grace said, walking in behind him. Adam turned to smile at her. 'They are cute.'

'Not as cute as us,' my brother told her.

I rolled my eyes. 'And you have the cheek to moan at us.'

Adam laughed. It was nice to see him happy. And to feel this happy, too.

'Okay, I'm off,' Grace said. 'I'm meeting Beth to talk about our plans,' she said excitedly. Beth was keen to get her involved with the events at Glendale Hall, maybe even strike up a partnership, which was really exciting. 'Good luck, call me later,' she said.

'I will,' Adam promised.

'Good luck to you, too!' I called after her.

'Heads-up, guys,' Adam said, nodding out of the window then. We turned to see a car driving in through the gates. Our first guests had arrived. I hoped they would be the first of many.

'Let's go and greet them,' I said to my brother.

'I'll put the kettle on,' Finlay said, hurrying off to the kitchen.

I walked outside with Adam, waving as our first guests parked their car, and I smiled and waved as I recognised them.

'Betty, I'm so glad you could come,' I called out as Betty, Dove House's previous owner, stepped out of the car with her daughter. She looked up at the house. And I was relieved to see her smile at what she saw.

'Right, I'll help with the bags,' Adam said with a happy grin, and he stepped out from the door to go over.

Then the second car arrived, and Finlay's uncle and his wife drove in through the gates. My nerves faded as I walked out to say hello to them because this was what we had worked so hard for, and there was no time for nerves. It was about to be a new year and a new beginning, and I couldn't wait to start this new chapter.

I remembered how I'd felt at the end of summer: single and feeling like I'd never find love, bored and unchallenged at work and wondering what to do about it, wondering if I'd ever get to do what I wanted. But somehow, it had all worked out and come together. And the journey to get here with all its up and downs and wobbles and moments when I'd questioned everything, were all worth it. My mum had always said that things would work out, that everything would be okay, that what was meant to be would be, and I had been unsure whether to believe her, but as always, she had been right.

'Welcome to Dove House,' I said as our four guests walked towards the front door. 'I really hope you're going to enjoy your stay with us.'

Epilogue

It was autumn, my favourite season. The village was covered in crisp golden and burnt-orange leaves, shiny conkers rolled around on the ground and the sky was clear with golden sunshine bathing my home village.

'Are you ready?' Adam asked me as I walked downstairs. He was wearing his morning suit and looking nervous but happy.

'As I'll ever be,' I replied, walking gingerly down the stairs so I didn't stand on my dress.

'You sure we should walk?'

'It's a tradition,' I replied. We always walked to church, and I didn't see why today should be any different.

'Let's go then.' He held out his arm and I took it, leaving Dove House with him and walking through the High Street towards the church as we had done so many times before. We hadn't done this before, though.

I had butterflies in my stomach as we walked, but the familiar sight of Glendale calmed me and I glanced across at my brother to see if he was nervous too but he smiled happily back. The church soon greeted us, the steeple rising up into the cloudless sky. I could hear the church band playing as we reached the doorway and there waiting for us outside was our family.

'You look beautiful,' my mum said, dabbing her eyes as she turned around and saw me. She took in my long white dress. 'An absolute princess.'

'You look lovely,' Kathleen agreed as she handed me my bouquet. We had matching ones in beautiful autumnal colours of deep reds, oranges and yellows, and her dress was a lovely maroon colour that suited her perfectly.

'Gorgeous,' Grace and Anna agreed in their matching dresses. Grace gave my brother a smile that showed she was remembering their wedding day in the summer.

But today was mine and Finlay's day.

'Ready, Lorna?' my dad asked in his suit, offering me his arm.

I took in a breath. 'Let's go.'

Mum and Adam led the way and then Grace and Anna walked in as the music in the church changed to the wedding march. My dad and I followed them closely and I looked around as we walked down the aisle, which was lined with gorgeous autumn flowers that matched our bouquets, at the familiar faces – people I had grown up with and known forever. We passed friends from school, Adam's rugby team, the Dove House builders, Cameron smiling at Anna, Beth and Drew, everyone from Glendale Hall: they were all there, and mixed in were Finlay's guests – his uncle, his aunt who had flown in from Australia, his uni friends, and Jack Smith was there grinning – and I felt love all around us as my dad kissed me and I stepped up to the altar where Finlay was waiting.

He had never looked more handsome in his tux as his eyes lit up and he took my hand. Definitely more Superman than Clark Kent in this moment, I thought. 'I love you,' he mouthed as Brodie stepped forward and welcomed everyone to the church.

I had grown up dreaming of my wedding day, of getting married in this church, and my eyes welled as I looked across at the man who was going to be my husband, and I couldn't quite believe I had found my soulmate.

We had so much to look forward to. Finlay had just signed his first book deal, and I couldn't wait to hold a copy of his first novel in my hands. The bed and breakfast was fully booked for our first Christmas, and I couldn't wait to celebrate the season with all our guests. And decorate Dove House, of course. Grace lived with us too now, and the four of us had so much fun together. It was a real family home and business, which me and Adam had always wanted it to be. Kathleen worked with us one day a week now, while baby Drew was at nursery, and she loved it.

And the best part was, whatever happened this year and the next and in the years to come, I knew I had the best people to share my life with, and through the ups and downs. That was what mattered.

'I love you too,' I mouthed back to Finlay as Brodie talked about the power of love, and I knew that he was not only talking about me and Finlay, but the love of our family and friends, of this community, of Glendale, and I knew that I wouldn't be here in this moment and be this happy without their love. They had supported me, they had encouraged me to believe in myself when I was struggling. They had helped me create the life that I had always wanted.

Dreams do come true, I thought to myself, and I hoped that anyone who needed to know that would, in this very moment, know it too.

A letter from Victoria

It always feels like I'm coming home when I return to Glendale and I hope that you feel the same way as you're reading this book. I can't believe this is the fifth Glendale Hall novel – it's been a dream come true to write this series, which is why I wanted to dedicate it to anyone who has a dream. If you need inspiration to make yours come true, I hope this book will be it.

Lorna first appeared in Always and Forever at Glendale Hall making friends with Anna and I wanted to follow her on her journey to find what she was looking for in life. It was about time that the village had a place for people to stay and Lorna felt like the perfect person to make it happen along with her family, and the Glendale community lending a helping hand as usual. There are lots of new characters, and a gorgeous new property, that I fell in love with while I was writing, but all our favourites appear too and the Glendale magic is in full force as we open the book in Lorna's, and my, favourite season – autumn.

I really hope you enjoy returning to Glendale and reading Lorna's story, but most of all, I hope that your dreams come true.

Love, Victoria

Acknowledgments

Special thanks to my agent Hannah Ferguson and my editor Keshini Naidoo for being by my side through writing the whole Glendale series, cheering me on along the way! Thank you for making my dreams come true.

I have a wonderful team that work on the Glendale books and I am so grateful for all your hard work, enthusiasm and support… thank you so much to everyone at Hera and Canelo, and Hardman and Swainson. Thank you also Jenny Page, Aimee Coveney, Vicki McKay and Suzanne Juby.

As always, I'm blown away by the love that readers have for Glendale and I want to thank everyone who is reading this for supporting the series and making writing it so very special. Thank you to all the book bloggers, reviewers, retailers and everyone who has helped to spread the word about Glendale in any way. You're all stars!

So much love to all my family and friends for supporting and encouraging me, and for always being there. Thank you for everything.